"SUPERLATIVE . . . A PAGE-TURNER!"
—*Anniston Star*

A call girl who wrote detailed letters about her work to her young daughter . . . a picture-poster cop on the take . . . a female psychotherapist with intimacies to share and maybe to hide . . . a pillar of respectability involved with a beautiful black transsexual . . . a vulnerable woman cop hoping to meet Mr. Right even while she drifted into a tawdry affair . . . a hit team of a shadow agency that made the Mafia look like lambs . . . a very private video of a very public figure . . . and a city where the most shocking sins could be chic and the most monstrous crimes covered up . . .

Put them all together—and you didn't have the stuff that dreams were made of. More like a waking nightmare. . . .

DAYDREAMS

DAYDREAMS

A NOVEL BY

MITCHELL SMITH

AN ONYX BOOK

To Linda, my wife

ONYX
Published by the Penguin Group
Penguin Books USA Inc., 375 Hudson Street,
New York, New York 10014, U.S.A.
Penguin Books Ltd, 27 Wrights Lane,
London W8 5TZ, England
Penguin Books Australia Ltd, Ringwood,
Victoria, Australia
Penguin Books Canada Ltd, 2801 John Street,
Markham, Ontario, Canada L3R 1B4
Penguin Books (N.Z.) Ltd, 182–190 Wairau Road,
Auckland 10, New Zealand

Penguin Books Ltd, Registered Offices:
Harmondsworth, Middlesex, England

Published by Onyx, an imprint of New American Library,
a division of Penguin Books USA Inc.

This is an authorized reprint of a hardcover edition published by
McGraw-Hill Book Company.

First Onyx Printing, August, 1988
12 11 10 9 8 7 6 5 4

Printed in the United States of America

PUBLISHER'S NOTE
This is a work of fiction. Names, characters, places, and incidents either are the product of the author's imagination or are used fictitiously, and any resemblance to actual persons, living or dead, events, or locales is entirely coincidental.

CHAPTER 1

Sally Gaither had been waiting to be found for a day and a night, sitting naked, wired to her folding chair in a small, shifting storm of steam and hot water, the pink spauldeen bulging fat between her teeth.

She'd been alive the first few hours—in the most extraordinary agony for two. Then, scalded, her neat pale skin turned sagging, pouched, blistered, finally peeling slowly away in slender strips—her youth turned to desperate age, her eyes rolled back, the pupils out of sight, Sally had gone mad. Insane, she became more complicated, had wonderful dreams in which she flew with flying flowers—was herself a tangerine rose, no longer moaning past the muffling ball. After a while of this, she died dreaming.

For the last of that day, she sat in her shower, and through the night as well. Then, Monday morning, company. Sue Elva Jacks used her key, and came on in.

"There's the Chief's blow job." Keneally, in the bathroom, was speaking in mingled pique at Ellie Klein's make-work position on the Commissioner's Squad—where she served at the pleasure of the Chief of the Department—and out of a distinct pleasure of his own, the words allowing him to imagine her crouched on stockinged knees before Chief Delgado in his corner office downtown, ministering to that squat, aging man with snorting, gobbling noises.

"Up yours . . ." breathed a heavy breath in Keneally's ear, and he looked over his shoulder to see Nardone's thick, unpleasant face, his sticky black eyes. In the living room, Ellie Klein was talking to the patrolman first-on-scene. They could hear her clear, breathless voice.

Keneally presented a finger, then stepped enough aside for Nardone to wedge himself in. The bathroom was packed with bulky, armed men—one with the Crime Scene Investigative Unit, one from Nineteenth Precinct, and Keneally and his commander from District Homicide—all watching as an assistant medical examiner named Greenstein gently extracted a thoroughly cooked banana (shriveled and smaller than it had been, its skin still on) from Sally Gaither's vagina. The small pink rubber ball had been wrenched from her mouth with some difficulty earlier, after the pictures, leaving the lolling corpse with a mighty, gaping grin.

"What are you doing here?" Maxfield to Nardone. Maxfield was black, gray-haired and slender, and the senior detective in Division Homicide—a juicy post, leading straight as the Seventh Avenue subway to an inspector's shield. Maxfield was generally regarded in the Department as stupid, but a cutie—riding the black bandwagon for all it was worth.

"What's it to you?" Nardone to Maxfield. Nardone a devout Catholic, a righteous brute—ex-shoofly and present attendant spirit and guard dog to Ellie Klein. He and Klein had come to the Commissioner's Squad by different routes—Nardone by shooting a connected-up dealer down—and, after that, in Internal Affairs, by turning too many sinful comrades in. So, shoot-out to shoofly, to gilded exile from the real Force onto the Commissioner's Queens. —Special events, sensitives, errands, and ass kissing, all orchestrated by Chief of the Department Delgado, himself beloved of the Commissioner.

Ellie's had been another path. —Public relations. The "Klein" was an accident of marriage to a tall, thin young attorney with inquiring eyes, and not an authentic ethnicity. Ellie was WASP, maiden name Bowden, and was, if not beautiful, still quite pretty in a lanky, pale blond, slightly lantern-jawed way. Eyes equally pale, a puzzled, washed-out blue.

An oddity on the Force, these days. And not entirely a successful one. Good grades at the Academy; thought at first to be a comer. A crisp pistol shot—none of the wavering overcontrol most ladies indulged in. Spirited in hand-to-hand, though it was difficult to be certain of a fair test there, the males taking it easier, the females making it harder for her as they struggled, sweating on the mats. She had an odd, yelping, jumping style of combat, intrinsically dissimilar to the grim dark determination the Italian and black girls showed, the nasty hysterical violence of the Irish. —Still, perfectly all right there, all right in hand-to-hand. And absolutely first class in law and regulations—a winner as well in formation, and the Department's organizational charts.

Something of a failure in the locker room. There, in a sweat-dank ditch of women, where lovely breasts and buttocks jostled with tough talk, waste cans loaded with soaked tampons, an occasional towel-snapping bully—in that damp garden Ellie Klein failed to shine. The women noticed a certain delicacy of approach, almost reproach, carefully concealed behind a lattice of macha grunts and curses.

She wasn't comfortable with them. —Not with any excuse of daintier class. Her father was, or had been, a carpenter out in Far Rockaway, and the family had never seen better days, except, perhaps, when a distant ancestor had owned a few hundred acres of Long Island, and that had been so long ago that the land had been more a malarial health menace than real estate gold. Nor was she educated beyond them. One year at Sarah Lawrence on scholarship—she'd left at the beginning of her sophomore year, gone down to the Village to paint, and, a year later, met Nate Klein at a party—meant not much to hardworking girls who'd slogged through four years at Brooklyn College, CCNY, or NYU.

Hers was simply a slightly different rhythm. Just different enough to irritate. The others weren't cruel to her—everyone, after all, was grownup, busy, intent on graduating, getting on the force. Some were pleasant to her, and one of them liked her very much.

The instructors, always alert for the oddball, if not too much else, picked up those vibes, on and off the mat, and let the tall blonde through with all her good grades, but with no corresponding word of mouth: here comes a solid cop.

They weren't wrong.

Her first assignment was administrative, Personnel waiting to see if she had a friend downtown—a rabbi. Ellie had no friend, but at the time still had a husband. Klein spoke to a fellow lawyer—a senior partner in Temple, Wright, Wright and Sharecroft—and the man, amused by Ellie's choice of profession, mentioned her career lag to a captain in Tactical Command—like the attorney, a dedicated bridge player. In this way, Ellie was relieved of her responsibilities in the Property Clerk's office, and put on patrol.

She lasted two years with one of the lowest arrest records in her precinct—an admittedly low-action area in Queens—and then blotted her sheet badly, within a week or two of summer vacation.

A very large black detective named Bayard Drew had, with his partner, stopped two handsome long-haired white boys on a corner. —Bayard had seen an inescapable outline of switchblade in one boy's pocket, and being out of temper for personal reasons, stood the boy and his friend up against a wall for a look-see. Broad daylight, with passersby. Ellie, on her one foot-patrol shift in the week, passed by just in time to make her mistake.

As Drew patted the boy down, the young man became suddenly and furiously violent, and got his knife out. Drew, grappling with him in embarrassed surprise, twice the boy's size, made a distracted grab for the knife-wrist, missed it, and received a serious wound—a cut up along his forearm that sliced veins and arteries in two.

At that, Drew raised his other fist, hit the boy a collected punch, and knocked him into the building wall and unconscious. Then he attempted to stanch the flow of blood. His partner was occupied with the other boy, who had seen an opportunity in the confusion, and determined to take advantage of it.

It was up to Officer Klein, and she muffed it.

Given time, just a moment or two to consider, Ellie would certainly have done what she should—taken out her sap (frowned on, but more effective in a tussle than the stick), closed with the boy still struggling, struck him hard on the head several times to assist in subduing him—and then gone to the aid of the injured officer, applying pressure to the site of bleeding, using a folded or wadded cloth if necessary, while summoning aid with her belt radio.

But Ellie wasn't given time to consider. She came to the corner—mildly curious because of an elderly couple standing in the middle of the street staring at something happening out of her sight—cleared the corner, and saw Drew cut and the blood come spurting out.

He'd barely had time to punch the boy when she rushed to him, fluttering, crying out—reaching to touch his draining arm, then withdraw her hand as quickly. Her cries were, in fact, just the ones she'd offered when trying three years before to attack Marie Valonte, kick her in the groin, strike her across the throat with the edge of her hand, take her on the hip, and throw her to the mat to kneel on her head and subdue her utterly. Marie had been a sweet-tempered chunky girl, very religious, and had cooperatively collapsed under Ellie's assault, but shifted her dark-curled head abruptly when Ellie, kneeling, had pressed upon an earring.

These cries, then, without the attendant violence, were much the same that Ellie now employed in succoring Detective Drew. She pawed, touched the arm, and leaped away, uttering cries. She was also weeping.

This spectacle, this extraordinary behavior observed by so many interested people on the corner and in the street adjacent, and a cause of terrific chagrin for both Detective Drew and his breathless partner—the one gripping his own arm in the fiercest way, the other more relaxed, with his prisoner kneeling peaceful at his feet, the short muzzle of a .38 Detective Special touching the boy gently on his right ear—resulted in Ellie Klein's swift transfer to Manhattan, to a children's shelter program there, as Department Liaison.

Here also, she muddied her sheet in many minor ways—getting once into a furious dispute with a Puerto Rican mother who had seared a particular devil out of her little girl on the big back burner of her stove. Ellie was accused of striking this lady, and in front of a witness, a social worker—almost the worst thing a police officer can do. Had the social worker not been a veteran of those wars, and kind to cops, Ellie Klein would have been up on charges and out on her ass.

So things stood in her career—her commander, answering an inspector from District who had inquired who the pussy might be, and how good a cop, had replied that she was a nice girl—meaning that she was competent at daily police work, intelligent, industrious, honest, and not to be relied upon in an emergency.

So she was ruined, judged as simply the wrong material for the job—when, abruptly, she was given her chance, and given with it a few moments to prepare.

She and Klein had been divorced for two years when a tenement in the barrio, at East 108th Street, caught fire from tattered wiring in its old boiler room, and burned. The divorce had been painful for Ellie, who had thought herself in love with her handsome, clever husband. They had been together for six years, Klein almost always humorous, joking with her over thousands of small matters, but grimly and pleasantly serious in bed. He had occasionally taken advantage of her long legs to have her parade before him in high-heeled shoes, garter belt, and wide-brim straw hat, kicking and prancing like a horse, which motions made her small breasts shake, her pale buttocks, already slightly slack, tremble whitely in the shadowed light of their bedroom lamp. Or he would ask her to march through the whole of their neat apartment—to no music but her soft panting, her faint gasps of effort as she danced.

After such performances, he had the habit of taking her strongly. Twice, he'd annointed her between the buttocks and entered her there, pleasing himself and hurting her, then pleasing them both.

The divorce had come, for Ellie, from a nearly cloudless sky—hazed only a little by their not having had children. A decision—to postpone—they'd both agreed to, Ellie then as ambitious as her husband, though less fitted for it. "I like you, El . . ." he'd said. "I probably still love you—but you simply don't interest me anymore." He'd said that as merrily as he'd joked and jibed with her for many years. He'd smiled.

Ellie thought of killing herself with her service revolver; then, in a day or two, thought of killing him—but did neither.

Klein moved out, leaving the apartment to her. In the

years that followed, Ellie saw him eleven times—twice in the street (by accident), once on divorce business, and a number of times by waiting under a dry cleaner's marquee across from his firm's offices off Wall Street. She didn't try to speak to him on those occasions of observation, didn't let him see her—and finally, on the last of these, saw him walk from the building with a small, beautiful, dark-haired woman in a handsome charcoal-silk suit.

On the day the tenement burned, a summer day and blazing, Ellie had left the Juvenile Authority office—had been there for an hour and a half talking with Elena Munoz about a boy named Elacio, who'd molested another, younger child—left the office, and was walking west on 109th when she'd heard a dying siren, saw in the next block a small gray-black plume of smoke, and went to the scene.

The Fire Department had been there almost an hour, the men hustling over a flooded street among pythons of hose, hurrying in and out through the building's main doorway—and at the corner, by short extension ladder through a smashed-in second-story window—all of them clanking with tanks and tools. Four patrol cars from the precinct were now at the scene as well, and Ellie, in plainclothes so as not to overawe the children in her work—a blue print dress today—went over to the near car, showed her badge to a freckled sergeant, and asked if she could help. He, comfortable in the passenger seat, gave her a look at once surprised and bored, talked with her for politeness' sake awhile, then went back to his notebook, jotting this and that.

Ellie wandered then across the street to join the casual crowd, and after watching the firemen at their duty for a few minutes, looked up the building's side, along high rows of windows, some whole and neat, others charred and broken in or out. Then, in one of the neat ones—closed to the level of a rust-stained air conditioner—she saw, or thought she saw, a very small brown face, eyes wide, peering down. Two windows away from this, to the left, through an empty window frame, smoke rolled out solid and black as a small tornado, but silent.

The firemen were busy in the street (one, a firewoman

and fairly small, wrestling hose with the rest); the massive pumper—parked half-turned from the uptown corner—stood unmanned, its nozzles dripping. Ellie ran back across to the fire captain, a short, wiry man with a neat mustache. She interrupted him as he was talking on his hand radio, and when he turned from her still talking—he had a man, one of his men, down with chest pains on the seventh floor—she reached out and tugged at his rubber jacket.

"Goddamn you, lady," he said. "—Get your hands off me!" And was not impressed when she showed her badge, pinned now to the bosom of her dress. Indeed, he looked around for a cop to get this cop off his back. Like many firemen, whose jobs are—statistically—so much more dangerous, the captain had a certain contempt for policemen, and policewomen. Ellie persisted, pestering him about the small brown face. She'd become child-sensitized in her work, and, perhaps because of her childlessness, was quick to assume a guardian stance.

The firemen, as it happened, had already cleared the building quite thoroughly—it was a smoky fire, not an inferno, though not much less dangerous for that—and two men were now bringing Richie Rollins down seven floors of smoldering stairs in the near pitch dark, carrying him on their shoulders while trying to keep his breather mask straight on his face. Rollins had peed on them, and was dying, his heart shaking uselessly in his chest.

The captain spoke to his building boss, who was on the third floor and climbing to help with Rollins, directing him to lower the man from the north-side corner window to save the time on the last two flights of stairs. The captain also had a problem with water. The pressure—due to hydrant-opening by the foolish and broiling poor—might not permit him to cope if the building burst into flame. He was calling in another alarm, therefore, simply for more hose length, and was embarrassed by the necessity, since this was only a shitty little fire, nothing special, isolated in this one building—no spread at all. He'd had no serious injuries, only one man, an inhaler, taken gasping away to Metropolitan . . . a second, Packwood, who'd lost a fingertip in glass, and another man in the basement who'd sustained an electrical burn. This man had refused to come out of the basement work, so the captain assumed the burn was only minor—one of those flashy zaps that would happen when a person ripped live wires out of a roasting wall with a steel prybar or the backhook of an ax.

When this woman kept bothering him—raising her voice, gesturing more violently—the captain stepped away from her, over the jungle of hose, gesturing for someone to come deal with her.

One of the patrolmen in the cars had watched much of this—nudging his partner, who was reading a paperback Western, to make him watch, too.

"Look at this shit," the patrolman said. "—Isn't she a cop?"

As he said it—and out in the street Ellie began to shout, then reached again for the sleeve of the fire captain's jacket—a fireman climbed down off Unit #557, came up to the policewoman, and took her by the arm.

"I'm a police officer—"

"I don't give a shit what you are"—pointing to the fire captain. "—See that guy you been talkin' to? Well, leave him the fuck alone."

Ellie crossed the street, and thought of going back to speak to the sergeant—thought of looking for the firewoman . . . did, and didn't see her. She stood at the edge of the marveling crowd, looked way, way up, and was certain she'd found the window again. It had the recalled small air conditioner, its side panels crinkled in to fit it to the window's paint-flaked frame. She looked up at this window, seeing, in her peripheral vision, a silent column of smoke pouring out thick and slow from the window two down, on the left.

She stood and stared, feeling foolish, recalling the contempt in the fire captain's glance, tugged from talking on his radio. She had just recalled this face, when, looking up, she saw for an instant another one remembered, tiny with distance, dark brown, barely visible through dusty glass, peering just over the air conditioner . . . gazing at the spectacle below.

Two, three years old. A baby. Must have climbed on a couch . . . a chair, to look out. . . .

Ellie considered, standing jostled on the sidewalk in

the searing sun, watching the movement, the bright noontime colors of the equipment in the street, and decided what to do. She ran out of the crowd and across the swollen vines of hose, behind a fire engine's massive rear bumper, which—superb, polished, heavy-duty chrome—reflected three blurred suns and the vista of the block in multiples curved in concert with its own rich curves, reflected her as she ran by, splashed a quick step up from the flooded gutter, on up the building's stoop past two firemen coming out, through the door, and in. She dropped her purse at the foot of the stairs.

Ellie'd had no notion of the oddness of a burning world, its stink and dimness, its damp and surprising rearrangements. She climbed the first flight of stairs fast enough—past a fireman coming down, who turned to stare up after her, his air tank clanging on the cracked plaster wall beside him. He'd seen her rising to him—long, white lady's face (firm jaw, long nose, pale blue eyes wide with excitement). Neat blue summer dress, stockings, blue high-heeled pumps. —All brushed past, and, as he turned half around, the *clang,* and slender lady's legs vanishing disembodied into a ceiling of smoke.

"You get the hell back down here . . . !"

High above him, fifteen feet at least, Ellie, climbing into a darker world, heard an echo of that call. She'd thought she could hold her breath for almost the whole climb—the window had been on the fifth floor—if she were quick. But effort and fear now neatly pulled er breath away as a couple of cheerful boys might yank an old woman's purse from her, and taunt her, going. Ellie wheezed out the last of her precious breath (taken so long ago out in the hot and sunny street), held her throat with one hand as she climbed endless steps in darkness almost absolute, as though by that light grip she could control any substance going in or out—and doing so, put herself to climbing faster.

She knew she was past the second floor—certainly past the second—and had heard that in smoky fires the trick was to crawl, so got obediently down on all fours and continued with her climb, her hands soon slippery with ancient dirt, wet and dripping with hose water. Ellie could see no more, traveling in this fashion, than she had in that, but when she tried a little sipping breath, she was able to keep the dark stuff down. Her hands then splatted on a landing, knee bumped a riser hard enough to bruise. —The third floor, she thought, surely, fumbled blind around a newel post, and recommenced her climb. Here there was glass, and Ellie felt its sudden bright bites into her hands and knees. Still on all fours, she straightened her legs to keep her knees up out of the slivers, and climbed that way for a number of steps on hands and feet, like a kindergarten child playing bear, her face down for dubious breathing, her buttocks in the air. Her hands continued to be cut, for she still went on them, not being able to bring herself to stand up into the all-smoke.

Even so, the smoke pressed upon her personally; it stopped her mouth like a large soft hand smelling of toasted wood, no matter how low she bowed. Crawling up steps, weary, slumped back now onto her sliced knees, she became so concerned with breathing she began to forget why she'd come in, began to doubt the reality of the day outside, the superb trucks and hurrying people. She thought she heard shouts below her.

Sanchez and Potts, brown and black under their mighty hats, were coming up after her, furious—ordered in and up by the fire captain as he ran to kneel by his heart-dead man and puff and blow into his mouth while the resuscitator was hustled from the pumper . . . an ambulance far, far away, whooped down the avenue.

The parked policemen, not having happened to see Ellie's entrance, stayed in their cars, or held casually the margins of the crowd, taking care not to stare at the dead fireman and his brothers and sister, all odd in black rubber with bright green stripes and numbers painted on it.

Ellie was halfway up to four, falling from side to side as she crawled up, in grave difficulty. Her lungs were hurting her, a pain lancing into them like a sharpened point, sticking into her every time she tried a breath.

She reached, after the longest time, the landing for four—slipped in water and recovered, but lost her shoe, hobbled, then kicked off the other and turned the stair's corner to climb again. Seven stairs up, she screamed at last, a breathless bleat, and stood up into deeper darkness, screaming softly, fluttering her bleeding fingers before her eyes so as to be able to see anything. —She saw nothing at all but blackness so black she supposed something from the fire, some chemical, had made her blind—and in panic began to run and stumble up the steps, thinking she might reach the roof of the building so far above her, break out of this darkness into light, regain her vision, and gratefully jump out and down into bright air. Now, falling held no terror for her.

She ran up, struck her face on an empty old fire-hose box bolted to the landing wall—she would never know what it was—and fractured her right cheekbone. She staggered away from this, felt a doorway, and pulled herself into the fifth-floor hall. Here her life was saved by a draft drumming up from a back stairwell forty feet away. It heaved the heavy smoke aside as it blew, and showed her dimly—seeing one-eyed now, her vision damaged by the blow that broke the bone—a long row of doors, most kicked open, several shut.

Down this shaded hall she ran, gulping air and smoke together, and then—the finest thing she was to do—stopped, panting, thought . . . and realized she was in the wrong corridor, going deeper into the building rather than parallel to its front. She remembered the possible child's face for the first time in some time, turned around—leaving a red handprint on a blackened door—and went back the way she'd come, into a feathery, drifting dark gray wall of smoke.

Men were shouting below her.

Potts and Sanchez, using their lamps, had found her shoe on the fourth-floor landing. Small, narrow, and blue, with blood on it. Raging, they stormed down the corridor a floor beneath her.

Ellie, in this more likely hall, in air hot enough to sting like bees, breathed in smoke and stood the pain, felt blindly at doorways on her left along her way. Hot paint flaked under her fingers, the doors were wet sometimes with water, sometimes oven-dry, a little sticky soon from her cut hands. Many of these doors were closed. The second, third, and fifth were certainly closed. She heard an odd, deep humming, almost music when she couldn't breathe, and when that music faltered in the least, she felt her heart commence to skip and pause. The sixth door was half open. The seventh door was closed; she fumbled for the knob; the door was locked. Ellie wished that she could see. She kicked at it, tried to call, kicked again and fell, crawled a long way to the eighth, found the frame, reached up through darkness to the knob and tried it. Pushed, and the door opened, but not much. She shoved with her shoulder and then crawled in over a scorching floor to light at last, and raised herself on stiffened arms to take a breath.

Then a little child came out of the light, its diaper damp with shit, and grappled to her, small, potbellied, soft, and warm.

"You fuckin' bitch!" cried Sanchez, Potts beside him, as they kicked and chopped their passage through the fourth, below. The small blue shoe was on their minds.

Far down the hall behind them, in the black rolling chimney of the stairwell, Ellie, strangling—Hector Nunos clutched, fenced firmly in her arms—fell rolling down the stairs to that landing, made the turn, tripped, and fell down the stairs again, curled to guard the child.

Edward McGinnis, small, plump, fresh-faced as a boy, was a stringer-photographer for the *News*. He'd run across the street to get a picture of the ambulance loading the dead fireman. He made that, covered it with a second—ducked out of the way of a fireman who rushed him, redfaced, yelling—turned, and saw the Pulitzer Prize come stumbling out of smoke, bleeding, onto the stoop of the building. He got the shot.

It was, as often, a time of some crisis for the Department. A gambling operation in the Bronx had been shown to have continued in very profitable operation with the forbearance of numbers of patrolmen, sergeants, and the officers of two precincts.

This was a disaster involving indictments and trials to follow—to the fury of the Mayor, facing reelection in less than a year. —A mayor who then might find it politic to request the resignation of one and the appointment of another Commissioner of NYPD. This public relations *Titanic* had occurred only two weeks before Ellie Klein appeared at the entrance to a burning building, cheek blackly bruised, blond hair (smoke smudged) floating loose about her shoulders, and bleeding hands clutching to her blue-flowered breast (where her bright badge hung) a weeping little child.

And so appeared on the front page of the *Daily News,* the third page of *The New York Times,* and, very briefly, in newspapers and on television across the country.

"An absolute *godsend,* sugar," as Lieutenant Eastman—gay as a jay, but tolerated for his quick wit as assistant to the assistant head of Departmental Public Affairs—represented it to his chief, a civilian, a lady, and an ex-reporter. She agreed.

Ellie—made Queen of Metropolitan Hospital—was visited there, briefly, by both the Mayor and Commissioner, on separate visits. People took her picture with each man, Ellie being something of a picture herself, thanks to Lieutenant Eastman—her swollen cheek carefully powdered, her pale eyes lined and shadowed by the Lieutenant himself, her pretty hair down and fanned white-gold against the pillow. And a patrolman's cap hung artfully off a chair-back beside her bed.

So, she tasted the odd wine of celebrity, a very small glass and quickly swallowed, but vintage nonetheless. The attention, noise, and visitors—the hope, a humiliation still, that Nate Klein would at last be sorry, and might possibly come to the hospital one night, get some way past the nurses to lay his sleek and handsome head down on the bed sheet to weep and beg her pardon—these events and imaginings excited and exhausted her, so that she found herself half dreaming in daytime, acting for every visitor the part they'd come to see.

She considered this foolishness one evening, flushed with shame—the Departmental surgeon had held her hospitalized for several extra days as photo opportunity (on orders and against his will, it should be said). This had been reported to Ellie by the night nurse, an angelically naive young girl from Nebraska, perpetually agog at the doings in New York. Ellie, while mulling over this embarrassment, found she had to get up and pee. There, in the bathroom's cramped and dizzying white, she sat and found some comfort in the coolness of the toilet seat. The side of her face still hurt her; the cuts on her hands and knees hardly hurt at all. "Expect some sinus trouble later on, with this," a specialist had told her, pressing with his cold and furry hands across her cheek as she winced away.

Now, in the bathroom, relaxing, sorting out, discarding the later fuss, she considered the saving of the child. She thought she had done that pretty well, and might do as well again, if she had to. She thought that for once she had not made a fool of herself.

On release from the hospital, Ellie received a promotion to detective third-grade, a medal from the Mayor—awarded at Gracie Mansion—a letter from the Governor that he had signed himself, and, after some delay, an appointment to the Commissioner's Squad. —This last she assumed, as did a few other innocents on the Force, to be a signal honor.

This was not to say the Commissioner's Squad was not composed of competent police officers, eleven detectives in all. It was. And the Squad was effective in its chores: minor bodyguarding of minor VIP's, errand-running for the Chief of the Department's office, following up a few long-term investigations the regular divisional squads had filed as unproductive—and, their most demanding duty, keeping a rather feeble surveilling eye on Internal Affairs, monitoring the activities of these unpopular shooflies in various divisions, to keep the cop-watchers aware that they, also, were watched.

To compensate for these less than demanding (or rewarding) duties, the Squad found recompense in the close company of the great—the Department's administrative offices only one flight up—and in an unusually gentle work schedule (mimicking the brass they served) consisting of regular day shifts, one- or two-man night watches, and extraordinary demands infrequent.

It was all legitimate police work, and not to be despised, but it wasn't what Ellie had expected. The Squad handled no big cases, no difficult cases—not, at least, in a fashion likely to cross the lines of regular investigative or enforcement units. It was gradually borne upon her, as it had in their times been borne upon all the more veteran members of the Squad, that they were held in amused contempt by many of those in the Department that were "wised up"—a term adopted from organized crime. The Commissioner's Squad was often a high-class dump, position on it a kick upstairs to nowhere. Most members had, after some usually public feat, been offered to the precinct commands as prize packages—and been turned down for this reason and that, occasionally from sheer superstition, as was the case with Graham, who'd had two partners killed through no fault at all of his own. Usually, though, the reason was a better one than that.

Ellie's package had circulated the districts, and been shipwrecked on two rocks: her failure to come effectively to the aid of Detective Drew and his partner four years before—and the bitter complaint addressed to the Department (and included in her file by a sullen lady clerk at Headquarters) from the office of the Manhattan Commander of the New York City Fire Department. It was the first rock, however, that really wrecked her ship; the fireman's complaint was regarded as simple sour grapes.

Doing the Fire Department's job better than it did was well and good, but of no great account to these grim officers, captains and commanders. However, failing for whatever reason to succor an officer in distress—to fail, as a civilian might put it, to aid a cop in danger—was of the greatest possible account. It was unforgivable, however minor, however long ago. They refused to take her.

"Ouch," the Chief of the Department said, with unusual levity, as his assistant, a cool captain with a law degree and a masters in criminology as well, pointed to the comments column referring to that incident in her file. This assistant, named Anderson, was a lean, handsome man and recently divorced. In a year or so, Anderson would astonish Ellie, having called her up to his office to discuss a report she'd written on another report already on file concerning corruption at a construction site on Thirty-second Street. Internal Affairs had discovered a police sergeant involved in insurance fraud at that site, helping to steal, peddle, and set up recovery payoffs on heavy equipment. —During this meeting, Anderson will suddenly get up from behind his desk, come around to sit on its edge, lean forward to touch her face with his hand, her injured cheek, and ask if it still hurt her. Then, stroking her there gently with his fingertips, say, "You're a sad and complicated girl, aren't you?"

Ellie was to sit there for a moment, under the Captain's hand—then turn her head aside, get up, her clipboard held against her breast, and leave the office. In the ladies' room, afterward, she would smoke a cigarette—one of her last, in fact; she would by then almost have stopped smoking—and look into the mirror, thinking it odd he had called her a girl. In the mirror, water-spotted, cracked at a corner, she would see a tall, thin, tired woman. Tired. Pale, bony blond. Going dry.

Anderson now indicated the distressing entry, the comments column. "—Want me to pull that out of there . . . ?" offering to contravene Departmental regulations against such interference. Delgado sighed and shook his massive head. He, with a sensitive and more experienced nose, scented that where one such fault in the heroine stood revealed and commented on, more were likely to exist, or in future to occur.

The Captain was quick. "Clevenger is out, sir," referring to a woman detective promoted suddenly years before out of a daring drug-buy setup. A bank record's check shortly thereafter had revealed to the Treasury people, working in cooperation, that Detective Second-grade Clevenger, a short, stocky black woman with a high IQ (a darling of the black brass), had recently deposited forty-seven thousand dollars in an account at Marine Midland under the name Henrietta Christophe.

Followed a bad day at the U.S. Attorney's office, where the formidable Detective Clevenger was frightened to tears—and followed that, a serious fuss at Headquarters, with the result that the cash was donated to the Treasury's Ongoing Operations Fund, and Detective Clevenger, chastened and hastened away, was appointed to the Commissioner's Squad.

This clever woman was now dying of leukemia in Memorial Hospital.

"What about putting Klein in?" The Captain.

"Perhaps," the Chief said, who, a deeply conservative officer, would have preferred to have somewhat less flawed subordinates than custom allowed him. He was tired of cracked eggs—even for shit work. "We'll see," he said, and his captain let it lie.

But the Commissioner, when Chief Delgado mentioned this most minor matter to him very much in passing—they were going to different restaurants for lunch—said, "—Why not?"

CHAPTER 2

Six or seven hundred a month maintenance, Ellie thought, since it was owned. . . . The apartment—decorated very nicely in greens and dark golds, a handy one-bedroom, one-bath, large living room—smelled like the Times Square Nathan's, the damp air rich with the odor of cooking frankfurters . . . and some spoilage.

The patrolman was balding young, and sweating along his brow. —Perhaps because of the smell. Or, he might have the whore's book jammed into a back trouser pocket, along with his notebook, pens, and sap.

"The super let you in . . . ?"

"Nah . . . it was open. The colored lady was screamin' in the hall." He took out a crumpled ball of blue bandanna, shook it open, and wiped his brow. He was going bald fast; his hair was thinning even at the sides.

"When you went in there, the water was still on . . . ?"

"Oh, yeah—still goin'."

"Hot?"

"What do ya mean?"

"Was it running very hot, or just warm, when you turned it off?"

"Oh—it was hot. Plenty hot. —Got a lot of hot water in this buildin'." He tried a smile.

Murmurs from the bathroom, a muffled cheer. —There, Greenstein had discovered another banana, this in the corpse's anus, and removed it. In the echo of this cheer, two of the M.E.'s men came into the apartment pushing a rattling gurney, a green plastic bag folded neatly on its narrow sheet. A photographer left the bathroom, reloading, and stood aside for the cart.

"You turned it off . . . ?"

"Yeah, right then." The patrolman took a deep breath—and regretted it. Ellie saw he'd be more comfortable in the hall. The detectives were leaving the bathroom, too, making room for the coroner's men. Nardone started to come over to her, but Ellie glanced him away.

"Where was her book?" she said.

"What book?"

"Don't give me that shit," Ellie said. "This whore's book—that's what book. Where'd you find it?"

"I didn't. I didn't see any book."

Had sure as hell looked, though, seeking that annuity in a drawer, a class whore's date book. "If you don't tell me the truth right now," Ellie said, "—I'll bust your balls for you, Officer. Now, hand over that fucking book and take a commendation for good response . . . safeguarding evidence."

"I didn't." Sullen face.

Years before, Ellie would have let it go at that. —She turned to beckon Nardone, and when he came over, said, "He picked up her book; we're going to have to take him in. . . ."

"Hey—hey, c'mon!" Staring wide-eyed at Nardone, who looked sleepy. "—That's fuckin' bullshit!" Nardone took the patrolman by the arm and tugged him toward the door. "Hey—c'mon! You can fuckin' search me!" Nardone felt growing resistance in the arm he held, a telltale sign.

"So you say," Nardone said, and let him go.

"I didn't find any damn book," the balding patrolman said, rubbing his arm where Nardone had gripped it.

"Where'd you look?" Ellie said.

"All over the fuckin' place," the patrolman said, and the three of them laughed.

There was a soft, farting sound from the bathroom.

"Can I go?" Pearls of sweat stood on the patrolman's brow.

"Go ask Keneally," Nardone said, and the patrolman went to do it.

The coroner's men, with Greenstein following carrying two small plastic bags, rolled the loaded gurney out of the bathroom into the living room, and out the door. Sally

Gaither, strapped into her bag, moved a little with the motion of the cart.

Keneally, potbellied, ginger-haired, his face a flushed drinker's mottle, strolled from the bathroom to them, gave Ellie a casual nod, and said to Nardone, "Where's the book?—Maxfield wants it."

"Well, he can't have it, Kenny," Nardone said.

"We haven't turned the apartment yet," Ellie said. "But any book goes downtown—not to Maxfield."

"You tell him then, sugar-lips," Keneally said, and walked away.

Sally Gaither had been a very neat whore. The doorman, Driscoll, had confided as much to the District Homicide team when Maxfield, dapper in a gray sharkskin summer suit, had led his people in. Driscoll had grinned and winked to let them in on this and that—an odd sight, since he was old enough to be any of their grandfathers. This old man had rattled on—he had not, however, gone into the apartment to see what was smelling like that. "—Smells like cookin', don't it? Took the nigger maid's word for that. Super's business, anyway." Didn't discuss his hundred dollars a month, either, and didn't have to. It was typical doorman's wages for letting johns go nicely by—no glances, smirks, or difficulties of any kind. A hundred for him, another for the night man. Circumspection in these matters being enforced by Ms. Gaither's ownership of her apartment, the management had confided to Maxfield first thing—not simply a tenant at all.

Two detectives were across the river talking to the night man—not with any hope. Neither that man nor Driscoll had seen anyone come to visit. Nobody asking for Gaither Saturday night, or all day Sunday. A slow day, Saturday must have been for Sally, a slow night, too, no doubt. But, according to Greenstein, a very busy Sunday morning. —And the delivery door had been wide open at the back of the building all day. Carpet cleaners scheduled to work weekends for the month—and now, of course, to be closely questioned.

As for the sturdy super, Correa—who had loudly prayed over the dead woman when he found her, prayers punctuated by the black lady's screams from the hall—he was under some suspicion because of these same prayers;

Maxfield and Keneally of the opinion they showed an unhealthy interest in the dead woman's spiritual welfare—which Correa might, for example, have sought to guarantee by an early departure to purgatory. District Homicide had seen many stranger motives than that.

Mr. Correa, blissfully unaware of his equivocal status, performed now as super, and with a long-shanked screwdriver, forced a simple skeleton lock on the bedroom closet door—though the key no doubt lay somewhere about the room. Mr. Correa had also wanted to shut off the hot water showering down on the corpse upon discovery, both to spare the dead woman further insult, and—it was his job—to save hot water. The building boiler, a wonder when new, was now very old and uncertain. He'd wanted to shut the water off, but fortunately for Correa-as-suspect, had not.

The big closet was packed with clothes, and Ellie, with some pleasure, thanked Correa, and stepping into an air of rose potpourri, and out of one less pleasant, leafed through a row of crowded hangers one by one, fingering swiftly for little bags pinned among the cloth, or perhaps a heavy pocket sagging a suit. Sally Gaither had had good taste—and been a sharp shopper for it—almost all discount copies, downtown sales and clearances. Only twelve uptown labels, and none of these in the gaudy row of a binge-shop at Saks or Bendel's. Neat, and close with a buck. Ellie smelled something of the woman among her clothes, and found with that faint odor a momentary fantasy of Sally Gaither with a client, or perhaps two—doing something awkard, with a groan.

Ellie had noticed, when she'd swiftly looked, still-faced, into the bathroom at Sally, and seen the small woman's predicament, that her delicate finger and toenails had been neatly painted a pale, pale pink. Her hair, a soaked clot of yellow, soggy on a spoiling scalp, had slipped a little backward from her brow, from under which cooked eyes with wrinkled whites gazed up.

Ellie imagined the woman alive, naked, slight and lissom, at play with one man—tall, with humorous ways—on the broad bed, while another, stockier, looked on.

Ellie took two bandboxes down from the closet shelf, and went through a heap of scented handkerchiefs—Irish lace along the edges, a tiny *S* embroidered at a corner (money spent on those, at least)—and a stack of boxes of costume jewelry, necklaces, pins, brooches and bracelets in all styles. To one small ornamented hair clip a single strand of ash-blond hair still clung, fine as a child's. It occurred to Ellie that the man who'd killed this prostitute had wrecked a particularly lovely creature—and it seemed odd to her that men, willing so often to murder to possess such perfection, could just as willingly destroy it.

The second bandbox held (tucked under packaged panty hose) fourteen thousand dollars in cash, divided and stacked, each denomination circled by a narrow red rubber band. Ellie counted the money twice, then carried the box out into the living room.

Maxfield was talking to another of his detectives (a man Ellie didn't know) while the fingerprint team was finishing up in the living room just ahead of Nardone and Keneally, who were searching side by side. Two CSIU men were having a discussion with Correa at the apartment door. Correa appeared upset.

"I have fourteen thousand dollars here, Lieutenant," Ellie said, and showed the box. Maxfield, bittersweet brown, elegant in his sharkskin suit, looked over, frowned, and nodded. Homicide had no great reputation as thieves; still, cash was cash, and deserved to be treated less publicly. When Ellie went back into the bedroom, Keneally—burrowing under the sofa cushions—stood and leaned over to speak with Nardone, who lay stretched on the floor examining the bottom of an end table (he had found the world full of cute cabinetry, little hidey-holes here and there). "—That's some partner you got. You ain't goin' to get rich, pal."

They found no book.

Not in the living room, the bedroom—(Fingerprints pouting at the handled bandboxes: "Look, the perp already did a wipe . . . will you people pretty-fuckin'-please stop addin' to the problem?")—nor in the bath. The folding chair (one of a set of four from the tiny breakfast nook) and its attendant twisted coat hangers remained in the tub. The small chair's blue vinyl seat had cheerfully shed the hours of scalding water, the steam, Sally's sticky flesh and feces. It looked like new.

Not in the kitchen, either. Ellie and the nameless detective went over it carefully, unloaded the refrigerator shelves, the cabinets, stripped off shelf paper, checked under the counter, took the top off a large coffee maker there, and every pot and pan, dumped mayonnaise and raspberry jam into the sink in search of a safe-deposit key, and emptied the ice cubes into the sink as well, and melted them with hot water.

They found no book, and no way to it.

"We have a number of cases of this kind," the Chief of the Department had said earlier that afternoon, "—all unsavory." The Chief's chins crowded the collar of his uniform shirt. He was a short, dark man, shaped like a bar of soap that had softened, then hardened again. "An individual, a prostitute of the more expensive type, has been the victim of a homicide."

"Today . . . ?"

"Discovered today." The Chief of the Department gave Ellie a surprised look, as if he weren't certain he'd seen her before. He stared at her for a moment. In three years on the Squad, Ellie had not discovered what the Chief thought of her—if indeed he thought of her, or any of the Squad, at all. Delgado was not close to his people. His round body, his warm brown eyes, his easy, coarse old New York accent, all misled. The Chief was cold as the moon and as remote. It was rumored the Commissioner was very fond of him—but it was difficult to see how that could be so. Most of Delgado's business dealt with the day-to-day direction of the New York City Police Department, particularly its uniformed men, and there were very few of the approximately thirty thousand employees of that massive and stony organization who did not fear him. The less important, very peripheral tasks of his office, such as the nominal supervision of the Squad, the Chief left to his clever captain, Anderson. It was highly unusual for any Squad member, including its commander, Lieutenant Leahy, to be called upstairs and down the corridor to Delgado's big corner office—invariably curtained from daylight—to walk the deep-pile gray carpet, to sit in the leather-bottomed straight-backed chairs.

Ellie had sat in the office that afternoon, her fourth

time there in three years, with Nardone and a detective named Morris Classman. Classman was a painfully thin, quiet, thoughtful man who'd been involved in a shooting. "Righteous," as television policemen, and perhaps Los Angeles policemen say, but odd nonetheless. He had, as a veteran patrolman more than a year before, killed two young perpetrators in the Bronx as these young men were exiting Colonial Liquors—the first with a paper bag filled with small bills, and, in his other hand, a .22 caliber revolver made in West Germany. He had a close friend with him, armed with a more formidable American-made .44 caliber weapon.

Classman had come upon the scene on foot patrol—car men were usually safer from such encounters—had called the first man and killed him when he offered fight. So far, so fine. Then witnesses began to differ. One, a black lady, stating that the second "perp" had whirled and presented his Continental Bulldog—two other witnesses, however, that this sad turkey, unmanned by the death of his friend, had begun to weep, leaned down and put his expensive handgun on the sidewalk—and had then, standing, unarmed and in tears, been shot to death by Patrolman Classman, whose face looked strange.

The Department—and, after a pause, the newspapers—had decided to believe the lady. Even so, Classman would have been a goner, headed for a career clerking at the Queen's auto pound—but for an uncle, Inspector Michael Classman, a Fordham graduate and ex-head of Central Robery Division. Mike Classman had made many friends in his thirty years on the Force—besides having once, in 1962, subdued and rescued from the top of the Manhattan tower of the Brooklyn Bridge a large man shouting a personal message from the prophet Zoroaster, and preparing to validate this communication by leaping to his death. Mike Classman had balanced along a cable, up there with the wind and the gulls, and had then abruptly fallen upon this proselyte, taken a severe cut across the face from the fellow's butcher knife, and, sneezing bright blood, had subdued and rescued him. Inspector Classman's many friends were not about to see Mike humiliated in the year of his retirement.

Morris Classman, therefore, went to the Squad, where

an occasional eye was kept on him, more because of his puzzling dullness—a nasal niceness that never varied—than because of any sudden odd humors, any toying with his new, short-barreled detective's revolver. He proved an exemplary investigator, careful and hardworking, and, after almost a year, the younger officers were convinced that the black woman had been the reliable witness in the affair.

The older men didn't believe it for a minute, and were carefully courteous whenever they spoke to him.

This thin, stooped man, who wore spectacles for reading, and lounged like a plain Henry Fonda playing a Jew, had sat, like Ellie and Nardone, painfully upright in his straight-backed leather-bottomed chair and listened to what the Chief of the Department had to say. The three of them were the shortest time-in-grades on the Squad, except for two young black men assigned temporarily and hardly seen in the squad room at all. Captain Anderson, standing behind Delgado's right shoulder, smiled down at them in a friendly way. He had never seemed to hold against Ellie her lack of response to his caressing hand. She thought of it almost every time she looked at him, but he seemed not to remember it at all.

"This woman might have kept a client book of some kind," Delgado had said, his gaze drifting away from Ellie to touch Nardone, "—lists of johns, descriptions, charges. If she did keep that sort of record—and some prostitutes with limited clientele do not—we want that material sequestered. From long experience, we've found these situations tend to become very involved, affect a number of people who might be embarrassed for little cause. . . ." He slid a red-veined marble paperweight slightly back and forth on the glossy walnut desktop. "—We think it best that any book, or diary or notes or whatever, if they exist, don't circulate for the pleasure of the press. If the perpetrator has that material, we want it. —If somebody else has it, we want it." He glanced at Classman. "I understand this officer has a source that might be helpful to you. . . ." The gaze, mournful, muddy, cold as deep water, swung back to Ellie and Nardone. "Now, it's your case—you two have it. Keep in mind this is to be a *focused* investigation, confidential, concentrating on this woman's killer—not peripheral issues. Do you understand me?"

"Yes, sir," Nardone said.

"Captain Anderson will be fully informed by Lieutenant Leahy as to progress—in detail."

"Yes, sir," Nardone said again. Lieutenant Leahy had not been invited to the office for this meeting.

After a few moments, it had seemed Delgado had nothing more to say, and first Nardone and then Ellie and Classman got to their feet and started out of the room. When they reached the door, the Chief cleared his throat, and they stopped to listen to him. He paused, however, to light a cigarette. Delgado smoked heavily—and an amused Anderson had described to Lieutenant Leahy the Chief's response in the Four Seasons when the maitre d' had asked him not to.

With the three detectives pausing at the door, Delgado had drawn a faintly wheezing drag on a Winston and said, "If you do find paper—don't make any copies." Behind his master, Anderson had smiled and made a friendly face.

It would be unpleasant, after such extraordinary, ranking attention, to disappoint, and since Ellie and Nardone had found nothing—and the patrolman first on scene had not stolen it, as he hadn't—then the whore's book (that handy list of suspects) likely didn't exist at all, or, if it did, might be snug in the insulation of the coil compartment of the killer's refrigerator, might be nested in his mattress springs. Might have gone to the sanitation people in a sack of garbage for landfill in the Bronx, or barged out for debris to litter the ocean floor.

"I don't give a damn what crap is coming out of downtown, about you people taking this case," Maxfield said to Ellie and her partner as they prepared to leave the scene, both looking forward to a different air, though they hadn't said so to each other, "—if you find something—you find out something, you pass it to us right-a-fuckin' way—and no pages missing! I don't care if she was balling the mayor's boyfriend!" Brave talk, and nothing more. Maxfield watched too much TV.

Neither Ellie nor Nardone replied, except that Nardone

gave Keneally, talking to Fingerprints across the room, a casual finger in farewell. It was a delayed response to Keneally's, given in the bathroom more than two hours before. Nardone always remembered that sort of thing. He and Keneally disliked each other, but both good Catholics, they did retreat at Avondale upstate every year, and it was a slender bond between them. They had never eaten at each other's houses, though their wives urged it annually, after each retreat. At Avondale, one morning, Nardone had seen Keneally come weeping from the Host.

It was late, almost seven, when they stood out on the corner of Second and Sixty-eighth Street, breathing a cooler, relieving air. "Want to go downtown and find Classman?" said Nardone.

It had taken Ellie months to realize that Nardone's zeal was a matter of duty, strictly, rather than the pleasures of action on the streets—and the displeasures of their homes—that held many detectives to their work past time. Nardone wanted badly to be home in Brooklyn with Connie and his daughter—and so proposed an evening with Classman and his report on Frankie Odum's possible contribution to the Gaither thing (Frankie having been a major madam in a four-apartment shop just west of the garment center). —In this way, Ellie and Nardone were, as partners, poorly matched. He had something beside the work, and she didn't.

"No," she said, "—it's too late, and I'm tired, Tommy."

Nardone nodded, said, "Well, take it easy," and leaned forward to kiss her on the cheek. His breath smelled faintly of Tic Tacs. Then he walked away west on Sixty-eighth, heading for the subway; they'd hitched a ride uptown with a detective named Burke, from Forensic, to avoid the trip all the way back downtown to the garage. Nardone had his head down as he walked, thinking, and Ellie saw people step out of his bulky way. Tourists, seeing sometimes in summer the bulge of his revolver at his hip, blousing out the fabric of his short-sleeve shirt—seeing his thick, black curly hair, his blunt, swarthy face and brutal build, would take Nardone for a big-city gangster, a Mafia person. New Yorkers, who knew cheap shoes when they saw them, knew he was no such thing, but stepped aside for him in any case.

Nardone used the subway every day to get in and out of town. He was the only detective Ellie knew who lived in Brooklyn and didn't drive into Manhattan. He left the car (an Oldsmobile with frequent transmission trouble) for Connie to use, shopping.

When, after slow weeks of acquaintance, of working together, Nardone had shown Ellie increasing care and tenderness, she had assumed he might be falling in love with her. She was surprised and flattered to discover it wasn't so. Nardone simply liked her. He liked her very much—the first man who had liked her, as far as she knew. Certainly the first man who had liked her very much. This made the big man dear to her, and Connie Nardone—a gentle, dark, plump pigeon—sensing she had nothing to fear from this blond American partnering Tommy all over town—had welcomed Ellie into her home and cooked for her. For a few months Ellie had spent a good deal of time in Brooklyn, had eaten many dinners with them, and had taken her turn exercising Marie, crouching on the living-room floor alongside the silent child, moving the meager arms and legs in the sequence of a crawl—then, once the edge of the rug was reached, reversing direction back across the room toward the TV.

Marie's eyes, dark and deep as cups of coffee, would seem to Ellie to belong to a different person than did those fragile, disconnected arms and legs. Marie, staring at her, made her feel odd—as if the braindamaged child commanded Ellie to come and crawl. Once, after she and Clara had had some drinks, Ellie dreamed that Marie Nardone stood up and danced, a quick snappy little prancing step, every evening after Ellie left their house.

For several months Ellie was close to the Nardones, and met their friends, and went on dates with Connie's brother, a recorder in the borough court. Gradually, though, very gradually, she went to Brooklyn less. At first she was ashamed, thinking it was because of Marie, that the crippled child upset her—but she soon realized it wasn't that at all, only the closeness of the Nardones that left no room for another person close to them. Connie's brother, a very nice man, had been the one to reassure her, to tell her that.

"Connie and Tommy," he'd said in his car on the way to Roosevelt Island after a hockey game. "—Tommy and Connie. Nobody could ever get in there edgewise from high school, you name it. Those two were *the* item—ask anybody. So, don't feel bad."

Charlie Corsaro was a decent man, burdened by his looks. Goodnatured, generous, and competent in his work, he was small, bald, and big-nosed. "A Walt Disney rat," he'd said to Ellie once, smiling, "—that's what I look like." He'd said that in a Chinese restaurant, the Hu-Nan. Later, weeks later, after they'd gone on several dates, he'd driven her over the causeway onto the island one evening, parked in the street outside Ellie's apartment, and asked if he could come in for a while, for coffee. She'd felt he was becoming too fond of her, and said no . . . that she was tired. Charlie had sat in the car and smiled at her, a hard-edged shadow thrown by a streetlight slicing down across his face. "Would you believe," he said to her, "—would you believe that inside this body there's a tall, nice-lookin' guy . . . who cares for you?" Ellie saw there were tears in his eyes, and decided not to see him again.

Charlie had called her several times after that, then stopped. When she went to the Nardone's thereafter, he was never there. Connie said something only once, while they were in the kitchen, and Tommy, with Marie on his lap, was watching television. When Connie mentioned her brother, Ellie told her she liked Charlie very much, but couldn't care for him more than that. —This may have pushed her a little farther from the Nardones, though Connie was always kind and welcoming to her, and gave her recipes.

Now, Tommy was lost down the block. Ellie couldn't see him through the evening crowd anymore. She waited for the light, crossed the street, and walked downtown toward Bloomingdale's.

There, she drifted in lambent gloom through the boutiques along the ground-floor entrance, seeing herself, counters of luscious goods, other drifting women reflected in dark mirrors at every turn. Snowy gloves in soft stacks.

She picked up a pair, smoothing the fine blanched kid in her fingers, feeling the slight roughness of stitched decoration, the tiny supple roll of turned border paired along the sides of every finger. Ellie had gloves, though none as fine as these, and never wore them. It was still a little too early for gloves, even if she had the occasion. She walked through dreaming women to the scarves, and found buried in a furled banner of them one fine Italian silk in a small blue and white print—little white heraldic animals, leopards and lions rampant on a field of Prussian blue. A minor tag at the corner read $32. A larger label, off-white, loosely sewn, Linette. The clerk, fat and in her twenties, with a dark pageboy haircut and an unfortunate horizontally-striped green sweater-dress, came over to her, took her credit card and the scarf, folded the silk into a Bloomingdale's box, and left it on the counter while she marked the charge, processed the card, and handed Ellie her receipt, her card, and the box. —It just fit into Ellie's purse, and she walked away pleased with it. At such times, the whole massive structure of the Police Department was a reassurance to her, a guarantee of her credit, of every sensible purchase. And the retirement was certain. Ellie once, years before, had imagined the Department as her husband, a new husband, powerful and slow.

The scarf a small treasure in her purse—where it pressed close to her shield case and ID, and a stainless Smith & Wesson Bodyguard .38 (an expensive little revolver, too difficult for many policewomen, some policemen, too, to fire accurately for quick second and third shots)—Ellie took the stairs, and then an escalator up two floors.

At Sweaters she asked a girl for Rebecca Platt, and the clerk pointed through an aisle of cotton cable knits to the opposite side wall. There, behind a long beige screen, Ellie found Mrs. Platt amid a sample of the fall collection—shawls, vests, and leg warmers in rust, taupe, and tweed.

"Rebecca, you're rushing the season. —It's still late summer out there."

Rebecca Platt looked up from her work—a white plastic countertop display tree of leg warmers—and pretended she hadn't known Ellie was there. "Jesus, it's the Queen of the Cops!" She smiled at Ellie as though she liked her.

Ellie had known Rebecca since her assignment in liaison with the Child Welfare people. Then, Rebecca's husband, a wire man with Con Ed, had beaten their little boy to death, and been arrested, tried, and sent to prison for it. Rebecca had played the addled female, a loyal and terrified innocent married to a brute. Ellie, as had most of the others dealing with the case, found Rebecca convincing. —A social worker named Lennie Spears, had, however, not found her so—and had introduced Ellie to a playmate of the martyred boy. That playmate, Jessie Chaiken, seven, had described the loyal Rebecca beating her deceased six-year-old's bare feet with a coat hanger and a toilet plunger handle, while her husband, the brute, sniveling, held Justin firmly to the floor.

This information, whispered to Ellie by the small witness in Lennie Spears' office, had led her to approach Rebecca—whom she then recognized as a thug, savage as any, but cocooned in a social shape both apparently harmless and respectable—with the notion of making a source of her. This person, Mrs. Platt, was a handsome woman in her forties, black-haired, dark-complexioned, nervous, bangled, quick-motioned, humorous and capable. Successful in her profession, standing strong against a tidal flood of talented homosexual men, she countered their refinement with an extraordinary capacity for work. Rebecca also, as she confided once to Ellie over coffee, fucked like a bunny—and had, by these muscular surrenders, made familiars of several executives in the store.

"But if I don't get my gun," she'd said to Ellie over a second cup, "—to hell with them. I give, but I've got to get, too." She'd winked, and pursed bright lips in a little kiss.

Early in their relationship, Ellie, unable to prevent herself, mentioned what she knew of Rebecca's cooperation, at least, in the destruction of her child. The result of this, introduced while they were walking together over to Second Avenue, had been no dreadful yawning of the pit, but only a glance at once weary and amused. "—You didn't have any kids, did you?" Disturbing in the finality of its tense, indicating no hope for Ellie Klein ever to have a child to murmur to.

"No," Ellie said.

"Well, sweetie, let me tell you, kids are wonderful—but angels, they're not. Justin, may God keep and bless the small son-of-a-bitch, was a difficult little boy." She'd sighed, and stopped to look into Liberty of London's shop window. "Jesus—look at that cute kitsch! —And don't tell me where you got your little made-up horror story. Dollars to doughnuts it was that tiny turd, Jessie Chaiken." Another swift glance. "—Justin wasn't much, but he was perfect compared with that little nose-picking horror. —Well, if you met the mother, you'd understand. I caught the oh-so-shy Jessie with my Justin in a closet once, and I mean deep in a closet, tooting on my Justin's tiny wee-wee to beat the band. —Thank God Matt never knew about that one—he'd have been up the river that much sooner!" She'd taken Ellie's arm to cross the street, and noticed a girl walking in front of them. "—Jesus, look at that poor thing. She's screwed herself bowlegged! *Men.* Men and kids . . . Truth is, there's not that much to any of them; a blow job or a peanut-butter sandwich, and they're satisfied."

This woman, who, after investigation in Records, Ellie found had been an occasional prostitute and sometime small-time dealer in cocaine years before, became for Ellie a minor source, too casual to be called an informant—too employed and tough-minded, as well. Ellie had, in a roundabout way, threatened Rebecca with disclosure and indictment—Spears had urged it, and on the evidence of two other children beside Jessie Chaiken—but Rebecca had not been frightened.

"Listen, dear, I went to New York once"—she meant the hospital—"with a broken arm, and Mathew Platt broke it, and told Dr. Nussman he had. If I ever do get to court, believe me, once I've told the jury the hell I went through with that maniac and that creep of a kid—believe you me, they'll be on the train to Ossining to tear the bastard's nuts right off. Then they'll come back, go out to Mount Zion, and dance on that little asshole's grave. —I'm not afraid of any New York jury. . . ."

Still, she'd told Ellie what little she had to tell, but in the fashion of a gossiping friend. —Her ancient tribulations with a madam who didn't know a twat from a turnip; the clothes she'd had stolen by a man who envied her style and determined to emulate it in massive drag; the so-called dope dealers who'd embarrassed her with a fake mule trip to the Bahamas. . . . These matters—and a few others—she chatted about, gesturing violently, her bracelets musical. And occasionally, if Ellie persisted (and bought lunch), Rebecca would relate some oblique tale of plans, of probabilities, of perhapses in criminal endeavor on the Upper East Side. Call girls and their various sorts of johns; odd and angular plots to bring cocaine into the country—none of these very credible, and all laced with revelations of the great: this singer, and what pleased him; that Superior Court Justice, so desperate to be cleaned, powdered, and diapered, once he'd moaned and made poo-poo; and politicians innumerable, local and national, in all their spotted nudity. —These stories, a few true, Rebecca garnered from old friends lonely for a companionable dinner in an uptown restaurant—or from new friends, expensive young prostitutes still exultant in their release from secretarial pools, word processing, schoolteaching or first marriages, drifting on word of mouth to Rebecca, who took considerable fees in payment for personal and cultural remakes and do-overs of volcanic thoroughness, lasting weeks. Concerts, fine restaurants, museums, classic films at the Modern, elocution, makeup, clothes, aerobics and dance. *Sofa*—not couch; *curtains*—not drapes; *pictures*—not paintings; wool, silk, linen, and cotton for clothes—and for Christ's sake, read a book!

From this inconsequential source, Ellie received little of value. In three years of Rebecca Platt, she was able to pass on sufficient information to a joint antidrug task force to facilitate a minor arrest at La Guardia, a matter of no interest to the Department—and, almost a year later, to report to the office of the Chief of the Department (in the person of Captain Anderson) that an important member of city government was behaving foolishly with a black transsexual prostitute named Audrey Walker, this last of definite interest to the Department.

For these slight returns, Ellie had bought Rebecca two or three dozen lunches, resisted letting her see the apartment on Roosevelt Island—Rebecca was urgent about decoration, deeply interested in Ellie's private life—and suffered numerous suggestions regarding her clothes, her jewelry (costume), and her finances. "I know," Rebecca had said once at a table at Sign of the Dove, "—a guy would pay five hundred, cash on the barrelhead, to spend a night with a lady detective on the cops. Give him the long legs, the real blond muff, he might go seven-fifty. Of course, you're no kid—you have some sags, some imperfections. . . . Still, I say seven-fifty. I can get you that. —You like money?" Rebecca, Ellie had noticed then, had a tiny bright-yellow wedge in the pupil of her dark left eye. "Well?" she'd said, "what about it . . . ?"

"For God's sake, Eleanor," Rebecca draped the last leg warmer, "—don't bother me today. It's been a ten-hour day, and another couple hours to go." She stepped back to look at the display-tree of leg warmers. "—Ever see such shit in your life? Can you believe women will wear these damn things another year?"

"Let's go somewhere where we can talk."

"We can talk right here," Rebecca said, lifting a stack of folded plaid shawls from a tub-cart. "Now these are all right, if you want to look like Mother Machree. I've told Robinson a dozen times—leave the plaids downstairs for the drifters. Serious shoppers don't shop plaids!"

Ellie picked up one of the shawls, heather and gold. It was soft, light, and beautiful, but there was a lot of fringe. "—Did you know a woman named Sally Gaither?"

"Put that down; you'd look like shit in it with all that fringe. You're too late for the blond love-child bit, sweetheart." Rebecca began draping shawls over a transparent S-curved display rack. "—Do I?" She cocked an eye at Ellie while draping. "—*Did* I? Is little Gaither a goner?"

"How well did you know her?" Ellie, surprised and pleased. Something from a source—probably more than Classman would get from his big-time madam. "—See her lately?"

"So," Rebecca said, "—Gaither is a goner." She unfolded another shawl—green plaid ground, orange added. "Now, that is a surprise." She draped the green and orange just over the edge of the heather and gold. "Odd for a john to go ape over that package. . . ."

"Why not? Why wouldn't he? —She must have been pretty."

"Pretty—but a purse, from what I heard. You know what that means?" Rebecca reached down into the tub for another shawl. "It means she was nothing but business. Fun, but business—and she let the men know it. That was the dumb part, letting the assholes know it. No romancing. A man'll bang a purse once or twice, pay the cash—and take the chill. Then they'll try for a girl who at least acts like she's falling in love."

"She made a good living at it."

Rebecca draped. "Damn good, I'd say. I'd say that little piece never spent a dime if she could help it, either." She finished the last of the shawls, stepped back to look, then in to shake out a fringe and drape again. "—This fucking fringe."

Ellie was tired of standing; she walked to the counter beside the legwarmer tree and leaned against it, watching Rebecca searching in the depths of the cart.

"Did you know her well?"

"Ah," said Rebecca, "—the jewels of the collection." She bent into the cart, grunting with effort, and came up with a handful of tam-o'shanters, all in the same plaids as the shawls, all topped by bright burnt-orange balls of yarn. "Would you believe this crap? Thank God I don't have to sell it. I'd be ashamed to face a customer and try to sell her this garbage. . . . Can you imagine a grown woman with this shit on her head? —Maybe a college girl, looks juicy in anything, but can you imagine a grown-up in something like this—with the shawl?" There was another white plastic tree at the other end of the counter, and Rebecca began putting the tams on it, pausing every now and then to change the bonnets' places to avoid too fierce a clash of patterns, or unfortunate conjunctions of greens and bright blues, yellows and vivid pinks. "—Do you believe this stuff? Can you believe it? Robinson's got one lover-boy too many up there, that's all there is to it. Those boys are sucking his brains right out!"

"You see much of Sally, Rebecca?"

Rebecca paused at the plastic tree, trying to choose the top tam. "I saw that little chinch just twice—and that was enough for me." She looked down, choosing between a blue and rust, and a yellow, green, and mauve. "What the hell. . . ." She spun the blue and rust on her forefinger, then hung it over the looped armature at the top of the display-tree. Tossed the yellow, green, and mauve back into the cart. "There's some crap I won't display. —I tried to help the little bitch—but no way. All she was looking for were discounts. She was a piece, though, one of those little cute-as-a-button types, good for playing Daddy's daughter, except she was too old for it. . . ." Rebecca searched the tub-cart for anything she might have overlooked. "Little girl—a six. Who the hell killed her? —You might as well strangle a wallet!"

"One of her clients, I suppose," Ellie said. "—He scalded her to death in her shower."

Rebecca straightened up from the cart, and stood for a few moments looking at the back side of the beige screen that separated her task from the rest of the floor. Her throat worked as if she were drinking something.

"Poor baby," she said. "—Poor little baby . . ." She turned and looked at Ellie, her eyes dry, black, and bright as a bird's, and cleared her throat. "Men are such assholes," she said.

Ellie heard a woman shopper, just beyond the screen, asking a salesgirl if she had a cable knit that tied in front, with open side pockets, that could be used as a casual jacket. Ellie happened to have a dark brown sweater almost like that. . . . The salesgirl's reply was almost inaudible. Ellie thought she said she had two styles that front-tied—and something else about pockets. Ellie couldn't quite hear that.

Rebecca walked back and forth in front of the new display, surveying her work. "—Does this say 'autumn' to you?" She rattled her bracelets.

"It says you're rushing the season."

"Would it say 'autumn' to you in a couple of weeks?"

"I guess so. . . ."

"What if I had Signs make me a sign that said 'Rush the Season with Cozy Wool!' . . . ? Yellow, brown, and gold—you know? Leaves. Fallen leaves. —That's what I call making a virtue out of bullshit."

"I suppose so. . . ." Ellie was feeling tired enough to go to sleep right there. Seeing Sally Gaither sitting that way in her shower, all ruined, had made Ellie tired, worn her out. . . .

"But not really, right?"

"Sure," Ellie said, making an effort. "—I think it's better for you to say you're rushing the season, than have them say it."

"You're right," Rebecca said. "—I'm right. Signs is closed, but I'll get Jake to do it in the morning. Now I've got to go up to Robes and dress dummies. Want to come up with me, and we can go have dinner when I'm through?"

"No," Ellie said, trying to think of an excuse. "—I've got a date."

"Who with . . . ? Not another cop?" Rebecca stared at Ellie, trying to find out a secret, her head cocked to one side.

"No."

"Thank God. It's bad enough being one, without going out with them. —Who is he?"

"Nobody you know."

"Then he's nobody. I know every guy on the make on the East Side. Every guy with money, anyway. . . ." Rebecca began to maneuver the tub-cart out from behind the screen.

"You said you only saw Sally twice. —What was the other time?"

"Same as first." Rebecca began pushing the cart back toward the fitting rooms. "Come on, follow me. Don't be ashamed to be seen with a woman doing honest work."

Ellie's feet were hurting. She followed Rebecca, seeing two women look their way. The women were mother and daughter, both neat, stocky, with noses that had a small bulb of flesh at the end—not enough to spoil their looks, but noticeable. The two women took identical marching sideways steps to try to peer behind the edge of the screen to see what Rebecca had put on display. "Will you look at that?" Rebecca said. "They're crazy about that crap. Let me see, let me see. . . ." She turned the cart into the last aisle in the row. "—Second time was the same thing. She wanted to know about designer markdowns, the days they were released—so she could get downtown early, you know? I told her, 'Honey—if I knew the day each designer was releasing, I would tell *nobody*, except for big money.' —Susan brought her by.

Susan brought her the first time, too. Introduced her. Both times at the store, and that was it—didn't even spring for lunch."

Rebecca used the front of the cart to butt open a door to the right of the fitting rooms. Beyond was a wide gray corridor with closed freight elevator doors at the far end of it.

"Who's Susan . . .?"

Rebecca shoved the cart up against the corridor wall. "You want that shitty hat? . . . Take it." She reached down into the cart with a grunt.

"No, thanks."

"Bullshit." Rebecca straightened up with the tam in her hand. "It's ugly, but it could look cute. You know—a snowy day in the woods up in Connecticut. You jump around in the snow throwing snowballs at some jerk with nice eyes. Then it would look cute, you know. Wouldn't make any difference if it was ugly."

"No, thanks . . ."

"Will you take it! You want to hurt my feelings? You want to hurt Alfred's feelings?" She meant the late Alfred Bloomingdale. "It's ugly; it needs somebody. Take it!"

"No thanks, Rebecca."

"Oh, all right," Rebecca said. "I don't blame you. Nobody'd look good in this piece of shit." She threw the tam back into the cart.

"Did you ever mention Susan to me before?"

"Hell, yes—Susan Margolies; she teaches at NYU. She's the psychologist. Maybe she met Gaither at school down there; she said Sally was always taking courses. . . ."

"Birnbaum," Ellie said, pleased. Todd Birnbaum had been the mayor's political aide, fallen madly in love with Audrey Walker—once a black man, a plumber's assistant—later, and likely still, a beautiful woman with endless slender legs, lovely breasts, black eyes blacker than her soft skin, and blood buzzing with injected hormones.

"Now you got it—that's right! Susan and Audrey are buddies, been buddies for ages. —I told you . . . Susan's friends with everybody. I thought maybe she and Sally were having a thing, you know? Sally's cute. —She was . . . Very *femme,* except where cash was concerned. But now, I don't think so. —I don't think Susan kisses kitty; she's got too much sense of humor, you know?"

"You have her address?"

"Hell, no. She's in the book."

Ellie's legs were aching, just behind her knees. "—Well, thanks, Rebecca. I really appreciate it. —You've been a help."

"Anytime, sweetheart." Rebecca leaned close and kissed Ellie on the cheek. She had hard lips. "You know I like to help; you cops need all the help you can get. You're getting swamped. —Listen, they changed your duty? You on Homicide, now?"—holding her head to one side, listening with great attention.

"No," Ellie said, "—this is something else."

"Still on that Mickey Mouse downtown thing? —They ought to put you on something else, one of the regular squads. They're wasting a smart gal."

It occurred to Ellie, not for the first time, that Rebecca must talk to many people, perhaps to other people in the Department.

"I'm tired, Rebecca; I want to get home."

"—Get ready for the big date, huh?" Rebecca stared at her, smiling, seeing that Ellie had lied, enjoying having caught her at it.

"That's right." Ellie turned away and tugged the corridor door open. "Thanks a lot; I really do appreciate it."

"Oh, anytime . . ." Rebecca said, standing by the cart, smiling at her. "—Lunch Friday?"

Ellie was tired of Rebecca, tired of talking with her. She didn't want to keep her company on Friday. She didn't want another lunch, with Rebecca sitting across from her, staring at her, fuller of questions than Ellie was.

"All right. —Maybe. I'll leave a message for you." Rebecca had recently gotten a phone-answering machine, and was very proud of it. Ellie walked away into the store, heard Rebecca say, very distinctly, "It's a date . . ." as the door closed behind her.

On Fifty-ninth Street, the evening was becoming night, but slowly. The dirty peach and purples of New York's September sunsets dusted the west sides of East Side buildings. As she walked over toward the tram station,

Ellie passed a hot-dog cart, its yellow-and-blue umbrella folded, being wheeled along the gutter by a tired young Greek, heading for the warehouse downtown. The cart's odor reminded Ellie of Sally Gaither, and how she'd gone.

The trams were up in the darkening air—sailing past each other on their cables high over the East River. Ellie deposited her token and joined the small crowd gathered on the second-story platform of the station's small concrete castle. Two young children, brother and sister, came and stood beside her; Ellie heard their mother murmuring to them from their other side. She glanced that way, and the woman looked back, smiling over the bright heads of her children. Then they all looked up, and watched the small gondola come gliding down out of fading sunset light, down over building roofs, over the avenue, and into its berth before them.

Its sliding doors opened, its passengers filed out, and Ellie walked in with the others, reached up to grip one of the handholds, and stood swaying slightly, watching through a wide window as the gondola trembled and ran smoothly up into the air. The lights were on along the East River Drive, reflecting, shimmering at the edges of dark water. The East River ran flat black far beneath them as they reeled along.

On Roosevelt Island, Ellie took the small bus for its short route, got off, walked past the liquor store and a travel-agency office—the store still open, the office closed—past another apartment building, and into hers. Through the lobby—the security man, just come on duty, nodded and smiled—and straight on down the ground-floor corridor to the last door on the left.

She heard Mayo calling, cursing her as she took out her key. When the door swung open, the small Siamese, not much larger than a kitten, ran swiftly out into the hallway, as though expecting someone else. This temperamental game, a result of too many hours of solitude, was liable to continue through several minutes of calling and coaxing, with the cat skittering along the corridor from door to door, sounding its hoarse complaint.

Ellie took a step, stooped, caught the Siamese as he started off, and held him against her for a moment, until he quieted, kneading at her breast with soft, strong paws, the claws only very slightly extended. She carried him inside and shut the door—remembering, as it closed behind her, that she'd had shopping to do. Milk . . . bread. Some pineapple sherbet. Something else she couldn't remember. . . . She put the cat down to turn on the hall light, and he began to march slowly around her, tail in the air (bent at the tip), talking to himself.

Ellie'd had two cats. The other—a fat half-Persian—had died of a kidney ailment, and left Mayo, who'd hated her, bereft. Ellie'd thought of getting another, but consideration of odors, snagged upholstery, another pair of perfect, empty eyes to watch her from the back of the couch, had prevented it.

She put her purse down on the hall table, checked her answering machine—there were no messages—then turned right at the end of the short hallway, went into the bedroom, and put on the bedside lamp. She kicked off her shoes, hitched up her skirt, and tugged her panty hose down and off—then reached under her skirt again, and gently drew the lips of her vulva apart, feeling a cool, momentary kiss of air. She had read long ago that fresh air was necessary for those tissues, that it was bad to keep them compressed, closed, and heated hour after hour until infection began to cook. Either she'd read that, or come to the conclusion on her own. Both Klein and Spears, in their time, had caught her at it—the quick little motion of her fingers there when she undressed—and made fun. Spears said she was spoiling the taste.

Ellie took off her summer suit and hung it in the closet—thinking she'd heat up the rice and one of the small cans of chili—bent forward slightly, arms winged back, delicate shoulder blades in relief, unhooked her bra, and tossed it on the bed. She stood, absently caressing her small breasts, lifting them up with a gentle stroking motion as if to counteract in that way all the sullen weight of gravity upon them throughout the day. —She used wire-edged bras to support them, make them seem a little bigger, even though Clara said she shouldn't, and these left red marks engraved. She went into the bathroom and turned on the light, leaving the door open on the empty apartment—sat on the john, and, after a moment's relaxation, farted and began to pee. The fart was soft, high-pitched, and querulous, and Ellie smiled at its resemblance to Mayo's cries. —There had been several months after Klein had left her, during which she had once or twice communed with farts she produced, answering soprano with soprano, gruff with gruff reply. She had also spent a lot of money getting her hair done, particularly shampooed, so as to enjoy the touch of another person's hands. —That was, Ellie supposed, wiping herself, much the same use Sally Gaither's men had made of her. A small, cool woman, murdered hot. Possibly some poor maniac, disappointed by Sally's chill, had resolved to warm her under water.

Ellie reached back to flush, got up, put on her shower cap, and stepped into the tub to turn the shower on and balance its temperature. She made it cooler than usual.

Soaped and rinsed, she soaped her legs again, took a throwaway razor from the corner of the tub, and taking care around the bones of her ankles, began to shave her legs. She heard Mayo, and through the translucent shower curtain, water-stippled, dripping, saw his small silhouette pacing back and forth on the bathroom carpet. Ellie flicked at the curtain with her finger, but he paid no attention. She heard his muttering over the drumming water. —Ellie enjoyed shaving her legs, the length and general smoothness of them—though she also enjoyed the fine felt of blond down that grew along her shins, when, on vacations at the beach in summer, she didn't shave. She was fond of the memory of her legs' smoothness and perfection when she was younger. —Now, and for years, she had watched with interest the fine traceries of tiny veins clustering beneath the sheer skin behind her knees. The faintest touch of the same turquoise could be seen on her left calf, in proper light, when she wore no hose. Ellie found, though, she didn't mind these slowly gathering imperfections. They interested her, as if her legs belonged to another woman, had been very beautiful, and were now slowly being spoiled.

She turned off the water, shoved the shower curtain back, selected the less used of two canary-yellow towels—but used enough to have a faint bite to its odor when she held it to her face—and dried herself. The phone rang as she finished.

Ellie went into the bedroom, wrapping the towel around her, Mayo snaking through her feet. She picked up the phone and sat on the edge of the bed. Her father's picture, in an oval tortoise-shell frame, stood on the bureau top facing her. The photograph, her father smiling into the camera, had been taken almost a year before he died. Ellie had never sketched him.

"El?"

"Hi, Clara."

"Listen, can you come over tonight?" It was a quiet, round, full, humming voice, as if its owner were about to chuckle.

"Oh, I can't, Clara. I'm exhausted—I had an unbelievable day. Worse than usual." Her father smiled at her, squinting a little in the sunlight. Ellie had taken the picture herself, in the backyard of the house in Queens; a section of the brickwork showed in the photograph, just above her father's left shoulder.

The voice hummed softly in her ear. Clara almost always spoke softly. "A lawyer's trick," she'd said, "—it makes them listen up."

"No . . ." Ellie said. She reached down, picked up the Siamese, and put him in her lap. "—I'm going to have some leftover rice and chili, and I'm going to sleep. No. —No way . . ." She listened a few moments more. "Yes, I will," she said, and hung up. She stood, the cat leaping softly down, and tugged the towel from her hips as she went to the closet for her dark green robe, put it on, and walked out to the kitchen, Mayo stalking behind.

Ellie took a can of Nine Lives from the cupboard over the counter, opened it, scooped the stuff into a saucer with a spoon, and slid the saucer just under the small kitchen table, where Mayo, safe in this shadow den, ran to it and began to eat. Ellie bent for a moment and stroked him, feeling the fragile configurations of his bones beneath her fingertips.

Then she opened the refrigerator, took out the plastic container of cooked rice, and began to search the cabinets for a can of chili. She found one behind the can of cherry pie filling—opened it, mixed the rice and chili together in a small saucepan, added some warm water, butter, Tabasco sauce and a dollop of ketchup, and had just set it on the burner on low when the phone rang. She answered it out in the hall.

"You cunt," Clara said. "—Do you have somebody there?"

"No," Ellie said, and hung up the phone.

When she finished her supper, she went to the hall, got her purse, and took it into the bedroom. She sat on the bed, took the .38 out, and put it on the bedside table. Then she took out the Bloomingdale's package, unwrapped it, and unfolded the scarf. She sat for a while, looking at it, smoothing the blue silk and holding the material up to the light so the small white animals stood out in bold relief. Ellie stood up so she could see herself in the bureau mirror, and draped her scarf around her neck. It clashed with the bathrobe's green, and she took it off, folded it, went to the bureau, and put it in the top right-hand drawer. Then she took off her robe, draped it over the foot of the bed, turned off the bedside lamp, tugged the covers down, and got into bed.

Ellie lay still for some time, enjoying the darkness, then turned on her left side, stroked the soft edge of the pillowcase for a moment, and fell asleep.

She slept, quite still, for hours—kept company by the small electric clock's slow sweeping hands, its constant faint hum—almost below the range of hearing, and, silent now in darkness, Mayo, pacing the apartment wide awake, slipping under chairs, ranging the couch, sliding through the gloomy hall—hunting for creatures never found, of which he had no clear notion as to sight or size or scent, his superb slit pupils stretched to perfect ponds of black.

An hour more, and Ellie woke, turned to feel a cool, smooth surface of sheet beneath her hip, and went to sleep again. She dreamed her father had called to her, and she walked and drifted from the side of the house where she'd been watching flowers, and saw him in the backyard, measuring a window frame for glass. Sheets of glass stood behind him, glittering, flashing in the sunlight.

Ellie thought she asked him why he wasn't working in the garage, but if she had, he didn't hear her. He measured, then let the rule-tape retract with a flicker of white.

"Eleanor," he said, looking down into a sheet of glass. "Eleanor . . ." He turned and looked at her, smiling. She'd forgotten how nice-looking he was, even with his blue workshirt sweated through, a light frost of beard stubble on his face. His eyes were as gray as she remembered. His fingernails were bruised blue from his work.

"Sugar-bear," her father said, "—you visiting? Or goin' to stay awhile?"

Ellie moved in some wrong way, and was in the kitchen, though she wanted to stay and talk with him. It was empty; her mother had left it clean and dark. She looked out a strange window, and saw her father talking to a man with bare feet. Her father pointed to the window, and the man turned and looked across the yard—and was able to see her, even though she stepped back into shadows. Then he began to dance, barefoot, a slow dance while he looked at her, raising his knees high, changing to a swift little sideways shuffle. She'd never seen his face before.

Outside the apartment building, down past the western edge of the island, out across the deep, slow estuary tide, a bright knotted cord of light snaked in from the north, moving, twinkling as the East River Drive began to murmur in darkness, to hum, to tremble, to vibrate with the weight of traffic. There, more and more machines were rolling, speeding, thumping past potholes, booming over steel slab and black pavement, rushing, rushing into the shaking city.

Far from this disturbance, the earth spun slowly to morning along the shifting sea, and the Colonel and his men flew into Kennedy out of the sun.

CHAPTER 3

"By the short hairs," said the First Deputy Commissioner. Francis Connell was a very large man with eyes the color of pencil lead.

"So—if they got us, we got them." John Cherusco, an Assistant Chief and Commander of Intelligence.

"We have shorter hairs," said Chief of the Department Delgado.

These three men, three lords of the New York City Police Department—Connell and Delgado rough equals, Cherusco not—sat almost at ease in the First Deputy's large corner office, where glass walls gave the city to them on two sides, its buildings, its morning light reflecting in little in the glass-fronted desk photographs of the First Deputy's wife and two daughters, in the glass covering his citations and honors along the office walls—his diploma from Fordham, his honoraries from NYU and Binghamton, the group portraits with men and women of Democratic Party politics throughout the city and state.

With all this, still he sat in service of a greater.

"What does the P.C. say?" Cherusco—slight, fierce, dark-eyed, big-nosed, shifty-headed as a hungry bird. Though a respected man, he did not ordinarily spend much time in the First Deputy's office. His two stars, enough to frighten twenty thousand lesser ranks in the Department, counted for little on this floor of Headquarters, for less in this corner office.

"The Commissioner," the First Deputy spoke of his boyhood friend, his lifelong friend, only as the Commissioner, "—the Commissioner put a stop to this operation two years ago, right after he was appointed." A comfort, as well as some slight discomfort always in speaking of his friend, who had, when both were thirteen years old and masturbating together in Mr. Kramer's basement, said, "Oh . . . Frank," and, his narrow hand at his own part traced slimly with silver, laid his handsome head for a moment into the angle of the future First Deputy's throat and shoulder. —A memory that, now and then, still drifted though Francis Connell like a breeze, sometimes chill, sometimes warmer.

"Stopped it four months after he was appointed." Cherusco's dark, hectoring voice had all the Bronx ground up in it.

"The Commissioner put a complete stop to that operation as soon as he was apprised of it!" For the record, if not quite true.

"Almost," said Chief of the Department Delgado. The Chief, uniformed as the other two were not, his stout bulk crowded into fine dark blue, his buttons gold-plated for eternal polish, sat in the dimmest portion of the room—the corner where some architecture high above cast a long shadow through the left-side wall of glass—his familiar practice even in these airy new spaces, where most morning shadows amounted to little. "—Let's not kid ourselves on this one. This one could be a problem."

"How long is this meetin' goin' to take?" Cherusco said, not famous for deference. "—I killed three appointments for this. I got people waitin' for me, right now."

"We all have people waiting for us, John," Delgado said, reproof in the lack of any sounding.

Cherusco closed his mouth.

A pause in the conversation. These three men did not, as most men do, appear to fade when sitting silent. These three had, however many years before, been accustomed in line of duty to struggle physically with other determined and dangerous men—striking them, slugging, wrestling them down—kneeling, if necessary, on the downed man's neck to hold and subdue him on filthy pavement while many people watched. Two had drawn and fired their revolvers in those days. One had killed a man. —These experiences, though long past, had left a coarse practicality behind, a ready knowledge of the men and women in hiding beneath clothing, behind faces—of the way this person or that would feel to the hands if struck, if seized and wrestled down, struggling, weeping, begging them to let him go . . . let her go.

All three men, despite their maturity, their grand positions, were armed.

The First Deputy's wonderful black leather chair—a nine-hundred-dollar item in the Department's budget—cupped and held him, for all his size, as easily and surely as a giant Negro mother might, when he leaned suddenly back from his desk as if taken faint and needing to nearly recline.

"Whose idea was it? Who thought the damn thing up?" The First Deputy had a heavy voice, and rather loud. A firearms instructor many, many years before, he had suffered some slight hearing loss.

The question rhetorical, since the idea had been realized under the previous administration, all of four years before, and by some Captain Nobody in the Public Morals Division. That Nobody and his small crew had—when the Intelligence Division rapidly took Operation Godiva over—received promotions with alacrity, solid (if obscure) assignments, and warnings dire concerning Departmental security.

"And why the hell did Frankenthaler let those federal people in? I thought Norm had more sense than that!" Frankenthaler having then been an officer in the Intelligence Division, and rising.

"The Army people were surveillin' that Russian; they followed him right to the woman's apartment. —I don't see Norm had any choice." Cherusco glanced at Delgado to see if this was permissible utterance.

The Chief of the Department sat still in his slight shadow, unperturbed.

"Anyway, this thing is all cleaned up," Cherusco said. "—A long time ago. Took out the two-ways and mikes, plastered the wall back up and everything. Watch apartment's been rented to some jerk for almost two years, now."

"Mention Costello, John," the Chief said.

"O.K. There's that. Costello already got a complaint from Goodman for taking District Homicide off the Gaither thing—givin' it to the fuckups. Goodman told him Major Crime is Major Crime.—And, the guy's got a point."

Sad news, since George Costello, who yearned to be the next Commissioner—and was presently Chief of Detectives—posed as adamantly upright, and was a bad man to cross.

"Who the hell is Goodman?" said the First Deputy.

Delgado gazed through plate glass, out into mazy morning air high across Park Row to the Federal Courthouse. The rich, late-summer sun was drenching that building in gold. "—Inspector, East Division Homicide," he said.

"What is he—trying to make trouble?"

"Goodman's O.K.," Cherusco said. "—He was just curious. It's not a usual thing to get a case pulled away from his guys like that."

"It's not his *business* to be curious about Departmental decisions," the First Deputy said. "—He sounds like a big-nose, to me."

"No, he's all right," Cherusco said, illustrating by this one of his pleasanter traits—a reluctance to do a fellow officer dirt. "He's an O.K. guy. His people were wonderin' about it, that's all. —He went to Costello . . . Costello sent him to me . . . I set him straight—told him we were givin' the oddballs downstairs a little waltz, remind them they were detectives—plus that class whore might have been screwin' some state senator or somethin' . . . didn't want that in the *News*."

"Dumb," the First Deputy said.

"Smart," said Delgado, entranced by the Federal Courthouse, the long, long reach of Park Row. He noted, as well, two cars double-parked along the western side—resolved to mention it to Ed Lauterbach, Chief of Patrol.

"I figured," Cherusco said, "—it was better they think we're coverin' small . . . nothin' out of the ordinary." He nodded to himself, a quick pecking motion, confirming the sense of this. "—Should be my people handlin' it, though—not those fuck-ups downstairs."

"We want those fuck-ups downstairs handling it, John," Delgado said, watching a third car double-park—far down the block after next. Looked like a rented limo. "—We want a limited inquiry, a limited paper trail." He turned back to the room, looking at Cherusco, blinking once at the change of light. Tapped the arm of his chair as if this were his office, not the First Deputy's. "We want it all kept right here, where my man"—he meant Captain Anderson—"can keep his eye on it."

"O.K.," Cherusco said. "—All right."

"We want this one to just drift away, John," the First Deputy said. He made a gentle fluttering gesture with the fingers of his raised right hand. The hand was red, and huge, and bristled with gray-black fur, but the motions it made were rather subtle, delicate, and controlled. "—Just drift away . . ."

"You keep out of this, John," Delgado said, and Cherusco shrugged and spread his hands apart to show how far the Intelligence Division now stood from interfering in the matter in any way.

"I don't see," he said, "why it has to be such a big deal. That particular shit was more than three years ago, for Christ's sake! No way is anybody goin' to find out about that. —The guy was just some candidate for the Senate. —Wasn't even elected yet! Nobody special."

"He's special, now," Delgado said.

The First Deputy sighed and exercised his wonderful chair, swinging full forward upright without a squeak.

"Who is this Goodman with the mouth, complained to Costello? —Is that Buddy Goodman?" The First Deputy was a persistent man.

"No," Cherusco said. "He's an Irish guy. Pat Goodman."

"Ah . . . I got him. He's a brain—right?"

"That's right."

"He better be careful he doesn't get to be a nose. He'll do a lot better when he learns to mind his own business."

The Commander of Intelligence decided to let it ride. —It was unlikely, now, he'd be free this afternoon in time to meet Joyce at the Hilton. Wouldn't get to see those small breasts—long nipples on them, the rest of that soft meat white as cream cheese—revealed for him, trembling, when she climbed up on the bed. One big bite each—that's all. And that smile—so sweet you wouldn't think she even knew what a fuck was. You knew it when she got those skinny little legs in the air, though. Then you knew she loved it. . . . And there was more to the whole thing than that, even if she hadn't said a word, give her credit. They were feeling closer and closer—and complications were coming. He knew it, and she knew it, but the little sweetheart hadn't said a word, had never bugged him, not once. —The Department didn't like divorces among senior officers. Showed a man couldn't handle a problem—couldn't live with one, either. Both, prerequisites for high command.

He had a weakness, of course, just like everybody did. He knew that. Enjoying trouble was his weakness. Dorothy would be shocked—really stunned—just like when he'd reached across the table with Jennifer watching (Jennifer four at the time) and hit her in the mouth over that high school reunion thing. Knocked a tooth out for her. Got her attention. —This was probably going to get her attention again. Would sure as shit break the monotony.

"Costello," the First Deputy said. "—What did he have to say?"

"Costello said he didn't remember talkin' to Goodman about it . . . said he wouldn't remember talkin' to me about it . . . said if I ever mentioned it to him again, I'd be sorry."

"Smart," said Delgado from his almost shade.

"Too fucking smart," the First Deputy said, who rarely used the vulgar word. The First Deputy considered Costello a threat, though still distant, to the Commissioner—preening himself as he did on his rectitude, giving news conferences. . . . Costello, who'd been a hero-cop—exchanging gunfire at a range of ten feet with a perpetrator who'd just killed a bank messenger—had then been adopted by a senior commander of the Tactical Division (a black man), who, years later, had become Commissioner under the city's last white mayor. Costello (Irish on both sides) had risen with his rabbi, and was known therefore, by some white and Hispanic officers, as the Easter Egg—born of a chocolate bunny.

"Let's have them in," Delgado said. "—I'm due uptown at eleven."

The First Deputy opened the shallow center drawer in his wide mahogany desk, looked for something, and didn't find it. "—This is not a subject for discussion at the meeting," he said, meaning the regular executive board meeting on Tuesday afternoons, which all deputy commissioners attended—commissioners of Legal, of Departmental Trials, of Administration, of Community Affairs, of Organized Crime Control.

"I hope to hell not." —Cherusco, who would not be invited to attend in any case, meaning, as did the First Deputy, particularly the Deputy Commissioner for Community Affairs, Jorge Molina, an ex-journalist and desperate police buff with wacky notions of making mayor someday. This young Hispanic, handsome as a demigod and clever at his job, had proved to have a mouth the size of the Holland Tunnel.

"You heard what Molina did last week?" Cherusco said—the question rhetorical, since they certainly had, but their silence indicating some interest in Intelligence's version.

The Deputy for Community Affairs, taking advantage of his technical elevation to peace officer, though intrinsically civilian, had purchased a large military-model automatic pistol in gleaming stainless steel, and was pleased to brandish it while answering any possible call for response overheard on his limousine radio before his patrolman driver could manage to reach over and change channels. —This change too late, the call overheard in the back seat, the Deputy for Community Affairs might instantly order a response—siren yodeling, tires squealing at the turns—and would, his driver swore, have the big automatic drawn, its numerous safeties and switches clicked this way and that, its fat grip ponderous with innumerable rounds of high-speed hollow-points, its sneering muzzle swinging at times in the excited hand to cover the back of the patrolman's head, so that he hunched lower and lower in his seat as he drove.

On arrival at the scene, the Deputy for Community Affairs would leap from his limo all ready for action, making most circumspect any cop within pistol range—demanding the situation, his sleek, handsome head swiveling for possible newspeople, for microphones, for cameras—and then go bounding up any steps present, preceded by his baleful glittering great gun, which made men part like the Red Sea before him.

Cherusco related the latest and best—how the Deputy for Community Affairs, last week, on Wednesday, having caught a call to *Assist Officer* before his driver could obscure it, had responded with great speed, to discover on Henry Street a parked patrol car, and, inside the entranceway of a small apartment building there, one patrolman standing at the open door of a first-floor apartment—and his partner within, talking in a small living room with a fat man holding a kitchen knife to his young daughter's throat.

Her father had already cut her, lightly, along the side of her neck (apparently for insisting on continuing a relationship of which he disapproved) and still seemed quite upset. The girl, held firmly at his side, was only glum, though her blouse was ruined by the blood.

All, to this point, was perfectly proper. One patrolman inside, talking, and the other—so as not to overheat a situation already warm enough—just outside in the hall, visible, but not too close. They were waiting for a Hostage Team—expert talkers, delayers, understanders, sympathizers, and sudden seizers.

Enter the Deputy Commissioner for Community Affairs, who, to do him justice, might have behaved quite correctly had he not seen a columnist for *The Village Voice*—not ordinarily the man to be answering police calls (but, as it happened, a resident nearby)—come trotting along the sidewalk to see what was up, evidently having recognized the Deputy's handsomeness and shining weapon.

With that small, sweatshirted man hurrying behind him, then, the Deputy came to the apartment doorway, took in the situation, shouldered past the astonished patrolman at the door—the cop reached out and grabbed the Deputy's jacket tail (gray Italian silk) and, afraid to tear it, let go when the Deputy angrily jerked away—and entered the room, a Superior Officer taking charge. Didn't seem to him there was time, considering the girl's bloody neck, her ruined blouse, to wait for the Hostage Team at all.

The patrolman beside him in the living room reduced to silence by surprise, the Deputy was enabled to deal with the troubled sire as only a truly practiced public speaker could—rapidly reassuring the fat man that children, however loved, could plague a decent person to death, were such a responsibility, were so foolish, so ignorant of what was best for them, it was no wonder even the most loving father might lose his temper—and so on and on, and not to no effect. The troubled parent—his knife blade trembling with eagerness at his daughter's throat, as if the steel had requirements of its own, impatient of fulfillment—listened and appeared to ease until he stood somewhat slack, his attention equally divided between the stream of murmured commiseration issuing from the movie-star face, and the wandering small bright circle of the automatic's muzzle.

From the street outside, faintly, the soft whimpers of brakes as the Hostage Team came, siren-less, to rest.

At this, the Deputy for Community Affairs abruptly snapped his fingers, said, "I'll take that knife," reached out, took it, tossed it behind him onto a dark green sofa, then holstered his heavy weapon inside his jacket, deep down under his left armpit. Emergency over. Life saved. *The Voice* reporter witnessing all.

The Deputy, as the Hostage Team came down the hall, held out a manicured hand to the sullen teenager so saved, and said, "It's all over, sugar—you come over here to me." —And upon those words, received from her fat father a sudden, awkward, whacking punch that struck him in the mouth quite hard.

The patrolman near him, released from awe, jumped past the shocked Deputy (posed with both hands to his lips in the echo of the blow), seized the fat man, spun him, kicked his feet out from under, threw him on the floor—and, relaxed, knelt on his neck while attaching the cuffs.

This, while the Deputy Commissioner for Community Affairs turned for any sort of help—to the small columnist for *The Village Voice,* to the lieutenant commanding the Hostage Team, just entered—and displayed a face pale as paper, a small spatter of bright blood on his sculpted lower lip, and a neat, comic black gap where the left of his two upper front teeth had been. Tears in his fine eyes.

His tooth he held in his right hand, having spit it into that palm to look at—to see if it could be true. Having seen, he clutched it (and would continue to do so for some time, refusing to have it pried away, until—almost an hour later—a young nurse, in soft Spanish, soothed it from him). This handsome creature, foolish, shocked, and helpless as an injured child, now required the services of all grown-ups present, and they gave it instinctively as any grown-ups would. The fat man, a prayer cushion on the floor, was quite ignored. His sullen daughter, also.

This tale, gaining continually in the telling, was no longer new—though Cherusco had discovered (not Chief of Intelligence for nothing) or had invented the hour-long clutching of the tooth. Still, it remained a refreshment for all real police officers in their dealings with those odd civilians occasionally appointed to be their superiors in this peripheral division or that. The tale of Molina's Tooth had the added advantage of being continually refreshed by the appearances of the man himself, smiling bravely with his plastic prosthesis (the best that Dr. Bimstein could do until the gum was less swollen).

This plastic tooth was of an unconvincing whiteness that put the Deputy's other handsome teeth to shame. Blue-white, and much bigger than it should have been, standing slightly in advance of the row of others, it was a constant reminder of foolishness and frailty signaled to all he spoke with in the past few days. Above this large plastic tooth, the handsome lip, the perfect nose, Molina's interlocutors saw velvet eyes, swimming in shame.

The First Deputy swung a little to the side in his fine chair, cheered by the repetition of that cautionary tale, smiled, and shook his head. In such a manner, and by all the reporters, buffs, clerical employees, the policemen and -women that staffed and swarmed through Headquarters, that manned the thousands of division and precinct posts, the Academy, the shops, garages, ranges, armories and stables, the helicopters and harbor launches—through all these, the tale of Molina's tooth would continue to propagate, flourish, and add its slight fiber to the ancient dense-woven macramé of the Department.

"Well, this Operation Godiva thing is not to be brought up in any way, shape, or form in the meeting," the First Deputy said. "—It's too touchy."

"We'll have enough on our plate in there with the budget," Delgado said. A sore point, since the mayor, a good Democrat and supposed friend to the police, though black, had proposed a budget of the most stringent sort, the City Council reluctantly approving.

"That jigaboo doesn't care if the city slides right into the river," Cherusco said.

"John," said the First Deputy, "—be quiet."

"There *are* some priorities in that budget, Frank," Delgado said. "—There's stuff that can get cut and not hurt the Department at all."

"You will keep that opinion to yourself, won't you, Tony?"

"Except in proper company—yes, sir," Delgado said, the honorary sounding odd from his dark snapping-turtle's face. He shifted in his chair, hitched up, and as he moved, revealed for an instant something under his left trouser cuff. —Where most chiefs of the New York City Police Department had scorned to carry any armament but their princely office, Delgado gave no weapon away. He wore a .32-caliber Seecamp pistol, a very small, neat piece, in a patch holster of elastic at the inside of his left ankle—a slender ankle for his weight, blue-veined, black-haired, black-socked.

This weapon, from that holster (his wife and widowed sister downstairs cooking dinner in the big, stuccoed house in Forest Hills) Delgado would secretly seize in practice draws—the draws complex, involving, as he stood, a suddenly lifted left leg crossed in the air before him, then a snatching beneath the trouser cuff with the right hand—after which, more often than not, the Chief stood armed and ready, his little pistol pointed at the stomach of a squat aging man in a straining uniform, framed in Delgado's bedroom closet mirror.

"Fact is, though," Delgado, quietly, after only the slightest pause, "—fact is that training is getting shorted more than a million of that budget. Closer to two. Lawrence says so, and I say so."

"Lawrence never has enough money—"

"That's right," Delgado said, as if the First Deputy had just agreed with him. "They need a new floor in that gym; they need to hire at least four more permanent instructors—"

"Will you get serious?"

"Lawrence needs them, Frank." Delgado spoke softly, but suddenly leaned forward in his chair as if in an instant he might come bounding out of it, and—despite the disparity in size—reach across Connell's dark, polished desk to take him by his suit lapels. "—And I told him I would personally see he got that money."

"Then you told him shit, Tony." The First Deputy was cursing today. Godiva had upset him. "The Commissioner is going to make those allocations. Not you—not me."

Cherusco, pleased to be witness to this battle of elephants, stayed still and quiet as a child afraid of being noticed and sent from the room.

"Then let him consider this, Frank." The Chief's voice was almost too low to hear. "The Department is only as good as the quality of its personnel—and that's only as good as their training. I will be damned if I allow future New York City police officers to be sent out onto those streets without the finest training that budget will buy. And if that means fewer helicopters and limos, if it means fewer trips to London and Tokyo to those bullshit conferences—or if we have to keep the old green-shift patrol cars for another year—then that's what it'll have to mean. Because there will be no compromise on the quality of training."

He sat back in his chair, and looked out through the plate glass once more, as if his real interest lay in that vacancy. —One of the doubleparked cars down Park Row had left.

"Why don't you save that crap for the *Times,* Tony?" The First Deputy smiled. "The Commissioner appreciates your position—hell, I appreciate it. We're not going to gut Lawrence and the other guys down there. You know that—right?" He reached to a small red-lacquered box at the front edge of his desk, lifted the lid, then lowered it again.

"A new floor for that gym," Delgado said. "Four new permanent instructors—Breedman couldn't teach Wyatt Earp to shoot on that range—and we need a senior legal instructor, an experienced criminal attorney, not those part-timers from John Jay."

"You got to be kidding! —We're going to put out for a

full-time attorney, just to instruct? —No way!" The First Deputy's cheeks showed the faintest flush.

Cherusco, a quick learner, was learning it might be unfortunate to observe too severe a disagreement between superiors. The loser would remember the witness.

Delgado turned from the transparent wall. "Frank," he said, almost whispering, "—false arrests, arraignment discharges, cases dismissed last year cost the City and the Department just over three million dollars. —And I'm not even talking about man-hours lost because our patrolmen and detectives were not up on whatever crap the courts handed down last year. An experienced attorney, instructing full-time at the Academy, will save us about a million a year."

"So you say, Tony. So you say. —But those are your figures. I doubt very much if they're the Department's." The First Deputy's big hands, flushed the same faint maroon as his cheeks, lay on his desk like small dogs meeting.

Delgado turned back to his view. "O.K. Check 'em. —Ask Busoni at the meeting." Armenio Busoni being Deputy Commissioner for Administration.

"You bet your ass I will," the First Deputy said—and realized, just as he said it, that he'd obligated himself to request figures from Buster Busoni, who owed to Delgado all that he'd become—and would not, now, fail to repay.

Delgado waited at his view until the First Deputy had come to that conclusion, then turned his bulky head and said, "Am I being too much a son-of-a-bitch on this, Frank?—Don't you agree with me it's important?"

"You *are* a son-of-a-bitch," the First Deputy said, "—and someday, you're going to get a little too cute, Tony."

Delgado smiled, and turned back to the glass wall. Another car had come to double-park down there. Two of them. —Two more than there had been. There was no excuse for it.

A heavy silence. Cherusco pretended he wasn't there.

"O.K.," the First Deputy said. "—Let's have these people in. We all have other things to do." He sat up straight behind his desk. "I don't know why the hell

Frankenthaler isn't here. —He let those people in on it in the first place. I thought he was a shrewd guy."

"Shrewd enough," Delgado said from his wall. "—Shrewd enough to put in his papers damn fast after that operation shut down."

"Well—once they blew Godiva, I don't think he had any choice about lettin' the Army guys in," Cherusco said. A safe subject, and thank God for it.

"He could give us some information on them, anyway."

"I talked to him this mornin'," Cherusco said, "—and I was lucky he told me his name. Norm says he only talks through his lawyer about that—and he's forgettin' as fast as he can."

"Great."

"I got a phone call from Washington on this," Delgado said. "—I believe the P.C. got one as well."

The First Deputy didn't say the Commissioner had, or hadn't.

"These people belong to somebody," Delgado said.

"My information," Cherusco said, "—is that they were assigned DIA"—by which he meant the Defense Intelligence Agency. "We don't know if they're regular with them, or not—but somebody up there likes 'em."

"Same people were on Godiva?"

"That's right. —At least the Colonel was. Frankenthaler said he was an asshole. —Had a smart sergeant."

"All right," the First Deputy said, "—let's have them in." He reached to touch the third button in a row of nine at the side of his desktop—as he did, shutting his mouth to suppress to silence a burp returned from his heavy breakfast . . . so it fumed out, soundless, through his nose.

The Colonel and his lieutenant, both neatly dressed in business suits—the Colonel's a pin-stripe gray, the Lieutenant's a light summer blue—had been sitting side by side on a waiting-room sofa, quite content, each reading a *National Geographic*. —"Brazil, a Nation of Futures" . . . "Along the Malapang Trail . . ."

A plain brown leather briefcase was leaning against the Lieutenant's right leg.

These two, so neatly dressed, might almost have been

civilians, and taken as such by the detectives and Department secretaries around them, except for their short hair, the slight creases at their jackets' left armpits, beneath which handguns rested. The office people believed them to be Treasury men (a great grinding case of securities theft currently looming large enough to come to the attention of the highest brass). —Those, or Bureau people, though they'd shown no ID, had only introduced themselves as Mr. Mathews (the Colonel), and Mr. Cates, and said they were expected by the First Deputy Commissioner.

Now, a good while later, on the approach and nod of one of the many bulky detectives first class strolling in shirtsleeves up and down the wide aisles of cubicled desks—their short-barreled Colts, Smith & Wessons, and Rugers riding their massive hips like tickbirds—at a nod from one of these men, the Colonel and his lieutenant rose together, the Lieutenant lifting his briefcase with him, and walked behind the Nodder down the long corridor toward the First Deputy Commissioner's office.

At a wide doorframe, past which white walls turned to paneled, smooth carpet to plush, the Nodder stepped aside, and an even bigger man (but elderly), blue-blazered, his smooth, plump cheeks crimson satin, his hair whipped cream, introduced himself as Inspector Mahon, shook the Colonel's hand, and addressed him as Mr. Mathews. He did not offer to shake the Lieutenant's hand—divining their relationship, perhaps, by his bearing of the briefcase—and, murmuring easy Irish courtesies, ushered the visitors the last thirty-five feet of panel and plush to Francis Connell's office, walking before them with a gait as generous and rhythmic as a sailor's—an old beat cop's walk, in fact, hardly seen anymore.

None of the men in the First Deputy's office rose to greet the Colonel and his lieutenant—indeed, each of them outranked the Colonel in the only measures he or they respected—the number of armed men commanded, the length of time in grade in those commands.

The Colonel and his Lieutenant were content to accept their white-haired usher's introductions standing, smiling, replying with "Gentlemen" to the nods received from the

First Deputy on his leather throne, from Cherusco, from the Chief of the Department by his shaded wall of glass.

"Thank you, Terry," the First Deputy said to the old man, and that minion strolled out of the office in his sailor's roll, closing the heavy door behind him so softly no latch click could be heard.

The First Deputy indicated two chairs to his right, across from John Cherusco.

The Colonel settled himself in the slightly more isolated of these, and crossed his left leg over his right knee, so that his tasseled, black left loafer drooped toe-down toward the carpet's Prussian blue. Then the Lieutenant took his seat.

The Colonel, older than he seemed at first, with short, pale brown hair, and pale brown eyes to match, looked like one of the more mature male models used to advertise fine tweed overcoats. A wide mouth. A well-cut jaw.

The Lieutenant, taller, something of a gawk, his eyes a milky blue, sat up straight, knees at ninety degrees, shins parallel, his hands folded in his lap. The brown briefcase, like an affectionate cat, leaned against his right leg.

The First Deputy, affable, at ease, mentioned Washington's heat when he had last visited that city, and remarked that New York's summer heat had slackened at last into autumn.

The Colonel, speaking in the slow, swooping cadences of the deep Middle West, agreed, found New York's temperature quite pleasant. "—Those few hundred miles north make quite a difference." But found, or one of his people had found, the ragweed pollen blowing east from New Jersey pretty trying.

"Oh, yeah . . . oh, yeah," said the First Deputy. "People live in a big city, they think you get away from nature. —No way, though. More trees, more things like that around than people realize."

Silence after that, almost companionable. None of the policemen had anything more to say.

"Suppose we ought to get down to business," the Colonel said.

"This is pretty old business," said Cherusco.

"We feel," said the Colonel, "—we feel that that old business just got dug up. The Gaither woman's death comes close to laying everybody's balls right out on the table."

To this hearty introduction, there was no immediate reply.

After an uneasy moment, John Cherusco said, "That is strictly an NYPD case," his Bronxed voice distinctly unpleasant after the Colonel's prairie music.

The Colonel, also, had attended many conferences. "—Your Chief of Department doesn't agree, Commander," he said, and left that small poisoned needle to glitter where it fell. "I think this matter might very seriously affect our organization as well as yours—would certainly affect some of us personally—and would damn well affect the present national administration, the present government of the United States."

"Mr. Mathews called me from Washington," Delgado said serenely to the First Deputy. "—It seemed best for both parties to be agreed on the handling of this one."

"Right. Right on," the Colonel said, and his lieutenant nodded.

"All right," the First Deputy said, "—to an extent."

"Absolutely," the Colonel said, and looked up at the ceiling for a moment, revealing an almost youthful throat. "—And we appreciate that." He paused for a little, still looking up at the ceiling, then looked down at his hands, his Academy ring. "This operation has, until now, remained so secure that frankly we haven't worried about it, despite the obvious political repercussions." The Lieutenant nodded very slightly to support the "repercussions." "—The fact that, legally, there was no wrongdoing whatsoever involved, that we all had good security reasons for using the woman, the other people, for making the tapes—Soviet involvement directly out of the U.N. and so forth, Organized Crime . . . wonderful intelligence for you people as well. And by no means the first occasion where male and female prostitutes were used. —I was informed at the time, I hope correctly, that tap-and-tape warrants were proper and current, the ones we were shown."

"They were," Cherusco said.

"Well, then," said the Colonel, "—there's no legal difficulty."

"We're not here discussing legal difficulties," the First Deputy said. "—You can take it we know our business."

"No offense," the Colonel said. "—Just getting that out of our way." He lightly lifted his left leg, put it down, and recrossed his legs the other way, right over left. "Our joint concern, now, is the possbility of some untoward revelation—in the press, for example—if and when this woman's murderer is caught . . . or some written evidence is introduced. A diary or whatever."

"If the guy that killed her got anything like that," Cherusco said, "it's under his refrigerator or in a plastic bag in his toilet tank. Even if he's got it, he can't ever show it, because it'll get his ass convicted. —So come on, now—what's the problem?"

"If he gets caught," the Colonel said. His lieutenant nodded again, very slightly. "—If he gets caught, that would be problem enough. Witnesses to previous activities might be called . . . a good deal of information would come to light. —Wouldn't it?"

"If there were any such witnesses . . . if there was any such material," Delgado said. "—If he does get caught."

"I wouldn't care," the Colonel commenced, reflective, and began to slowly raise and lower the foot of his crossed right leg. The tassels on his black loafer swayed slightly back and forth. "I certainly wouldn't care to hazard the existence of the present administration of my country . . . my personal future . . . the personal futures of all of us, on their being nothing concerning Godiva produced in a murder trial of that kind. —I surely wouldn't. I don't think any reasonable person would want to hazard that. —If it wasn't Soviets from the Mission who performed that termination."

"That's a lot of crap," Cherusco said, his bird's beak poised to peck. "The Russians . . . ? Those U.N. Russians can't find their way to the toilet! The KGB and those Red Army guys send every faggot they got to the U.N. Mission just to try an' keep us busy. Their real guys come out of L.A. and Washington. —I know that, and you people"—a bird's cock-headed stare at the Colonel—"should damn well know it!"

"John," Delgado said.

Cherusco sat back into his chair, his feathers settling, beak softly chattering.

After a pause, the Colonel said, "Everyone else in Godiva was shelved years ago. The other two women are living on the West Coast. One of the two males involved is terminally ill." At this, Delgado and the First Deputy exchanged a glance. "—All shelved until this killing." He smiled in a friendly way at Cherusco. "Of course, if KGB or GRU questioned and then terminated the Gaither woman, we can assume they have everything she had. —Not a pleasant prospect, that's for sure."

The three police officers simultaneously assumed that bored expression seen on doctors at dinner parties, when lay people express some possible diagnosis.

"This homicide is a *relationship* homicide, Colonel," Cherusco said, not troubling with the "Mr. Mathews." "—The perpetrator is one of the whore's johns, or at least somebody knew her personally. —O.K.? Now, will you please stop tryin' to tell us our business? That Russian asshole Matuchek is long gone, and you got nothin' on him anyway except he had a big dick and wanted an office with a window. —So give us a break."

The Colonel took no apparent offense, though his lieutenant did, displaying a thinned mouth, his mild blue eyes now chilly, resting on this slight and big-nosed wop—a typical piece of New York trash, and likely with the police rather than the Mafia only for the pension.

"The Soviets," the Colonel said, "have longer memories than we do," his leisurely voice as pleasant as ever—the tassels on his suspended loafer jiggling, however, in an agitated way.

"Horseshit," said Cherusco, playing bad-cop to the elbow.

"That's enough of that, now, John." The First Deputy, good-cop through and through. "—These gentlemen are very right to be concerned." He opened the small red-lacquered box on his desk. "You gentlemen smoke?"

"No, thank you," the Colonel said, for both of them.

The First Deputy lowered the box lid. "Good for you. It took me a solid year to break my habit. —Nobody can tell me nicotine isn't addicting. Took me a solid year."

"More," Delgado said, "—took you more than a year."

"You're still smoking, Tony—you've got no right to comment."

"And intend to continue smoking," Delgado said, "—and live forever, too."

The Colonel and Lieutenant smiled.

"A year . . . maybe a year and a half," the First Deputy said. "Torture . . . and let me tell you, I put on maybe twenty pounds of flab doing it."

"A tough one to break," the Colonel said, his jittery loafer now at ease. "—It's possible, you know, that the Soviets might have staged the killing to appear to be a personal one. I understand there were some bizarre elements."

"She had a banana up her ass," Cherusco said. "—I can just see Bodrun Shulamof from the U.N. up there in her apartment with his perfume and his hairnet, choosin' the right banana while his boyfriends do the job on her in the shower. —Shulamof would have tossed his cookies all over her carpet, and his boyfriends would be in the Mission clinic flat on their backs gettin' vitamin shots and beet soup. I told you—those U.N. guys aren't up to it. And their Army guys are just as sad."

"The U.N. people are not the only agents the Soviet—"

"Look—I *told* you. You think my people don't know what the Russians are doin' in this city? I know all the shit they're doin' in this city. —O.K.? Now, why don't you just get off it."

"John," the First Deputy said, though pleased enough to see his man pecking Washington, "—that's enough of that."

"Yes, sir," the bad-cop said, put his head beneath his wing, and dozed.

The Colonel cruised on, a lean warship sliding through ructious tides. "—Of course, there were others," he said, by which he meant several criminals of some importance; seven or eight politicians—local and national, minor and major—a justice of the New York State Supreme Court; some forty or fifty businessmen, foreign and domestic; two movie stars (man and wife—both of great reputation and, as it happened, disappointing performance); and several important and less important attachés, intelligence officers, representatives and functionaries of the

United Nations. "—There are," the Colonel said, "several of these individuals quite capable of violence. The congressman, for example . . ." Referring to one of the notable clients, a retired politician from the South widely believed in intelligence and law enforcement circles to have murdered his daughter—the motive as unpleasant as could be.

"That guy wasn't even in town last week," Cherusco said. "It was a way different M.O. Plus, he banged this Gaither just once, years ago. He didn't have any problem with her at all."

"And the gangsters?" The Lieutenant, speaking up at last, spoke up Southern. He'd played basketball in high school in Birmingham, and done well—but had been too slow up and down the court to be offered any but a tuitioned place at Clemson. —So, the Army and Officer's Candidate School.

The policemen smiled together at "gangsters," and the First Deputy leaned forward in his splendid chair. "Those men," he said, meaning his opposite numbers in Organized Crime, "—those men don't usually have any reason to murder prostitutes. Those people usually don't talk about their business with whores—they just enjoy themselves. Prostitutes and those people understand each other very well; they keep each other company."

"And," Cherusco said, "—and, if a wise guy did want a whore dead for some oddball reason—maybe he couldn't get it up, didn't want her telling his buddies—he'd just get some meatball to shoot her in the ear." The Colonel started to say something, but Cherusco rode right over him. "—Those guys aren't perverts, you know—they're not goin' to go stick a banana up some woman's po-po."

"Po-po?" said the Colonel.

"Vaginal area," the Lieutenant said.

"I know that—I thought it was put in her anal area."

"She was a two-banana girl," Cherusco said. "—You understand what I'm sayin'? We're talkin' about an emotional thing, here. A personal killing. We probably got love involved here—O.K.?"

"Even if you're right, Commander," the Colonel said. "—Suppose you're right, and this killing of an ex-Godiva operational person—who had as her clients a number of

Soviets and Cosa Nostra people—even if her killing was, nonetheless, just a personal thing by some sickie . . . even if that's true, it doesn't solve our problem. Our problem is the possible publicity—the possible revelations coming out of this! Frankly, at this point, DOD simply does not care *who* murdered the woman."

"Right," the Lieutenant said.

"We do care that the woman's activities for us in those years not become public knowledge—for reasons we all know very well. Washington is very definite on a firm lid being kept on this case . . . this whole matter. They are very serious about it, which is why I've been sent back here. —Now, we have certain assets I would be happy to offer to help in damage control. We'll be in town for as long as it takes. —We're staying over at the Algonquin—"

"Great," Cherusco said. "That's all we need."

"I have to tell you . . . Mr. Mathews," the First Deputy said, "—that I do feel it would be best for your people to stay out of the case. It would almost certainly do more harm than good. —A matter of too many cooks."

The Colonel uncrossed his legs and sat up straight. "Of course," he said, "if you prefer we stand aside for the time being . . ."

"You bet," said Cherusco.

"The Department," Delgado said—he'd been gazing out through his wall, now turned toward them, blinking at the lesser light—"the Department has had considerable experience handling delicate cases."

"Not this delicate, I'll bet," the Colonel said. And to the First Deputy: "Have you seen the tape?"

"I read the file on all the tapes. I'm familiar with our particular problem."

"But you didn't view the tape. . . ." The Colonel nodded to his lieutenant. "With your permission—"

"We know the problem," Delgado said.

"Even so," said the Colonel, and nodded to his lieutenant again. "With your permission . . ."

The Lieutenant rose, his briefcase in his hand, went to the near corner, where a massive Sony console squatted, knelt beside it, opened his briefcase, and took out a small video cassette player and a short coil of cable. He put those down on the carpet, then reached behind the console for connections.

"The difficulty of this matter is," the Colonel said, "that any revelation at all—routine investigative reports, court records, gossip, newspapers . . . anything like that at all . . ."

"A special squad is handling this," Delgado said.

"Yes," the Colonel said. "—I wish I could say I found that reassuring."

Delgado sat in his filmy shade (near his left foot, the climbing sun had laid a lemon-yellow shelf of light along the floor), looked at the Colonel, but said nothing further.

"May I ask what those 'special squad' people have been told?" the Colonel said.

"That it's a confidential case. To keep their mouths shut." Cherusco said. "—That's what they've been told."

"Heaven knows that's the truth," the Colonel said. "—And minimal record-keeping, I hope. Not necessarily any resolution of the case at all . . . ?"

"Could be," Cherusco said.

The Lieutenant finished his connections behind the Sony, stood, and said, "Ready, sir."

"I hope you didn't screw up that set," the First Deputy said. "There's a perfectly good VCR right in the console, in the top."

"Let her roll, Bob," the Colonel said.

The Lieutenant bent, took a cassette from the open briefcase, snapped it into the recorder, pushed the start button, then stood and took an easy stance at parade rest beside the TV, carefully clear of sight lines.

"This is a copy of Godiva tape four hundred and twenty-three," he said. "There was no sound taken for this tape." The Southern Lieutenant had done many briefings—had done a course at Fort Sill on how to conduct them—and possessed a light, pleasantly penetrating tenor voice, full of pending information, though, in this case, he had nothing more to say.

"We have copies of all this shit," Cherusco said.

The Sony's screen had meanwhile expressed a sheet of fine-grained white, then faded to the same, but with letters printed in thick black across it.

SECRET—VERIFIED EYES ONLY

Log. 4771—Video File 676UI—881
New York City Police Department
Auth. Max. Tr.
GODIVA—Oct. 4, 1987 (Frankenthaler) (Lt.)

These titles held for a number of seconds.

"That's cute," Cherusco said. "You guys must have forgot to label this one Department of Defense."

"We have all these tapes ID'd under DOD regulation logs," the Lieutenant said.

"Sure you do," Cherusco said. "—You guys wouldn't be plannin' to leave us holdin' the nasty bag, would you?"

"We have no such intention," the Colonel said as the titles flickered and faded, revealing—in slightly fuzzy black and white—a small, slender blond woman, short-haired and very pretty. Seen, by the slight softness of her narrow upper arms, her slim thighs, to be at least in her early thirties, she sat at the edge of a very wide bed in her bra and panties, watching with a sort of abstracted attention a monumental and moving geometry at the bed's center.

There, in profile to the immobile camera's lens, muscled, naked, and balding, a white man with an intent harsh-featured face and pale furry buttocks, was kneeling in attendance to the large, near flaccid penis of a lean, beautiful young black man, also nude, and distinguished by neat and lovely breasts.

This activity, rendered impressive rather than shocking by the strenuous tenderness the white man proved in his caresses, was nonetheless a confounding sight; the white man having been, at the time, a candidate for the Senate from Illinois. Being now, the Vice President of the United States.

"Can't say the guy don't care," Cherusco said.

On the television screen, silent, softened by the uncertain light, the difficult conditions of filming, by duplication as well—the three people changed their positions, and held almost still on the broad bed, resting for a moment.

Then, viewed somewhat nearer in a change of lens that incidental pause apparently made time for, the lover—his guarded adult's eyes now seen wide and wondering, certain as a baby's to be pleased—reached out to the black man and recommenced his ardencies, and the blond woman, closer to them, pale as the sheet on which they played, stretched a slender left arm out and under to grasp the white man's rigid sex and hold it—as if to anchor him from floating away, arched and kicking, out of consciousness from sheer delight.

"Turn that dirt off," said the First Deputy.

As if hearing, and on cue—her companions distracted—the blond woman turned her head to confront the hidden camera's vantage, and, her narrow face forthcoming as a child's, grinned, and merrily rolled her eyes.

The Lieutenant, who hadn't moved to the First Deputy's command, stooped with alacrity when his Colonel nodded—and pushed a button to OFF.

Silence—into which the Lieutenant introduced small sounds, disconnecting and packing up.

Then, the First Deputy, struck by the superior weight of witness over report, said, "Holy Mary . . ." reached to his red-lacquered box, opened it, and took out a cigarette.

CHAPTER 4

"Two buttered bagels, four Danish—a prune, all the others I'm takin' cheese. Five coffees and a tea. Lemon."

The refreshment-cart woman—a small, slender young black girl with slanted eyes, who wore her hair straightened to seem to hang softly to her shoulders—refused to take the long detour down the supply corridor to the Squad's office, which meant that the morning duty officer (Serrano, this week) had to go out to the hall every morning at eleven to get the orders.

She stood now, silent, unfriendly, looking at her own dark reflection in the coffee urn's bright, curved steel while Serrano collected his order, took a throwaway paper tray from the stack beside the wooden stirrers, loaded his goods, then handed her a twenty to change.

"How you doin', honey?" he said. Serrano was a friendly man, balding, dark, small, and diffident. —Nothing from her, though (perhaps an expression of slight distaste, then back to her own reflection). Appeared to believe he was coming on to her. —Fat chance. He hadn't stooped that low, that he'd try to make a cart woman—especially a stuck-up black one. It was too bad; she was nice-looking, or would be, if she'd smile a little.

Serrano wanted people to like him, and didn't see why they shouldn't. He felt he was a pretty nice-looking guy. —Getting a little thin on top, but still a nice-looking guy. He'd never let himself go—never started to act like a son-of-a-bitch on the job, either. Never roughed anybody up he didn't have to. . . . He'd been married, once, when he was a kid.

She handed him his change, bent to the wide handle and shoved the heavy cart into motion, brushing past him, heading down the long strip of indoor-outdoor gray carpet, past the elevators—service elevators in this corridor—heading way down the hall to Accounting and Personnel. —Those offices, she took her cart into.

"Take it easy, sweetheart!" She'd come around. It was a question of time. People could tell when other people meant no harm. —After all, she didn't know him. No way she could know what kind of guy he was, just ordering coffees and shit like that.

When Serrano came back with the food and coffee, Ellie was already stuck in Leahy's office, wishing she'd smoothed her skirt better before she sat down; it was almost new, a summer stripe in light pink-and-gray linen that went with her gray blazer perfectly, and she was probably sitting nice big wrinkles into it. Ellie could hear Serrano's distribution through the open door. —By the time she got out there, her coffee would be cold.

She had the only chair in the little room, except for Leahy's burdened swivel. The squad commander's office had been the large walk-in sink-and-storage closet for the much larger L-shaped supply room. The Commissioner's Squad occupied the supply room; their commander, this storage closet. The big sink, flanked now by a small metal-legged Formica table supporting a hot plate, yellow plastic cups, plastic sugar dispenser and a small coffeepot, was the Squad's kitchen—traffic to and from it constantly wearing away the Lieutenant's solitary dignity.

A detective would knock, and—if a tough guy like Nardone or Samuelson—would then come lurching in without a say-so, banging the door open, bearing a plastic glass with a spoonful of instant pink lemonade waiting on its bottom. Use the sink—not a word of apology—and barge right out again, stirring his lemonade with a white plastic spoon hoarded from the coffee cart.

Lieutenant Leahy was a fat man in his fifties, with a rosebud mouth and small, upturned Irish nose. A girl had once told him he looked like Captain Bligh—by which she meant the old Charles Laughton version on TV. Leahy had hard, china-blue eyes, and an odd handshake; first, one felt a cushioned squeezing, unpleasantly soft with fat—then, surfacing against one's palm like weights of metal pressing through a pillow, a considerable pressure of bone and muscle. Leahy always held his grip long enough, on a handshake, to be certain that these last were felt.

It was a numbing grip, unpleasantly challenging—a bully's grip—and had likely been learned as a fat boy's offensive defense in a tough Newark high school. The Lieutenant was from New Jersey, originally.

This surprising handshake, and his manner on the job—brusque and tough-talking—were Leahy's only social aggressions. Even with his latent physical power, so perfectly cloaked by the fat swelling in every motion within his trouser thighs, tugging inside his shirt to open it despite his buttons, pouring softly over his collar all around—even possessing this submerged, potent muscle and bone, his position as commander of the Squad, the Lieutenant was shy as a turtle in any but his purely professional capacity—there, he was occasionally stubborn, often angry, never cruel.

After his wife had left him, she phoned him one Sunday afternoon, out of the blue, and said awful things.

This fat man, who had struggled with great courage from the beginning of his service in the Department to deal with the tidal urges of his appetite, managing by heroic measures of starvation and denial to meet and pass physical examinations that might have ruined his career if he had not been able to lose, from time to time, twenty pounds . . . thirty pounds . . . fifty or sixty pounds of fat barely in time for his annual visits to the police surgeon's office—this obese man, exhausted rather than strengthened by these struggles, and whose great reliance had always been on a steady and energetic talent for proper paperwork, now sat sausaged into his clothes, waiting with Ellie for snack comfort (his prune Danish, his coffee with three sugars) while looking up from his swivel chair to accept from Captain Anderson—tall, lean (almost bony), handsome in a light-gray summer-weight wool suit—a small stack of reports, one by one.

Ellie sat and Nardone stood against the wall behind her, waiting. The four of them crowded the storage closet.

"What about Harrison?" Ellie and Nardone had been working on and off for some weeks on the case of Wilfred Harrison, a British Member of Parliament for Iseley who was a registered heroin addict and a spokesman for the conservative wing of the Labor Party. Harrison—invited to the city with a British trade delegation (Aquascutum, Burberrys, etc.) to arrive in October—presented a nice problem in law enforcement, since, NYPD had been informed, he intended to carry his British-legal supply of pop with him—to shoot up, possibly, in Gracie Mansion, right after lunch.

The newspapers had had this story for some time, and were not being helpful.

"Fuck Harrison," said Lieutenant Leahy.

"—But don't give him lunch," joked Captain Anderson in his pleasing baritone, handing Leahy the last of the files. Anderson glanced at Ellie to see if she got it, and saw that she did. He was wearing a blue-and-cream tie, a white shirt. "We need your activity reports on these," he said. "Some Internal Affairs people are spending way too much money."

"But, what about the Gaither thing?" Ellie could see that important case already flown out of their hands, back to the regular squads.

"You two have that," Anderson said. "—They still have that one, don't they, Ed?" Leahy's full name was Phillip Edwin Leahy.

"Oh, sure," Leahy said, "—they're assigned to that."

"We don't expect anything fast on that one," Anderson said.

"No?" Nardone, from the wall.

"We want you to take your time on that one. Careful handling. —No use embarrassing a few honest citizens for wetting their wee-wees until we really have a solid case made. Chief wants this one handled in a grown-up kind of way—no reporters at all. Absolutely no leaks, no bullshit."

Nardone said, "Uh-huh."

"Any questions at all develop on that one, you check with Ed, or you check with me. O.K.? —Now, the Internal Affairs problems are a little more front-and-center. We want to get on that one fast, so I'll need your activity reports and summaries upstairs every couple of days. —All right, Ed?"

"You'll get 'em," Leahy said, and sat back a little in

his suffering chair. He was wearing a light-blue sports jacket that couldn't close and button across his shirt front. "—We'll turn 'em out." He picked up the stack of reports, and held them out across his desktop. Ellie stood up, took them, and remained standing to see if Leahy had anything more to say.

"That's it," he said. "—Get on 'em."

"Won't hurt," Anderson said as Ellie turned to go, Nardone heaved forward off the wall, "—won't hurt to be a tad obvious about these investigations. We're as interested in correcting behavior as getting indictments."

Ellie picked up her bagel and coffee at her desk (Serrano had left them beside the phone with a note—*You owe me twenty cents)* and crossed the squad room's narrow aisle to Nardone. They were lucky, their desks resting in the long leg of the squad-room L, where there were two vents along the back wall (decorated otherwise with bulletin boards and blackboards) though no windows. The short leg, around the corner to the right, was a four-desk cubby, and airless. No vents. There, Graham and Classman sat crowded in with two young black detectives, only nominally members of the Squad. Nobody knew these young men's assignment, which was believed to involve some scandal in the pari-mutuel system as odds were computed. And that notion might be mistaken, since the young men spoke very little, and were hardly ever in the office.

Nardone was sitting straight up at his desk, leafing through the reports on the Internal Affairs people. Nardone always had tea at the morning break, never coffee, and never anything to eat, though when they went out he was liable to stop at the first Sabrett's and buy three of the skinny, damp little hot dogs and eat them without onions or mustard—nothing to drink, either.

"What a load this stuff is," he said. "—I don't know why we even got this shit. Here's a guy; his wife's aunt says he's a crook. Says he's buyin' sports cars like they're goin' out of style. —Says she don't want to make trouble, but it's her taxes, too."

"Don't use that word *taxes*. Don't use that word in my presence," Samuelson said, walking by. Samuelson was the biggest detective on the Squad (salt-and-pepper hair cropped in an archaic crew cut, his nose jutting from a raptor's great heavy-boned head very like the beak of one of those high-flying hunters) and, unlike many big, powerful men, he had a hasty temper. He'd been assigned to the Squad several years before for beating up a sergeant from Traffic after that officer attempted to extort money from Samuelson's father (whose two delivery trucks had had no option but to double-park at his underwear business on Thirty-seventh off Seventh Avenue). Nathan Samuelson had never been much of a businessman, but he'd been very gentle, and his huge son had loved him dearly. —Therefore the confrontation with the sergeant from Traffic, considerable of a horse himself (an ex-St. Joseph's football player named Mike Grew).

The fight ensuing remained something of a legend in Manhattan West, occurring as it had in the public purlieus of the precinct locker room. A row of lockers had been dented, the sergeant dented even more, and the matter had gone straight up the ladder to the Grand Hair-bags at Headquarters, had been mulled, turned and polished there, and finally adjusted and put away. The sergeant (his jaw lightly wired to heal) was told to wise up. Samuelson was transferred from Stake-out, where he had already assisted in killing two perps, to the Commissioner's Squad, where his regular duty was to escort and safely convoy through the shoals and reefs of Manhattan a succession of visiting firemen—important and less so.

These men, small, often brown or pale orange, Samuelson usually led, ponderous and protecting, from Bruno's Pen & Pencil to a Soho disco named Peabody's, and finally, often, to Harriet Picunis' large apartment on Sixty-first Street—after a precautionary call to Morals to be certain of no pending harassment. There, amid a forest of white plastic Art Deco, Samuelson would sit on the lime-upholstered living-room sofa reading paperback science fiction (until sufficient customers had arrived to make up a game of gin) while his charge or charges sported with whatever Puerto Rican girls Harriet was then supplied.

Occasionally, pleased and weary, ready to go home to the Hilton, these foreigners—sons of Thailand or Korea, Brazil or the Philippines—would emerge from a back bedroom (having been told of a certain confused, shy admiration held for them by a girl who'd thought herself lost to that sort of feeling forever) to discover their watchdog, mountainous in a folding chair, at play of gin with a choice selection of the City. —Attorneys, businessmen, politicians, criminals, and an occasional officer of the Fire or Sanitation Departments.

These games, with the occasional Sanitation man already in over his head, would sometimes last till morning—and the foreign visitor too timid to brave the night streets alone after so comforting a companion through the evening, found no alternative but to go to the kitchen for a sandwich and beer, and, later, to fall asleep on the sofa to a riverine murmur of card talk, the masculine comforts of curses, burps, farts unrestrained, and cigar smoke whiffed from the table of play.

It was odd how good company might improve a man. Often, by morning, that same creature who'd trotted like a spaniel behind Samuelson's bulk the evening before, would, under the civilizing influence of women, cards, beer, and roast-beef sandwiches paved with horseradish and mayonnaise, stand revealed as not such a bad fellow at all, a man of some experience, and no fool. —And occasionally, no fool at cards.

"Taxes killed my dad," Samuelson said, "and the fuckers are on their way to killing me"—and walked on his way. His desk was the last in the left-hand row, across from a slender, aging black detective named Murray, generally believed by the Squad to be a queer, and to have been caught at it.

It was known that Samuelson and Harriet Picunis had had a thing for a year or two, and some Squad members had bet it would destroy Samuelson's marriage. But the thing was over, apparently, and no harm done. Nobody knew if Ruth had known about it or not. —If she had, she'd apparently decided to let it pass.

Samuelson had built his family a cottage up in Otsego County—perhaps as a peace offering—and had then been struck, in those bosky environs, by a new school tax of brutal weight.

Ellie smoothed her skirt—it had been badly wrinkled across the back—and perched comfortably enough on the side of Nardone's desk, absently enjoying the light armor of her panty hose taut around her bottom, at her knees when she crossed her legs.

"Look at this shit." Nardone extracted another report. (The fluorescents of the squad room seemed, when one first walked in, to pour down a flood of white-yellow light, almost bright as the day outside—but, on the surfaces of paper, this brightness turned a dull violet, difficult to read by.) Ellie bent slightly, unwrapping her bagel, and was able, holding her head at the proper angle, to make out in the dense type that a detective named Johnson had been observed by a fellow officer to enter the establishment of a bookmaker named Porfirio Cruz, pause in those premises for thirty minutes and a little more, then leave.

"Are they kiddin' us," Nardone said, "—or what?"

"Is that all they have?" Ellie said. The bagel had butter oozing out its edges.

"Look at this . . . 'Officer observed. . . .' What kind of crap is that? What are we supposed to do—surveil this Johnson? Go talk to this Cruz guy?—What the hell's that goin' to get us?"

"That'll get us nothing," Ellie said, and took her first bite.

"That's it. That's just what it's goin' to get us." Nardone took the top off his tea.

"We could talk to that witness; he could know more than Johnson just going in there."

"Yeah, we could talk to him—if you can find his name in here." He shook the report as if the man's name might fall out onto his desk, might just miss his tea. "—You find that witness's name in here, I'll buy you lunch."

"Why are we getting this crap?—We have a major case to work!"

Nardone's phone rang, a minor addition to background conversations the singing of other phones throughout the squad room, the rattle and click of processor keys as two detectives across the aisle and two desks down entered and edited their previous day's activity reports. —Second thoughts, emendations, corrections, completions. Leahy liked his file reports perfect—and provided only with those, would, more often than not, leave a man (or woman) alone.

As Nardone commenced a conversation with an old informant calling from loneliness, Ellie took a second bite of bagel, pried the top from her coffee cup, took a paper of Nardone's sugar, tore and poured it in, then tore a creamer paper and added that. She took the thin wood stirrer from his tea—though he tried to protect it, phoning—and mixed her coffee to light tan. It tasted slightly from the Styrofoam at first, then rushed over her tongue to soak the second bite of buttered bagel, joining with that rich flavor as if two veteran lovers, soft and kissing loose, had come to lie in Ellie's mouth.

"What about Classman?"

Nardone covered the phone's mouthpiece. "He called me at home last night. Said Frankie Odum never met Gaither. Heard about her from some john or other, and that's it. Didn't know she was dead, and didn't care one way or another."

"Nothing."

"Nothin'." Nardone took his hand off the phone's mouthpiece, and said, "Marty, you always been straight with me—I always been straight with you. We don't have the budget to be sendin' you to Miami, no matter who's down there. I don't care what they're doin'. Let the Miami cops sweat that out. It's . . . it's—I'm tryin' to tell you it's none of our business. And we couldn't afford it, anyway. You get somethin' on Midtown construction; you get some Internal guy lookin' the other way—that's a different matter. I'll be happy to talk to you." Nardone sat listening while Ellie ate the rest of her bagel. It took five bites. "I'm—I'm always glad to talk to you," Nardone said. "It's a pleasure. Umm-humm . . . Right. Yeah. Now you got it. —Hell, you don't like those assholes any better than I do. A bunch of animals. Do you owe them anything? You sure as hell don't owe them anything. Umm-humm. That—that's exactly right. Right . . ."

Nardone rolled his eyes up at Ellie, but he stayed very patiently on the phone, listening to a voice high-pitched and harsh enough so that Ellie could almost make out its words. Nardone had a reputation of being soft with his sources—overpaying them, too.

Ellie drank her coffee down, picked up the damp stirrer from the desktop and stuck it back in Nardone's tea.

Nardone told his informant to give Jennifer a hug for him, told him to tell her to treat him right, or Nardone would be coming after her. "She's got a good man," Nardone said. "—She's got the best. She's got a guy with some balls." Then Nardone said, "Take it easy, Marty," and hung up.

"Would you believe," he said, "—that Marty B is dead drunk before noon? We're talkin' about a guy there hasn't got any liver left."

"He's scared."

"And I don't blame him," Nardone said. "I was in his position, I'd be scared, too. I was in his shoes, I'd be terrified. —You want to go out to Queens? This Ambrosio thing?"

Charles Ambrosio was the detective accused by his wife's aunt of buying sports cars on a salary that shouldn't have permitted it.

Ellie read more of that report, down to the bottom of the second page. (It was getting uncomfortable to be sitting on the edge of the desk.) There didn't seem to be much against Ambrosio but his wife's aunt's accusation.

"Not much to it," Ellie said. "The old woman probably hates him for criticizing her cooking. —I wanted to check the Gaither place again."

"Let's do this shit first. We'll do Queens first, keep Leahy off our backs." He sipped his tea. "—Marty talked this stuff cold," he said. "Poor guy. They're goin' to smell the sweat on him someday, and shoot him right in the head. Then what the hell's goin' to happen to Jennifer? —She's damn near retarded—you know that?"

"No," Ellie said, "I didn't. . . . I knew she wasn't very bright."

"Who wasn't very bright?" said Samuelson, stirring a cigar-smelling breeze as he trundled by again.

They checked out the bronze Ford in the basement garage—Ellie trying the slap-on light, Nardone, as he always did, opening the car's trunk to be sure of the spare and tools, and to work the action of the Remington twelve-gauge, check the loads. Neither of them had ever had to use, or even brandish the big shotgun, though they'd fired it on the range to qualify.

Ellie thought it a good sign for the afternoon, that they'd gotten the old Ford. It was their usual ride, comfortable, and didn't look as cop-ey as some of the cars. The ford had a severe dent in the right front fender—someone had hit them trying to parallel-park while they were having breakfast in Brooklyn months before. The garage boss, the king of that echoing cavern—a civilian named Ramirez—had wanted them to pay for the damage, because Ellie had told him the truth about how it happened, and no way was that line-of-duty. Maybe once—not anymore. The Department, pinched for cash, was now trying to save in such little ways—occasionally out of the pockets of its people.

The Ford smelled faintly of both of them, so that climbing into it was something like coming back to a small, messy home with grimy windows.

Nardone asked Ellie if she wanted to drive, and though she did (felt like gunning the sedan around) she said no, knowing that he enjoyed it, liked sitting behind the wheel in easy competence, steering through the city's noisy tangle. The thicker, the more brutal and impatient the traffic, the more Nardone appeared to relax in it, like a wealthy businessman in a warm and tumultuous Jacuzzi.

They rode up and out into a warm and muffled afternoon (that smelled lightly of bus exhaust and some residue of garbage), the sunlight so diffused it was difficult to make out people's faces at much more than half a block. This haze made all New Yorkers strangers at a distance, though a friend or lover might recognize a walk, or an attitude, a manner of window-shopping, a way of looking out across an intersection before crossing.

There was a buzz in the Ford's plastic trim, somewhere above the radio, that sounded loudest when Nardone accelerated after a stop for red; once they were cruising, the buzz faded softly away.

Ellie properly watched the right, as Nardone, while driving, watched the left. They considered the people by their ways of moving—looking, without thinking of it, for odd breaks in rhythm—sudden jolts and starts along the sidewalks, faster movements, bursts of speed, running

. . . people looking after the runner, mouths open in surprise.

So, Ellie and Nardone, rolling by in noisy, shifting traffic, watched the people as they passed. Ellie had, when she first became a detective, greatly enjoyed observing people, guarding them without their knowledge. She'd thought of herself as a sheepdog (a large, pretty female, with silky white fur like a sled dog's—powerful, sharp-toothed, and part of a greater pack of protectors trotting through the city).

She no longer thought that sort of thing, but still felt pleased, comfortable, gazing out her side window as they drove uptown. It was a long ride out to Bayside.

Just as they entered the tunnel, swinging swiftly into it (having barely beaten the light)—and were only a few yards onto the slight downslope in warm, close, thrumming air—the Colonel, in tan summer slacks and white polo shirt, sitting at an early lunch at his hotel-suite table, said, "Try the Jewish guy—more likely to accept cash payment."

His lieutenant, sitting across from him, having ordered a club sandwich, which the Algonquin did very well, nodded and took a toothpick out of his next section of toast, chicken, lettuce, toast, bacon, tomato and toast. The toothpick had a little cluster of yellow plastic threads at its tip to catch the eater's eye, warning of the sharp sliver—a nicety no longer often seen. The Colonel was having shrimp salad.

His commander's instruction had come in answer to the Lieutenant's suggestion that a second source, a source "closer to the trenches," might be useful in monitoring NYPD activity in the delicate matter to hand.

"And for heaven's sake," the Colonel said, reaching for his iced tea, "get a receipt. Give him one hundred dollars to start . . . a bottle of something—some of that sweet wine they like, or a bottle of Scotch with a fancy label." The Colonel put back his head slightly, and took a deep swallow of his tea. His throat was so closely, so cleanly shaven, that the Lieutenant couldn't see where his beard might have begun.

"Right," the Lieutenant said, took a bite of his sandwich and chewed it. When he'd swallowed, he turned in his chair to look at three sergeants in summer-weight sports coats and slacks. They were sitting on the sofa, crowded as three big birds on a short branch. —Tall, bony Mason on the left; Budreau, stockier, on the right; Master Sergeant Tucker (the biggest bird, and black) in the middle.

"Reminds me. —You people listen up, now," the Lieutenant said. "Just because we're in New York City, doesn't mean you can go hog wild on per diem. Your rooms are prorated and paid for, and each one of you has got exactly thirty-six dollars a day for food and transportation—and that's plenty. You overspend that, and it will for damn sure come out of your pockets. —Just don't . . . don't come whining to me you got robbed by some nasty hooker! You will get short shit from me if I hear anything like that. . . ." He paused to look down and tuck a small tongue of bacon back into his sandwich, and when he looked at the sofa again, saw that the two sergeants to the left and right were nodding their understanding and obedience. Master Sergeant Tucker, in the middle, sat stiff and upright, smoothly rounded out, large, solid and black as any ebony idol. He was looking at the Lieutenant in an unpleasant way, through gold-rimmed spectacles.

"I'm referring to these men, Sergeant, of course," the Lieutenant said, and would have apologized further, but Sergeant Tucker stood up abruptly, flicked the men to either side of him lightly on their shoulders with his thumbs and forefingers (as if they'd had flies on their shirts, there) and when they rose, said, "With your permission, sir," to the Colonel, then led his men to the door of the suite, and out. —Budreau, stocky, black-haired, almost as wide as the jamb, was last through, and closed the door softly behind him.

The Lieutenant didn't know what to say, after that. He had talked to black people all his life, and knew how to talk to them—better than any Northerner ever would. The Sergeant had been rude—had been out of line, no other damn word for it. Now, the Colonel sat smiling at him from across the table, chewing on a mouthful of shrimp salad. When the Colonel had swallowed, he said, "It's best, usually, to let a Field First handle his men. —If he can't do that, of course, you have to get a new Field

First." The Colonel sprinkled more salt on his salad. "—You know, Bob," he said. "Tucker was with me on Godiva. He's familiar with the city. . . . And I do think we can ease up on the chicken this trip." He pursed his lips. "—It's just that this one, this trip is a make-or-breaker. I don't have to tell you that. This one's a make-or-breaker. . . ."

"That's for damn sure," his lieutenant said, eyeing the Colonel's ring with some distaste. If the Academy people had a serious fault—it was being snotty. A V.M.I. guy could count on a lot of lectures. —A lot of shit, was what he could count on. *"It's best, usually . . ."* following which, a guy would receive bullshit on handling men up the ying-yang, just as if he hadn't gone to a better school. Same damn school General George C. Marshall went to. —The Lieutenant had a vision of himself confronting Sergeant Tucker, and getting that jig squared away. "—Sergeant, we all make mistakes. I made one when I braced your men on that per diem thing without going through you. —Then you made one, Tucker. A real bad one. You left me with shit on my face in front of the C.O." . . . A little pause to let that sink in. "—And shit, Sergeant, rolls downhill. You lay an attitude like that on me again—I will personally put the peg to you . . . and I mean right on through to the ground!—You read me?"

See what Mr. Wise-ass four-eyes tar baby said to that.

Off the boulevard, the sky unfolded over Queens, sunlight flooding freely over the long rows of one-story houses, the low red-brick buildings of small shopping districts, used-car lots, dentists' offices, lawyers' offices upstairs. It was not far from here to Ellie's house, the house she'd grown up in. A mile—a couple of miles—and they'd be there.

"Want to go look at your house?" Her partner.

"We don't have time," Ellie said. "—I want to get back to New York and take another look at that apartment."

"Nothin' much to find, there. —That place was turned pretty good."

The air smelled different now, away from the city, nearly a small town's air. The edge of the Ford's window, the narrow complication of panels, strips, the slit well for the glass, pressed up against Ellie's forearm; she thought perhaps she hadn't put the window all the way down, but wasn't uncomfortable enough to move her arm to see. The warm air poured into the car as they drove, stirring loose strands of hair behind her ears. She had her hair gathered back in a French knot, out of the way.

Ellie thought of someone she might meet someday . . . a man touching her at the back of her neck, lightly as this wind. Not a lawyer. No one on the Force. A man at a party . . . looking different from the others. —Not very tall. Just a little taller than she was. A businessman . . . beautifully dressed in a blue-black pin-stripe suit . . . maroon tie. Gray eyes, deep . . . adult. Amused. "You're not the type, are you," he'd say, "—for police work? I'm sure you handle the job very well—but that's not the real point, is it? *Comfort* is the point, isn't it? Whether the job really fits you . . . whether you fit the job. You seem to me a little too gentle for that kind of work. A little too fragile. . . ." He liked her . . . thought she was interesting; Ellie could tell. He stopped a waitress, took two canapés off the tray—liver pâté, with pimiento across the top—handed one to Ellie and ate the other, hungry as a boy. An important businessman; the hostess would tell her that in the kitchen. —No, not in the kitchen. Ladies' room. A maid was there, a Central American girl in a black-and-white uniform, sitting in a chair against the wall, waiting beside a small stack of folded beige towels. The party was in a beautiful apartment just off the park. No, it was in a town house—the downstairs parlors in ivory, cream, and gold. Oak paneling, textured French paper for the dining room. "Jack's a banker with interests in Europe. —A very important man. . . ." The hostess would smile into the mirror at Ellie as they made up . . . the sounds of the party barely audible. "—And *very* attractive. . . ." In the front parlor, after dinner, he'd come to her again, tell her funny stories about banking in Brazil. —Wide-shouldered, stocky, and strong. Bronze hair, streaked gray from his hairline back. He was ten years older than she was. Older, with younger eyes. —After they'd talked for a while, he'd put his hand on her arm, on her bare arm. She was wearing a Giles Bascombe dress, silver, trimmed in black lace. She'd saved and saved for it. —Now, it was just right. Ellie tried to think who the woman giving the party might be, but it was too much trouble. —Some friend of Clara's. And after the party, he (Jack . . .) wouldn't call her or get in touch or anything. Nothing, nothing for months. She would almost forget him, but then remember him again in the morning, or while she was sitting stake-out at some construction site, Midtown. —Then, one day, Anderson would call her upstairs, and Jack would be there, looking handsomer than Anderson—much better dressed.

"The Commissioner gave me a hand finding you. —We're old friends. . . ." Deep, soft voice, a harsh buzz to it beneath. Anderson just standing there looking like nothing at all. "—It's been a long wait. I've been in . . . China." Would hold out his hand to her. Tough face, tanned, a little tired from traveling. His grip even stronger than Tommy Nardone's. —A slight scent of shaving lotion. It would smell like new-cut grass. . . .

At Jarnigan Street, after waiting for a Holsum bread truck to make the turn before him, Nardone took a left.

"Connie's makin' a big dinner," he said. "A friend of hers from high school, Patty, is comin' into town. Patty Daley. Lives in Chicago—a buyer for Marshall Field's. Big career girl. Connie hates her . . . Connie loves her." Ellie laughed. "—No, I mean it! This girl is a career girl plus. She's got an office—she's got a secretary, even! Connie's green, I can tell you that."

"She wouldn't give up what she's got—you and Marie—for anything."

"No . . . but that don't mean she wouldn't want for Patty to fall on her face, just a little bit."

"Well, I guess it's nice if you can do both, have a wonderful family, and have some kind of career, too."

"Patty don't do both. That's strictly . . . she's strictly a businesswoman, you know? That's it for her whole life, period. —She's gone with guys, but they come in strictly second."

"Well . . . it's not easy to have a profession—for a woman—and have a family, too."

"Oh, yeah." Nardone said, agreeing quickly, worried that he'd hurt her. "Oh, yeah. —Not easy." He slowed the car almost opposite a low duplex in white aluminum siding, its two front entrances short flights of brick steps. There was a tricycle in the left front yard; a bronze St. Francis with a small bird on his shoulder stood in the yard on the right. The house number on the black double mailbox was 1181—83, in small brass numerals. Above that, in cursive brass letters, *Dukakis—Ambrosio.*

"That's our guy," Nardone said, "—the right side. His kids are too old for that stuff." (By which he meant the tricycle.) He turned the Ford up and onto the concrete driveway on the right. The driveway was in good shape; so were the lawns.

"Owns the whole house," Nardone said, setting the emergency brake and turning off the ignition. "—Looks like he keeps it good."

They got out of the car, and Ellie went up the steps to the door, Nardone loitering by the driveway.

The doorbell was musical chimes.

A child with dark hair cut fairly short—hard to tell if it was a little boy or girl—moved a curtain inside the left front window to peep out. Then, Ellie saw a woman's face (dimly through the screen door) appearing at the small square lookout cut into the front door's heavy wood. Locks clicked and clacked, and this swung open. A thin young woman with a big blade of a nose, close-pinched mouth, beautiful chocolate-brown eyes.

"You want somethin'?" A hoarse, rich voice, a smoker's voice—once so common, now unusual. The woman had a stiff, vibrant permanent, thick with burnt-orange curls over traces of black, where luxuriant roots of hair, heavy, oily, dark and dense, had grown out swiftly. She was wearing very expensive clothes—a Bendel's flowered silk, or something just as nice, and a cashmere sweater with mother-of-pearl buttons (something against the heavy chill of air-conditioning pouring slowly past her out the open door). She wore a square-cut tourmaline set in gold—Fortunoff's, Ellie thought—on the ring finger of her right hand. Then and there, Ellie figured that Charley Ambrosio had gotten his beak a little wet.

"Hey!" the woman said. "—I asked you somethin'. I asked you did you want somethin'."

"I'm on the cops," Ellie said, took her buzzer case

from her purse to show her shield, then put it away again. "I wondered if Charley was at home . . . we could have a talk." The thin woman gave Ellie the look, circular, then direct, that questioned whether Charley Ambrosio had been fucking this piece that went around all day with guys, pretending to do a man's work just to get some stuff between her legs . . . maybe steal a decent woman's husband.

"It's business," Ellie said. "—Not bullshit."

"So?—Then go see Charley where he works. He's at work. —What are you? What division are you from?"

"O.K. if I come in?"

The thin woman put her skinny left arm up on the doorjamb to show that was not O.K. She still wore, on her left hand, the tiny diamond chip of her original engagement ring and a very thin circlet of gold. "I asked you a question," she said. "Where the hell are you from? —You want to talk to my husband—you go see him on the job. My husband don't bring his work home—you understand?" Movement caught her eye, and she ducked her narrow head, its wealth of hairdo, close to the screen door to see Nardone wander away from the Ford and up the drive alongside the house.

"Where's he goin'? —What the hell's he doin'?"

"He's just looking around," Ellie said. "—O.K. if I come in?"

"Huh?—No." The orange curls brushed the door screen as she craned her neck. "Where the hell's he goin'!"

"Just around the back," Ellie said. "O.K. if I come in?"

"What?—Listen—fuck you. You ain't gettin' into this house. Get the fuck out of here!" Despite this tough talk, her slender, fine-boned hand trembled at the doorframe. Ellie supposed she was frightened of what Charley Ambrosio would think if she let big-noses into the house, cops or not. —Maybe especially cops.

"Calm down," Ellie said, "—we have no problem here. Take it easy."

"Then you get that . . . you get him out of the back of the house!" The thin woman suddenly shifted back from the doorway, turned her head, and called, "Char—" remembered her husband was gone from home, and instead called, "Gramma . . . *Gramma!*" in a voice piercing as a jungle bird's in a Tarzan movie. "Watch the back! Watch the back—a guy's back there!"

"Will you take it easy?" Ellie said, seeing the child, boy or girl, still at the parted curtain to the left, wide-eyed. "We're just here on the job—we're not going to bother you. Call your husband on the phone . . . maybe he can drive out here for a few minutes, talk with us."

The thin woman, panting, listened to none of it. "Are you goin' to get out of here? —Are you goin' to get out? You better get the fuck out of here—I'm tellin' you!"

She seized the inside handle to the screen door with both hands, wrenched at it—then suddenly shoved it partly open to strike against Ellie's raised arm, slammed it shut again, then open-and-shut in Ellie's face several times, as if that would force her off the steps, drive her away.

Ellie saw herself wrestling with this frantic woman, struggling with her in front of her child . . . a screaming child seeing its mother knocked down, knelt on, handcuffed . . . all the neighbors watching from across the street.

The screen door flying half open at her again, Ellie kicked it shut, hard, leaned into it to keep it closed, and said to the woman, their faces very close, screen separated, "—If you don't shut your mouth and step back, I'm going to drag your ass out here and put the cuffs on you in front of the whole fucking neighborhood!"

Their faces were close enough that Ellie could smell the woman's breath, a little sour with her smoking, her fright. Charley Ambrosio must be a grim husband.

"All right, now—*let go that door.*"

The thin woman avoided Ellie's eyes, then took her hands off the door handle.

"You O.K., now?" Ellie said. "—You finished making a fool of yourself? In front of your kid?"

The thin woman looked at the floor. She seemed a sort of brittle girl, nothing much behind her bluff. Ellie supposed, though, that Ambrosio loved her, to dress her up that way. She wasn't bad-looking. She had nice eyes, anyway.

"Are you calmed down, now?"

The woman nodded, still looking down at the floor.

"We're not here to bother you," Ellie said. "O.K.?"

The thin woman cleared her throat, and nodded.

"What's your name?"

"Doris." Tears waiting.

"Doris—you tell your husband that we came by. We're from Headquarters, downtown. You tell him we hear he's spending a lot of money. —You know what I mean?"

Doris had nothing more to say. Wouldn't raise her head, either.

Ellie saw the curtain in the left front window shift and fall closed. The child, boy or girl, was now seeing Mama quiet.

Nardone had heard some yelling from the front—raised voices—and supposed that Ellie was busy with the ladies of the house, whatever. He'd seen a big new bass boat, with white Kevlar swivel chairs fore and aft, parked on its trailer just behind the house. —First thing he'd seen. Looked like Sergeant Ambrosio took his vacations upstate, spent a lot of time out on the lakes. —Second thing seen was a brand-new Buick (a LeSabre, four-door, cream and dark blue) parked alongside their garage. The big garage door was locked, had a padlock on it. Nardone didn't see himself busting a guy's padlock—not if he could help it.

Voices still from the front.

The bass boat and Buick filled Ambrosio's yard right up; guy was out of room, except for the garage. Nardone walked around to the left side, and found the window there covered with brown paper. —Man was a private sort of guy, apparently. Nardone walked to the back of the small yard, and started to squeeze along between the back of the garage and a low chain-link fence. There looked to be a little window back there, high up.

"So, what's goin' on?"

Nardone turned, wedged in, and saw an old Jewish guy across the fence, sitting in a lawn chair in his bathing suit under a leafed-out grape arbor in the next yard. The old man had been reading the *Post;* now, he put it down and looked at Nardone.

"I'm a police officer. —We got a report there was vandals back in the yard here. Kids." Nardone got his ID case out, showed the tin, and the old guy squinted to see it. He had glasses thick as bottle bottoms.

"That's a good one," the old guy said. "That'll be the day—vandals go in that yard!"

Nardone stepped sideways between the fence and the back of the garage until he got to the window. The window was too high to look into, standing there. "—What's so special about this yard?" He reached up, got his hands on the narrow sill, and chinned himself up so he could just see in.

"You ever meet that guy?" the old man said. "—Ambrosio?"

"No." There was a Nissan in the garage, a new Z car. It was medium green or blue—hard to tell with no light in there. "No, I never met him."

"You met the guy, you wouldn't ask."

Nardone lowered himself, brushed off his hands, sidled back along the chain-link fence. "Rough guy, huh?"

"He's a cop."

"I'm a cop. —I'm a nice guy."

"That's a good one," the old man said. "—I was assistant court clerk in Brooklyn. Tell me how nice cops are, makin' cases. —You go meet Mr. Ambrosio; you tell me you want him to catch you in his yard sometime."

"Lousy neighbor, huh?"

"I'm not sayin' anything."

"He's got some nice stuff here," Nardone said, but the old man quickly picked up the *Post,* high enough to cover his face, and began to read it. He said something from behind the paper, but Nardone didn't catch it. —There was something else, though, some kind of muttering talk back by the house. At first, Nardone thought it came from the front, Ellie and somebody there, but it was closer. He walked down the side of the garage, and there was an old lady, must have been eighty or ninety years old—very old—standing there in a blue housedress with lace on the collar. Nice-looking old lady, very old, white hair up on her head. She was staring at him, talking in Italian, not loud, conversational . . . some sort of old-country talk. Real peasant stuff.

The old woman put her finger up to her left eye and

pulled the lower lid down and goggled the eye at him. —She was cursing him out like mad; he got that, all right. Bad stuff, too. His balls . . . she was talking about his balls. —How they should dry up and rot off him. Real old-country shit. She wasn't embarrassed to be saying it, either. There she was, looking like she belonged in some old folks' home or something, just cursing everything he had . . . balls, whatever. Now, she wanted his eyes . . . the juice in his eyes to turn into pus.

"Listen," Nardone said to her in very bad Italian. He hardly knew any real Italian at all, just street stuff from when he was a kid. "Listen—you're makin' an asshole out of yourself. Go back inside."

The old lady reacted badly to hearing that. —Nardone was afraid she was going to drop dead right there in front of him. She kept it up with the curses, though, and began to goggle both eyes at him, pulling down on the lower lids so the red showed like a big dog's. —And all the time going with the curses. Now, she was giving him cancer.

It was a no-win thing. —Strictly a no-winner.

Nardone gave the old lady the horns with his right thumb and little finger, just in case it might help, and headed back down the drive. He heard the old Jewish guy laughing from the other yard, because the old lady was right behind him, still talking that conversational Italian to his back. She was after any kids he had, now, very unpleasant. It wasn't so funny to hear somebody cursing your kid. It was like that was what had happened to Marie—this old asshole's curses got back in time and did that to her.

There was nothing pleasant about it. —He would have liked to turn around and kick that old lady's ass, was what he would have liked.

Nardone got to the Ford, jumped in behind the wheel, and put up the side window right in the witch's face. —A nice-looking old lady, too. Not so nice goggling her eyes and spitting on his side window. Looked like she wanted to tear him apart.

Ellie came around the front of the car—paying no attention to the old lady—and climbed in the passenger side. Nardone could see she was trying not to laugh—

must have been watching the old woman chase him down the driveway.

"It's not as funny as you think," he said. Then she laughed.

"I'm sorry, Tommy," she said. But she didn't stop laughing, on and off, until they parked at Gandy's Bayside and went in for lunch.

While they waited for their orders—Reubens and coffees—Ellie said, "Well, that's a hot spot; his wife is wearing a mint, and she's real scared."

"Forget that; the guy's got maybe sixty thousand bucks worth of new stuff in the back. And whatever he's drivin' to work can tow a boat . . . and you can bet it's brand-new, too. —He's a fuckin' thief, that's all. Him and his buddies grabbed some cops steppin' back for some gambler—"

"—And he's stepping back for the cops."

"That's exactly right. The man is a thief, period."

The waitress—a pleasant Puerto Rican girl with frosted hair and a slight mustache—brought their coffees, and sweetener for Ellie. Her uniform was very clean, starched—it was a well-run restaurant. The booths were new white vinyl.

"We could make a case on that guy," Ellie said.

"They're not makin' cases on these people—they're throwin' scares. —Last thing the Department needs right now is more cases against cops. Not goin' to do it. So we can forget that. —So listen, Connie's doin' a big dinner a week from this Sunday. She's doin' it for this Patty; a couple other people'll be there, and she wants you to come. But Charley's goin' to be there. Patty and him were buddies."

"That's all right; I want to come. —I like Charley. Connie shouldn't worry—"

"Well, you know . . . an awkward thing. Awkward for both of you. You know."

"There's no problem. Tell Connie I'm happy to come."

"O.K. One week after this comin' Sunday, six o'clock. Connie says don't bring anything. Nothin'. No wine, nothin'."

"Right."

"I mean it. Don't bring anything. She's gettin' the wine; she's gettin' everything."

"O.K."

The waitress came with their sandwiches, potato chips and pickles on the side. "You want water?"

"Yeah," Nardone said, "bring us some when you come back, O.K.?"

"O.K." She walked back toward the kitchen, her tray tucked under her arm.

"Mustard?" Ellie passed it to him.

Nardone tried to pry up the top piece of toast on his sandwich. "This thing isn't comin' apart—I'll skip the mustard. Whatever I got in here, that's what I'm goin' with."

"We head back to the East Side?"

"We eat, we're on our way. —Figure we're goin' to make headlines with that little whore, right? —Prostitute."

"It's a real case, Tommy. —I don't know why they gave it to us, but I'm grateful for it."

"That's easy. —We got it so they can keep tabs. They're scared who she was sleepin' with, that's all. It's bullshit."

"But it's a real case, just the same."

"Oh, yeah. It's a homicide case—no bullshit about that."

"It was a terrible way to go . . . what happened to her," Ellie said, and ate a piece of pickle.

"You tell me a good way," Nardone said, took a bite of his Reuben, chewed and swallowed, "—and that's the way I'm goin'."

The tram swung steadily up out of night into evening. At this height, the setting sun still shone, the upper air yet held the light, while below, deep in darkness, the sluggish river lay like lead as they crossed over. Ellie, tired, leaned from a strap alongside a man carrying a little girl, asleep, on his shoulder.

Keneally had walked into the apartment—which still smelled slightly of cooking—while she and Tommy were peeling back the carpets. He'd thought that pretty funny. "It's the new Homicide guys—checkin' the rugs! I saw your shitty car out front. Let me ask you guys somethin',

O.K.?" He'd sat on the couch with a grunt. "—You aces think to check her phone?"

"We'll get the records at the phone company, tomorrow."

"Honey—you aren't goin' to get shit at the phone company, tomorrow. I figured I'd do you a favor and check, and found out just what I figured. —This whore used Eddie's. You know Eddie's—the registry?"

"We know it, Kenny. —Why don't you get the fuck out of here?" Nardone, grimy, jacket off, shirtsleeves rolled up, kneeling half under the runner in the hall.

"I was talkin' to the lady—but if you know it, hotshot, maybe you know that registry's got twenty phones goin' day and night; got maybe eighty, a hundred subscribers each phone; get maybe five, ten calls a day each one. —You figure it out, foolin' around with that rug, there. You can figure maybe half those calls are pay phones, too. Figure all that out, wise guy—tell me you don't have maybe ten thousand calls goin' through in a week or two. Eddie's don't keep no numbers records." Keneally shook a cigarette out of a pack, and lit it with a transparent lighter, a green one, almost out of fuel. "You guys figure it out. —Jack the Ripper could have called this whore—you guys'll never know it."

"We'll check with the registry, anyway," Ellie had said.

Keneally, bulky in an ugly brown-plaid summer suit, had given her an odd, measuring look, his lumpy, red face intent as if he faced a suspect. "—That's O.K.," he said. "Go ahead, waste your time, you don't figure I'm tellin' you the truth—tryin' to make you look bad or somethin'."

"I didn't mean that."

"Shit you didn't. —Let me tell you guys, Maxfield's little brown nuts are bangin' together over havin' this case pulled. He went to Goodman about it. You guys haven't made any buddy out of Maxfield."

"Oh, dear . . . oh, goodness gracious," Nardone said from the hall.

"Well, don't say I didn't tell you. —You find anythin' in here?"

"Get the fuck out of here, Kenny." Nardone got up,

hauled at the long runner so that it flapped heavily and fell folding to the left along the hall wall.

"You ever hear of anybody hidin' somethin' under a friggin' hall runner?" Keneally had glanced at Ellie and winked at her.

"Sergeant, why don't you get out of here?" Ellie said to him. "—This is not Homicide's case anymore."

"You want me to go—right?" Grinning at her from the couch. An uneasy grin.

"You got it." Nardone walked into the living room.

"Please," Ellie said.

"O.K. —All right." He heaved himself up. "O.K. You guys know all about it—don't need any help, right?"

"Not from that asshole, Maxfield," Nardone said, moving an armchair off the living-room carpet. "—You tell him that for me."

"I'm not here for Maxfield," Keneally said.

"Sure. —You just take off O.K.?"

"Why don't you mind your own business, Tommy?" Keneally said, and stubbed his cigarette out into a round white china ashtray with a blue flower painted in its bowl. "—I was talkin' to the lady. I came up to give her a hand—an' fuck you." He'd winked at Ellie again, and strolled out to the hall.

At the front door, he'd called back, "Who the hell was this pig screwin'? —The Mayor?"

Ellie listened for the door closing. "—Can't we tell that watch cop not to let those people in here?" The watch cop, a stocky patrolman stationed in the corridor to protect the scene, had been discovered sitting in a chair provided by the building management, drinking coffee and reading an old copy of *Field & Stream*—had hopes, he'd confided, of going on the Stake-out squad.

"We can tell him; he still isn't goin' to keep a regular District guy out."

"It's not fair. —They gave us the job; why don't they stay the fuck off our backs?"

Nardone was crouched, looking under the edge of the living-room carpet. "Kenny . . . he probably wasn't here nosin' for Maxfield. He hates Maxfield's guts. He doesn't like any black guys."

"Then why is he hanging around?"

Nardone had pulled up another length of carpet. This had been tacked down, and he tore the carpet edge up with a continuous popping sound. "Got me," he said. "—Don't ask me why Kenny hangs around. . . ."

The tram-car slid into its berth, humming, and Ellie saw there was no bus at the stop. She pushed through the iron-pipe gate with the others—the man's daughter still lay across his shoulder like a soft stuffed toy, sound asleep—and set out to walk. It wasn't far—down and around on the road, up to the street and apartment buildings. The night was cooling the day's heat already. —An end-of-summer evening.

"We're not gettin' shit for new physical," Nardone had said, the carpeting torn up in every room. (He meant physical evidence.) "—And we won't have shit until we inventory every damn thing this woman had. . . . Who do we have to see next week?" Their two days off coincided with the weekend this month—unusual luck.

"We've got Rebecca on Monday, and a friend of Gaither's—Margolies. She's a psychologist."

"Rebecca—that bullshit artist."

"She's what we've got. —At least she met Gaither."

"We got ladies' day at the Turkish bath, that's what we got," Nardone had said, picking carpet lint off his furry forearm. "—Boy, I don't want to use the bathroom here to wash, I can tell you that. —This can's been spoiled for me."

"Why don't I talk to Rebecca, Monday, and I'll do the other lady, too. —The same time, if you want, you can check the registry, see what Fingerprints and Forensic have to say. . . ."

"You lookin' for me to do those shoofly checks, too—while you stay uptown havin' a ball? Leahy's goin' to want those reports. You didn't forget that?"

"Tommy, I'll get right back on that with you."

"Why is it I don't believe you? —I don't know what it is. . . ."

They'd said "So long" to the watch cop—due to be relieved in a few minutes, and sitting half-asleep—and Ellie had told him to pass it on that only she and Nardone were O.K. to go in, as far as detectives went. The watch cop, a nice young guy named Lehrman, had nodded and said "Right" (just as if he were going to bar the way, no matter what, no matter who) and woke up enough to start rereading an article on upland game as they walked away to the elevators.

Outside, it had been near full dark. Cooler.

Nardone had driven over to Second Avenue and down, to stop at the tram station. He said, "Listen, don't worry about this one. —We'll get it done," and leaned over to kiss her on the cheek, then open the door for her. "Take it easy."

When she watched him drive away, Ellie was sorry she hadn't gone down to the garage with him. Little things like that . . . stuff she should do. He did too many of the chores. —Monday morning, she'd enter the reports into the machine. He could drink his tea, and make fun of Serrano. . . .

Ellie met a woman—whose name she never remembered—out on the street in front of her apartment building, and they talked for a moment. While they talked (the woman complaining about how dirty the streets were—how clean they had been) Ellie was trying to remember if she needed groceries . . . food for Mayo. She remembered milk and bread, but didn't feel like shopping for them. She agreed with the woman—some name like Parry, or Perry—about the streets, then said "Bye-bye," and went into her building.

In the corridor, she heard music through her apartment door.

When she unlocked the door, went inside—and smelled shrimp . . . curry—Mayo stood in the hall, complaining, to greet her, and she saw a tall florist's basket of white roses on the small hall table, beside the phone and answering machine. A piece of white poster board was stuck in among the flowers. *Forgive me* had been printed on this in black marker.

Ellie put her purse beside the flowers, and walked down the hall. One of the chairs to the kitchen table had been put outside the kitchen door. There was another basket of roses—these light pink—on the chair. The note with them said, *Please.*

Clara Kersh, in a white blouse and the skirt to her cream linen suit, was standing barefoot, stirring something on the stove. She looked around at Ellie, then back to the stove without saying anything. When Ellie went over to her, Clara still didn't turn.

"Hell," Ellie said, "—it's O.K. I'm not mad. —I was, though."

Clara turned to her, and they hugged, Clara holding her stirring spoon away from Ellie's gray blazer.

"I know I shouldn't have just let myself in—after I made that remark on the phone. I couldn't believe I said it . . . made such an asshole of myself! But I figured—'if she hates me, then she hates me; I'm not going to throw the weekend away.' "

"I don't hate you. —What's that?"

"Shrimp Bengal."

"No." Ellie pointed a finger in the air.

"Oh, that. *Serenade to Music.* Vaughan Williams."

Clara loved the British composers, and would take Ellie's soft-rock tapes off the deck without even asking—put her tapes on.

"Pretty . . ."

Clara turned again from her shrimp Bengal, and kissed Ellie lightly on the cheek. "—You're not so bad, yourself," she said.

"Beautiful flowers . . ."

"I fed Mayo," Clara said.

Clara Kersh was four years younger than Ellie, and almost four inches shorter, a neat, small, coordinated woman (had been a gymnast at Yale) with short red-brown hair almost dark as boxwood honey, and as heavy, smooth, and shining. Brown-eyed Clara kept, it seemed by will alone, a mild but constant year-round tan, her skin still not too dark to contrast strongly with a neat pubic patch, which once, giggling almost like harness bells—a pretty thing she did—she had Ellie, also giggling, trim.

Ellie stood by Clara for a little while, watching her shake pepper and paprika into the shrimp, then went to her bedroom, took off her shoes, went back out to the hall, and checked her answering-machine for calls. There was one call from Rebecca Platt, and a call from Classman. Rebecca's was about lunch; Classman's was an apology for no news from Frankie Odum . . . a promise to give them anything that might turn up.

Ellie went to the bathroom to pee, missing Mayo's usual visits at such times. —It pleased him, she supposed, to confirm that these tall and eccentric creatures produced familiar variations of odor. Now, he would have drifted to the kitchen, be coiling around Clara's ankles, wishing for shrimp.

Ellie thought about it, sitting on the john, and while standing to tug her panty hose up decided it was true she wasn't angry at Clara. She had believed, as they grew closer, that Clara was a tough woman, severe and forward, who loved her. —That had given Ellie almost exactly the same firm, relaxing, pressed-down feeling that Klein had through their years of marriage, that Lennie Spears had for many months. It had been a constant, reassuring, occasionally uncomfortable sensation, as if Ellie were carrying a coil of mountaineer's rope—and feeling both heavier and lighter than she would be without it, had it always looped around her waist, for safety.

She had discovered since, that she was mistaken about Clara . . . had found that Clara was as uncertain as she. Was, perhaps, becoming less certain. Ellie supposed what Clara had said over the phone was because of that. *"You cunt . . ."*

They had met more than a year before, when Clara, as one of countless Assistant Manhattan D.A.'s, and on her next-to-last case—she was about to join a Federal Task Force with more dignified prosecutions to make concerning grand and complicated manipulations in the market—had called Ellie to testify in a case of collusive theft-by-taking. Then, having dismissed her after a long day's waiting, had met her in the corridor and apologized. They had found an opinion on Judge Hoff in common, enjoyed that laugh, and gone across the street for corned-beef dinners at Wellman's.

Almost a month after that, Clara had come up to Ellie in the lobby of the Federal Building, talked with her, and made a date for Sunday shopping and lunch.

Some weeks later, after two or three such expeditions, after Clara had joined Ellie at the Met, once, and at the Modern to see a Tregaskis show, she invited Ellie for supper on a Saturday night near Christmastime (homemade french fries, round-steak hamburgers on toasted Thomas' Muffins, butterscotch-vanilla ice cream) and, both warmed by cocktails before and wine with dinner, had kissed Ellie lightly on the mouth, and then less lightly.

It had seemed to Ellie that such kissing on Clara's couch—which went on and on, and finally involved strenuous and intimate dealings of their tongues—it seemed to her at last that such kissing was surrender enough to excuse any further, and ashamed and shaking, heart thumping hard, her vulva slippery wet, she'd followed (cold hand gently held) to Clara's queen-size bed.

There, after their undressing, slight Clara—first stroking, then sipping, then using (for the longest time) slender active fingers—had finally and at last employed her small fist and wrist in a determined way, producing in Ellie such considerable sensation that she cried out loud, and louder, and more than once, her joy being as much in the crying out as in the pleasure that caused it.

She had wept, afterward, relieved of a dreadful weight of loneliness, and Clara had comforted her.

They had been together ever since, sometimes serious, sometimes a little less so, Clara pleased by Ellie's shame, her shield, the weight of the small pistol in her purse—as much as by her long legs, her pleasant parts, her mild confusion when confronted—and was quick to tell Ellie she'd had men as well, more than a few, as though that news might comfort her, make the matter much less queer.

Ellie (though she lay embarrassed, flushed, eyes avoiding) often deeply enjoyed presenting herself, straddled, for Clara to see and handle—to invade her every privacy (Clara naked, crouched, intent). Ellie would have, if she could have, turned herself inside out on those occasions, so that no part of her would be left alone, left unseen—and was willing enough, afterward, to do what Clara wanted her to. Enjoyed doing those things—and the companionship, very much. Liked to take her easel out of the closet, set it up beside the couch, and sketch her lover, too, when Clara, a collected, fine-muscled miniature, would lie still for it. —Beside that, though, even with the woman's loveliness, her occasional merriment and quick wit, the riches of her fine education, Ellie found no fundamental sustenance. Clara was no happier than she—might be less happy. Also, Clara didn't really know her, though she thought she did—never spoke to her seriously, about serious things—and, not caring to know the real Ellie, couldn't very well claim she loved her. —In that way, Ellie thought, Clara was very like a man.

The shrimp Bengal was good—a little spicier than Ellie cared for, but more than good enough for two portions. Ellie ate them, not wanting Clara to think she was still angry with her.

"It was just bizarre," Clara said, "—coming on like some jealous bull dyke over the phone like that. Weird!" They were sharing a kiwi fruit for dessert. It was like eating a slice of a little green animal—something out of the ocean, and not quite dead. "Weird!" Clara said, "—and, I'm afraid, a stone bore."

"Clara, will you cut the crap?"

Clara stuck her tongue out at Ellie. "I'm trying to apologize—will you let me make my goddamn case?"

"You already apologized; if you want to really apologize, then go get us some Häagen-Dazs. Coffee." That was the right thing to say; Clara stuck her tongue out again, and got up happily enough to put on her shoes and suit jacket to go down the street.

Ellie thought she could afford one more pound before she'd have to diet a little. There were already two skirts that weren't really comfortable on her. —The trouble with women always saying how thin you were, was that you had to stay that way—or they'd be very happy to say you were getting fat.

She and Clara sat on the couch through the evening, watching TV and eating ice cream until the *Tonight* show came on. Mayo had gone to sleep in Ellie's lap during the early movie—a movie about twin sisters who were in love with the same man. (One of them was married to him.) The married sister died when the women were out sailing—drowned in a storm. After that, the other sister (Bette Davis played both of them) pretended to be the dead one so she could live as the man's wife. —Ellie loved these old movies, so full of shadows, of multiple views of everything that no modern movie seemed to have . . . worlds a person could go and live in, if she knew the way. This movie about the sisters was very good, and Bette Davis was wonderful in it.

They watched the beginning of the *Tonight* show, but the guests didn't look interesting (a man from the San Diego Zoo with a kangaroo on a leash, and, to follow, a rock groupie who'd written a book, and a man who'd been in the CIA). Ellie poured the cat off her lap—Mayo fell to the floor moaning—and Clara collected the ice-cream dishes and put them in the sink. They went to the bedroom, undressed, took a shower together, and went to bed.

Often, when they showered, they would soap each other, scrub each other's backs. Sometimes they'd fool around, do breast examinations on each other, for lumps. "—That was how I got into this gay crap," Clara once said, "fooling around in the showers with Jennifer Booth."

"In college?"

"In college. —And we were both getting screwed at the time, too."

"At Sarah Lawrence," Ellie had said, regretting her meager one year (barely college at all compared to graduating with honors from Yale, and then law school), "—there were boys in the showers, half the time."

This night, though, they didn't do any of that. Didn't soap each other. Just showered and went to bed. —Ellie supposed Clara still didn't feel comfortable, after the phone call.

Ellie'd thought she wouldn't sleep well—thought the discomfort between the two of them (it had gathered again while they were sitting silent, side by side, watching TV), thought this unease would keep her waiting, awake, for some kind of talk. —But she did sleep, after all. The night was cool enough for no air-conditioning, the single bedroom window half open to the narrow slant of grass stretching between the buildings down to the road and the river's edge. Cool air eased in, with the distant, constant, buffeting wind-sound of the FDR Drive, across the river. —After a while, Ellie dreamed of checkered cloth. She and some friend were shopping for a tablecloth for the country. Ellie seemed to have a house in New Jersey, north, in the hills. She could see colors in the cloth—so it was a dream with color. Red, and a color she'd never seen before.

After that dream—and after a long sleep not dreaming, or not remembering—Ellie heard Clara say something, quietly. Then Clara cuddled against her, snuggled along Ellie's back, naked, smooth and warm. Clara occasionally wore the same stockings or panty hose two days in a row, so the stocking feet sometimes smelled a little. Except for that, she was very clean . . . sweet-smelling. Even her perspiration smelled sweet.

"Do you love me?" Clara said, softly, into Ellie's ear, so as not to wake her if she were asleep. Ellie heard her very clearly, and started to say something to her, to say "Yes, I love you." But she didn't. She pretended to be sound asleep—and then was afraid Clara knew she wasn't, so muttered and shifted restlessly, as if she were dreaming. After a while, after listening to see if Clara would say anything else—louder, so she couldn't pretend not to hear it—Ellie fell asleep.

She dreamed again, later, and thought she was home with her mother. Her father was at work. Her mother was just the way she remembered her, short skirt, high-heel shoes—always dressed to go out, even when she stayed in the house all day.

Her mother was joking in the kitchen, saying all sorts of funny things about how she and Ellie's father had met. Their first date—their first serious one, after her mother had broken up with Karol Ferenz, whose father had been a Freedom Fighter,"—who was handsomer than your dad, and already set with the electrician's union. He wasn't—I'm sorry to say—what a woman would call a live wire in the sack. —An area of your dad I have nothing to complain about." Ellie's mother had made a funny face, and stuck out her tongue, the same way Clara did.

They were cooking something, after that, but Ellie never went to the stove to look and see what it was.

Toward morning . . . almost morning, the air smelling coolly of the river, Ellie began to wake to small strong hands tugging the sheet down, pushing at her hip so she lay flat on her stomach. The bed trembled as Clara crouched above her in the dark, then, seated lightly on

Ellie's buttocks, began to stroke her back with her fingertips—slowly, slowly all the way up, then down, then up again as Ellie woke . . . stroking so gently, so lightly it was difficult to feel the touch. Ellie thought that Clara kissed her on the small of her back, but wasn't sure.

This caressing continued for some time, with perhaps another kiss, then Clara said something too softly for Ellie to understand her . . . crouched back and lower—and, her hands holding hard, gripped Ellie's hips and turned her over . . . then stroked her, not as tenderly as before, murmured, bent, and after a few moments commenced to lap as neat as any cat—making in time, as if by magic, Ellie's thighs to slowly spread in presentation, her knees to slowly rise, and causing her at last, from the comfort of her pillow, to call into the dark.

CHAPTER 5

"What the hell is his name—what happened to that cute little intro they're supposed to do? What happened to waiting to see if the wine's O.K.?" Rebecca flicked the rim of her wineglass with a crimson fingernail. —It was inexpensive glassware, and made barely a *tink* as she did. "Crystal, my ass." Rebecca said.

"It tastes pretty good."

"On a salad, it would taste pretty good. I'm not pouring this upstate shit down my throat—not if I can help it." She pursed her lips and made a sharp, sudden kissing sound—loud enough, apparently. Ellie saw their waiter, heading past, quickly swerve toward them, a basket of rolls, a little plate of butter flowers in his hands.

"What's your name, honey? —Christ, he's young enough to be my kid."

"Raoul," the waiter said. He was slender, seemed gently gay, and presented damp dark eyes. His white cotton jacket was clean as new night snow.

"Now listen to me, Raoul," Rebecca said. "If I was paying for this lunch, I wouldn't dream of complaining about the upstate wine. —Since my friend is paying, and she's too ladylike to make noise, I have to tell you that this wine sucks."

Raoul nodded sympathetically. "It is a little sharp," he said.

Rebecca set the wineglass down on the butcher block with a *clack*. "Will you please go out to the kitchen, Raoul, and tell Tony—if Tony still works here—that it would be better to keep the vinegar where it belongs. And if he has a nice fat jug of some California Chablis, to for Christ's sake pour me a glass—and one for my friend—and put this New York State shit where the monkey put the pineapple! —And I don't want to hear some bull about a French wine. We don't want this, and we don't want some sour overpriced French crap. California wine, Raoul—O.K.?"

Raoul was not shaken. "No problem," he said. "—I've seen something obese on the shelf back there. Some kind of California Cellars . . ."

"Bring it."

As Raoul swung away with his rolls and butter, Rebecca said, "The best goddamn light table wine there is, and they keep trying to serve anything but! —What is that? The will to fuck up, or what?"

"I don't mind this," Ellie said.

"My fault," said Rebecca. "We should have gone to the Dove." She cocked her head slightly to the right, and seemed to look at Ellie harder with the advanced, left eye. "—Something bothering you—beside your lousy job?"

"No."

"You look like a guitar string ready to pop—you need to get laid, that's the answer to that. I've got a guy—nice good-looking Jewish guy, has a personality shlong and a long, strong back; he'd be happy to give you a ride. —No money in it, though."

"Will you cut that crap out?"

"So—get a vibrator. Don't get mad. —Get a bigger vibrator! Don't get mad; I'm your guest here."

"Eat your salad," Ellie said.

"This, they do pretty well," Rebecca said, carefully selected her smaller fork, and stuck it into a slice of avocado. "—House dressing's supposed to be O.K."

"What do you hear about the Gaither thing?"

"I hear that the regular Homicide guys think it's a bullshit case. A friend of mine—Larry Ergin? The bartender?—makes Raoul look like Clint Eastwood—says that some cops were talking about it at Clinkers. Drinking on the cuff, as usual. —And what the hell do they know? They were talking about that case . . . other cases, too. You're a smart gal; and that wop hoodlum you go around with—at least he has muscles. What they can do—you can do. Don't pay any attention to the fuckers; that's my advice. I learned a long time ago it doesn't pay to be scared of cops. It's just like dealing with some dog.

Show him you're scared, and he's all over you—kick him in the tush, and he leaves you alone."

"Don't ever try that kick on me," Ellie said, "—or that'll be your last free lunch." The avocado salad was pretty good; there were small slices of hard-boiled egg in it.

"Hell, you're a woman. You're a friend—not just a cop."

Depressing to hear. Ellie thought of poor Marty, Nardone's informant. So scared and lonely. Calling for company—likely spilling the beans for company, too, as much as for the helping hand if he took a fall. Ellie thought that perhaps Rebecca wasn't as impervious as she seemed. Not tough enough to be alone.

"Rebecca," she said, "—you are full of shit as a Christmas turkey."

"So . . . ? That makes me different?"

Raoul swooped up to their table for two—alongside the bare-brick wall—and set two glasses of white wine in front of them. "Compliments of the house," he said, and scooped up the other two glasses. "By the way—Tony quit. This is compliments of Frank Cosumo . . . new manager"—spun half around and slid gracefully away.

"Wheel that squeaks," Rebecca said, satisfied, and took a sip. Ellie noticed she left a faint print of lipstick on the glass rim. "O.K.—unless we get the kitchen revenge."

"What?"

"They spit in the food." Rebecca used her knife and salad fork to carefully fold and refold a leaf of lettuce into a pale-green little package, small enough to eat at a bite.

It had been a bad morning. Watching the meticulous leaf folding, Ellie felt that even lunch with Rebecca was better than the morning had been.

She'd been halfway through a report she and Nardone shouldn't have had to file at all—a follow-up on two state troopers who'd gotten into a fight at the Blackthorn Bar on Seventh Avenue the week before. The quarrel had begun over which game to watch on the bar TV, and, everyone involved being drunk (especially the troopers, who were in town celebrating the birth of one's son at

Presbyterian—the trooper's wife having had complications in Tarrytown, and been ambulanced down), the quarrel had turned to punching. No weapons had been shown but fists, and the officers responding had settled the fight, tuned the TV to a game show, and left, taking nobody in.

All well, and ending well—but the bar owner, a woman named Grace Aline Moran, had sued the troopers for damages, and, at least so far, had refused to listen to reason, citing a broken bar rail and long mirror, and two damaged tables.

Result: a necessary investigation and report—the report to be filed with the State Police in four copies, each signed by the investigating officers, and Lieutenant Leahy, and Captain Anderson. Nardone had called the troopers upstate the previous week and suggested a payout on the damages; the troopers had been willing. Their commander—unfortunately an asshole—wouldn't hear of it. Complained to Leahy, in fact, that Nardone's call had "tainted the inquiry."

It was the remnant of this silly case that required Ellie to process-in eleven pages—strictly by the book—of interviews: one cabby; three black rack pushers from the garment district (the men who'd come to fisticuffs with the troopers); the bartender; another customer (an incoherent alcoholic)—and the squad-car officers who'd responded.

The baby boy—Michael Edward Irwin—was back upstate with his mother, and doing fine.

There was this to finish, and the report on the Queens thing yesterday, and the additional at Sally Gaither's apartment yesterday afternoon—zip, but additional time to account for. All morning at the keyboard, was what it amounted to—and lunch with Rebecca to follow.

Ellie had been working on a proper explanation of why the alcoholic's testimony—that one of the troopers had been a small Puerto Rican youth who'd drawn a gravity knife during the disturbance—of why this testimony was unsound, and might be safely disregarded. She'd just decided to use the phrase *on interview, SUBJECT, a substance abuser, proved unreliable*—when she heard raised voices (raised even higher than usual) at the entrance to the squad room.

She turned from the computer—Nardone, in shirtsleeves, sat across the aisle at his ease, drinking his second cup of tea, and reading a follow-up sent in on Detective Johnson of Internal Affairs, and his acquaintance, Porfirio Cruz, bookmaker. "—The same shit as before," Nardone had already said. Ellie turned to look toward the noise, and saw a detective named Medina (with Buddy Serrano, the only other officers in the room) trying to reason with and restrain an angry man—a cop, by the way they were dealing with him.

"You get the fuck out of my way!" this man said, and followed that up by shoving Serrano against a desk. The strange cop was short, thick-chested in an expensive tan sports jacket; carefully cut blow-dried black hair framed a face as furious as an angry dog's.

"Where is this bitch?" he said, looked around, and saw Ellie down the aisle.

"You!" He shoved past Medina, and stood in the aisle, legs apart, and crooked his finger at her. "You—you fuckin' bitch. Come here!"

Before she thought—so peremptory was the order—Ellie stood up and took a step toward him. Nardone put down his tea and reached up to take her arm, hold it for a moment.

"Where you goin'?"

"*You* . . . !" The angry man crooked his finger at her again. "I want to talk to you . . . !"

"I think it's Ambrosio," Ellie said, and giggled.

Nardone looked over his shoulder down the aisle. "No bet," he said, picked up his tea, and went back to reading the Johnson report.

The cop, who was likely Sergeant Charles Ambrosio, shrugged Serrano's hand off his heavy shoulder and came down the aisle like a vehicle.

Ellie wished Tommy wouldn't just sit there. She wished Lieutenant Leahy would come back to the office. —He'd gone down the corridor to Personnel to complain about the month's roster, just distributed, which showed the two young black detectives working on the racing-odds scam as belonging to Division Bunko, rather than to C Squad, Headquarters—which they absolutely did.

"You're the fuckin' cunt came to my house, Friday!" The sergeant was pointing a thick finger into Ellie's face as he came up to her. He was a little shorter than she was, but that seemed to make no difference.

"You came to my goddamned house!" He had a hairy hand wide as both of Ellie's. "—Come out to my fuckin' house and scare my *wife*? Mess with my *mother*? My wife is expectin' a *kid*!" He was so angry, his voice was shaking. "Who the fuck you think you are . . . from this shit Squad—you fuckin' ass-kissers comin' out fuckin' with a man's *family*!"

"You go to hell," Ellie said, but not as loud as she'd wanted to.

Ambrosio reached out and took her by the arm—just above where Tommy had held her. With that grip, holding her firmly, but not hurting her, he began to shake her slightly back and forth. "You dirty cunt," he said, "—if you or any of your faggot buddies come out to my house again . . . An' you made goddamn sure I wasn't there. . . ."

Ellie saw Nardone put down his tea, the report on Johnson and the bookie.

"Tommy, don't," she said, ashamed. "—I'll handle it."

Ambrosio turned to look down at Nardone, and said, "You were out there, too—right? You, I don't have to go easy on. You get up outa that chair, you motherfucker, I'll break your fuckin' jaw!"

"Hey, now!" Serrano said, he and Medina standing just up the aisle. "Hey, now—take it easy, you guys."

Nardone, looking satisfied, stood up. "—That new kid's probably not yours, anyway, Sergeant," he said.

Ambrosio let go of Ellie's arm, turned, feinted a punch with a grunt—and kicked hard at Nardone's balls. He didn't quite have room enough to make it good.

Then, the sergeant—slugging, kicking—was seized and lifted into the air, shaken very severely, and thrown down hard across Ellie's desk (sending the computer sliding off and slamming to the floor, and crushing a coffee cup and prune Danish beneath the back of his fine sports jacket).

From the desktop, recumbent, Ambrosio swung up several punches which hurt and frightened Ellie when they hit Nardone's face and head, *smack, smack, smack*! so that she jumped forward and tried to wrestle in between them, but Nardone casually elbowed her back so powerfully that she slipped and fell on her rump in the aisle—startled, as she always was, by men's strength,

Serrano and Medina were also trying to grapple at the fight, but Nardone paid no attention to them. —Reaching down, he gripped Ambrosio's head in both hands (as an adult holds a child's head to lean down and kiss it). He raised the sergeant's head high—then slammed it back down on the desktop.

Nardone did that once, and still Ambrosio struck at him—and tried to draw up a heavy-muscled leg to kick, as well. Ellie was up, then, shouting at Nardone, trying with the other two detectives to wrestle him off. It was like handling moving machinery.

Nardone did it again—Ambrosio's head whacking solidly against the scarred wood (sounding like a softball, well hit). Ambrosio reached up, fumbling, to Nardone's wrists, trying to break his grip.

"*What the hell's goin' on here?*" Fat Leahy, just arrived, manhandling Medina to get past.

Nardone had lifted Ambrosio's head once more, and with a grunt of effort cracked it down onto the desktop even harder than he'd done before. —At that, the sergeant settled, and lay beneath him slack as a sated lover when Leahy came bustling to haul Nardone off and away.

Lieutenant Leahy, fresh from a minor victory over Captain Cahill of Personnel, and not intending to have that triumph wiped away by a trumpeting of this embarrassment (though news of it would certainly leak in time) took hold in a very creditable way. —Leading a stumbling Charles Ambrosio back into his small office (where the sergeant, slightly concussed, vomited into Leahy's sink), the Lieutenant had first asked if he wanted someone to come down from the P.S.'s office to take a look at him (Ambrosio said no)—and had then sat listening patiently to the details of the Sergeant's complaint, before informing Ambrosio that he was an asshole who was asking for official trouble that (believe Leahy) he wouldn't like—and suggesting that unless he wanted it widely known that he'd had his ass kicked in front of a whole squad room, including a woman officer, he'd be well advised to keep his big mouth shut. —And would be further well advised to sell that new bass boat, that new Z car, and that new Buick—and, in short, to stop being such a fucking thief.

This advisory, Ambrosio (seated, his mouth rinsed, his ears still ringing) listened to without replying. When Leahy finished talking, the sergeant rose, smoothed his mussed hair with both hands, and walked from the Lieutenant's tiny office, down the long squad-room aisle, and out—looking neither left nor right as he went.

"The salad was O.K.," Rebecca said. "—Good house dressing." She put her fork on her salad plate; she'd left nothing on the plate but half a radish. "Lots of garlic. You can always tell class salad—no skimping on the garlic." She wiped her mouth with her napkin. "Did you finish yours? You didn't finish yours. —Honey, the salad a girl can always eat; keeps you from making a pig of yourself with the rich stuff."

"Nothing keeps me from making a pig of myself with the rich stuff."

"It will; finish the damn thing," Rebecca said, and Ellie picked up her fork for another try. The morning had ruined her lunch—probably ruined her day, though Nardone had appeared to find it all funny. "—That head sounded hollow to me," he said more than once, to applause from the detectives as they drifted in to make phone calls, do their reports, lie to Leahy about progress here and there. It pleased the Squad that they had, in Tommy's person, achieved an impression on at least one regular Division guy, and a sergeant, at that.

As to any difficulties that might result from cracking another cop's head—albeit a thief of a cop—and right in a Headquarters squad room, too, Nardone didn't seem to consider it. "Oh, *thay* . . ." he'd said, doing his gay impression (something he did only when exhilarated), "—I thurely hope there won't be any *trouble*!" He had a cut on his upper lip, near the left corner of his mouth, and there was a dark smudge of bruise beneath his right eye. Ellie found it uncomfortable to imagine what it had felt like to be hit in the face by Charley Ambrosio. Hit in the face several times.

Nardone hadn't seemed to mind it, either, when Leahy, forms ready to hand, came out for his signature—reference the charges for the computer's repair or replacement. He'd signed with a flourish.

"Here we go," Rebecca said, and Raoul steered to them with entrées—curried chicken for Rebecca, salmon mousse for Ellie. "Small portions—but if it's as good as Bloomies does it," Rebecca prodded the chicken, "I won't complain."

Raoul raised an eyebrow to Ellie, refilled their water glasses, and slid away.

"Good news," Rebecca said, "—I talked to Susan Margolies, and she's *very* interested in meeting you." She ate a forkful of curried chicken.

Ellie put her knife and fork down hard, and a piece of salmon mousse fell off her plate onto the tablecloth.

"What in hell is the matter with you?" she said. "You're not stupid, Rebecca. —Are you trying to get cute with me, or what?"

"I knew you'd be pissed—will you just listen to me. . . ."

"I won't listen to shit, Rebecca—"

"This is not a woman you're going to scare! —Susan Margolies isn't scared of any cops. —What did you think? Did you think you were going up to her office and catch her off guard or something? Come on! We're talking a lady who's been around, here. —You're not going to scare her with a badge."

"I want you to keep your hands off my business," Ellie said. "You understand that? Just—"

"Oh, I understand. Rebecca's just a dummy—right? A friend buys her lunch, so Rebecca just lets her friend make an asshole of herself because she doesn't know the person involved?" Bite, chew, and swallow. Another swift bite.

"Just keep your hands off Department business."

"You came to me."

"That's right. —And not for you to start calling people."

"Look—I know something's bothering you. I know something's been bothering you. What happened—something bad?" She buttered a roll. "I tried to do you a favor; I didn't mean to *offend* you." Rebecca ate some of the roll, chewing with her mouth open. "But I don't mind—I really don't, because you'll see that I'm right the minute you meet Susan. —You'll say a couple of words to her, and you'll see right away that this lady may be a little wacko—but she's not scared of any cops. You weren't going to impress Susan, anyway, just showing up and sticking your badge in her face." She put down the roll and shifted her grip on her fork to pin a piece of chicken to her plate. "—Never happen."

"Listen to me," Ellie said. She didn't want any of the salmon mousse. The stuff looked like cat shit. "Next time I ask you for a source—*I* do the contact. Do you understand? You understand me?"

"Ordinarily," Rebecca said, and sipped her wine, "—ordinarily, you'd be right. Ordinarily, I'd be out of line. But not on this one. —Let me tell you something—I'd have made a pretty good cop, myself. I have a nose for that. So, when I tell you that Susan Margolies is not the kind of lady to get cute with—you can believe me. Susan's *interested* in you—she wants to meet you. Can you get closer than that?"

"Don't do it again," Ellie said, and ate a bite of her salmon. She wasn't going to sit there, upset, and watch Rebecca making a pig of herself. . . . The salmon tasted better than it looked.

"You should have had the chicken," Rebecca said. "If salmon isn't perfect, it's crap." She ate more of her chicken. "—Because you're being such a pain in the ass, I'm going to have the rum cake, too."

"Have what you want."

"Are you going to pout all the rest of this lunch?" Rebecca picked up her roll again. "—Let a nice lunch go to waste?" Her right hand was trembling on her wineglass stem. The monster was distressed.

"I didn't mean to upset you, Rebecca."

"Then don't give me that tough look. —You think I don't know who's the boss, here? You think I don't know I'm just a jerk, some kind of nasty stoolie, and you're the pretty blond cop. I know who's in charge in this friendship! Don't kid yourself I don't know that." She finished the roll. "—You ever think I'm lonely? You ever think maybe I don't enjoy blowing some creep in his office bathroom so I can decorate windows? —Just for fuckin' *money*! You don't know what a hard life is, sweetie. —I hope you never know." She ate the last of her curried chicken, ran the tines of her fork neatly around the plate's circumference for the few moist crumbs, raised the fork to her mouth, and licked it clean. "—That was O.K.," she said. "A little heavy on the curry. Bloomies has a lighter touch on the curry. —You still mad?"

"Rebecca—have the rum cake," Ellie said.

The faintest odor . . . hardly a smell at all . . . was woven lightly through the apartment when Ellie and Nardone walked in. Their passage roiled the air, and sent the slight frankfurter smell stirring.

At first, Ellie thought nothing had been disturbed—that Gaither's apartment was now entirely theirs. Then, starting into the bedroom, she saw seven shoe boxes lined neatly up alongside the living-room wall. The shoe boxes were from Gaither's closet floor; Ellie remembered the box labels—all sales stores, remainder outlets.

"Goddamn it!" She brushed past Nardone, heading out to the hall.

"What's the problem?" he said to her back as she went.

The watch cop this afternoon was a tall, black patrolman named McCann. He was standing, leaning against the corridor wall—asleep standing up, or almost.

"What the hell do you think you're doing—don't you know you're supposed to guard this goddamn scene?"

"I am guardin' it." Wide awake, now.

"Like hell! —Evidence has been fucked with in there!"

"Only people I let in was Homicide."

"Who'd you let in—did you let a detective in there? A big fat man with a red face?"

McCann paused, considering a lie.

"Did you?"

Nardone—swollen lip, ripe black eye—had come to the apartment door, and stood listening.

"He had a shield. —Him and his partner both."

Ellie felt herself vibrating with anger—as if there was electricity coming up into her out of the corridor carpet. She saw Keneally . . . Maxfield, all of them sitting in some bar, screwing the owner for free drinks, talking about her.

"This is our case—Commissioner's Squad! Do you understand that, Officer? On this case, we *are* Homicide. —Didn't you get those instructions? —*Didn't* you?"

" 'Unauthorized people' is what I got." McCann was looking sullen.

"Well—do you know better, now?"

"O.K." Very sullen.

"Hey." Nardone, from the doorway. "Get off the poor guy's case; I got a note here from your boyfriend."

. . . *Don't get your ass in an uproar.* Unsigned, but certainly by Keneally, in pencil. There was a P.S. . . . *You need to move this shit out of here.*

McCann was glad to see the apartment door close behind them. Content to stand at ease for another forty minutes, until his shift was done.

"What did they take?"

Nardone was kneeling, going through the shoe boxes. "They could have taken the store, but I bet he took nothin'. Looks like he arranged the stuff in here. —We got her letters in this one . . . bills . . . receipts in this one. Her jewelry and shit." He flicked that shoe box with a large forefinger. "An' if you think *this* is good news—CSIU already packed up all her stuff in the bedroom . . . probably finished Saturday. Man, I wasn't lookin' forward to doin' that for a couple of days."

"He could have taken something."

"He didn't take the book, if she had a goddamn book—which I'm startin' to doubt. That's one thing I know damn well wasn't here to take. —We didn't miss that one."

Ellie knelt beside him, fingered through Sally Gaither's jewelry. There wasn't much of it—all costume or cheapies, as far as she could tell (one playgirl who'd gotten no diamonds, no emeralds, no pearls . . .). Ellie'd assumed a call girl would want to have some good jewelry. Sort of an insurance policy, stuff she could sell if things got tough. —Not Sally Gaither. Or she'd had some fancy stuff once, and had to sell it.

"Strange woman . . ." Ellie said.

The jewelry had been inventoried on a folded sheet of typewriter paper—typed (probably on Gaither's old Smith-Corona), listed, and signed off by Micky Newsome, Keneally's partner, and countersigned and dated by Kenneth Keneally, in a loop-lettered scrawl.

"She had a buddy was even stranger," Nardone said. "—Guy wired her to that chair, an' turned the water on." He sat down on the floor and crossed his legs, studying a receipted bill.

"We need to take this stuff downtown, Tommy, keep it in second-floor Evidence. . . ."

"Some job Mick and Kenny did here," Nardone said, reading. "They finished out the inventory on all this shit. —Must have been in here all mornin'."

"And why the hell would they do that, except to get Maxfield's nose into our case?" . . . There was one pretty piece, a big brooch, an oval stone that looked almost like an opal—it glimmered when she turned and tilted it—a clear, watery gray, with a cracked thread of red running through the center.

"Kenny's crazy, is why," Nardone said, sitting at ease, his back against the wall, looking through a sheaf of Sally Gaither's bills. ". . . Big phone bills—big bill from that registry. Take a look at this." There were two envelopes of photographs, drugstore developed snapshots. Most were of a younger Sally Gaither—thin, long-haired, almost very beautiful, except that her eyes (blue-gray, they seemed, narrow, shy as a fox's) were very slightly too close together. In these pictures, she was dressed in cheap summer dresses, jeans, sweaters; friends as young as she stood beside her in many. One photograph had been torn diagonally across—leaving only her smiling face—fuller than it had been—her right shoulder in a figured blouse, the crook of her bare bent right arm.

"Could be somethin' there," Nardone said, and slid the pictures back into the envelopes, "but that's old stuff. No pictures of her family, her parents—notice that?" The flesh around Nardone's right eye was colored mottled plum. Small streaks of blood showed below the tar-black pupil. "—Don't ask me about Kenny . . . why he does anything." He smiled. "—Could be Kenny likes you."

"Oh, right—that's got to be it." Ellie's knees were starting to hurt, crouching there. She stood up. Clara had said she was crazy not to wear Light Support, instead of plain sheer. "Let's take all her stuff downtown. —That's the best advice we got from him. Maxfield wants to get into it down there, let him talk to Anderson about it—see how far he gets. We can load the car up—take two, three trips."

"Got her bank statements . . . all of 'em since the beginnin' of the year." Nardone put a bundle of those back into the second shoe box. "Let me tell you somethin' —it's real good we're not gettin' rushed on this one, because no way are we goin' through this case like a six-man Division team would do it. It's goin' to take us a month just to enter a real good workup on it, let alone we get a case Leahy's goin' to want to take upstairs."

"I know it."

"We better hope those ladies you're talkin' to can give us a boost . . . maybe put that book on the table, or a couple guys went with this whore. Prostitute. —We can't squeeze some of her johns, we got nothin' but bullshit paper'll take weeks and weeks to run down. Know what I mean. . . ?" He picked up a different bundle of paper, started riffling through it. "—That faggot from Fingerprints didn't sound too good about the way stuff was wiped down in here, either. —That's somethin' else; guy who did this wasn't a wild man; he was careful. Fingerprints guy told Kenny the perp did a damn good job dustin'." Nardone put the bundle of papers back into the third shoe box, picked up another. "O.K., here you go—medical shit. Got a receipted bill from a dentist—guy in Connecticut. Got a doctor's bill from here. Got a receipt from an optometrist—a pair of glasses . . . two pair. One's sunglasses." He stretched out, propped on an elbow, leafing through the bundle. "—Maybe the dentist killed her; those guys'll do anything. You got a dentist, you got a desperate guy, is my experience."

Ellie walked out of Headquarters into early evening. The sun, setting, lit the sidewalks at an extreme angle, so that the pavement, dull gold and glittering with a myriad of mica chips, seemed, as she glanced down, to rise rhythmically to strike her shoe soles as she stepped. She walked east, to the subway.

Al Torres, once a patrolman—until he'd been struck by a vehicle on Clarke Street; it was believed a deliberate hit-and-run—presently was Property & Evidence clerk on the second floor, where an additional records and storage area had been opened the year before, squeezing two long rooms of offices into one.

Torres had gimped actively back and forth behind the counter, producing this form and that form for both Ellie and Nardone to sign—the wall camera taking everybody's picture every twenty seconds, printing the time and date on each frame, to make property-room thefts too awkward, the Hair-bags hoped, for even small amounts of narcotics to be moved and removed before their court appearances.

In this way, with a constant exchange of paperwork, Nardone and Ellie had slid across the counter eleven paintings and prints—three of which Ellie had recognized as copies of Ricciardis, one as a Mondrian, a numbered limited run—and heavy plastic bags of clothing on hangers, of shoes taped in pairs, linens and towels; lighter plastic bags stuffed with panties, bras, washcloths, dish towels, T-shirts, blouses, slips, stockings, panty hose, gloves, scarves, and an exercise outfit (maroon, with white piping). —All this, the bed sheets particularly, to be vacuumed and examined for stray hairs, odd dander, tiny flakes of skin, minute blood spots, dried semen, and dried saliva, if Central Lab considered that useful.

Had slid as well, two Samsonite suitcases, a Samsonite makeup case (all in light blue), a sewing basket, and seven large cardboard cartons filled with paperback and hardcover books of all sorts (cheap romances, histories, biographies, novels, and paperback books of poetry) along with odd objects from the closet shelf, the closet floor, the dresser top, the top dresser drawer—six rented VCR tapes (*The Cruel Sea, Neon Nights, The Enchanted Cottage, The Other Side of Julie, Pandora's Mirror,* and *The Fallen Idol*); several bottles of perfume (Chanel No. 5, Ambiance, Fleuve, Mary Chess); brushes and combs (very fine wisps of blond hair caught in the bristles, the teeth, of these); old *Newsweek* magazines; two vibrators (one short and sleek, a slender white with fluted shaft, the other more brutal, thicker, its oily black-rubber surface ridged with improbable veins); *Chap Sticks,* lipsticks, lip gloss, cold cream, skin cream, deodorants—cream and roll-on, and a separate carton of makeup, nail clippers and scissors, files and emery boards, blushers, false eyelashes, nail polish (Misty Pink), nail-polish remover, pencils, pens, tweezers, fine brushes, powders, liquids, hair sprays and bottles of shampoo, brightener, two wigs in their own boxes (one wig long-haired and blond—one brunet and shorter); conditioner and moisturizers, with—in the same carton, but separate in a stapled plastic bag—the contents of her medicine cabinet: aspirin, Metamucil, a box of regular Tampax, bottles of multivitamins, calcium tablets, vitamin C, B vitamins, Anusol suppositories, Bufferin, Alka-Seltzer, Ivory soap, Vaseline, Kaopectate, Albolene, several boxes of Massengill douche, bottles of witch hazel, K-Y jelly, rubbing alcohol, and hydrogen peroxide lay jumbled among a dozen or more prescription medications, eye drops, tablets, capsules, antiseptic ointments, all in various bottles, plastic containers, and tubes—some brand-new, some so old their labels had worn away.

Ellie thought her possessions would be much the same, if they were someday paraded over Torres' counter, bagged, boxed, receipted and accounted for.

"Don't come in here, now," Torres said, as he had said many times before, and to Nardone and Ellie more than once, "—don't come in here and tell me you don't have your pinks. . . ." He meant the form copies of the receipts. "You don't have your pinks, you don't see shit in here; I don't care if you just brought it in. Then, you come in without 'em, you gotta go see Manugian." (That formidable Armenian was Headquarter's Inspector in charge of Records.) "—An' let me tell you, man—you don't want to go see Manugian . . . 'cause he sure as shit don't want to see you."

The little tram castle was crowded, and Ellie had to wait for a second car to come gliding in—the first had been too full. On the ride over, wedged between slightly swaying people avoiding each other's gaze, she'd been able to see only a distant stretch of the river far upstream, near the projects—the water dark gray in the shadows of buildings on the west bank, flashing crimson where the sunset light could touch it.

Ellie'd recognized two of the people riding the car. —A man standing on the same side, two people down, had asked her to dinner, once, when they'd parked side by side in the garage. He'd been married, and said so—had been very talkative, and seemed relieved when she'd said no. And there was an older woman standing near one of the cable car's windows. They'd spoken a couple of times in Gristede's. . . . Not even aquaintances, really. . . .

She caught Mayo with her right hand when he scooted out the apartment door as she opened it. He bent his head, pretended to bite at the base of her thumb—and did bite, a little. Ellie felt the long muscles of her back ease as she walked into her apartment, out of the sight of anybody. Alone and private. —As if she no longer had to stand so straight.

She set her purse on the hall table, dumped Mayo on the floor, doublelocked the door, and put her hand up under her hair to the back of her neck, rubbing there, rolling her head, hearing the subtle sounds the small linked bones made as they moved.

Mayo followed her into the kitchen, and sat watching while she opened the far left cabinet, chose Chicken Liver Delight for him, took the lid off, and served it to him out of the can, under the table. He would take treats out of hand anywhere, but the regular meal had to be set under the table. —Ellie had considered getting a female; neutered males were supposed to get too fat. But Mayo didn't get fat, no matter how much he ate. She thought the hunting he did, roaming the apartment at night—maybe all night—might be what kept him thin. He was small, too—even for a Siamese. Once the Persian (Woose) was dead, Mayo hunted alone.

Clara had suggested a live white mouse for Mayo's Christmas—let it loose in the apartment, so that the Siamese, hunting in the dark, might at last find a prey, have one startling, unforgettable success.

Blood on a corner of the carpet . . . little stains . . . little pieces. Mayo would have to do without it.

An image of the mouse came to Ellie—as she raked through Mayo's litter box, combing out his few small, neat turds (each coated with spearmint-scented sand so it looked like a tiny toffee rolled in crushed pecan)—the mouse, let loose at dark. White, fat, tiny, all its small extremities pink (Misty Pink?)—lost in a forest of great furniture, scurrying over moonlit streaks along the floor. Hearing . . . hearing with its fine sense that had survived a thousand generations in small cages, something odd, some soft steps somewhere nearer than they had been, commence—just over there—and stop. Stay silent long enough to be almost past remembering, then commence again. An acrid smell (not a mouse smell) drifting with those soft steps along the carpet pile, so rough, so difficult for the travel of a mouse.

Then, deeper into the night, after the longest silence of all, so long a silence that all had been forgotten—would come a sudden gusting breeze, and orange eyes.

Ellie heard the small can slide slightly, under the table. Mayo had almost finished his dinner.

Clara had left an envelope with *Ellie* on it by the phone. A letter inside, written in her sleek, racing hand. *I love you, my darling, my sweet girl. Great breakfast—great French toast. My tongue longs for your little belly button—but alas, I've got to go to Chicago instead. Again—forgive my asininity on the phone. The weekend was heaven, and your Clara will return in about two weeks, depending on how slowly the Prosecutorial staff of the Federal Fourth District considers. Play with Mayo's sister, darling, and dream of me. I swear I won't be bad with any creature in Chicago—even if she plays tennis!—Yours forever. C.* Clara liked to sit with Ellie on the couch, sometimes, and neck while they watched the women tennis champions play on television—Clara commenting on their grim faces . . . their wonderful tan, smooth, round-muscled arms and legs.

"How would you like those legs wrapped around you?" Clara would say, as one of these lionesses paced her back court. "—She'd eat you up."

Ellie checked her answering machine, found two messages on it—one from her aunt in Rochester, the other from Mary Gands, a friend, a social worker she'd met years before. Mary'd had a thing with Lennie Spears before Ellie'd had a thing with him. —Mary wanted to know if Ellie wanted to go see a movie this Wednesday night. Also had something to tell her about Joseph, and what he was up to, now. Joseph, a funny man, was an accountant and a drinker—and Mary had hopes of marriage.

Ellie went into the bedroom, smelled traces of Clara, her perfume still in it, sat on the edge of the bed, and took off her shoes. —Free toes.

She got up, went to the closet, and undressed, watching herself absently in the mirror. Ellie supposed it was a sign of something serious that she was so pleased to be alone—that she'd be annoyed if Clara had missed her plane, had had a change of plans, and so came smiling through the door with wine and delicatessen, or Chinese. It would be tiresome, if that happened.

Ellie walked to the bathroom naked, her hair still up, lifting her small breasts gently in her hands. In a few years, she'd probably need to have surgery there, if she wanted Clara, or a man, to squeeze and suckle at her. It was ridiculous, really, when you thought about it—grown-up people being so eager to suck and chew on each other. —Loneliness was what did it.

Ellie ran a tub, and sat on the toilet, peed, and tweezed two blond hairs from a small light-brown mole on the outside of her thigh. She didn't have many moles—not many freckles, either, no matter how long she stayed at the beach. As a little girl, she'd thought that moles were alive—tiny animals that lived on people's skin, and could hear things, even if they couldn't see.

She wiped herself, flushed, and climbed into the tub—easing back down into the hot water as deep as she could get without wetting her hair—it was too much trouble to wash it tonight. The water was very hot down near the faucet, and Ellie lifted her feet out and rested them on the tiles above. —Advantage of long legs. She supposed Sally Gaither had writhed in her chair when the steaming water fell, arched, tried to kick, to scream the smothering rubber ball away. . . . Ellie picked the soap out of its dish; it was pink, and shaped like a shell (she'd bought a box of them . . . couldn't remember where), lathered the washcloth with it, and raising up just a little, began to soap her armpits, and down her arms. She should have been able to keep Ambrosio and Tommy from fighting. —Been a lot firmer with Ambrosio. (*"You go to hell."* —In that wimpy little faggoty voice. She hadn't even yelled at him!) Maybe hit the son-of-a-bitch. That might have snapped him out of it—reminded him he wasn't talking to some whore on the street . . . or his wife. That poor woman—living with a hoodlum like that. Getting screwed by him whenever he wanted . . . pregnant.

Ellie sat up and put her feet back down into the water; it wasn't quite so hot. She soaped her throat and shoulders, reached around to do her back, then stroked the lather down to her breasts. —Poor soft little things, she thought. There was a pale bruise on her left breast, near the nipple. —Clara, being so damn macho. It would do Clara some good to have a guy like Charley Ambrosio after her. —Then, she'd know what tough was. Ellie looked for a bruise on her arm, where the sergeant had held her, but there was nothing there.

She lathered the washcloth again, closed her eyes, and soaped her face, scrubbing at her forehead, the sides of her nose. She felt for the small porcelain handle over the soap dish, to drape the washcloth over—and scooped up double handfuls of water to rinse her face, get all the soap off so she could open her eyes. Then, she lay back in the water—it was just right, now—and rested, lay listening to her own slow breathing. The soap had a nice perfume. —She remembered where she'd gotten it. She'd bought it at Tendencies—fourteen-fifty for the box. A dozen bars. Small bars. —She would like to have seen Clara in the squad room this morning. Facing him. Clara would have been damn glad Tommy Nardone was there. Probably wouldn't have said a word. —Just stood there, scared shitless.

She imagined Clara on a bed, on a white, tufted spread, kicking, trying to fight. Naked—with Charley Ambrosio, hairy as an animal, above her and bearing her down, beating her, his thing . . . his cock sticking out, angry. An angry cock. Clara scratching, trying to punch with her small fists. Then, she supposed, Clara—bruised, her lip bleeding a little, would lie still . . . let him do it to her. She pictured Clara, after a while, enjoying it—enjoying not having to be so tough anymore. Not having to be tough at all. Letting him do anything he wanted to do to her—and when he finished, he'd say he loved her. He'd cry—like a big dog or wild animal crying, and say he loved her. And he'd hug her until her ribs hurt, he was hugging her so hard. Then he'd guard her for the rest of her life; they'd be married, and she'd have babies with him—two fierce, dark little boys, very beautiful. She'd stay beautiful all those years, too, and find out that Charley was a wonderful, kind man, under all that savagery. All her friends would be jealous of her. Ellie, too, but not as much. —And when she stayed with them, because they both loved her (and she and Charley would laugh at how they met and the big fight with Tommy Nardone)—when she stayed there and played with the little boys who both loved her, she would lie in bed in the big guest room, looking out on the sea, and would hear Charley and Clara making love. Soft, gentle, special love. Laughing together, afterward.

And Clara and she would never talk about what they did together, before Charley. —But Charley would know, and one day would make a joke about it, about Ellie's good taste, like his, in loving Clara. After that, the three of them would be like a family—the boys, too. Then, one night, Charley and Clara would come to the guest room, smiling, very late, the boys asleep long ago . . . moonlight streaming in through the wide windows, shining in from over the sea, a soft sea wind blowing the curtains so they billowed gently in . . . they would come in and Clara would say, we love you as much as we love each other, and they would come to bed and wouldn't do anything, just hug her, and kiss her. Maybe there would be sex, later, if Charley got too excited, being in bed with both of them . . . such lovely women. . . .

Ellie soaped her legs—the left, then the right—tucked them back under the warm water as if it were a blanket, and lay back and rolled slightly in the tub to one side and then the other, to wash the last soap foam off her breasts, her belly. Then she sat up, dipped the washcloth into the water, and rinsed her throat, her arms, her shoulders.

She came into the kitchen in her bathrobe and slippers, stooped, with a little grunt, to reach under the table for the cat-food can, and dropped it into the trash bag under the sink.

There were two kinds of frozen pizza in the freezer compartment at the top of the refrigerator—both single servings. Extra cheese and pepperoni. Regular cheese and olive-and-onion. Ellie chose the olive-and-onion—they didn't put extra cheese on the pizzas, anyway; skimped on the pepperoni, too—took off the outer wrap, and put the pie in the oven at 375.

Then she went out to the hall, took her notebook out of her purse, found Susan Margolies' number and address—Rebecca, enunciating carefully, had dictated them to her over their coffee (and her rum cake)—and made the call. She was nervous, waiting for the woman to answer, and blamed Rebecca for being such a jackass, talking about her to this possible informant—giving this woman, Margolies, all the time in the world to come up with bullshit to anything that Ellie wanted to know. It was ridiculous. It was a joke, was what it was.

"Yes?"

"Mrs. Margolies?"

"Doctor," the woman said. "—Or Ms."

"This is Officer Klein."

"Oh, God!" The woman laughed. "Rebecca wasn't kidding! —Officer Klein!"

The woman sounded older than Ellie had expected—and with a sort of tough accent. Boston—someplace like that.

"Well, Officer Klein, I suppose you want to talk to me about Sally . . . ?"

Ellie said she did.

"Listen, are you a morning person? Because I am madly busy, and if you can come by in the morning—tomorrow morning?—it would be the best time. Is that possible?"

"What time?"

"Can you come at eight-thirty? Is that possible for you? I don't know how necessary—"

"I can do that."

"I didn't know if it was an emergency, or what."

"I can come tomorrow morning."

"Eight-thirty? That's not too early?"

"It's fine."

"Do you know the Donegal—off Riverside on Eighty-seventh?"

"I'll find it."

"Well, it's a huge place—you can't miss it. Apartment Seven D."

"Right. O.K."

"And listen, I can't keep calling you Officer Klein. Did I offend you, laughing like that? Some law-enforcement people get very tight-assed. —It's a stress thing."

"No. My name's Eleanor. Ellie."

"I like it. Rebecca says you're one of the prettiest policewomen in the city. —Is that true?"

"No," Ellie said. Rebecca had had enough fucking free lunches—and this woman was an asshole. "That's not true at all." The woman didn't say anything. "—I'm not."

"I'll judge for myself," Susan Margolies said. "Rebecca says you're a solitary person. Well, so am I. We should get along very well."

And she hung up.

"Fuck you," Ellie said to the phone, and put it down.

She was in the kitchen, checking on the pizza, when the phone rang.

"Was I too abrupt?" Susan Margolies.

"No," Ellie said.

"I don't do good-byes, though I suppose I should; people like to know when things are ending."

"No problem, Ms. Margolies."

"Well, good-bye." Click.

No more free lunches for Rebecca. Period.

Ellie called Brooklyn, and Connie answered. "Ellie—are you comin' next week?"

"Yes, I am—I told Tommy to tell you."

"I know, but I wanted to check—you know."

"Do you want me to bring anything? Let me bring some wine."

"Just yourself—that's all you have to bring. We're gettin' everything."

Ellie thought she'd bring some nice flowers. "—How's Marie?" she said.

"She's in a special exercise class—after school? An' she's doin' great. They do dances—group dances, you know? An' they're goin' to have a dance recital."

"When? I want to come to it. —Or is it just for parents?"

"No, no. It's for everybody. —You come; it's next month. Marie would love for you to see her." Ellie heard Connie draw a quick, soft, nervous breath. "You're goin' to be surprised, I'll tell you that. She's just like a regular little girl doin' it—you know? She just moves slower, doin' the steps."

"I want to go. I wouldn't miss it."

"An' we'll see you next Sunday?"

"O.K. I'll be there."

"Don't bring anything. —Want to talk to Tommy?"

"O.K. Yes—let me talk to him for a minute."

"O.K."

Ellie heard the phone clack onto the table. Voices. Heard Tommy pick it up.

"Ellie?"

"How are you feeling? How's your eye?" Connie hadn't mentioned the black eye . . . the cut lip.

"That's nothin'. Connie wanted to put some steak on it—I said that's just wastin' good meat. It's fine."

"Tommy—I'm going over to the West Side and see that Margolies woman. I'm going to see her tomorrow morning."

"All right. —You go do that, an' follow up if she gives you somethin'. But don't go see any guy, any assholes without I'm along."

"Right."

"You do that, I'll go up to Cruz's place. East Bronx. See if he's goin' to cooperate—if there's anythin' there."

"O.K. —Don't you go see any assholes alone, either."

"No problem. I talked to Nicky Bando; Cruz has been around a long time."

"All right."

"I get done, I'll go in and see the lab starts on Gaither's stuff, the sheets and stuff. Find out what's what from

Fingerprints and Forensic—if they got off the pot yet. Which I doubt."

"O.K. I'll check in with you tomorrow afternoon."

"You got it. —Connie tell you about Marie?"

"Yes. It sounds wonderful for her."

"Oh, it's the best thing in the world, there. Those people really know what they're doin'."

"I told Connie I was going to come see the recital."

"Oh, it's fantastic. We went to a demonstration the kids did? —Fantastic. Those kids got the guts to do anythin'."

"Marie's got the guts, all right. She's a sweetheart."

"Yeah, right. She is. —O.K., talk to you tomorrow."

"Take care."

"You take care."

Ellie got to the pizza just in time—slid it out of the oven onto a plate. It looked better than it smelled. She took a Miller's from the refrigerator, opened it, and got a fork from the silver drawer. Opened the refrigerator again, took out the container of powdered Parmesan, and sprinkled a lot of that on the pizza. Then she salted it, found the powdered garlic in the cabinet over the sink, and poured a little of that on. She bent down and sniffed. It didn't smell too bad. Pretty good. Took the crushed red pepper from the spice rack over the stove, and shook out some flakes of that.

She carried the pizza, some paper napkins, and the bottle of beer out to the living room and set them on the coffee table, turned the floor lamp on low, picked up the TV control, looked over her shoulder to see where she'd fall, sighed, and let herself topple back onto the couch.

Sergeant Budreau, parked in the east underground garage of Park West Village, off Ninety-sixth Street, blew his nose in a Kleenex, and moved the driver's seat all the way back. The car was a rented four-door Chevy; Budreau had picked it up at Avis himself, using ID and credit cards identifying William M. Turner, Waukegan, Illinois. —Sergeant Budreau had never been to Illinois, and considered that no loss. He hated cold weather, and he'd seen movies of Chicago's winters on TV. Miami—

O.K.; Nicaragua—O.K.; Williamsburg and Langley—O.K.; Baltimore—O.K. North of that—strictly shit.

Budreau took his new copy of *Sports Illustrated* out of the glove compartment. Pretty good lighting down here—enough to read by. Not like some garages, where a guy could go blind just looking at pictures. The Lieutenant had wanted him to park way, way back, against the wall. It was dark back there, and not only that, but he couldn't see the fucking elevator. They had a big discussion about it—then the Lieutenant let him park where he should have parked in the first place—got out of the car at long last, and went upstairs with Tucker and Mason to wait in the Jew-boy's apartment, routine shit to shake him up a little—walk in, find them waiting. And he was due. They got the call he was off duty a half hour ago.

"Hurry up and wait." That's what his dad had told him. Had that shit changed? —It had not. A man better learn to keep himself company, in this outfit.

Budreau blew his nose again—the hay fever was easing up, thank God. That shit wore you out.

There was an article on page thirty-two about pro linebacking—lots of diagrams and faggy artwork. There was some good stuff in it—you could tell the guy wrote it had talked to some people that played the position—but it was still a lot of bullshit. A guy didn't have to play with anything but a junior college team—especially a good team (regional division champs, good coaching)—to know how linebacker should be played. Maybe not quarter, maybe not offensive end. —A guy had to keep a lot in mind, playing those.

Mason had his head up his ass, always talking about the Big Ten—just like he hadn't got cut for a busted ankle and never played for Iowa after the first couple of months—not even baseball. Hadn't played service ball, either. He should have come down to Pennsylvania and played regional—would have got both ankles busted down there. A good-enough guy. He was O.K.—but he didn't know shit about football. Man didn't know about something, ought to keep his mouth shut about it. —How linebacker ought to be played. . . . A guy had to have a pair of balls on him, for starters, and real good lateral movement. And he had to be able to diagnose. That was the key right there. —You know the play—you know where it's going. That's the key right there. Than all you got to do is get over where you need to be, and kick ass.

Budreau turned the pages to another article, on the fighting problem in pro hockey, read a little of that—it wasn't very interesting; hockey players didn't know how to fight better than a drunk in a bar, knew no crippling strikes, didn't even know eyes-throat-and-nuts—then put the magazine back in the glove compartment, and sat watching the wide, stained concrete space in front of him. Rows of parked cars—most people home from work already—the narrow gray doors of the elevator far to the right.

Budreau began to do what he often did, think about things he'd done years ago. He could sometimes picture them in his head, as clear as if he was there. A game with . . . a game with Chalmers. Big game. *Big* high school game. On a very hot day. He'd tackled an all-state half-back in the second quarter—boy named Wilcox. That had been a hit, him coming off a block the tackle put on him and just sliding—had some luck, and never thought he didn't—just sliding right, and there was Wilcox (a big fucker for high school) head down and pumping through the line. Meat on the table. Hit that son-of-a-bitch so hard it made them both sick. Wilcox down on his back, trying to get his helmet off, trying to get a breath—and Ronnie Budreau not feeling too good, either, like his whole chest and his neck was asleep. But still on his fucking feet—you better believe it! One hell of a tackle. "—The single best stop that I've seen in fourteen years of coaching high school ball." That said by Coach, in public.

A man could wait a long time, and not have a better day than that one he had when he was just a kid. Very same day, by the way—that evening—that he got stoned enough at the senior dance to go up to Annette Shefflin and dance with her, and then ask her outside, and all the time stoned-out on pot and vodka both, and with a hard-on that wasn't about to quit.

Talk about getting put down, man! A man could have his ass whipped a dozen times—like, for example, when Sergeant Tucker had surprised him to shit by taking him down to the gym basement at Fort Peary and just kicking the cocky-doodee out of him. Damn near killed him. —And the same to Mason when he was assigned. Damn near killed him. Old Mason. "Hell, Ronnie—I'm used to guys droppin' turds for *me*. Now, let me tell you, that four-eyed black son-of-a-bitch has got me brownin' *my* Fruit of the Looms; and that's a fact, man. —You know that nigger never even took his glasses off?"

Tucker hadn't taken them off to beat up Budreau, either.

Well, a man could take a trashing, and think about it, and finally figure out he fucked up, or the other dude was just too much to handle. No matter how good you are, there's always some guy a little better. Every grown man knows that—and if he doesn't know it, then he isn't a grown man. A man can take that kind of stuff, and get it down and go on trucking. What a man'll *remember*, though, is just a word or two some girl stuck to him. —He'll remember that word or two forever.

"Ronnie," Annette had said—and we're talking about prime eating-pussy. We are talking about a *nice* girl, man—her daddy was mayor once. And we're talking about beautiful. We're talking about dark-haired and thin, with just a pretty good ass on her, and little pointy tits—and we're *still* talking about beautiful. Never had said a god-damn civil word to Ron L. Budreau in four years of high school. And we're talking about a Ron L. Budreau was a real big fat kid his first year, and would have about died if that girl had said "Hi" in the hall.

Too goddamned stoned to care—just took her outside, and gave her a hug so she could feel that big boner up against her. Out in the parking lot. Gave her a hug, and went to kiss her—and she put her hand up over her mouth so the back of her hand was all was kissed, and pushed away—no more strength to her than a little kid—and said, "I have . . . cared for you for a long time, Ronnie. I really do think there's a nice, gentle boy inside you, that a girl could really care for. But I was wasting my time. I have finally realized you're too damn scared to ever let that nice boy out."

Stepped away from those strong linebacker arms, and walked off like she was leaving a cow flop with flies on it.

If you think a few days go by that doesn't get thought

about, remembered . . . People think because a man is real strong, physically—that means that sort of stuff can't hurt him.

Budreau saw a blue VW, an old bug, come rolling down from the long entrance ramp, wheel on in, and swing a hard left into a parking place beside a pillar, across the garage passage from Budreau's Chevy, and about five or six cars to the left.

A tall, thin guy in gray pants and a cheap blue jacket, black hair with gray in it cut kind of long—the Jew-boy for sure—climbed out the driver's side, pulled the seat forward, reached into the back, and lifted out a sack—looked like groceries. Closed the car door, locked it, headed for the elevator.

Budreau slouched a little, picked the radio up from the passenger seat, thumbed the speak, and said, "R-1 to R-2—Subject's on A."

"Say again . . ." The Lieutenant, with lots of hiss. Budreau heard him say something to somebody else.

"R-1 to R-2—Subject's on A."

"I read," the Lieutenant said. "Out."

Budreau put down the radio, opened the glove compartment, and took out *Sports Illustrated* again. —The fighting problem in pro hockey was terrible. It was just terrible. One of these days, a guy was going to get hurt.

Mrs. Henry was cooking when the door buzzer sounded, and she turned down the heat under the potatoes, and covered the pot before she went to answer. "Don't you get up, now," she said. —Her sons, Hadji and Troy, were watching a car race on TV. "Don't you answer the door—don't you move for nothin'." She walked to the door—a slight, handsome black woman with a graying afro and wink of gold tooth at the right corner of her mouth—lifted the little cover of the peephole lens, peered through at Detective Classman's pleasant brown eyes, his long, bony face, and unlocked her door locks, thinking—not for the first time—that this man needed a wife to feed him, take care of him, a lot more than he needed that poor senile old lady upstairs.

Classman thanked her, said he wouldn't come in, was

sorry to bother her at dinnertime. And how was his mother?

"You sure you don't want to come on in—have some supper with us, Officer? —Your mama's all right. She's just fine. I was up there all afternoon—an' when I left to come cook supper, she was sound asleep in her bed. She's just fine. She was real good all day."

Classman thanked her, and said, "No . . . no, thanks." He thought he'd be going on up—fix some dinner upstairs. He'd bought some ground chuck and hamburger buns.

"Well, she loves those hamburgers," Mrs. Henry said. "—She'll like that." Mrs. Henry had been a full-time practical nurse at Roosevelt Hospital until phlebitis in the veins of her legs had gotten very bad. She looked after several old people in Park West.

Classman thanked her again for the invitation to dinner, stood thinking for a moment to be certain he'd paid her to the end of the month, then thanked her again, and left her to close and lock the door behind him.

He walked down to the elevators carrying his bag of groceries, rang, and stood waiting.

"O.K., this is going to be a relaxed contact," the Lieutenant had said. "—We're agents of the United States Government looking for cooperation in a matter of serious national security. —It's true, and that's what I'm going to tell him. I'll mention the money to him real casually—just for expenses. Tucker—when he's on stream, you remind me about the receipt. You know—just paperwork, routine . . ."

Tucker had nodded, said, "Mason—you go in that bedroom and try and keep her quiet. Talk to her." The old lady was mumbling to herself in there a mile a minute.

Mason went in to do it, smiling. —It was one chore Tucker sure didn't want; the old lady didn't like that black face at all. They'd had a funny problem with her. . . . It had taken Classman's mother a long time to open the door—probably had seen Tucker through the peep—but the Lieutenant had calmed her down, got her to open up.

Then, no sooner were they inside, than the old lady—

who looked like a skinny plucked chicken in her pink bathrobe—began to mumble at them (backed away when the Lieutenant tried to calm her down) and then let out a couple of little screams and scooted back into her bedroom. A complete veggie—senile, according to the Lieutenant—and that, they hadn't been told. —But Mason didn't mind talking to the old bag. He'd talk baseball with her.

Tucker and the Lieutenant sat in the living room, the Lieutenant toying with the radio, Tucker sitting still, as usual. The sergeant felt that restless movement was a sign of weakness and uncertainty, felt further that the aimlessness of this society's political and cultural movements expressed exactly the same. He didn't feel that that was a bad thing, necessarily—his was an observation, not a judgment.

The old lady apparently didn't care for Mason being in her bedroom; she came out a little while after Budreau radioed up, started walking back and forth in the wide entranceway, stopping every few turns to say something and point her finger at Tucker. The Lieutenant got up to calm her down.

"Come on, now, ma'am. Come on. —We just want to talk with your son, Mrs. Classman. This is official business."

"What's she talkin', Tucker?" Mason, very tall, lanky, with short ginger-red hair and hazel eyes, was standing behind the old lady, grinning. "—Sounds like she don't like bloods."

"Yiddish," Sergeant Tucker said, and stood up. Mrs. Classman pointed her finger at him again. She yelled something.

"Ma'am," the Lieutenant said, "—will you please just calm *down*?" He turned to Tucker. "Sergeant, I think you better go on in the kitchen, so she'll calm down." It was embarrassing.

Tucker didn't say a word, walked out of the living room and past them down the hall to the kitchen.

"Maybe you can put some coffee on in there," the Lieutenant said, and they heard Classman's key in the door. "Now," the Lieutenant said to Mrs. Classman, "—your boy's home. —O.K.?"

At that, Mrs. Classman drew in a breath and suddenly

screamed out loud, and Mason, startled, reached around from behind her and put his hand over her mouth as the door swung open and Classman stepped in with his bag of groceries cradled in his left arm.

"Take your hands off her for Christ's sake!" the Lieutenant said to Mason, and holding his hands out, palms up, a portrait of apology, stepped toward Classman, meaning to say, "—I'm really sorry; we had no idea that your mother was sick," but managed only to say he was sorry, and that word obscured, because Classman—seeing in a glance the two men, seeing his mother's eyes over the smothering hand—reached back under his jacket with his right hand while still holding his groceries in his left, drew his short-barreled revolver with remarkable speed, and fired one round into the Lieutenant's chest.

The blast was shocking, and rang so loud in that close space that no one heard the Lieutenant's shout as the bullet killed him—punching a small round hole through the bottom of his heart on its way to nick a back rib and exit.

Then Classman, his expression peculiar, spun half around like a clockwork man, his revolver's muzzle searching for something vital of Mason's as that tall sergeant ducked and withered behind Classman's moaning mother. Classman's pause for some target there was not much more than half a second—but just time enough for the Lieutenant to fall back into the foyer, his feet kicking left and right, his heels thumping a rum-te-tum on the polished floor. —Just time enough for Tucker, twelve feet behind Classman at the kitchen door, to draw an Italian pistol from under his left arm and fire one shot into the back of the detective's head.

Mrs. Classman, deafened by the shots, fallen silent as if satisfied, stood watching her slender son fold into death against the door, smearing the white paint down with brains.

Mason stood slowly straight, wiping her spit from his right palm onto the leg of his trousers.

Tucker walked over to him through a haze and odor of gunpowder, holstering his pistol. He said, "—See if the Lieutenant's dead," reached out, seized Mrs. Classman by her sparse blue hair, yanked her, bent her head so forcefully down that she stumbled to her knees, raised his left hand, fisted, high in the air—and struck down at the back of the old woman's neck.

When Tucker stepped over her corpse, then ran to the bedroom, Mason, an odd buzzing vibration through his whole body, went to the Lieutenant and found him lying dead, one eye wide and staring, the other sleepy, half-closed, about to wink. Mason heard noises in the bedroom—drawers hauled out, things broken—then Tucker came out running, said, "Pick him up!" and went himself to heave the living room's twenty-one-inch TV off its stand, onto his shoulder. *"Move!"*

Down the corridor they went, lumbering, trying to trot, lugging their disparate burdens past dadoes of silent, locked, and listening doors—the Lieutenant sagging over Mason's shoulder, heavier than the world—Tucker pacing behind, bent beneath the big TV. They staggered fast to the fire stairs, then down four steep, steep flights of concrete steps, Mason's sweat running with the single trickle of blood being jounced from the Lieutenant as they descended.

"Jesus!" Mason said at the first-floor landing, gasping, his voice an octave high. "—He sure as shit didn't have to do that!" He had stopped for just a second to get his balance. He hitched his burden higher up, and the Lieutenant's left brown loafer fell off onto the concrete. "—It wasn't my fuckin' fault!"

"Shut up and move," Tucker said—and, balancing the TV carefully, bent his knees, reached down with his left hand, and retrieved the shoe.

Then they were down the last flight and out the heavy door, laboring across the garage floor as Budreau came running to help them, quacking questions.

The Lieutenant, TV, and shoe dumped safe into the back with Mason—Tucker, beside Budreau, sitting composed, lips pursed—they drove up the long ramp and out into the sounds of the streetlamped night, casual traffic . . . the distant, yelping squad cars hurrying near.

CHAPTER 6

Already dressed, scrambling an egg to go with a piece of whole wheat toast, Ellie thought of driving over, then decided not to. It was more of a hassle to walk to the garage and get the car out, drive around and across the river and try to find a parking place on the West side, than just to take the tram over and catch a cab. —She missed the issue car, and Tommy driving, and no insurance problems in case of a fender bender.

. . . Needed to remember to put in for a new faucet in the kitchen—and, hopefully, for a new toilet seat. There was a little chip out of the side—out of whatever the thing was made of—that she'd tried to disguise with a dab of white paint. All that did was make you notice it more.

Maybe go to Zabar's afterward, bring some stuff home. If there was a pet store, get a rubber mouse or something for Mayo. A catnip mouse . . . ?

Ellie ate her breakfast standing up at the kitchen counter, had another half cup of coffee, and considered a second piece of toast, then decided not. She'd stopped using margarine after reading in *Consumer Reports* how it was made, and bought sweet butter instead. It was difficult not to have a second piece of toast with that butter.

Mayo, silent, wove through her ankles all during breakfast, and when Ellie'd finished eating, she got a Kitten Delight biscuit out of the box in the cabinet, and gave it to him. Then she sat at the kitchen table and put on her makeup, a little powder, pearl-pink lipstick, mascara, light blue eyeliner, same shade shadow.

Ellie walked out into a warm morning—ruffles of light gray clouds marching slowly overhead on steady, high western winds, allowing only intermittent flushes of sunshine, fading just as fast. She thought of going back for her umbrella—she was wearing a powder-blue cotton summer suit, and rain spots would look terrible on it—but the bus came (all seats taken) and she rode standing to the tram station, then took the next car up and over with the going-to-work crowd.

She'd been near the front of the line and gotten to stand by an upstream window to see the river below—an estuary, really, according to Serrano—flash and sparkle in the shuttling sunlight like sword blades, bayonets in some old military poem. She thought of riding the tram back and forth all day, or most of the day—maybe next weekend—painting the river. —Have to get permission from somebody. Paint streaming ghosts of river flowing over and under each other by different lights as the sun's light shifted. All of one day's rivers, morning to night—running, running down across the canvas with tugs, slender sailboats captured in it (dots and broken pieces of white and red-lead paint stuck in the iron and silver, flashes of gold). White gold, whiter than the water, even where it foamed. The sun and the river. Estuary. Call it *Estuary*. —Then in a small gallery on Seventy-first . . . Some woman noticing it, saying to the gay guy. "—Whose is this? Now, this one's *special.* Where in God's name have you been hiding it?" He'd be embarrassed. —Had given Ellie lots of shit about accepting "something from someone with no track record *whatsoever,* dear." Had accepted it finally, because it had "definition." "It does have something more than that," he'd said to her. "—Though heaven knows what." Now, he felt like a fool. "—I want my husband to come and see this." A rich, beautiful Jewish woman. European. Tanned. A face like a beautiful hawk's. She knew everybody. Had been a dancer when her husband saw her in a ballet in Monte Carlo. "—My husband has got to see this. Do you have anything else of hers—anything at all?"

"Of course; she's doing several things for us. . . ." Lying. He'd come to Roosevelt Island that evening—not even call, just talk his way past the night man and ring the bell—and not even come in, just stand in the doorway in his beautiful custard suit, and say, "Sweetie, you are lucky beyond *belief*—and you'd better turn in your badge and nightstick, or whatever, and get those pretty buns to hummin', because Sarah Rothstein loves your work. —That means, sweetie, you're going to be famous, and we both—thank *God*—are going to be rich." He brought champagne with him—so he did come in, and they had that. He had a cat, too, a part-Burmese. And turned out to be nice, under that snottiness . . . had lost his lover to AIDS. "—Well, it nearly killed me. Jerry and I were a great deal more than lovers. . . . That was the least of it."

He became a really good friend, very close. They'd go shopping together, Ellie so rich she could buy anything. —That wasn't important to her at all, anymore. She'd bought gifts for everybody. Bought Tommy and Connie a new car. —She and Sarah became friends, too. It was through Sarah Rothstein, at one of her parties, she met . . . the man who came to Anderson's office to get her, who'd been in China. Stocky, handsome, hair bronze-and-silver . . . Jack.

At one of her shows, Klein would be there with a tired-looking girl. Ellie'd be with Jack, talking to somebody important. Klein would come up to say hello, talk about his cases and bore poor Jack to death, but Ellie would be very nice to him . . . gracious.

The Donegal was a huge, quiet, slightly shabby apartment building built of streaked gray stone—the corridors twice as wide and almost twice as high as the halls in Ellie's building on the island. Plaster molding running along the sides of the corridor ceiling. Old maroon carpets. —Susan Margolies' door, like all the others, was painted nearly the deep worn red of the carpet.

Ellie buzzed—then, after a while, buzzed again. She heard faint sounds inside. Then coming closer. Pause. Ellie smiled at the little peep lens. The rattle and clack of the Fox lock. Another lock, before the door swung open.

"Oh, I think she was right!" Small bright blue eyes in a long, pale, wrinkled face. Some freckles. A really ugly dress, the wrong blue for her eyes—had green in it—white floral pattern. Susan Margolies was almost elderly, very tall, a big-boned woman, lanky, big-hipped. Seemed to be in her early sixties . . . iron-gray hair to her shoulders. A big, plain old woman. "—You have to be *one* of the best-looking, at least. You *are* pretty . . ." She watched Ellie like a cop, the talking not interfering with the watching. Then she smiled. "Well, we can continue our inventories inside, can't we?" and led Ellie in.

"Where did you get that purse? —I've been promising myself a new purse forever. It's too late to get myself a straw; but I'm determined to get a really good leather bag for autumn." She was leading down a long high-ceilinged hall with small, elegant lamp tables right and left along the way, eighteenth-century engravings, little ones (German or Austrian, Ellie thought) low on the walls between the lamps. Music-room scenes. Guests and musicians.

Then the woman walked before Ellie out into greater space, nimbused by the momentary sun in a living room twice the size of Ellie's. This had high cream ceilings, plants in fine china pots in rows along the deep window-sills of four big windows looking out over the Hudson. A small white-marble fireplace . . . Ellie doubted that it worked. Tall, glass-front bookcases along the walls on either side of the fireplace. Plants up on top of those, too—hard to water. And a wonderful big rug—Turkish or Persian with a whole flower garden woven into it, the pile dark green on the borders, and deep as grass. —If the rest of the apartment was like the living room, so big, airy, so perfectly done, then Ellie wished she had it. —Probably worth putting up with the trendy West Side to have it; it made hers, on the island, seem cramped. *Shitty* was the word.

The woman patted the top of the back of a long brown corduroy sofa. "Here," she said. "This is wonderfully comfortable. —Have you had breakfast?"

"Yes," Ellie said. The sofa was a deep bath of warm cloth and cushions.

"Well, I don't care; I'm toasting some bagels. We'll have cream cheese and jam with them. You want coffee or tea?"

"Whatever you're having."

"Tea, then. Coffee's just too harsh for me in the morning." Susan Margolies said the "harsh" in a very Boston-sounding way . . . *"haash."* She walked through a door at the other side of the room—another hall, Ellie supposed, to the kitchen—and said something as she went, but Ellie couldn't hear it well enough.

The apartment smelled faintly of some sort of potpourri, primrose . . . something woodsy. There was only one picture in the living room. A Hudson River School copy—probably a copy—over the fireplace. Green hills (looked like up past Tarrytown) rolling down very steeply to the river. The river was clear as glass. It looked from the sofa as though the artist had painted tiny fish under the water, near a skiff two men or boys in white shirts were fishing from. It was a pretty picture. —The sky not as good as the river. —As my river, Ellie thought. I could have streams of glassy clear threading through the white, off-white grays and charcoals. . . .

Susan walked back in carrying a wooden tray, set it down on the coffee table by the sofa, and sat on the other side in an armchair covered with the same brown corduroy. She'd put several toasted bagel halves on a big white dinner plate, most of a block of cream cheese with a butter knife on a smaller white plate beside it. And alongside that, a small stack of orange paper cocktail napkins. She'd forgotten the jam. Two teacups, pot, sugar and creamer in the same ornate pattern, gorgeous red, blue, and gold.

"You like that? Isn't that service pretty?"

"What is it?"

"Tobacco leaf—the store at the Met used to have it. I don't know if they still do. —Would you rather have lemon?"

Ellie would have, but didn't want to send the woman off on that long walk to the kitchen. "No—this is fine."

"Well, have a bagel—don't make me feel like a pig." Susan Margolies leaned over and picked a bagel half, then smeared the cream cheese on thick, using the butter-knife blade to sculpt the cheese around the toast's edges. Then she put the knife down, and holding her bagel in her left hand, poured the tea with her right. "Irish Breakfast," she said. Then: "I know it sounds stupid—but is there any chance at all there could be a mistake? You know, some other woman staying at her apartment, being killed . . . like in *Laura*?"

"I'm sorry," Ellie said. "The super knew her, and there were pictures of her in the apartment. I'm afraid it was definitely her."

"It's just so ridiculous," the big woman said, and put the teapot down. "She wasn't the *type* of woman to have that happen . . . ! She was always so damn funny . . . so lively. —Not one of those mopey types looking for some sordid tragedy." Susan Margolies' tone was indignation, and controlled, but tears began to leak from her small blue eyes, and two or three slowly followed the paths of pale, shallow wrinkles down her cheeks. "It's just a fucking farce—the whole damn thing. . . ." She picked up one of the cocktail napkins and wiped the tears away. "For one thing, she was beautiful." The tall woman blew her nose. "—There, the human comedy—no tribute of tears, without snot to follow." She wadded the napkin up and stuffed it into the left pocket of her dress. "Do you people know who did it?"

"Not yet."

"Well, I don't care what problem that bastard has—I hope he goes right into the electric chair. I hope they burn him. —Not a professional comment, I guess." She took out the wadded napkin, fiddled it open, and blew her nose again. "Oh, hell," she said, "let's eat."

When Ellie had her bagel, her tea in her hands—hoping she wouldn't spill on her skirt (she would have liked a bigger napkin)—Susan Margolies took two large bites of her toast in succession, then chewed her mouthful slowly, with satisfaction. She paused to sip some tea before she chewed again, then swallowed.

"It's fascinating, isn't it?" she said, "to watch someone eat. You learn a lot, doing that. —Whether they're enjoying at least that much of life, for openers. How aggressive they are? —That sort of thing. It's surprising how many people really hate to share their food—a bite from their cake, a section of a tangerine they're eating. Some people hold on to those morsels as if they'd starve without them. —Won't give their own kids a bite." She ate the rest of her bagel, filling her mouth full before she chewed and swallowed.

"Well—what do you think? Poor old bag, got nothing left but eating? Sort of greedy?" She laughed, showing an empty mouth, a still-coated tongue. "Dead right. —Not that I can't get laid, but you should see the creatures that agree to do it!"

Ellie smiled and finished her bagel-half—self-conscious, now, chewing. Had some tea. "You have a really beautiful apartment," she said.

"Thank you. —Would you like to see the rest? Well, after we talk? You wouldn't believe it to look at it now, but it used to be the most awful hole. I've put a hell of a lot of work into it, and money. *Money*. Carpenters . . . painters. You wouldn't believe the scenes I've had with those people. The cost of a love affair with rooms . . . hallways . . ." She drank some tea. "—Apartment's gotten prettier as I've gotten the reverse. Time"—she made a face—"and goddamn changes. I was never the handsome creature you are, but I swear there was a time men—at least in Massachusetts—found me attractive." She leaned forward to spread cheese on another bagel. "I hate it. I *hate* having that power taken away from me. —You better brace yourself for that change—very severe when it comes to good-looking women. One year you'll still be able to break their hearts, 'go swimming in their dreams,' as Ricki Misrahi puts it. —Have you read her? No? —Well, you should. One year, a heartbreaker . . . and the next year you're only a person—and not much of a person at that, unless you happen to have money."

She took two mouthfuls, chewed and swallowed, and drank some tea. "You're in for a real shock the day you realize even some desperate adolescent wouldn't have you on a plate in a peek-a-boo bra and black garter belt. —That's a loss, I think, a woman never really gets over. From then on, too often, it's only scheming. Scheming or slavery—that's what I see in my practice." She finished her tea. "Of course, that's what you see in your practice, too, I imagine—with occasional action-from-desperation thrown in."

Ellie put her teacup down.

"Some people know other people for a long time," she said, "and they're close—but not *really* friends. They don't really trust each other, you know? —Which kind of friend were you to Sally?"

"You have a pleasant style of interrogation," Susan

Margolies said. "You'd have done well in psychology." She looked at the plate of bagels, but didn't take another one. "—Sally and I were very good friends. I can't imagine anything I couldn't have told Sally. We've known—knew each other for years. . . . I met her through a patient of mine. And then I was able to recommend her to some other people."

"Kind of a sex therapist?"

"Call me Susan," Susan Margolies said. "—Can I call you Ellie? —It is Ellie?"

"Yes."

"Well," Susan said, "I might have to deny it in court, Ellie, if it ever came up. —It's a shaky situation, legally, although, God knows, it's done all the time. And you're really better off not using a prostitute, if you can avoid it. But, just between us—yes, I did send some people to her, and she was wonderful with them. A perfect little creature in bed, or so I was told." She sipped her tea, then put the beautiful cup down carefully. "I have to ask you something I don't want to ask you. Please be honest. —Please answer me honestly, if you can."

"O.K."

Susan Margolies sighed. "Was it as bad as the papers said? That awful? —She didn't suffer that much. . . ?"

"She had a very bad time," Ellie said.

"It couldn't have been any worse, is what you're saying." Long pale face, mournful as a sheep's.

"That's right."

"Oh, dear . . . oh, my God."

"I'm sorry. It's a terrible way to lose a friend. She must have been very nice—but, you know, Rebecca didn't like her."

"Poor Rebecca. —She only met Sally a couple of times. I think she had dreams of taking her on—you know, shopping for her, spending her money for her. But Sally wasn't one of Rebecca's usual dumb bunnies. —By the way, Rebecca told me of your involvement with that thing about her child. The death."

"She killed him," Ellie said.

"Oh, yes, I think so." Susan Margolies nodded, considering, small blue eyes dreamily fixed and looking away to Ellie's left. "—She certainly didn't like him. Did you know that Rebecca was seeing a married man at the time? A rich married man—apparently one of the store people where she worked." The sun had emerged from clouds again, and the room, flooded through wide windows, lightened from shade to bright cream yellow. Susan Margolies' face, in this light, looked like fine vellum, creased. "—I think she felt it would be opportune to get rid of her child—of her husband, too. She had *hopes,* I suppose. Not that her husband didn't help her do it. I don't think he liked the child, either. —Surprising, the number of parents who don't like their children."

"Would like to see them gone."

"That's right. —You don't have children, do you?"

"No."

"I do. A son—who, by the way, got as far as possible from Mom as fast as he could manage it. Oddly enough, I love the son-of-a-bitch . . . like him, too." She leaned forward to pour more tea into both their cups. "*And* I get angry if he doesn't call at least once a week. *And* I don't like his wife."

"I don't call my mother, either."

"Well, daughters and mothers . . ."

"When did you see Sally last?"

"Oh . . . I think about a week ago; I'm getting lousy on dates. We had dinner at her place . . . calf's liver and bacon. —She was a darling, but she was a lousy cook."

"She might have kept some sort of an appointment book. . . . Did you ever see her writing anything down—after she got a phone call, maybe?"

"Well—she had a little note pad by the phone, I think. I really don't know if she kept an appointment book. I doubt if she needed one; she didn't see *that* many clients in a week, and she had an excellent memory—for which I envied her. It's true, though, many of those girls did keep some sort of record. . . ."

"Beside sending people to her . . ." Ellie said.

"Oh, I only did that a few times. We got to be too close friends for me to keep sending patients to her. —I'd be treating the patient, and going into the success or lack of it with Sally, and it simply got too damn incestuous. Then—just between you and me—I found a graduate student who was interested in working with me as a therapist in dysfunctions of that sort. —Well, the girl enjoys it, probably, though most women really don't prefer multiple partners."

"Sally discussed her clients with you?"

"Oh, yes—every now and then she'd have some really unhappy individual, someone who simply wasn't capable of being pleased by her, or any woman. She'd ask me for suggestions, things to talk about with them, ways to make them more comfortable."

"Talking?"

"God, yes!" The tall woman sighed, leaned forward, and picked up a bagel half, the butter knife. "—The damn things are cold, and I don't care. I'm a fool for cream cheese. —God, yes. Talking . . . I know, you think it's all screwing for these women. Well, so did I, before I began to know them. For a few years, I had quite a practice of call girls, though Sally was never a patient. —This is the last one of these things I'm going to have. Won't you please have another one? —Share the guilt?"

"I really can't," Ellie said, "—I just finished breakfast before I came over."

"Well, I saw a number of call girls for a while, had that practice for a while, then got terribly bored with it." Two bites, then chewing. When she'd swallowed, she said, "Not only do call girls—mistresses, all expensive prostitutes, really—spend an inordinate amount of time talking to their customers, just being amusing company, listening to their troubles, giving them advice—more often than not, on how to get along better with their wives—but when they do have sex, they don't much enjoy it. —Not that they don't enjoy screwing—they do, most of them, orgasms and all, though that's not popularly supposed to be the case." She drank some tea. "It's simply that there's very little *romance* in their lives. Very little in the lives of most successful career women, truth be told. Doesn't seem to be the leisure for it." She put her teacup down. "—Listen, you want to see the apartment?"

"O.K. Yes, I'd like to."

They stood together—Susan Margolies much taller than Ellie, then stooping to pick up the two plates. "We'll leave the tea . . ." and started off to the door to the kitchen, Ellie following the long, narrow back, the ugly dress. *Peek-a-boo bra and black garter belt* . . . Hard to imagine. "—Very little romance. They're bored . . . they read a lot of cheap fiction, and they almost never have anything really interesting to complain about."

This hallway was narrow, painted the same light cream as the living room. Ellie followed Susan through a swinging door into the kitchen, and felt less envious of the apartment. The kitchen counters had been done in butcher block; the cabinets were brushed chrome, and must have cost a fortune—and it should have been a beautiful kitchen. But it was long and narrow as a subway car, and dark. There was only one window, over the sink.

"—But those girls love to have some sort of therapy going from time to time, like a lot of women with money, and no kids to keep them busy." She opened the dishwasher (brushed chrome, like the cabinets) and stacked the two plates inside, dropped the butter knife into a bunch of other dirty silverware. "—And for them, I suppose I provided the sort of sympathetic ear they had to act out themselves, professionally."

"And Sally was like that?"

"Oh, no." The big woman bent to make sure none of the silverware was blocking the dishwasher door, then swung it up into place. "—She wasn't like that at all; she was never bored. Sally was a little older than most of them, for one thing. She was an exception—very bright, always taking classes. History and English—trying to make up for her childhood, probably. Her parents had been working-class people in Chicago. Well . . . mine were working-class from Boston. People fascinated her. . . . Men. They were her field of interest. She was always exploring . . . discovering. —You know what she'd say? She'd say, 'I'm an interior astronaut.' —And she was, too."

"Then she found some alien in there, I suppose," Ellie said. "—Some creature she couldn't handle."

"That's a very good way to put it. . . ."

"It's a beautiful kitchen," Ellie said. "I love the cabinets."

"Well, the shape is *not* ideal—but I couldn't widen it because the guest bath is right behind the wall. Besides which, it would have cost a mint." She went to the sink and washed her hands, dried them on a yellow paper towel from the roll. "—Those prostitutes were very conventional women, for the most part. —Very conservative, very cautious. None of them stupid. —And they were *extremely* boring as patients. Fundamentally, very healthy young animals." She opened a cabinet under her sink, and threw the paper towel in the garbage bin there. "—Give me a monstrously married neurotic, anytime."

"You're describing a good profession to me? Good for women? —Is that it?"

"It's an excellent profession—or would be, if Americans didn't have shame on the brain." She walked to a door at the end of the kitchen, by the refrigerator. The refrigerator was brushed chrome, too, and huge. "Come on, I'll show you the bedrooms. Both big success stories, decorator-wise." And went through the door and out.

"I don't believe that," Ellie said, following her. "—I don't believe being a whore is a great profession—not for a minute."

"Shame," Susan Margolies said, crossing an entranceway and walking into a small, very beautiful bedroom in pinks and dusky rose, "—shame, and, if you'll forgive me, the despicable behavior of the police where these women are concerned. I know of several cases of the nastiest sort of sexual blackmail of these girls—one of which, by the way, took the amusing turn of true love, marriage, babies, and Massapequa. . . . How do you like this?"

"I love it. This is really a lovely room. —You decorated it—you did it all?"

"Every million-dollar inch."

"It's wonderful. Where did you find the beds? Have them made?" The two narrow, single brass steads, covered and bolstered in damask rose, were headed by crisscrossed slender bars of brass, polished to reflection.

"Nope. —Got 'em in Rhode Island."

"Well, they're beautiful. . . ."

"You like this room better than the kitchen."

"No . . . well, I suppose so."

"So do I. I can't fight that damn shape. A friend of mine—poor girl's terribly ill, now—suggested I just make an old-fashioned diner out of it and leave it alone—like the Metropole."

"It's not bad; it really isn't. But I love this. . . . And you were talking about happy women? Prostitutes. Going with any man who comes through the door? Any kind of creep . . ."

Susan Margolies laughed. She had a tiny bagel crumb below the right corner of her mouth. "—Have you taken a good look at the average husband, lately? Mine looked like a poodle—similar behavior, too." She glanced at Ellie's left hand. "I don't see any ring."

"I'm not married, but I was."

"I know; Rebecca told me. 'I have the impression of a handsome asshole' was the way she put it. Ah, ha—I see a smile! —Right? A handsome asshole? Well, at least he had looks."

"He was nice-looking. . . ."

"And you still have tender feelings . . . ?"

"No way."

"Never lie to a professional lie catcher," Susan said, and motioned Ellie before her out of the bedroom. "—That's why I haven't lied to you. —Go to the right."

"When she talked to you about her clients, did Sally mention names?" Susan Margolies was following close, her footsteps echoing Ellie's on the hardwood hall floor.

"No, no." Her voice coming high behind Ellie's left shoulder. "She'd use their first names sometimes—Ted, Georgie—that sort of thing." Ellie thought Margolies bent behind her and sniffed at her hair like a horse. "Here we are—go on in."

This was a much bigger bedroom, with a single wide, curtained four-poster bed in it—the room done all in shades of pearl. The armchair striped in shell-gray, the walls papered in satins, creams—the curtains shell-white, silver framing the dresser top, the dresser mirror—silver-backed brushes, silver combs, baby's breath in nacreous, slender vases by the bed. It was a room, two-windowed, high-ceilinged, cool and gorgeous, suited to hold a black-haired beauty while she slept.

"*Wow . . .*"

"Thank you."

"It's . . . spectacular. . . ."

"Yes, I think it is—and, of course, also ridiculous. It's a room for a very pretty young woman, not an ugly aging one. I like to imagine, some nights, that I *am* very pretty—one of those fairy-tale witches that turns into an old lady for the hell of it."

"It's a perfect room—a beautiful room for anyone."

"Well—not bad. Not bad. —The master bath's the same sort of thing—a sort of oceanic foam and silver sort of feeling. Usually, I've got my drawers and stockings hanging all over it, but I did a visitor-coming cleanup this morning. —Want to see it?"

"Yes, I would," Ellie said. "—You were saying about Sally's not using her clients' last names?"

"Yes; she just didn't do it." Susan Margolies went to the head of her beautiful bed, and began rearranging the baby's breath in the slender vase there, separating the delicate stalks with long, freckled fingers. "—I don't think I ever heard her mention a client's full name—even when we were working together with my patients. Well, I don't use full names either. I doubt if you do, with your informants. —It's just bad practice. And Sally was a professional, and proud of it. —If you want to know something about Sally—it's that. She was not ashamed of what she did. She thought it was very, very interesting."

"Sounds great for her," Ellie said, "—until she got put in that shower. She went with someone a little too interesting, I guess."

"I've heard that tone before." Susan Margolies turned from her flowers, her blue eyes a little brighter. "Isn't that the sound of satisfaction? —Of a woman pleased because another woman—more daring, perhaps more richly, more deeply involved in life, has tragically fallen?"

"I hope that's not true," Ellie said.

"Well, perhaps it isn't. Isn't all that unusual, anyway, dear. You can bet I had my hostilities, too, dealing with Sally—dealing with all those girls. There is *something* about a beautiful young woman earning enormous sums of money associating with a variety of men—some of them very interesting men, indeed—there is something about that that provokes just a little hostility in most women. —Me, too." She patted the flowers, appeared satisfied.

"Who killed her—do you know?"

"I haven't the slightest. If I did—I'd tell you like a shot. She . . . was very dear to me." The tall woman walked around the four-poster to attend to the flowers on the other bedside table. "—I will tell you this. Sally usually did not take as clients the sort of men who were ill, or dangerous. It occurred to me . . . it occurred to me she might have mistaken a man—might have underestimated how sick he was. . . ."

"She *must* have done that. —Right? Unless she was murdered for some other reason."

"Yes, that's true." She found a small twig of tiny blossoms that wouldn't behave, snapped it off. "It's an ancient profession—and I believe that many women are better off in it than in some of the occupations thought to be so natural, so respectable. But there are risks."

"Let me get this straight," Ellie said. "You're telling me you have absolutely no idea—no idea at *all*—who might have murdered your friend? —Just no idea at all. Not even a hint from her that she was in trouble . . . that she'd met somebody. Somebody different? Somebody who was worrying her?"

"Men didn't worry Sally. She knew them very well. She wasn't afraid of them." Susan stroked the trimmed stalk of baby's breath into place. "She wasn't afraid of anything that I know of—except the IRS. Most call girls are very frightened of them."

"We found money in her apartment."

"Hidden away, I suppose. —Where?"

"Up in her closet."

"Such an obvious place . . . Susan was afraid to put it in a bank—records and so forth. I think she mentioned investing with a client once, years ago—there were problems, and she lost a lot of money. . . ." Susan stood back a little, to get a better look at the vase of flowers. Seemed not quite satisfied. Ellie imagined Susan Margolies walking constantly through her halls, patrolling, regarding, straightening, correcting.

"Did Sally like to be beaten up? Did she enjoy having a man spank her, or anything like that?"

"You're thinking that might have gotten out of hand?"

"Damn right."

"No. No, I don't think Sally enjoyed roughness, except as most women occasionally enjoy it, in a very safe, controlled way. She was very normal, sexually." She went back to the bedside table, but didn't touch the flowers. Only turned the vase, slightly.

"Normal . . . Then she had affairs. —Did she mention the last names of these guys? What they did for a living? —Or was all that a professional secret, too?"

"Now, don't get mad," Susan Margolies said. "But I have to tell you—yes, I guess it was." Satisfied at last with the baby's breath, the slender vase. "I thought they were ex-clients—those were the men that Sally met, after all. And she became genuinely fond of a few of them, and they of her. I do know that a man named Fred wanted to marry her. —Was quite a guy, according to Sally—"

"Fred. —Just *Fred*? That's it?" Ellie felt herself flush, knew this Margolies woman was watching her face redden. "If you're trying to be funny, Susan—if you're trying to play games with me, you're going to regret it."

"Hey, now, don't get tough—don't blame me if Sally's men were just first names! Why the hell do you think they *were* just first names? Would *you* like to be arrested for prostitution? Would *you* like to be arrested for soliciting?" Freckles were standing out clearer across the woman's face. —A little pissed off herself, Ellie thought. "You police people have connived for years in this hypocrisy—used these women and their clients to play your own little career games. Don't blame me if those chickens come home to roost." Gave the snowy, figured bedspread a quick, light, arranging tug. "—Come look at the master bath."

Ellie followed her through a door beside the dresser. "—And the patients you sent her—what about those chickens, Susan? They just first names, too?"

The bathroom was unexpectedly big—almost three times the size of hers at home. Ellie thought she might like the apartment after all—do something else with that kitchen . . . get rid of the chrome . . . plain, white-painted wood. Relax the room, so it didn't look like the Long Island Railroad.

"As far as my patients are concerned, they are *no*

names, dear—not to you or to anybody else. Period. Under any circumstances. —Well, what do you think?"

"I think it must have cost a fortune." The bathroom, lit by two of the apartment's big windows—these looking out over Eighty-seventh Street—was tiled in textured bone-white, papered higher on the walls with a mingled white, silver, and dun pattern of seashells. The big, modern, sculpted bath, the toilet, sink, the built-in cabinets and small dressing table were all in pale, gleaming pink. —The color of the inside of shells, Ellie thought, when they were wet. The rug was rough woven wool, in light sand. "—It must have been a chore, matching the color for the dressing table and cabinets."

"A two-week chore. —That's metallic car paint from a spray shop over in Brooklyn." She tapped a towel rack the same color. "I'm sure they thought I was out of my mind. —About names and my patients . . . Just for your, for the police's peace of mind, I sent two, no—three men to Sally. All three of those referrals were more than two years ago—and none of those men were violent to any degree whatsoever. Also, none of them had anything to do with Sally once that phase of their treatment was over. That was understood and adhered to. —O.K.?" Susan slid a dark green towel off the pale pink rack, shook it out, and began to refold it.

"No—it's not O.K."

"Well, it's going to have to be, dear—unless you can get a judge that'll find good enough cause to force production of my patients' records . . . and, reaching that far back, I don't think you will."

"We'll do that if we have to, Susan—don't kid yourself."

"Oh, I stopped kidding myself a long time ago, dear." She put the folded towel back on its rack. "—And I'm not an idiot, either. I'm a very well-qualified clinical psychologist, with many years of practice and a number of publications in the field. None of those patients I referred to Sally either could, or would, have injured her in any way. Or even threatened her. —She would have told me."

"I'm not calling you a liar"—Ellie wondered if it would be possible to ask to pee in the perfect toilet—"I'm just saying that we have to satisfy ourselves about people.

Your say-so isn't enough. —Nobody's say-so would be enough."

"The hell with it, then," the tall woman said, smiled, and reached out to pat Ellie's arm. "We'll let some crook of a judge decide, if it comes to that. —Come on, you poor suffering creature. You've got one more showpiece to look at, then the tour'll be over."

"No, I'm enjoying it!"

"Then you've got only yourself to blame," Susan said, and led the way out of the bath and across the bedroom to the door, ushering Ellie ahead of her there, and trailing her down another high-ceilinged hall (this one painted royal blue, decorated with small, elegant pastels of wild flowers) and as she had before, walking close behind, sniffed once, as though she were starting to cry again. "You know," she said, "—I *thought* you were wearing two perfumes. I have a really good sense of smell; I only wish my eyesight was as good. —I thought so, and you are. You're wearing Sarabande—and there's something else in your hair. Really nice . . . Is it Tenue? Something like that. . . ?" She reached ahead of Ellie to a doorknob on the left as they came to the end of the hall—Ellie reflected there, blushing, in a tall, beveled glass above a small, fat vase of yellow silk flowers, the big woman looming just behind her. "Here we are."

"Well. . . ?" She raised her hands, opening them, palms up, to present the room. It was a small office-study in paneled blond wood. Desk chair, desktop, small sofa and facing armchair all in deep red-leather. Morocco. Built-in bookcases on two walls. It was a perfect room—like a display room in a fine furniture store. There was a small red-marble fireplace in the wall opposite the desk. "What do you think?" Susan Margolies said—then looked more attentively at Ellie. "What is it? Something wrong?"

"No. Nothing." —*Stupid,* Ellie thought. Clara and her ninety-dollars-an-ounce perfume. *Stupid* not to have washed my hair. . . . "—It's just perfect. Perfect. The paneling—"

"No, I can't take credit for that. The paneling was here when I first rented. I'm buying the place now, thank God—for a disgusting sum of money. Building went co-op this year—talk about Panic City! But, I was simply *not* going to leave. I was not going to scramble around trying to find some crappy little one-room-and-a-toilet studio I could afford somewhere. Live like a goddamn pig in a pen. —That, I did *not* intend to do."

"I don't blame you—it's a beautiful apartment."

"Well—it's my home. I can't see myself down in Delaware, living with Johnny, that ridiculous wife, and three kids."

"I don't blame you."

Susan Margolies leaned over and kissed Ellie lightly on the cheek, smelling faintly of jasmine powder. "Justification," she said. "—That's what I like to hear." She looked at her watch. "Damn—I think I have a patient in half an hour, and there was something else I wanted to ask you. —I'm developing an active forgetery." She went to sit down behind her handsome desk, and looked through a small calendar beside a brass-framed desk clock. "Sit down, dear—I really do apologize for dragging you through my palace. . . ."

Ellie sat in the facing armchair—the red leather felt smooth and cool, delicately textured against the palms of her hands. "No—I enjoyed it. Made me jealous. —My place is *strictly* functional."

Susan turned a page of her calendar. "I doubt that. It's probably charming. —O.K. Appointment in half an hour. A no-name . . ." She smiled at Ellie. "A no-name with problems about wide open spaces. —And I remember what I wanted to ask you. It may be out of line—I only met Sonia once, and that was by accident; ran into Sally shopping with her in Saks. I think Sally was upset by my meeting the girl. She liked the idea of Sonia growing up untouched by anything her mother might do—prostitution, in her case." She turned another page in her calendar, studied it carefully. "—Though I don't know if she'd have felt any different if she'd been a bank manager. She wanted Sonia to grow up as free of a case of the 'Moms' as possible—particularly since there was no father, no family in the picture. As free . . . as *individual* as possible—and prostitution, particularly, is emotionally loaded." She took a fat black fountain pen from the middle drawer of the desk, and made a note on her calendar. "Sonia knew what her mother did for a living, of course—but I think Sally didn't want her obsessed by it . . . troubled by it. She kept her separate from all her city friends, kept her out of the city. You notice there were no pictures of her in the apartment?"

"Sonia . . ." Ellie's heart was giving quick little bumps in her chest. *Bump, bump, bump*. She took a deep breath.

"And I was wondering—even though I hardly know the girl, whether there'd be any objection to my seeing her a few times. —I think I might make this dreadful thing a little easier for her to bear—reduce the trauma, if only slightly. It would give her someone to talk to." Susan Margolies stroked her leather desktop lightly with the fingers of her left hand. "—I knew her mother, after all, and loved her. It seemed to me it would be proper to help Sally's daughter, if I could."

"I don't see why that would be a problem," Ellie said. "I'll ask her if she'd like to talk with you. —I don't see that it would be a problem. . . ." The dentist's bill popped into her head as if Tommy Nardone were lying on the floor beside her armchair, propped on his elbow, and had just pulled it from Sally Gaither's shoe box, read it, and handed it up to her. "She's still in Connecticut, I think—I don't remember the name of the school. . . ."

"St. Christopher's," Susan Margolies said.

"That's it."

"I can tell you it cost Sally a ton of money. One of those Episcopal places. Very preppy, very small classes, subtle breezes of social superiority. —A *ton* of money. Sally spent beans for herself. Every dime was saved for Sonia. Probably more than a kid would ever need. . . ."

"Oh, God . . . oh, God, oh *God* . . ." The Colonel, the night before, lying on the sofa in his suite, reading *The New Yorker*—had let the magazine fall. . . . ("Not what it was, Sergeant," the Colonel had said the morning they checked in, tapping that issue . . . had also, then, downstairs, pointed out the place the Round Table had stood, and delivered a little lecture on that to Tucker as if Tucker were a Barbary ape, and had never heard of it, of Kaufman, Parker, and F.P.A.) —No lecture last night, however. All ears—except for the "Oh, God's" and *The New Yorker* sliding off his lap.

"How could that happen . . . how could that *happen*?"

"An Oedipal thing, I suppose," Tucker had said. "—And we surprised him."

The Colonel, sitting up in shirtsleeves, his tie tugged down for comfort—he'd come in from dinner only an hour before—had commenced to rock slowly back and forth, his hands folded at his chin. "Holy fucking cow," he said. "—How could you let it *happen*?"

"That cop was very quick," Tucker said. "—Doc Holliday couldn't have stopped it from happening."

"A stupid unbelievable snafu like this . . ." The wholesome ruddy then slowly drained from the Colonel's face, the change quite evident in the floor lamp's soft yellow light. Tucker assumed the Colonel had begun to consider consequences.

"Washington . . ." the Colonel said. "Jesus H. Christ."

"It's a problem, sir." Tucker standing before the sofa at a relaxed at-ease.

"A *problem* . . . ?"

The sergeant felt, as he had anticipated while Budreau drove up and out of the project garage, that comfort he derived from observing authority in trouble. It was a sort of rich, ancient, martyred satisfaction, that he assumed many other black people (women, mainly) had accustomed themselves to when these fragile lords and masters suffered their frequent collapses. —He had supported the Colonel once before, in Central America, when forty-two thousand dollars worth of military equipment (radios, binoculars, night-sights, Grid computers) had been stolen—and the Colonel signed off for it all. That difficulty had been made to disappear, with the empty shed, in a blast of plastic explosive, a few rounds fired at the tropic moon. —This "government attack" happily attested to by all, including a Contra captain who was no fool.

Since that incident, Tucker had been amused to observe the Colonel's efforts, constant, awkward . . . touching, to maintain his authority over his Master Sergeant—an authority certain as death, of course, in one way. But, in another, fragile as a consumptive Victorian child.

"They'll have no proof who did it, sir."

"A *could-be* is bad enough, Sergeant. A *could-be* is plenty bad enough! —What did you do with poor Bob?"

"The Lieutenant is buried out in the Meadowlands, sir. We stripped him."

"Great God in Zion . . . Washington's going to love this! O.K. . . . O.K."—an odd and sudden expression of sorrow. "—What the hell am I going to tell his people? He was just a kid!"

"Line of duty, sir—down in Central? Chopper accident?"

"Goddamn son-of-a-bitch! —Just like that jackass to go get himself shot. I can't believe it! —That goddamned Jew must have been crazy!"

"It *was* a hasty reaction. Maybe we could have been better briefed. . . ."

"That has to be the understatement of the year! Some fucking source . . . I suppose that fancy Dan could have planned it just to embarrass us. I wouldn't put it past any of them."

"No, sir. That cop wasn't expecting anything. —He just got the jump."

The Colonel had stood up, then, and commenced to pace from the sofa to the nearest window and back again. He was walking slightly hunched over. "How are the men taking this?"

"Budreau's all right. Mason was shook—the man almost killed him."

"*Mason* . . . Why in hell they don't give me better material to work with . . ." He made his turn, headed back toward the window.

"Would you want me to toss a little dust, sir?"

"Hell, yes—we have to do something! You think those hoods in uniform won't smell us in this thing. . . ? But Tucker, for God's sake, for the love of God—don't overdo!" He'd completed his second circuit as he said that, and headed away again, back toward the window.

"No, sir," Tucker said. "—I surely won't."

The Colonel had walked to the window, turned, paced back—still hunched over (like Quasimodo, Tucker thought) —then sat down on the sofa where he'd sat before. "—Bob didn't suffer, did he?"

"He knew what hit him—that's about all."

"Let me tell you something, Sergeant—when they say command is no fucking joke, they sure as hell know what they're talking about."

"Yes, sir."

"This is going to be a no-joy phone call."

"Well—it's really a jeopardy mission, sir."

"That's right," the Colonel said. "—That's right. Getting the job done is what counts on this one. —But Jesus Christ . . . it's a hell of a bad start, Tuck."

Riding the elevator down two floors to his room, Sergeant Tucker had wondered if room service was still available so late in the evening. He'd had coconut cream pie the day before, for lunch in the dining room. If room service was still serving, he'd order two pieces of that pie and a steak sandwich. If they weren't serving hot food so late, maybe have an egg-salad sandwich. Iced tea. —Get the Bobbsey Twins up for a little talk, before. Budreau carried a .38; that would do, through and through. . . . Mason could pack the Lieutenant's gear, pay his room bill. The Colonel had taken the Lieutenant's bye-bye hard. —It had been his habit in Central to be shaken at his people's funerals—although the only troopers lost had been two idiots crashed flying in beer. Tucker supposed he equated his lost men with his honor in some addled way. An oddball and flake. —Certainly never assigned regular troop commands . . . not in Field Grade.

Tucker checked his telltale, then went into his room, locked the door, and called room service first thing. —They were good for the coconut pie (double order), and the steak sandwich.

He undressed, put on his robe (a plain white terry cloth in extra-extra large), and called Mason and Budreau, who shared a room on the second floor. Then he unlocked his room door, went into the bathroom, and was taking a fine round shit when the men knocked and he called them into the room—and on into the can to be addressed—demonstrating one of the many advantages of a master's degree in history through the University of Maryland's extension courses. The Sun King had done such to display a majesty above shame. —Lyndon Johnson, too.

One of the tough old men behind Zabar's counter used a long slender-bladed knife to slice Ellie's salmon nearly thin as paper. Then scooped her a half pound of chive cream cheese, a half pound of creamed herring. —Now, after watching Margolies eat so much, Ellie was hungry.

She'd called the Squad from the corner booth, but Nardone's phone had been busy. Then she'd called the AAPS and gotten an address and phone number for St. Christopher's School, South Windham, Connecticut. The headmaster, a Reverend Peschek—sounding younger than she'd expected—listened to her, said, "Son-of-a-bitch—we don't get the New York papers"—and then said he'd tell Sonia Gaither her mother was dead, adding, "—You were afraid I'd make you do it, weren't you, Officer?" Ellie had said that was so.

The old Zabar's man tapped on the counter glass. "—Want anything else?"

"No," Ellie said, "—just bread."

"Over there," the old man said, and Ellie took her lox and herring and cream cheese over to the bread department, asked for a seeded rye, sliced, and a raisin pumpernickel.

On the street, she tried Nardone again from the same booth, and he answered. There was a lot of noise, talking, in the background.

"I got some serious news over here, Tommy."

"Hi. —You and me both."

"Go ahead . . ."

"No. —You first."

She told him, and Nardone said nothing. "It's tough news," Ellie said.

"That poor kid," said Nardone. "—They always get the shitty end of the stick in these fuckin' things. You goin' up to tell her?"

"No—I don't have to, thank God. They're going to tell her—"

"How old is she—the kid?"

"They said fifteen going on sixteen."

" 'Goin' on,' huh? That's great. —You goin' up there to talk to her? Poor kid might have somethin' for us. —Any daddy in the picture?"

"Nobody, according to Margolies. She has nobody."

"Shit," Nardone said. "Anyway, you couldn't go up today."

"Why not?"

"Because Leahy wants us to go up to the Bronx and wait for this Internal guy, Johnson, to go see Cruz and come out with money. Supposed to be his payday. —That's why not."

"That's just ridiculous! They're loading us up with all this crap. . . ."

"Hey—I know it. I got the feelin' they don't want too much shit comin' out on Gaither just now—after that gamblin' thing, and there was the black guy and the Mayor's guy last year. . . ."

"Well—if they don't leave us alone, nothing's what they're going to get."

"Listen, where are you? —I'll pick you up, we'll go up to the Bronx and get it done."

"I'm at Eightieth and Broadway. I have some groceries here; I was going to go home before I drove up to Connecticut."

"Stuff we can eat?"

"I suppose so."

"We'll eat it for lunch up there. I'll be up at Broadway for you in half an hour—I got one thing to clean up, here."

"Wait a minute—what was the big news? —We have to go up to the Bronx?"

"No. It's better I tell you when I see you."

"Tell me now—is it good or bad?"

"It's very bad. I'll tell you when I see you."

"For God's sake—will you just tell me?! I'm not going to fall down or something, Tommy."

Silence on the phone.

"Tommy . . . ?"

"See you less than half an hour." Click.

"Jesus Christ," Ellie said, and hung the phone up hard. When she left the booth, she stepped out into bright sunshine. The morning's high clouds had marched away over the Atlantic.

Susan Margolies had been right. After tears—snot. Ellie used her Kleenex.

"You O.K.? —Listen, this shit could happen to anybody. It was kind of an accident. —That's all it was. I was worried you'd see the papers; they're all comin' out with it, now, late mornin', makin' a big deal like a cop never got shot before."

They were in the Ford, heading uptown on Amsterdam—windows down, Nardone wheeling along with the traffic.

"You could have just *told* me, Tommy. I wasn't going to faint! I mean it—next time you have some bad news—just *tell* me. —O.K.? Don't play games with me. I've heard of cops getting killed before." She felt her nose running slightly, and wanted to blow, but it seemed the wrong time.

"Well . . . I knew you liked Morris. And he was on the Squad and all. . . ."

"O.K. All right. Just don't do it again, Tommy. O.K? —Who were they?"

"Assholes . . . nobody! Who the hell knows who they were? —It was a B an' E, or the old lady opened for 'em, and Morris just walked in on it. It was bad luck, that's all. Could happen to any citizen."

"Who's going to take care of his mother?" Ellie blew her nose.

"No need for that. . . . The old lady went out with her boy."

"They killed her?"

"Probably an accident . . . you know; they bopped her. . . ."

"This happened last night—why didn't the Squad at least get a call? They could have done that goddamn much." Ellie took out her compact to make sure she wasn't a complete disaster, then closed it and put it away.

"Because the precinct cars didn't have the floor right. —They got two calls—no names, you bet—and one jerk mentioned a floor number, but the cars got it wrong, checked the wrong floor—and nothing. This morning, two detectives went over there—precinct got another call—'How come the police weren't doin' their job?'—and this time they got the jerk made the call, lived right next door, and they went in and found out what happened."

"Why don't we just go over there, right now?"

"Because"—he made the right turn at 110th Street—"because Leahy said the word was to keep our nose out of it. It's West Division's business—it's not our business.

The Major Crime people are not interested in any more shit from the Squad—was the way Leahy put it."

"And that's that—one of our own?"

"Well . . . I guess Samuelson is goin' to stick his nose in a little. Maybe we'll stick our nose in a little, we hear somethin'. But it better *be* a little, or Fatty's goin' to cut some noses off. Leahy's not happy about this Gaither thing, for starters. —He doesn't think we got any business messin' with it."

"And Morris shot one?"

"Shot the shit out of him, it looks like." Nardone's bulky right hand did a little finger-dance along the top of the steering wheel. "Denny Neill's on West, and he called Samuelson and said there was a trail of blood all the way down to the garage. Morris nailed one of 'em, all right. —Samuelson said Neill said the jerk next door saw one of 'em through the peep when they took off, right after shots-fired. Caught a glimpse of just one of 'em. The fucker was carryin' the fuckin' TV—you believe that? Kill a cop and an old lady—and waltz the fuck out with a fuckin' TV! Big black guy with glasses, the jerk thinks. —You don't see too good through those peeps."

"What a damn rotten thing. He was such a sad guy. . . . He was always so quiet."

"Ummm . . ."

"What does that mean?"

"He was a nice guy—but, let's face it, he was a little wacky. He was goin' to get in some kind of trouble sometime."

"The hell he was! —What do you mean, Tommy? He's a dead cop—he was shot in a crime!"

Nardone turned left, up Third Avenue. "Hey—will you calm down? He was a nice guy—he was a good detective. God bless the guy, the way he went. But he was an unstable person—that's all I'm sayin'. Someday somebody was goin' to say somethin' wrong to him, and boom—there was goin' to be trouble."

"That's a lot of shit. —I'm surprised at you, Tommy. He was a very sweet man!"

"Yeah, that's for sure. He was a nice guy."

"Yes," Ellie said. "He was. —He didn't suffer?"

"Samuelson said Neill said 'through the noggin.' He didn't suffer. —What did you bring?"

"I got some rye bread, some lox and cream cheese. I was going to take it right home."

"Here we go." Nardone swung into 117th, drove halfway down the block, then backed in to parallel-park in front of an *empanada* stand. "This is great—it'll take everybody about ten seconds flat to make us for cops."

"We could neck," Ellie said. Nardone looked embarrassed.

Across the street, farther east toward the corner, a narrow magazine stand stood open to business, three doors from a corner *bodega.* Some papers were stacked on the sidewalk there, two racks of magazines—most Spanish-language—a revolving display of picture postcards out front as well. This small store appeared to be taking only its proper share of passing customers. "There you go," Nardone said, nodding toward it, then fished from the pocket of his blue polyester suit jacket a small square photograph, and handed it to Ellie. Officer Johnson, as a patrolman, had been a squirrel-cheeked, earnest-eyed young man. Light brown hair.

"How old is he, now?"

"A young guy," Nardone said. "An idiot. —Leahy says take this guy in. —I guess they figure to really nail one."

They sat parked at the curb for almost three hours, windows down for a while—then up, the engine and air-conditioning on as the day grew hotter, listening to *Go Slow Jazz 'n Rock* on the radio—against regulations—and talking cases (particularly the New York State Trooper thing, from which Ellie expected continued trouble) —talking, as well, Squad politics and Department politics, Marie's dance classes, Sally Gaither's child, and the hoped-for reports from Fingerprints (so sadly overrated by civilians) and Records; the last bound to be minor, since the computer revealed no arrest sheet on Gaither. —Not even a complaint.

They said little more about Morris Classman's death, that event resonating, nonetheless, beneath all other conversation, except to discuss Connors, the detective in charge of the Classman thing—a captain and an ace—

regarded as one of the best homicide men on the Force, now starring for Division West. "—That guy gets on a perp, he can kiss his ass good-bye," Nardone said.

Ellie reported on her morning with Margolies.

"A cutie," Ellie said, "—she spent a lot of time showing me her apartment, bathrooms and everything. —Damnit, I meant to ask her about that Audrey guy! Rebecca said they were buddies. . . ."

"So you're sayin' you got nothin'?"

"Not much."

"It doesn't make sense; I'll tell you that. —Somethin' wrong. I don't care what that whore—that prostitute was tryin' to keep on the QT. Ladies are friends—they're friends. They find out about each other."

"Margolies talks a lot—"

"—And she doesn't say shit. Am I right? Look—we give her a week, maybe a little more, so she feels pretty good . . . then we both go back an' lean on her. —She isn't goin' to show me her friggin' toilet."

All this while, they attracted to the Ford no particular adult attention in the rush of passing traffic, the ins and outs of delivery trucks, pedestrians ambling, hurrying by—Puerto Ricans, mainly, with occasional taller people, paler, the men more heavily mustached, from Colombia, Honduras, Costa Rica, Mexico.

Once, Nardone had had to move back so a man driving a frozen-chicken van could double-park and deliver to the corner *bodega.* A number of young boys in the blaze-orange T-shirts of some PAL team—skipping school for such a pleasant, warm, early autumn day—had stood along the *empanada* stand's front, watching this maneuver, and keeping an eye on blond Ellie sitting in the Ford, as they kept an eye on all present and passing.

"I think they think I'm a prostitute," she said. "—Hit me, and they'll be sure." She was half joking, but Nardone—always open to professional suggestions during police work—nodded, leaned over to her, drew back his hand, and hit her, as if hard, across her face. "—You owe me *money,* bitch!" he said pretty loud, his face unpleasant. The boys were pleased with that, though likely puzzled by the Ford—so improbable a pimp's vehicle—and watched Ellie through her side window as she pretended to protest the blow, to cry. Later, when she left the car to get Cokes at the *empanada* stand, the boys regarded her with fresh attention—one, very small and dark, gripping a meager groin and making a kissing sound as she walked by with the drinks. "How much you suck my cock?" he said.

"Find it, first," said Ellie, and got in the car to merriment from his treacherous friends.

These boys, after another while growing bored by their location, suddenly—at some cue unknown—turned together like a school of tropic fish, flashed their bright colors, and were gone.

Almost an hour after that, while Ellie and Nardone were listening to police calls (the radio turned up), judging trouble and response in this busy precinct, hoping for some overriding call to action, a big man—or one who looked big sitting behind his steering wheel—had pulled up alongside them in a new Plymouth Fury, honked his horn, and gestured to them to move out—apparently of his accustomed space. Nardone had gazed placidly out the driver's side window at this person, pleased by the comedy—even happier when the big man (who was very big, with a large belly neatly draped in a frilled-front white Cuban shirt) got out of the Plymouth, leaving it to block traffic, came around the front of his car to the Ford, and said some harsh things in Spanish. —Nardone, like most policemen, spoke a few phrases of street Spanish, but now pretended not to. —Only put his window down to hear better, and sat behind the wheel gazing up at the angry man, listening, amused.

There quickly came a time—having run out of personal things to say—when the big man had to decide what to do. Nardone's silence, his continued calm, his mildly interested and pleased detachment apparently rang some alarm then, for the big man said only one thing more, and that remark directed to the air. —Delivered that, turned, went back to his car (now a cork in a bottle of roaring horns), climbed in, and drove away.

"Let's have lunch," Nardone said, and swayed to the right to lift his heavy left buttock slightly off his back pocket, where he kept a Boy Scout knife for all sorts of minor chores. "We havin' the rye?"

"You can have the rye. Or pumpernickel."

"Which one you want to save?"

"I don't care, Tommy—we'll have what you want."

"Well, we'll have the rye. You can save the pumpernickel."

Silence, but for the rattle of heavy paper, as Nardone, with short, thick, powerful fingers, pleased as a birthday child, unwrapped the packages from Zabar's. "You're sure the rye's O.K.? —You want to save it, we'll save it."

"Tommy, will you please just have some of that bread. I got it to eat. —Have some."

"What's this . . . herring?"

"Creamed herring."

Nardone observed the herring, but didn't molest it.

"This is cream cheese with chives. The other one's lox."

"There you go! O.K." More unwrapping. Nardone then opened the larger blade of his small knife, carved a deep, richly white-and-green half-moon of cheese up out of the carton, and placed it, only slightly spread, on a thick slice of seeded rye. A strip of salmon—delicate, pink, translucent—selected, separated from the small damp stack, was very carefully draped across. Then another one, as precisely, rested right alongside. The covering slice of rye laid gently over . . . and all then lightly pressed together, as if he were closing a thick and favorite book.

Ellie had thought of being funny—of pretending she believed this labor of love had been made for her—then was glad she hadn't, as her partner, already rummaging amid the cartons for more, handed his construction over to her as swiftly and naturally as a mother bird thrusts a beetle into its baby's beak.

As if, from courtesy, he'd waited just the additional half hour for them to finish their lunch, Detective Johnson ("There's the schmuck!") at that time exited the passenger side of a freshly double-parked brown Chevrolet across the street and two spaces down from the magazine stand. He hadn't changed much from his photograph, though now wearing tailored summer-weight gray wool, a light striped tie.

"Don't look around, asshole," Nardone said. "—Just go in and get your fuckin' money! —Will you look at that guy? He don't give a shit if the Commissioner is standin' there with a camera. —Just does not give a shit." Ellie saw Nardone's glowering reflection faintly on the inside of the windshield. "—There he goes." Detective Johnson had hopped up the store's single step off the sidewalk, and disappeared into the narrow dark. "Will you tell me what's with these guys? —They're gettin' greedy as fuckin' doctors!"

Nardone opened the car door on his side, held it ajar. Ellie pulled her purse strap up over her right shoulder, unsnapped the purse, and opened her door, too.

"I want to get that asshole," Nardone said. "O.K. with you to hold the partner?"

"That's all right," Ellie said, feeling a litle breathless as usual in these circumstances. She'd mentioned it to Nardone once, just after they'd started to work together—saying she supposed she was afraid. "Shit, no," he'd said. "It's upsettin', that's all. —This stuff is goin' to upset any lady."

"Come *on*. . . !" Nardone said to the store's doorway. "What the fuck you doin'? —Countin' it?" He was hunched forward in his seat, as intent on that entrance as Mayo on an opening can of cat food. —She'd forgotten to get the Siamese something. It had been a long time since she'd brought any surprise—

"Go!" And—as the young detective appeared, stepping from the store's doorway—Nardone was out of the car, letting the car door swing half shut behind him, charging across into the traffic, his cheap suit jacket flapping back as he ran into the street, heavy shoulders rolling like a running bull's.

"Look out!" Ellie shouted—meaning for the passing cars—jumped out her side, ran around the back of the Ford and out across the street toward the double-parked Chevy. She got her hand in her bag as she ran, fumbled past her compact, the revolver, and found her shield case.

The man at the wheel of the Chevrolet was staring

across the front seat at her as she ran toward him. A square, handsome older face, gray-white hair.

"Don't you fuckin' move!" Nardone shouting down the street. Ellie didn't look that way—she saw the driver reaching down to put the car in drive—and she was at the passenger-side window, her buzzer case out and open, and as the car lurched and began to roll, grabbed the door handle and hit the window glass with the case as hard as she could, cracking the brass against it so the white-haired man glanced over to see her trotting faster and faster alongside, her shield against the glass, glaring in at him, shaking her head *no* in as grim a fashion as she could.

He pulled the car up then—no more than twenty feet traveled, and sat there hitting the steering wheel with his fist.

Ellie pulled the passenger-side door open and jumped in. "You motherfucker!" she said. "—You were trying to kill me!"

"No—I wasn't!" the cop (very handsome, in his fifties) was defensive, frightened as any civilian. "—It was an accident! I swear I didn't know you were a cop!"

"You're a fucking liar," Ellie said, "—and your ass is under arrest. Give me your fucking gun—give me your shield. —Come on! *Come on*!" She snapped her fingers at him, hustling him, hurrying him while he was scared, and the white-haired detective reached under his coat lapel and took out his shield case and gave it to her. "Come *on*!" Ellie said, and tucked the case under her leg on the seat. The detective reached around under his jacket to his belt, took out his revolver, and handed it over. Ellie dropped the .38 on the floor at her feet, and dug into her purse for her cuffs. When the detective saw the cuffs, he said, "Oh, Jesus . . . don't do that!" and drew his hands away and up against the door on his side like a child fearing they'd be slapped.

"What the hell *is* this?" he said. "What are the *charges*, for Christ's sake?"

"You have the right to remain silent—"

"Don't *say* that! —What the hell are the *charges*?"

"We have felony bribery—four, five misdemeanor counts of accepting . . ." Ellie looked through the windshield, and saw Nardone and the other detective standing beside a display shelf of oranges at the *bodega* near the corner. Nardone had the young detective by the arm, and the man was trying to pull away . . . starting to struggle. He threw a punch.

"Shit." Ellie reached over and took the keys out of the ignition, and gave the white-haired man the hardest look she could. "—I'm going out of here for a minute." She opened the passenger-side door. "I'm telling you—if you move one fucking inch! If you get one fucking inch out of this car—"

"I won't," the detective said. "—Just let me talk to you!"

Ellie bent, picked up the man's revolver, got out of the car, and ran down toward the corner as fast as she could, stuffing the revolver into her purse—was almost hit when a Yellow Cab came speeding down the street just past her.

There were people watching on the corner—but standing back. Oranges rolling everywhere, rolling along the gutters. Ellie jumped up on the sidewalk behind two parked delivery bikes, and ran to see Nardone sitting on top of the young detective amid more oranges, hitting the young man rapidly back and forth across the face with a long, fat manila envelope, from which, at each blow, a few twenty-dollar bills went wafting. The young man's jacket was open as he lay there, his holstered revolver showing. He had his hands up, trying to protect his face.

A number of people were watching—more all the time. A woman with a baby . . . Ellie got hold of Nardone's arm, and hauled at it to make him stop hitting the young cop. Money was drifting everywhere, but nobody was stepping forward to pick it up.

"Tommy! *Tommy—goddamnit*!" He paid no attention, so Ellie kicked him in the side as hard as she could, and Nardone grunted and looked up at her.

"Get off him! —Get *off* him!"

"He resisted—"

"Get *off* him!"

Nardone got to his feet—giving the young man a last smack with the envelope—then bent to haul him lightly up, and took his revolver away. A man in the crowd cheered, said something in Spanish, but none of the others said anything.

Ellie started picking up the money, and an old man in a white apron, the *bodega* man, helped her, grunting each time he stooped over to pick up a bill.

Three of the twenties were lying near a young woman's foot—she was wearing high-heel blue open-toed shoes—and she stepped back a little as Ellie bent to pick the money up.

"Are you a cop?" she said. She had such a heavy accent that Ellie didn't understand at first, and the woman asked her again.

"Yes," Ellie said, "—I am."

The young woman nodded, and watched while Ellie duck-walked over to the curb to pick up another twenty. —Too many twenties for just two cops. It was a bag job, was what it was.

"Got it all?" Nardone said, standing beside the young cop. He had the cuffs on him, and the young detective was weeping furious tears. "You cocksucker," he said to Nardone.

"That's a shame," a woman said. "—He beat him up." Someone else said something in Spanish.

The old *bodega* man handed Ellie a handful of twenty-dollar bills, and Ellie said, "I have it all, I think."

"Come on." Nardone shoved the young cop ahead of him down the street, stepping through bright rolling oranges. Ellie, following, turned to some people trailing along, and said, "You people go mind your own business, now." These people stood for a few moments where they were—staring after—then wandered away, obedient.

At the Chevrolet, Nardone opened the passenger-side front door, and shoved the young detective into the car—then motioned Ellie into the back and climbed in after her.

"You" he said to the white-haired man, "—drive downtown."

"Tommy?" the white-haired man said. He turned to look into the back. "*Tommy* . . . I thought it was you. Thank Jesus God!" The young detective wasn't crying anymore. He was sitting hunched over, his head resting on the dashboard.

"Oh, shit," Nardone said. "Pauly. —You fuckin' asshole!"

"Tommy—I swear on the living God. I swear on my soul we're just pickin' up. Just pickin' *up*! We don't get shit outta this!"

"Who does?"

"I'm not goin' to tell you. I *can't* tell you. You're goin' to get me shot!"

"Well, goddamnit," Nardone said, "—you got to!"

"Please don't do this, Tommy," the white-haired man, Pauly, said. "Don't do it for my sake—do it for Gracie's. It'll *kill* her, Tommy. Please don't do this . . . please, *please* don't *do* it!" His face was hydrant red; he was breathing in an odd, galloping way. The young detective sat still, silent, his forehead on the dash.

"Take it easy . . . come on, now," Ellie said.

"Tommy . . . oh, Tommy . . . it'll *kill* her. I'm beggin' you—oh, I'm *beggin'* you." No tears, but his heavy face a deeper and deeper red.

"If you got somethin' to tell me, Pauly . . ."

The older detective turned farther in his seat, furious. "You're tryin' to get me killed! You want to get me *killed*!—I can't tell you, goddamnit!"

The young detective—Johnson—lifted his head off the dashboard and sat up straight. "Don't beg him anymore, Pauly," he said.

"For Gracie, Tommy—not for me. —Don't kill my Gracie. . . !" Handsome Pauly was taking deeper and deeper breaths, plucking at the front of his shirt with his thumb and forefinger.

"Come on, now," Ellie said. "Come on, now—take it easy. . . ."

She glanced at Nardone. He was sitting beside her, silent, his heavy hands on his knees, staring at the white-haired detective as if he'd never seen the man before. He looked frightened. —She couldn't bear it. "Whatever you say, Tommy," she said to him. "—I figure they got some shit scared out of them. . . ." Nardone gave her the saddest look.

After another few moments, the car quiet except for Pauly's breathing, Nardone said, "No, sweetheart—it's not your business. You got nothin' to do with this." He leaned forward so suddenly she was startled, and hit the white-haired detective hard across the side of the face with his open left hand. It made a loud noise in the car. —Three men and a woman had been standing on the sidewalk, looking into the car to see what the fuss on the corner had been about. Seeing the blow, they lifted their heads like startled grazing animals, and angled away in hasty highstepping walks.

"You fuckin' thief," Nardone said, "—you're makin' a lousy *crook* outta me! You were my friend, an' you're ruinin' me here, Pauly. 'For Gracie'—huh? You bet your fuckin' ass it's for Gracie! It sure as shit is not for you. . . !"

The white-haired detective sat still, taking his deep breaths, plucking at his shirt, Nardone's fingerprints ivory-white across his right cheek. "Go ahead," Nardone said, "—die."

The young detective said, "You got no—"

"Be quiet—you!" Ellie said. "Don't press your luck."

Nardone turned to him. "You fuckin'-a, you little scum bag—takin' money from a fuckin' thief, handin' it out to a bunch of fuckin' thieves make us all look like *shit*!" He bent over the seat, reached down behind the young man's back, and unlocked the cuffs.

"Tommy," Ellie said, "—there's liable to be a precinct car coming by from that trouble—"

"You got some of that money?" Nardone said to her.

"Yes."

"Give it here." He took the folded twenties, stuffed them back into the battered manila envelope. He tore the paper a little. "—I'm givin' this shit back to that asshole in there," he said to the men in the front seat. "—An' if I catch either one of you in this fuckin' *neighborhood,* I'm gonna' turn you in. —We all go down! You understand me. . . ?" The white-haired detective only sat, but the young man nodded. "—So, you tell those creeps you're baggin' for, they better send harder guys next time. Ain't gonna be any more fuckin' free rides." He opened his door and got out into the street, then leaned back inside. "Pauly, don't you ever show me your face again. —For me, you're a dead guy."

When his door was closed, he was lumbering on his way to the curb, Ellie said, "—You're going to be sorry, doing this to him." Then she took the white-haired detective's .38 from her purse, dropped it on the floor of the back seat, got out of the car, closed the door, and hurried to catch Nardone at the magazine stand, listening for a patrol car coming to see about a fight, some money flying around.

Porfirio Cruz was an elderly, brown-skinned man with bifocal glasses and a neat, small salt-and-pepper beard. He was standing behind his small cigar counter at the dusky back of the store, dressed in slacks, a green shirt, and a brown tie—when Nardone came in with the envelope in his hand, Ellie hurrying behind him. Two phones were ringing in the back, and Cruz was already shaking his head, *No, he didn't know that envelope,* when Nardone held it out under his nose, then dropped it onto the glass countertop.

"You take this," Nardone said, "—an' shove it up your ass. I catch you givin' this to any more cops—I'll come in here and pull down your pants and shove it up your ass *for* you—I give you my word of honor, on Holy Mother."

A big, thick-shouldered Puerto Rican with a round, flat-nosed face was standing against the store wall to the left of the cigar counter. He was wearing a bright blue-and-yellow Hawaiian shirt. He glanced over at Señor Cruz, then stood straighter, and stepped away from the wall.

"Are you kiddin' me?" Nardone said. "—I couldn't get *that* lucky." Cruz raised his forefinger and the round-faced man leaned back against the wall.

"Are you a tough guy?" Ellie said to the round-faced man in her scraps of Spanish, and stepped up to him. She had her hand in her purse, on the Smith & Wesson. *"You look more like a queer, to me,"* she said, her Spanish good enough for that.

"Gracie Donaher was real nice to Connie when we had the baby . . . we had Marie," Nardone said. He was driving down Second Avenue in a crowd of traffic. The day remained summer warm—Ellie had the air-conditioning on. "—A nice woman, you know. She came over a lot.

Her sister's a nurse . . . she's the one got us over to Beth Israel . . . got us goin' on the exercises. . . ."

"Tommy—you did the right thing. I would have done exactly the same thing."

"An' you'd be dead wrong," Nardone said, and changed lanes to pass a bus. "—I made a bad mistake. I just made a bad mistake, back there. I could get you in a lot of trouble." He stayed in the center lane, didn't give a cab room to shove in ahead of them.

"Tommy, we all decide all the time to take somebody in or let them go! —It's not such a big deal."

"I never let a couple thieves go like that—with the money right in their fuckin' hands. I never let that go in my life." He glanced at Ellie, then back to the traffic. "—Why do you think I'm on this shit squad? You think because I let guys *go*?"

He said nothing more while they traveled (accelerate, slow, and stop—accelerate, slow, and stop) down several blocks.

"This traffic is god-awful," Ellie said. "—It's rush hour all the time, now." A couple—a bald, bearded man and a pretty woman in a white short-sleeved blouse—had passed them, were driving just ahead of them, shifting from one lane to the other and back. It was a junker rental car; they drove like tourists. —This couple, still in front of them, stopped late for the light at Sixty-sixth Street, and came close to nudging a tall, good-looking woman in an exercise outfit, crossing with a shaggy sheepdog on a leash.

The woman called to them, "Learn to drive!" She shouted it loud enough to be heard through the Ford's closed windows. They heard the pretty woman call back, "He is!" and the rental rolled late on green.

"I wish I didn't think those guys were laughin', back there," Nardone said. "—I wish I didn't think they were laughin' at me."

CHAPTER 7

"It's beauty and the beast!" The speaker—Avril Reedy, a *Post* reporter—had been a policeman himself, long ago, was injured in a patrol-car accident and invalided out. He was now lounging against the corridor wall at the door to the squad room, with another reporter Ellie'd seen in the building, but didn't know by name. —A *News* man, she thought.

Reedy was black, but his accent was solid Brooklyn, with none of the Southern slurring many New York blacks refreshed as children visiting relatives in Alabama and Mississippi. "—This company you got in there—is this on the Classman killing?"

Nardone walked past him as if Reedy had turned to wallpaper. But Ellie paused and said, "What company? —What's going on?"

"That's what I call a great source," Reedy said to the other man—a short white man, younger than Reedy. Then said, "—If you don't know, honey, damn if I can tell you. . . ."

Ellie started to follow Nardone through the squad-room door, then turned. "Why don't you come in?"

"Because, sweetie," Reedy said. "—Leahy ain't *lettin'* us come in!"

The squad room was crowded with cops—doing their entries and paperwork—and come in to make and take their afternoon phone calls to and from sources just beginning to stir, girlfriends for dates that evening, their wives to schedule dinner. They were there in such numbers, also, because of the death of one of their own—to share what they knew or thought they knew about Morris Classman's killing . . . to hang around, to be on the scene.

Nardone tapped a detective named LaPlace on the shoulder, said, "Frank—what's goin' on?"

LaPlace, taller than Nardone, but very slender, sporting a handsome madras jacket, a handlebar mustache, said, "Leahy wants you guys—he's steamin'."

When Nardone pushed open Leahy's office door, Ellie behind him, that fat officer did glance up in exasperation, said something to three people crowded around his desk, rose, and managed to sidle his way to the door and out, bellying Nardone and Ellie from the doorway, out into the squad room.

"I was real glad," Leahy said to them, "to hear that thief Johnson is down in holdin'—goin' right across town, gettin' booked."

Nardone said nothing.

"I think he made us," Ellie said. "—We saw him circle the block a couple of times . . . couldn't see the driver. Then, he just took off."

"No pickup?"

"We didn't see it," Ellie said. "—We figured you didn't want him brought in for a no-hold charge."

"I wanted that thief brought in!" Leahy said. "—Now, you're tellin' me the guy just took off like a friggin' bird!"

"That's right," Ellie said.

"Why aren't you talkin'?" Leahy said to Nardone. He had to raise his voice over the noise of the computers, the conversations. "*Hey—keep it down in here!* Well . . . ?" he said to Nardone. "—You got somethin' to say?"

"No," Nardone said.

"Oh—that's *very* nice. . . ." Leahy glared up at Nardone in unaccustomed anger, fat and furious—while his object, face closed as a vault, stared over the short man's head, as if to great distance.

"There was no use making a no-cause arrest, Lieutenant," Ellie said. "—It would just be kicked out. There wouldn't have been any evidence!"

"So you say," Leahy said. "—An' I notice this guy is sayin' nothin' at all. If it was any but you two . . . I'd figure you for takin', have your asses up on charges. —You understand me?" His blue eyes were bulging like a china pig's, and he blinked twice, then again.

"What *for*?" Ellie said, wishing that Tommy would say something—at least back her up.

"You know what for," Leahy said, quietly. "—You people were told who, what, where, and when. And you go out there and you come back with nothin'. —Now, *I* got to explain why," and he looked up toward the floor above. "You guys left me holdin' the shitty end—and I don't even want to know why you did it." Furious blinking. "—But I'll tell you this—the next cops I send you after, you better bring those fuckers in on a fuckin' plate!" The Lieutenant turned away, then turned back again. "—An' right now, you two come in and listen to some bullshit on that whore thing. A fuckin' waste of time, is what that is!" and marched away before them, back into his office.

"Tommy, come on, now," Ellie said, softly, "for God's sake. —You almost got us into trouble there."

"I'm sorry."

"Don't be sorry—but Jesus, speak up next time. . . ."

The closet office seemed packed with seven people in it—the three in front of the desk; Leahy just wedging himself behind it; Serrano—unseen before—leaning against the near wall; now Ellie and Nardone crowded in, closing the door behind them.

Sitting before the desk was a worried horse-faced man in an expensive brown-checked summer suit. He cut a glance at Ellie and Nardone as they came in, then looked back down at his lap. A short, thick-armed woman with heavy, shoulder-length black hair and narrow, dark green eyes, sat beside him; she wore a fine lime-green challis dress, matching top, simple heavy gold jewelry. An attorney—one Ellie had never seen before, but unmistakable in his alert concern, his lack of anger, lack of fear—sat on the other side of the woman, against the far wall.

"Listen," Leahy said to the horse-faced man, "these officers"—he indicated Ellie and Nardone—"these officers are workin' on the Gaither case." He made a gentle encouraging gesture with his left hand. "Why don't you just go over this for them—O.K.?"

The man looked up at Nardone, then Ellie, and stayed with her. "Miss . . ." he said. "Officer . . . what happened is that I . . . associated with Miss Gaither." He moved his long jaw sideways, left and right, as if imitating the animal he resembled. "I live in the same building. I . . . heard some gossip. I heard about her."

"Then he spoke to this prostitute in Gristede's," the short woman said; she had a voice unlike her looks, it was soft and treble as a girl's. "—And he arranged to 'associate' with her. Twice. —He says twice. For two hundred dollars each time. —Isn't that right?" she said to the man. "Wasn't it two hundred dollars each time? —She must have been crazy about *you.* She must have found you *very* attractive!"

"No," the man said, "I suppose she didn't—but she was very nice." He looked at Ellie, then looked away toward the little table with the coffeepot on it. "Then, I read about what had happened—and I thought I'd better come in. . . ."

"What an incredible wimp you are," his wife said, and seemed to give out deadly rays as she sat.

"What's your name?" Nardone said. "—You try to get her to do somethin' she didn't want? You smack her around a little? Warm her up? Get that juice goin'?"

"That's a laugh," the man's wife said.

"I never hurt her," the man said, "I didn't do anything like that."

"There's no need for questions of that sort," the attorney said. "My client came voluntarily to reveal his limited knowledge—"

"Didn't you hear me or somethin'?" Nardone said to the horse-faced man. "—What the fuck is your name?"

"Barry," the man said. "Barry Crowell. I'm in investment counseling."

"And she did everythin' you wanted—just like that? Wasn't anythin' she wouldn't do for you? Nothin' too dirty for her, huh?"

"She was very nice," Crowell said. "—I'm not ashamed of what I did."

"Well, I got to tell you, Barry," Nardone said, and went over to lean on Leahy's desk beside Crowell's chair, "—my opinion, a lot of these prostitutes are better off dead, you know? Lots of times, it's a favor. I mean it! You know, when we found her, she was smilin'—like she was glad she went. She looked peaceful. . . ."

"I don't see what good—" the attorney said, but Nardone didn't let him finish.

"I know—and you know what that means, too, Barry. It means the guy put her away knew what he was doin'. And what he was doin' was somethin' just had to be done. It was for her good—for everybody's good. —Right? Let me tell you somethin'—takes quite a guy to see somethin' tough like that, and get it done, and to hell with what people think."

"Lieutenant," the attorney said to Leahy, "—we're not going to hold still for this sort of questioning."

"What questioning?" Leahy said. "If you want, we can hold Mr. Crowell as a material witness—call Reedy in from the *Post*. They can take his picture. . . . Is that what you want? —You know, Counselor, best thing is just to cooperate here. Nobody's goin' to push your client around."

Nardone reached down and put his hand on Crowell's shoulder. "—They don't even know what we're talkin' about, do they?" He shook Crowell's shoulder gently, as if he were waking him. "We're talkin' about a guy with the kind of guts . . . everybody's goin' to wind up lovin' that guy for doin' what that poor woman really wanted. What she needed done, so she'd go out clean—stop makin' everything so fuckin' filthy. I can tell your wife doesn't understand, here," he said, "—but she will. A lot of guys do somethin' special, it takes awhile for people to catch up to 'em—you know? Everybody doesn't get it, not right off. . . ."

Nardone bent over Crowell. "Let me ask you somethin' —just for me, none of this official bullshit. Let me ask you somethin'. It wasn't easy—was it, Barry? Took a lot out of you, took a lot of your strength, just to get it done. . . ?"

Crowell stared up at Nardone as if the detective were a cloud that had come drifting over him.

"No," he said. "I didn't—"

"But you tried, didn't you. —At least you gave it a try."

"No," Crowell said. "—I never thought of it."

"Ooooh . . . uh-oh, now you're lyin' to me, Barry. —You never even *thought* about it?"

"No. Really. —And I couldn't have, anyway. I was on Long Island."

"All last weekend, Sunday mornin' and Monday, too? —All *day*? Hey, Barry—come *on*. It's not summertime anymore." Nardone counted on his fingers. "Gee, that's a *lot* of time on Long Island, Barry. Didn't you have to come into the office? —Just for a few hours? Take the train in?"

"No . . . no, I didn't. I was in Southampton for five days! I was seeing clients. —I was there when that happened to her!"

"And what about you?" Nardone said to the man's wife. "—You goin' to go to jail for a couple years to back up that bullshit?"

"All right, now—that's enough," the attorney said, and made to get up out of his chair.

"Relax, Counselor," Nardone said, "—your clients came in here to cooperate, right? I mean if you want to take 'em out of here, then take 'em out of here! An' we'll come get 'em later." He put his hand back on Crowell's shoulder. "—But Barry's got some stuff to get off his chest . . . he's been doin' some things with this prostitute behind his wife's back—and she's mad and I don't blame her—because it looks like that's all there is to it . . . just some dirty stuff he wanted, and this woman would do it for money." He squeezed Crowell's shoulder gently, leaning over him. "But, what I think . . . is that Barry is not that kind of a guy. I think he had somethin' else in mind all the time. —Not that dirty stuff. I think he had somethin' real serious on his mind all the time—and I'd like to hear about it, because this doesn't look like a perverted guy to me."

"I'm not," Mr. Crowell said. "It was just . . . lovemaking."

"Poor woman," his wife said. "—She should have charged three hundred."

"We can just stop this right now, Lieutenant," the attorney said to Leahy, who was leaning back in his chair, looking sleepy—and was; he'd had three cheeseburgers and a jumbo fries for lunch. A large Pepsi, too. "—We can bring this to a close, I think. Mr. Crowell had some information to volunteer concerning this case—and only peripheral information at that—and he has done so." He leaned over to pick up his briefcase.

"Bullshit," Nardone said. "—He's here, and you're here, because he left his fingerprints all over a murdered lady's apartment. I was in his shoes, I'd be up here, too, cooperatin' my ass off!"—and walked back to the wall by Leahy's only window, and leaned against it.

"He is here doing his goddamn duty as a citizen!" the attorney said, "—at the cost of very considerable embarrassment, and damage to his marital relationship!"

"Calm down, Counselor," Ellie said, "—there's no problem here. If Mrs. Crowell's going to swear her husband never came into the city—and, of course, we don't find evidence he hired some people to murder this woman—well, then there's no problem. If she commits perjury, she's going to prison. That's all this officer is saying. —You saying she *won't* go to prison for lying about a murder in court?" Ellie sat on the edge of Leahy's desk where Nardone had been, and said to Mrs. Crowell, "I'm sure your attorney never said you *wouldn't* go to prison for perjury if you lied under oath in this case? He didn't tell you that, did he?" Ellie leaned down and patted the green-eyed woman on the knee. She had round, fat knees. The dress material was heavy and smooth as old linen. "—You see, you'd have to have knowledge of his whereabouts every hour you were out there. He never went shopping alone? Never went to the beach? Never went to play tennis? Never left the house in the middle of the night—while you were asleep? —If you can swear all that under oath, then maybe you have no problem." She patted the woman's knee again.

"Mrs. Crowell has no problem in any case," the attorney said.

"Is that what he's been telling you?" Ellie said to the woman. "—That you'd have no problem, no matter what?"

The woman didn't answer her. She didn't look frightened; she looked tired.

"That is not what I told her," the attorney said, "—and you better be pretty careful, or you're going to find yourself defending a suit for damages to my professional—"

"That'll be the day," Ellie said. "That'll be a first—a damages case over questions, and not a single statement to effect by me or this other officer." She smiled at the woman. "—Are you satisfied you have the best representation you can afford . . . ?"

The green-eyed woman suddenly laughed—a trilling, high-pitched young girl's laugh. —It made her face prettier, so Ellie could see why Crowell had loved her, married her so many years before. "I hate to say it," the woman said, "but this jackass wasn't really out of my sight much last weekend, and we had house guests—some people from Detroit, clients of Barry's. The Shrellenbachs. You can check with them—Michael and Dorothy Shrellenbach. —They'd love this!" She shook her head, revealing, under heavy black hair, gold seashells curled at the lobes of her ears. "I hate to say it, but he really didn't have time to come into town and kill that poor creature."

"Or have it done?" Ellie said. "—If she were threatening to tell you, for example . . . had a little blackmail going?"

"Not a chance, dear," the woman said. "—Barry doesn't know anybody who'd dream of arranging such a thing. None of his friends are that interesting." She reached over, took Crowell's hand, and held it. "—He's just a cowardly sneak."

"Nothin'?" Leahy said, when the three were gone, Serrano gone before to block Reedy and the *News* man.

"Nothin'," Nardone said. "—That guy never did anything."

"And will his prints show up on the report, after all?" Ellie said.

"No way," Leahy and Nardone said, almost together.

"Check with the phone company, anyhow," Leahy said. "—See if the guy was callin' people his wife didn't know he knew. He could have made a couple calls from Long Island. Maybe did some investments for some wise guy owed him a favor. . . ."

"We'll call the Detroit people, too—see what they have to say," Ellie said.

"By the way, I don't see any board out there on this Gaither thing," Leahy said.

"We're using the machine," Ellie said. "—We put everything we get on the computer."

"Let me tell you somethin'—a pin board is goin' to give you a better look at what you got."

"Maybe . . ." Ellie said. "I guess we could put one up."

"Do it. . . . O.K., enough of that shit," Leahy said, and picked up a paper from his desk. "I got a letter here—guy's too paralyzed to use the friggin' phone—from that trooper commander upstate." Leahy's lower lip, damp and raspberry red, protruded as he looked the letter over. "—Says you have submitted an incomplete record of questions and replies from witness Bostwick, Charles W."

"That moron," Ellie said. "—Bostwick is an alcoholic! He's a mess. —He's incontinent, for God's sake! He ID'd one of those troopers as a Puerto Rican kid with a gravity knife!"

"Why don't we send that witness up to Albany, send him to the commander up there—let him interview him?" Nardone said.

Leahy smiled. "Oh—that's a good one. Send the jerk up on a bus—I'll give 'em a call he's comin' up, they can meet him. Let him shit all over one of those fancy cars they like to drive a hundred up there in the woods." He put the letter on his desk. "—Let me think about it—see can we afford the ticket for the jerk."

"Bill the State guys—it's their interview," Nardone said.

"Another good idea!" Leahy said. "How come you weren't so smart up in the Bronx today? —Don't think that one has slipped my mind, just because I didn't make a big deal out of it. It hasn't slipped my mind. —Which brings up somethin' else. . . ." He riffled through the papers on his desk, plump hands shuttling as an experienced gambler shuffled cards—found what he wanted, and passed it over to Ellie. "—This guy wasn't on that other sheet; this is new shit."

"Is this you wanting this, Lieutenant?"

"No, Klein," Leahy said, "it's Anderson. Upstairs wants this stuff checked out. You want to argue with me? —Go argue with them."

"Tommy, you're not going to believe this one—it's an Internal guy suspected of Observing."

"Give me a break."

"No—Observing. The cop has a telescope set up on his apartment-house roof on Grand Concourse—two complaints from people in the building directly across the Concourse, that he's peeping. Man—one of the complaints—came across the street, went up to the roof of this cop's apartment building, says he caught him with the scope pointed across the street aimed at his bedroom."

"Leahy—is this a joke, or what?"

"I'll tell you what it *is,* Tommy—it's exactly what you fuckin' deserve. It's penance, is what it *is.* —Now, why don't you two prima donnas forget about your big homicide case for the rest of this shift, get your asses back up to the Bronx—and this time, do what you're supposed to do."

"Listen to this," Ellie said, reading. " 'Complainant confronted Officer Gershon, stated his accusation—and was thereupon threatened with arrest by Officer Gershon on a charge of Public Display, Lewd Conduct, and Sodomy—the officer stating he had been gathering evidence of several acts of public sodomy committed by complainant on the bedroom balcony of his apartment."

"Well," Nardone said, "I got to admit that's not too bad. —That's a pretty good one. We got to waste time, that's a good one to do it."

" 'An assault and battery occurred.' "

"I'll bet," Nardone said. "Two assaults—two batteries."

"So," Leahy said, "get out of my office and go to work."

" 'Car responded—' "

"Go investigate it," Leahy said, "—I got work to do."

Nardone turned at the door. "What's new on Morris?"

"There's nothin' new on Classman," Leahy said, "—except his funeral is up in Woodlawn tomorrow, five o'clock. They're puttin' his mother and him in together." The fat man began to stack reports from the left side of his desk to the right. "They picked up some prints—an old lady, a friend of his mother's—an' a black lady nursed her, some others there's no records of at all."

"No record of at all?" Ellie said.

"I notice," Nardone said, "they got to the Bureau for a fast report on *those* prints—right?"

"Come on," Leahy said, "we're talkin' about a cop-killin' here. For that, even those assholes work a little faster. —An' it doesn't make any difference, anyway. It was just rotten luck, that's all. They'll get those guys. Assholes like that—killed a cop—they'll get drunk, they'll get stoned and shoot their mouths off, one of their ladies'll give us a call and turn 'em for a hundred bucks. —Don't worry about that case—worry about the astronomer on Grand Concourse."

"I don't think he's going to make trouble about this morning," Ellie said. Nardone steering the bronze Ford back uptown, going up Third. This was the beginning of real rush-hour traffic, impatient, furious, hustling away uptown under a reddening sun.

"He isn't goin' to do shit," Nardone said. "A good commander would have had us on charges right there. —*They made us, so they drove away*. . . . You think a real commander would have stood still for that?"

"Jesus, Tommy—then I'm glad Leahy's not so good."

"He's not a bad guy—just too easy. The guy does not have what it takes—"

"Tommy—do you *want* to get your ass in a sling because of what happened up there? —If you feel that goddamn bad about it, will you remember it's my ass in a sling, too? You did not do anything so *awful*. —Is he the first crook you ever knew on the Force?"

"That's not the point, El—"

"Yes it is—it *is* the point!"

"O.K. Year I went on the cops, there *was* a lot of guys takin'. But, now—he just surprised me, you know? The Pauly I knew, he wouldn't have done that . . . begged me like that."

"So? —It wasn't the worse thing you ever saw, was it? It was just an upsetting thing. . . ." She watched a group of black boys walking behind an old lady down the block between 103rd and 104th streets. The old woman, her ankles swollen over the edges of her shoes, was carrying a small net bag of groceries, a shiny black patent-leather purse. The boys caught up to her . . . then passed her, ambling on their way. "—All you're telling me, Tommy, is that when you knew Donaher, you didn't know the guy as well as you thought. Let me tell you, that's no reason to go looking to get up on charges for something like that. —That's just crazy. Maybe he was a nice guy—and a taker. Friends don't have to be perfect, Tommy."

Ellie looked over, saw Nardone watching his side of the avenue, thinking about it.

"You going all the way up on the East Side?"

"Yeah."

While they rode up the Concourse, Ellie checked the building numbers on her side for the address.

"Got another two, three blocks," she said. "I wish we could have caught this guy outside—before he got up to his place. This way, there's his wife . . . and he's got kids."

"How many kids?"

"Two kids. Boys. —It's late; they'll be home from school."

"We'll ask him to step out, that's all. Business."

"Well, I hope to hell he steps," Ellie said. "It's been a long day."

"Yeah—and I was a pain in the ass, right?"

"No, you weren't, Tommy."

"I could have got you in bad trouble," Nardone said.

"There we go," Ellie said. "It's that one—that building."

"No place. —I'm goin' to park up the block. We can walk back."

"Let's see if we can get him to come outside the apartment. —Either that, or we could have a mess."

Mrs. Gershon answered the bell. She was a tall woman with a heart-shaped face, long, graying red hair twisted into a French knot at the back of her neck. She wore glasses and an old-fashioned blue A-line dress. —The sheet had said she taught junior high. Mrs. Gershon looked at Ellie, then Nardone, then called, "Harry! —Two officers here to see you!" She smiled at Ellie. "Come in."

Inside the apartment, a boy called, "Pop!"

"No, thanks," Ellie said. "We don't have time. —We just need a quick word with Harry."

"You're sure? —You wouldn't like some coffee? I baked some crumb cake—and despite what the boys say, it isn't bad."

"Sounds great," Nardone said, "and I'd say the kids are wrong—but we just don't have the time, Mrs. Gershon."

"What is it, Lil?" Harry Gershon, in white sports shirt and tan slacks, looked younger than his wife, and was slightly shorter. He was a handsome man, thin, strong-nosed, deeply tanned—his face lined, weather-marked just enough for character. He had light gray eyes, and examined Ellie and Nardone, and identified them, with the same unconcern his wife had shown.

"You guys from this district?" he said, and motioned them in with his head. "—Come on in."

"They don't want to try the crumb cake, Harry."

"Then they can't be smart cops," Gershon said, "whoever they are." He beckoned. "—Come in!"

"No, Harry, we haven't got time—we got to get goin'," Nardone said. "This is Officer Klein—my name's Nardone."

"O.K.," Gershon said. "Be back in a minute, honey." He came out into the hall. "Come on—I'll show you my observatory. . . ."

"Harry . . . don't be gone an hour, O.K.?" His wife smiled at Ellie and Nardone. "If you're in a hurry, don't let him start with the stars. We got that telescope for the kids—and who uses it?"

"Right . . . right. Be back in a few minutes, honey." He led the way down the corridor. "Come on—we'll use the fire stairs. That elevator this time of day—we'll be waiting forever."

He led them through the fire door at the end of the hall, and on up the stairs. "Just a couple of flights."

"We're from downtown, Harry," Nardone said, as they climbed.

"I know where you're from," Gershon said, "—and it's no big deal." He led up the second flight. "—You're up here on the peeping thing—right?"

"That's right," Ellie said, relieved that Gershon didn't sound like the begging type. "A complaint's been filed—and a preliminary."

"That fuck," Gershon said, then went up the last flight of stairs fast, two at a time, shoved open the heavy door at the top, and was out onto the roof. Ellie climbed fast behind him (she didn't like the idea of Gershon being up there alone)—and Nardone took three-riser strides up past her, and through the door.

Gershon, no longer in a hurry, was waiting for them,

standing on a very wide, flat prairie of roofing tar, its pebbled surface—petroleum black at first sight—faintly iridescent on change of view. He threw a long, long shadow from the setting sun. "What did you think—I was going to do a Brody?" He turned and walked across the roof, heading for the upwelling roar of Concourse traffic.

"Here you go," he said. A considerable telescope—a large white-barreled instrument with a complicated eyepiece—was perched on a heavy tripod just back from the six-course brick wall bordering the roof edge. The barrel of the scope was padlocked to the tripod. The tripod was chained to a vent pipe sticking up out of the roof five feet away.

"If I didn't lock the son-of-a-bitch up," Gershon said, "—there are some assholes in this building would rip it off for money to recarpet. As it is, I can't have it out here in any kind of bad weather. —Too hot—too cold. Rain." He stroked the instrument's white barrel, touched a bright steel knob at the top of the tripod. "It's a delicate thing. I shouldn't have it out here all day today—heat's no good for it, affects the sealing stuff around the lenses. I keep the lens caps on, but that doesn't have anything to do with the heat. I'm figuring on putting a shelter up here. —The landlord and me are going around and around on that little question."

"Well, it's nice," Ellie said. "—It's a beautiful instrument."

"You're looking at just about eight hundred dollars worth of glass. —Lenses are what cost."

"Not eight hundred for the whole thing, though?"

"Hell, no. Try one thousand, two."

"Can you get a good look at a planet with this—I mean really see somethin'?" Nardone said.

"Damn if I know—I guess you could."

"You don't use it to look at stars?" Ellie said.

"You kidding me?" Gershon said. "I look at pussy. —If you'll pardon my French."

"Wait a minute," Ellie said. "—You're telling us you use this to peep over there at women across the street?"

"Across the *street*? Honey—this thing brings them in from a quarter mile! Here . . ." Gershon busied himself at the telescope, pulled the lens caps off, unlocked the padlock holding the instrument's barrel to the tripod—then swung the long tube around to cover an apartment building more than halfway down the block on the other side of the Concourse.

Nardone winked at Ellie as Gershon bent over his fine eyepiece—fiddled with adjustments here and there, then slowly rose on his toes to center his focus perfectly on some distant object. —Then he briskly stood up, twisted a screw knob to hold his field, and gestured Ellie to the eyepiece. "I got these ladies timed out pretty good," he said. "This one comes home from work—she always does her exercises—except on weekends. I don't know where she goes, weekends."

Ellie, in a wavering circular world of bright, uncertain light, followed a round of lucent white within the field, pressing her eye to the eyepiece cup—but saw no woman just home from work. "I don't see anything," she said.

"You wear glasses?"

"No—I don't."

Gershon came up and gently pushed her away from his machine, bent to the eyepiece, and grunted. Then made a slight adjustment. "Everybody's eye is a little bit different," he said. "O.K."—straightened up and stood away.

Ellie bent to the view again—saw her white, bright disk, saw it slowly roll away, as if in introduction, and then (faintly trembling in her view) a pretty girl, naked, half facing her—slightly fat, tanned to coffee brown, gleaming with sweat and oil, her hair wrapped in a white towel—standing exercising in a deeply rhythmic way (apparently to music). Her nudity occasionally obscured by the narrow, horizontal white pipes of the side of her balcony rail, she was doing stretches—and, as she swept down spread-legged to reach between her knees, then straightened, arched, arms up, to lean far back, straining at that posture till her breasts nearly disappeared, flattened into the flexed muscle of her chest, Ellie saw the soaked black chevron at her crotch.

"Isn't she a beauty?" Gershon said. "—No light areas on her. Tanned all over. Always tans nude."

"Yes," Ellie said, straightening up, "—she's very pretty."

"Trying to exercise that baby fat off," Gershon said. "It's just ridiculous. She's perfect, now."

"Are you two kiddin' me, or what?" Nardone came to bend over the eyepiece.

"That adjusted right for you?" Gershon said.

"Son-of-a-bitch . . . no wonder we got so many rapes!"

"Isn't she pretty, Tommy?"

Nardone straightened up, slightly flushed. "She's makin' a goddamned spectacle of herself."

"Well," Gershon said, "—you have to remember, nobody can see her but me."

"Man," Nardone said, "—don't you realize you're in trouble here? You're committin' an offense here?"

"Hell, yes," Gershon said. "—You don't know my captain. I'm definitely going on a Departmental from that fucker's complaint."

"Then what are you doing still up here on this roof?" Ellie said. "You're making all kinds of admissions . . . !"

"Not in that hearing, I'm not," Gershon said. "Take a look at this one . . ." and bent to his eyepiece.

"Will you cut that shit out!" Nardone said, "—or this is goin' on our report!"

"Oh . . ." Gershon said, swinging the telescope around to point more directly across the street, "—I don't figure you guys want to spend a couple afternoons at the hearing, listening to a lot of bullshit. I figure you're just going to file a we-saw-the-telescope-but-subject-denied, and go on about your business. If you don't—if you want to be assholes about it—I'll just deny on the machine, and say you solicited some cash. I have a philosophy—somebody screws you—you screw them, too." He found his view, bent to the eyepiece again, and fiddled. "—Of course, this is nothing to nighttime. I just get a couple of them late afternoon like this. Evening shift. —At night, this is spectacular, I'm telling you."

"Let me tell you," Nardone said. "You got anything more to say threatenin' us, sayin' we solicited—and I will throw that fuckin' thing right off the roof, and we'll take your ass downtown under arrest."

Gershon looked up, smiling. "Well," he said, "—seeing you're such a tough guy, I'll get off the subject."

"Doesn't your wife object to this?" Ellie said. "—Does she know about it?"

Gershon bent again to his eyepiece. "This is a tough

one; sometimes she doesn't come out at all. . . . Has to be a nice sunny day." He was quiet for a few moments, concentrating. "—My wife . . . let me tell you about my wife. First place, I don't know what my wife knows. —You think I'm so stupid I'm going to ask a woman what she knows? Second place—I come down off this roof some nights, come down early, and we send the boys to their cousins . . . to a movie . . . and we have the best time two people can have together. You think that girl over there was pretty—you ought to see my Lillian, she gets excited." He straightened up. "—That's got it. It's on her place—she's not out yet. You know—I figure, things so beautiful, so really special, you know?—It seems like a waste not to pay some attention. I understand there's a privacy problem. Believe me, I understand that very well—that a woman needs some privacy, needs to be left alone, you know. And the prettier they are, I figure they need the privacy even more—"

"Gershon—you are out of your mind!" Ellie said. "—You're really sick, you know? I mean it."

"Sure, you think that, because you're a woman. You just don't understand—you have no understanding of the hunger, the hunger for physical beauty! The stuff women just walk around with like it was nothing at all." He smiled at Ellie. "I guess it's sort of a burden to you, isn't it?—You're a pretty woman—don't you have any idea what I'm talking about?"

"I know what you're talking about," Ellie said. "—And people have rights you're *not* talking about. Women have rights for you to leave them the fuck alone—and not use that thing on them when they think they're by themselves."

"In short," Nardone said, "—you're actin' like a friggin' pervert, and you're headin' for a shit-load of trouble."

"Could be," Gershon said. "—I won't be the first guy got in trouble going crazy over beauty, not being able to get enough of it—and besides, I got some astronomy books out of the library. By the time that hearing comes around, I'm going to know a hell of a lot of astronomy—I'm going to snow those guys with orbits and moons of Jupiter and phases and parsecs till it's coming out their asses. They'll think I'm a weirdo, all right—but not a peeper."

"Very cute," Nardone said, "—and you intend keepin' doin' this shit up here?"

Gershon sighed. "I guess not. I guess I won't be able to.—Couldn't take another complaint." He bent to check the eyepiece. "You know," he said as he fiddled, "—that fucker Stillman that started this mess . . . you should have seen that jerk with his wife over there. His wife is a beautiful girl . . . long light brown hair . . . legs up to here. A goddess could look like that and be very happy. Incredible you think a girl like that just walks around this huge stinking city—and nobody notices. And here comes this loudmouth making a fucking mess.—You should see what he does, trying to make love to that girl. It's just a shame. It's such a *waste.* Guy has a regular dick—excuse my French, Klein—but he just doesn't know what to do with it! He doesn't even know how to please her—you can see it in her face, she's puzzled. '—What the hell is going on?' is what she's thinking." He was silent, attentive to the eyepiece. "Ah," he said, "I was worried this one wouldn't come out—but here she comes. She's black . . . a skinny little sweetheart. Little darling . . . Whoops, she went back in again! It's like she's made out of licorice—you know, so smooth and nice; she just comes out and reads—wears shorts and a little halter, that's it. I sort of keep her company, you know; never saw a guy over there, no lady, either. —All that prettiness, just wasted."

"We saw the telescope—and he denied."

"Right," Nardone said.

The bronze Ford (radio muttering occasional calls) was rolling downtown under sunset colors glowing over Broadway, flame orange, flamingo pinks flooding down between the buildings to fill the street. Ellie thought how such colors might be mixed on a palette. —The flamingo pink was very difficult. Too difficult. She was tired, her legs aching a little behind her knees.

"Some days are long days, and some go like lightning."

"This was a long one," Nardone said. "—But keep that lady in mind—Margolies. We'll give her a week, then we'll look her up again—see if she's rememberin' better."

"O.K."

"Goin' up to Connecticut tomorrow?"

"Yes—I'll go up in the morning, unless you want me to come in, enter the reports."

"I can do that shit myself."

"Tommy . . ."

"I know, I know. —I'll enter it right. 'Subject with another Subject, unidentified, possibly observing officers Klein and Nardone at location, left scene without commitment.' —And then we got, 'Observed telescope—Subject denied. . . .' " He blew his horn at a Toyota sedan moving slowly in front of them. "—Why a guy would drive in this city, and not have any friggin' notion of what he's doin' . . . Yeah, we had a big day, today. We straightened this town out. . . ."

"Maybe Leahy was right about the pin board," Ellie said. "—It would keep things together for us on the case. We put stuff on the computer, and it just gets lost unless we keep notebooks anyway—"

"O.K.—Could be a help. I'll go down, see if I can get a big one out of supply. Little one's no good—it gets to be a mess you can't find anything. . . . Prints said the Bureau held them up, by the way. Said all fingerprint reports should be in tomorrow."

"Bullshit."

"Now you got it."

"Do those guys need help?" Ellie said.

A patrol car was double-parked on the right side of the avenue, the two officers out and standing on the sidewalk, one of them talking with a heavyset middle-aged woman wearing what looked like a baseball uniform. A young white man with a dirty blond ponytail was sitting on the curb near them, his head in his hands.

"They don't need help," Nardone said. "—They already sent for a pickup car for that guy, probably. Guy looks like he was hurt."

He pulled up anyway, and Ellie rolled her window down, dug in her purse for her shield, and held it up as one of the officers turned to look at them.

The cop, a freckled young woman with big hips made bigger by her equipment belt, came over to the Ford. "No problem," she said. She had a stony Irish voice . . . sounded like the girls Ellie had grown up with. Gloria.

—She looked a little like Gloria Rooney, too. "—Got a jerk here tried to rip this lady off in the street." The freckled girl smiled. She was a plain, wide-faced young woman, but she had beautiful, even teeth. "He took a try—an' she hit him with a bat.—Comin' in from playin' softball in the park."

"Handy," Nardone said from behind the wheel.

"Somebody's coming for him?" Ellie said.

"Oh, yeah. We got him for a knife, too. —She gave him a hell of a whack. She was scared she killed him. When we got here, he was lyin' in the gutter on some dog turds. . . ."

The young woman seemed gleeful, pleased to be what and where she was. She had a wedding ring, and an engagement ring with a tiny stone together on her sturdy third finger—the finger as freckled as her face.

"Well—take it easy," Ellie said. The young man sitting on the curb looked sick. There was no blood on his face, but his skin was white as vanilla ice cream.

Nardone pulled away into the traffic, and they rolled past a small group of onlookers standing staring at the young man, the two cops, and the woman in the red-and-white softball uniform. She had *Riverside* stitched across the front of her uniform in large red letters.

"That was a good one," Ellie said.

"One of the best . . . playin' softball. . . . Couldn't that moron see she was carryin' a bat? What the hell these guys *think* about . . ."

As they slowed for the next red light, Ellie, not realizing she'd heard their call code till she'd reached down and picked up the mike, responded. They didn't get many car calls.

"603 Teacup tango," the dispatcher said, "you have a report-to-scene request, 139th Street and St. Ann's Avenue. Repeat 139th Street and St. Ann's Avenue."

Ellie acknowledged.

"What now?" Nardone said, and wheeled a left turn on Seventy-fourth Street, preparatory to another left uptown.

They arrived with night—only the western sky still streaked with sunset as Nardone pulled into a fierce zone of light behind a rumbling generator truck, the last in a line of Department vehicles parked at the curb along a long vacant lot, hillocked with rubble, the roasted ruin of a six-story building rising behind it. Phantoms, murmuring, calling, running through the surrounding dark, watched from across the avenue, where streetlights had been stoned or shot out. A white T-shirt here and there was revealed in reflection from the police work lights strung along the lot, and a distant pair of light-colored socks scissoring along, their owner almost invisible above them.

Autumn hadn't reached this section yet. Here, the Bronx still baked in summer, smelling of acres of dry weeds, spilled garbage, burned wood.

Ellie and Nardone got out of the Ford, and were locking it, when a man walked up behind Ellie in silhouette out of a softly sizzling halation of arc light.

"It's the homicide aces," Keneally said.

"What's goin' on, Kenny?" Nardone said.

"I asked Ben to put in a call to you guys—figured you might want to see one of the people put Classman away." He strolled out of silhouette into the glare of light. He was wearing another summer suit with a big checked pattern. This one was lighter brown, closer to burnt orange. "—Come on, I'm goin' to give you the tour, but keep it in mind you're only in on a pass. —Me, too. This is Upper East Division's shit, strictly Bronx South."

He turned to lead the way across a tangle of electric cable, then off the cracked, weed-grown sidewalk and out into the arc-lit lot, climbing carefully across the first rise of collapsed masonry, splintered wood, mounded broken bricks. A line of police officers, some in uniform, some plainclothes, was combing slowly across an area almost the size of a football field, each man casting several shifting shadows, variously dark, under the confluent beams of area lights, searchlights, and spots.

"Looks like they're puttin' out for this one," Nardone said.

"Those assholes shouldn't have killed a cop," Keneally said.

"Hey—Nardone! *Nardone!*" A tall bald man (late fifties, early sixties, scalp reflective under the lights), his gold shield pinned to his jacket lapel. "—What in the world is a Headquarter's troglodyte doing out so late—and uptown?" The detective trudged over the rubble as Nardone turned to meet him.

"Fancy company," Keneally said, walking on. "—I could drop dead before Connors would come over, talk to me."

"They arrested the perp here? —Or is he dead?" Ellie said, and stumbled slightly over a concrete shelf among the rubble—a ledge of foundation . . . perhaps the sill of some entranceway.

Keneally dropped back beside her, and took hold of her right arm above the elbow in a supporting grip, as if he were her husband, or a lover. Ellie didn't like the touch of his hand on her—though Keneally's grip, in contradiction to his bulky, red-faced, heated look, was relaxed and gentle—but didn't want to hurt his feelings by pulling away.

"He's dead, all right," Keneally said. "—Gotta be the guy Classman put a slug in; he's got a hole in him through an' through, looks like a thirty-eight." Keneally, with his free hand, patted his beer belly low on the right side. "—Looks like his buddies didn't want him goin' to no hospital. Brought him up here this mornin'—and threw him off the roof. Guy's been cookin' in the sun all day."

After a few more steps, Ellie said, "I'm O.K.," and was relieved when Keneally let go of her arm. She heard Nardone's heavy, hasty stride behind them, trampling loose bricks aside, catching up.

"You heard what this is?"

"Yes," Ellie said, and to Keneally, "Anybody know this guy—the dead guy?"

"Yeah," Keneally said. "Brabauer knew him—knew his brother, anyway." He paused to shove a roll of rusted wire aside with his foot. "Will you look at all this shit? —Guy's brother is a bad guy. Bobby Chavez. He's away right now—goin' to stay away maybe another ten years up in Ossining."

"What's this one? What's his name?" Nardone said. They'd come to the side of the ruined building, and Keneally, staggering like a drunk, picked his way over the uneven rubble along the windowless, fire-stained brick wall—the surface sprayed, here and there, with huge, cursive, incomprehensible phrases—in white paint, high—in yellow paint, low. He was heading toward a group of men standing in a white-ribboned enclosure farther along.

"Jesus Chavez, Brabauer says," Keneally said, "—a junkie, Brabauer says. —They got the TV set, too. The assholes left it inside the building, in the back." He forged on toward the ribboned fold.

The glaring lights, their electric buzz, the swift haze of insects circling in their radiance, the wide field so illuminated—and this particular play occurring before her in a cluster of intent males—reminded Ellie powerfully of football nights in high school, when she and her friends, in short white pleated skirts, white boots, and Schuyler High's cardinal-red tops, strutted, leaped, and cheered, playing princesses of the night.

She and Keneally stopped at the ribbon, but Nardone ducked under and lifted it higher for her to follow him. She went through, but Keneally stayed behind. —As Ellie straightened up, she saw Anderson among the other officers, and saw him glance up to see her and Nardone. She thought he looked annoyed, but then he smiled at her, caught Nardone's eye, and beckoned them both over.

"That's Carey, over there," Nardone said, indicating with a movement of his head a short, stout, mustached black man two men down from Anderson. Inspector Carey had dual reputations in the Department—one earned by killing a man who'd just shot another officer to death (and who shot Carey, too, before dying, leaving that young officer with a smashed hip to plague him all his days)—the other, less enviable, for functioning now as a hatchet man under the Deputy Commissioner for Administration, sallying out into the field to monitor precinct captains at their work—and, in more than one instance, to replace them peremptorily.

To this short, stout officer, all present were deferring as they stood in a casual loose-linked circle around a dead man.

Jesús Chávez seemed to have been a pleasant person—even now, with both eyes nearly closed, his dirty shirt, his crumpled chinos burst open as if the air had roughly molested him in flight, had determined to expose his brown, hairless chest, his soft paunch (a lighter brown), and the small black pit, twin to his navel, dappled with dry blood and located a few inches to the right of it—even now, his expression was quizzical, relaxed, and easy.

His front was fine—only his back, the back of his legs, the back of his head, had had swiftly to conform to the ruined concrete, the bricks beneath him.

He hadn't been a young man, even on the roof.

An M.I.'s man was kneeling beside the corpse, had a worn and dirty bandage (Chávez') laid out, and a kit still open before him—wads of gauze, sponges, small vials.

"They can take him off," one of the detectives said. "We're done with him. —Pictures all done, Toby?"

Toby, a tall detective with a mournful face, nodded, and said, "Yes."

"Hey," Nardone said, amid these senior figures, "—what the hell was the guy doin' up here?"

"His friend or friends brought him up here, Tommy," Captain Anderson said, inviting no continuation. Inspector Carey, two men down, had left off talking to his neighbor to listen.

"What the hell for?" Nardone said. "—I mean what the hell did they tell the guy?" Ellie reached out and tugged his sleeve.

"What did they *tell* the guy?" The tall detective, Toby. "—They told him they were bringin' him up to some hincty spic doctor was goin' to fix him up just fine. —That's what they told this fucker."

"You step out of a car around here with some meatballs killed a cop with you—you believe you're goin' to a doctor?" Nardone said. "You believe that? —I sure as shit wouldn't believe it."

"Come on, Tommy," Ellie said—as quietly as she could, and still be sure he heard her.

"Could be they didn't give him the option—just brought him up. . . ." Another detective, this man very senior, a man in his early sixties.

"I guess that could be," Nardone said. "They could have hauled him up here. But more likely, if it wasn't for him bein' shot, injured that way—I'd figure maybe they got him up here to deal. . . ."

A third officer listening, also an older man, said to a companion, "What's *this* shit . . . ?"

"Are you on District Homicide or what?" the very senior detective said.

"No, I'm not," Nardone said, and the detective turned away to talk with another.

"Nardone . . . Klein," Captain Anderson said. "—Let me have a word with you. . . ." And stepped back a few steps to wait for them in some seclusion against the strand of white ribbon.

"You are here," he said, "—and why you're here, I really don't know—but you two are here on a pass. You understand me?"

"Yes, sir," Ellie said.

"Samuelson was up here before—now you two are up here—and enough is enough. These officers don't require any advice whatsoever from you, Nardone. Is that really clear to you? —Is that clear to you both?" He waited for a reply, so Ellie said, "Yes, sir."

"I appreciate your concern—the Squad's concern that Classman's killers get what's coming to them. And, believe me, they will. But the investigation is none of your business. —O.K.? You understand me?"

"Yes, sir," Ellie said.

"Now, why don't you two get back to work," Anderson said. "—I believe you people have some things to do. . . ."

Keneally was waiting for them a few yards beyond the ribbon, his hands in his trouser pockets. "—Can't I take you fuckin' guys anywhere? You people are poison! You"—to Nardone—"you got a mouth on you, Tommy, that's right out of this world. You know the guys you were bullshittin' to, back there? Any one of those guys could turn you into a fuckin' meter maid with one report." Keneally shook his head. "—What a pair you two are. . . . You two are one of a kind. . . ."

"How about shovin' it, Kenny?" Nardone said, amiably enough, and set off trudging along the building wall, over rubble and drifts of time-laundered garbage tossed down from high windows long ago, when the building and block swarmed with noisy life. "Let's go in here—take a look."

Ellie—almost alone in the tram as it swept up in moonlight, humming high over the river, rocking slightly as it rode its cable—was able still to smell the breath of the ruined building on her clothes, odors of dank and stinking corridors, rooms, and stairways (pitch black where no police lights shone, lit there only by Keneally's tiny pencil flash), their walls ripped and smashed as if by bulky animals raging blind. —The building had reminded her of the building in the fire, and made her nervous, so that Nardone and Keneally, sensing it, had climbed closer to her on the stairs, walked alongside through endless butchered corridors, many written on along their walls, painted with names, swastikas, yard-long curved knives, blue stars, huge initials as elaborately doubled and shaded as any on subway cars, and—these revealed only for an instant, Keneally flicking the slight light aside—outlined naked girls half a wall high, their knees spread wide, their gaping vulvas in fine detail, their faces a single swift and empty circle.

They had, after some time, found the room where Classman's TV had been discovered. Two patrolmen were there on hands and knees, searching by work light for anything else. . . .

Ellie stood by a tram window, aching behind her knees, and searched the black water beneath for the moon's reflection. She couldn't find it—as if the river (the estuary) had tugged the reflection underwater to join the bony wreckage of small ships, tugs and barges, the tatters of long-dead gangsters streaming slowly above rotting chunks of cement. She thought of a nighttime painting, to match the day's—the river by night, in the night, throughout the night, carrying dark ships on darker tides—the moonlight threading through in zinc white and silver, streams of light flowing through and under wider streams of darkness. The moon rolling above, drinking its own light . . . endlessly drunk with its light, giving none of it to the surface of the river. Giving light only to the streams beneath . . . like veins of silver through a mine of coal.

Philip Murtagh had once told Ellie, in his life class at the Art Students League long ago, "You have a nice feeling for color, Miss Whatever-Your-Name-Is—but you can't draw worth a damn." Ellie, fresh down from Sarah Lawrence, waiting tables at Sorrento, had been unable to disbelieve him.

She took the bus from the tram station for its short, circling ride—only three other people on it—and got off at her stop, in front of the travel agency.

Mayo didn't meet her at her apartment door. Closing it behind her, locking it, Ellie heard regular, spaced, soft thumpings from the bedroom, as if two very gentle people were making love. She put her purse down beside the hall phone, went into the bedroom, turned on the light, and saw the Siamese at his infrequent game of leaping from the floor up onto the bed, scratching hastily once or twice at an already damaged and mended place on the blue bedspread . . . whirling and leaping with a thump down to the floor—then jumping back up on the bed at once to scratch again at that particular spot, only for an instant. Then down to the floor again. . . .

"Pussy smells pussy," Clara had said of this performance—adding that Mayo, male though neutered, felt something missing, scented nearly that something in the female odor on the sheets. —The Romans, Clara had said in her humming voice—standing at the time in her bathrobe beside Ellie at the bedroom door—had been able to train leopards to have sex with women captives, criminals, Christians. The women—she said—sometimes spoiled for human intercourse, thereafter. Haunting the cages . . . filthy . . . smeared with periodical blood. Prostituting themselves to the trainers to be allowed nights in the narrow, pitch-black, stinking dens.—To lie on their backs on wet stone paving in the dark, anticipatory, their legs up, up and back, spread wide to pose themselves properly for the great restless padding cats, smelling, like them, of piss and blood. —Or, crouched on all fours in the other fashion, their faces pressed down amid ruined meat, feeling first in darkness the hot breath at their presented buttocks—then, if he were pleased, the rough and painful surface of his tongue, abrading, cleaning their asses, their swollen, troubled sexes, preparatory to a sudden and shocking mount (great claws barely extended, lightly, lightly hooking at their ribs . . . a narrow roiling weight as dense as bronze, fur-cushioned, bearing upon their backs) from which pain and pleasure came tearing themselves apart, and later joined together.

Roman men and women would pay money, Clara said

at the time, lightly stroking the back of Ellie's neck as they watched the Siamese . . . would pay money to come down to those cellars beneath the arena, late at night (after parties, perhaps) to stand in the dark, masturbating, listening to the cries of any such woman as the beast seized upon her, and her beast seized upon itself.

Clara had spanked Ellie the night she told that story, and Ellie—though enraged the day after—had then, hot, lain still, taken her spanking, and done Clara favors afterward. . . .

She plucked Mayo off the bed, took him—hanging suspended from her hand, inanimate, staring at nothing as he was carried by—and dropped him in the hall, where he marched away toward the kitchen, commencing to cry for his dinner.

Ellie undressed, stood naked at her closet for a while, considering what to wear in the morning—it would have to do for Connecticut, then for Classman's funeral in the afternoon—and decided on a dark blue suit, blue shoes, white blouse, blue tie. —Her civilian uniform, she thought of it. She made sure she had one blouse out and clean—the other, she knew, was at the dry cleaners—and thought of buying a third, maybe on Wednesday, if she could get off early enough for shopping. A blouse, and another skirt. —If they didn't get more cases loaded on. *—I believe you people have some things to do. . . .* Anderson, unpleasant—looking even more handsome, angry.

What if she hadn't gotten up and gone out of the office that time he'd touched her cheek? What then? Ellie thought of him standing beside her chair, after she stayed still while he stroked her—standing, and reaching down very casually to unzip himself, to reach in and open his underwear, tug himself out, show himself—to see what she would do.

Ellie's breasts were tender when she touched them, walking to the bathroom; she thought her period might be coming a day or two early—she felt a slight discomfort, a mild full ache under her belly. Felt tired. Too tired for a bath. She ran the shower, dialed the water only lukewarm, and stepped under the near needle spray, turning slowly left, then right, her arms up to let it lave her, almost stinging at her underarms, her nipples.

She soaped quickly, rinsed—not making the water hotter—then wet her hair, soaked it, bent to pick up her shampoo (Seedling Pine), squirted a little into her palm, and massaged it into her hair with both hands, content under the hissing water, under the obedient attentions of her fingers.

Ellie shampooed twice, and rinsed very thoroughly, wringing her long blond hair out, stripping the water from the length of it through gentle fists. She dried herself, then gathered her hair up under her towel before stepping out onto the bathroom carpet, picking up her dryer at the side of the sink. Standing naked at her mirror, watching herself with no affection, Ellie found her big red comb in the top drawer under the counter, unwrapped the towel, and commenced to dry her hair, absorbed by the soft roar of the dryer, the repetitive motions of her right arm as she combed and combed fine fluttering white-blond under its heated breath. Could see her scalp occasionally, in swift pale pink lines as her hair wafted this way and that, lifted, and fell over. More delicate hair than it had been, easier to break . . . split ends. No longer a girl's careless, shining, supple fur.

Ellie supposed if she didn't have a child soon—she wouldn't have one at all.

Her hair finally dry, five small drops of baby oil gently brushed into it, Ellie sat and shat a small, brown, rough-skinned snake into the toilet bowl, wiped, then flushed it away, stood, and washed her hands.

She picked her warm maroon winter bathrobe from the bedroom closet, then went to the hall, moved the thermostat to extra-cool—to enjoy being cozy in coolness—and checked her answering machine. There were three calls—one from her dentist's office about a nearly due appointment for cleaning; one from a woman named Janet Ahearn, a friend of Clara's whom Ellie'd met a few times; and one from Lennie Spears—"Just checking up on you, honey. . . . You O.K.?"

"Thanks a lot," she said to his voice, "—you son-of-a-bitch."

Ellie stood leaning against the wall—listening to Mayo complaining in the kitchen—and called her mother.

Gordon answered, and Ellie was nice to him, asked

how the real estate business was going in Buffalo, asked if he was taking his insulin. —Business was not bad at all, he said, and he hoped to go on oral, though his doctor, Sonnenburg, was skeptical.

Ellie's mother came on the phone in her guarded way, as if she spoke into the mouthpiece at a slant. Clara had spoken to Ellie's mother several times, and at length, very patient with the older woman's complaints, avoidances, irrelevancies. "—Harriet and I understand each other very well," Clara said, after one such phone call. "She knows I'm shtupping her daughter—and she doesn't give a damn. With age, we ladies do turn into bags of shit, don't we?"

Ellie's mother told her what the mayor of Buffalo had said on TV about the welfare problem in the city. —That it had to be dealt with. "—And none too soon," Ellie's mother said. "That unemployment, too. They just use it to strike and bite the hand that feeds them"—forgetting, apparently, those distant days when, the young wife of a union carpenter occasionally unemployed, she had found such assistance handy. This was, for Ellie, like listening to a stranger who had come to inhabit her mother's body—that vigorous, sexual, amusing and untrustworthy young woman had been replaced by a caricature, aging, shriveled, and stupid.

Harriet—her voice still slightly distant—asked about the weather in New York, mentioned that Buffalo was already becoming cool, the leaves turning yellow, the price of fuel oil climbing thanks to that greaseball in Albany.

"I'm working on an interesting case," Ellie said.

"Well, it's about time," her mother said. "I suppose New York is full of interesting cases. Probably a new one every minute. —You couldn't pay me to live in that place. The last time I came in"—it had been three years before—"I thought I was in Timbuktu or something. I didn't see a white face from Fifty-fifth Street down Broadway. You couldn't pay me enough to live there. . . ."

They talked about Gordon's diabetes. "Sonnenburg says they might have to cut off his foot . . . not right away, but someday. —They say Jews are good doctors, but you better be ready to pay through the nose. Be happy to cut poor Gordy in pieces as long as he got his money.—Did Gordy give you that stuff about going on oral?"

"He mentioned that he wanted to—"

"Baloney—that's all that is! That's just baloney. You know he still doesn't like giving himself that shot? A grown man more than sixty years old? He wanted me to do it. I said, 'Oh-no! If something goes wrong, who's goin' to get in trouble? —Not me.' "

"It's probably just as well," Ellie said, wishing she'd called her mother on the bedroom extension. She was tired of standing.

"You better believe that," her mother said. "It's his diabetes, and he can take care of it better than I can. I'm the one that runs this house—which is the biggest white elephant in the world, and an unbelievable waste of money. I measure out his meals—well, you saw what a pain that is. I do what I'm supposed to do, and that's all I do. The only advice I've got to give you is, if you ever do get married again—which I guess you won't, now—then don't marry a man with bad health. I love Gordy and all that—but he's heading to be an invalid, and what am I supposed to do, then?"

"I think you take pretty good care of him, now," Ellie said.

"I take wonderful care of him. I think he could use a better doctor. Ellen Cord—you never met her—has some sugar and she goes to a wonderful young doctor who doesn't try and take her for every dime she has; she gets billed by his computer through the clinic—and it isn't cheap; it costs a little more. But it's a group practice, very holistic, and they give her free literature every time she goes. —I don't care though, I don't care. If he wants to pay through the nose with one of the Chosen People, that's his business. It's his money—if he wants to waste it, it's up to him."

"How's Tony?"

"Well, Tony's wonderful. He's the best company a person could have. —Whenever I'm blue, he just knows it right away, and comes out to the kitchen and jumps up on his chair and gives me that look—you know? Gives me that 'How ya doin', Mama?' look."

"He's nice."

"Nice? Listen—people say Scotties aren't affectionate? —They're crazy. They ought to come and spend a day in this big white elephant—this house is forty years old, and, believe me, it's falling apart!—With Gordy gone at the office, and me alone trying to show this retarded girl from the Catholic Society how to clean a carpet—you know? Shampoo it?—They ought to just spend the day, and see what a support Tony is. Whenever I'm blue—there he is, on his special chair in the kitchen, seeing that Mama's O.K., seeing if she'll give him a treat. —If anybody says that Scotties aren't affectionate, you just tell them to come up here and spend the day at 121 Brush Street, and they'll see."

"He's a sweetie—"

"It's the only argument I know that there's a God," her mother said. "—You won't see that in a human being; you can bet your bottom dollar on that. An animal's love is the purest love there is—because an animal knows you. It doesn't know *about* you. —It knows you. And if it loves you anyway—that's a terrific compliment."

"That's right."

"I'm not a perfect person. We both know I'm not perfect. —Who is? I probably shouldn't have done some things I did. But Tony doesn't care—I'm his Mama, no matter what."

"That's right."

"Well—what are you up to?"

"I'm working on an interesting case."

"Good. You couldn't pay me to live in that town. I hear they're coming out to Queens, now. —How's your friend, what's her name . . . Miss Kersh?"

"She's fine."

"Good. She's very bright, isn't she? —A lawyer?"

"That's right."

"Well, she likes you a lot—if she was a man, you'd be all set."

"What do you mean by that, Mother?"

"Time goes by, you know. You think you have forever, but you don't. —That job you have, Eleanor, running around with a lot of men with a gun in your purse, is all right for a young woman, you know. They probably look out for you. It won't be so hot when your looks are gone, and you're just some hard-looking old woman with no family, no kids. Nobody will want you around, then. Thank God I've got Tony and Gordy. —You just remember I warned you about it. Don't say I didn't warn you."

"I won't. . . ."

Ellie went to the kitchen, the conditioned air cool around her legs, trying to think of something she wanted for dinner. Mayo, tired of crying for his food, now sat enraged, silent, still as an Egyptian statuette, staring at the space under the kitchen table where his food should have been, while she searched the right side cabinet for a Puss 'n Boots tuna for him. There were several livers—no tuna. She opened one, spooned the stuff onto a saucer, put that down under the table, and threw the can into the trash.

The Siamese looked at his food, but stayed sitting where he was.

"Starve," Ellie said, opened the refrigerator and took out a small jar of olives. "The caviar of the poor," Klein had called them, and used to eat them by the spoonful. Ellie ate several, then put the jar back in the refrigerator, and looked for something else. She'd left the herring and cream cheese in Leahy's little cooler. It would have to be peanut butter, blackberry jam.

She heard the saucer move under the table while she was making her sandwich beside the sink. Mayo could hold out only so long. . . . He forgot his grievance after a few minutes, she supposed, then was puzzled trying to remember it—then went about his business.

She put her sandwich on a small plate, took a can of Sprite from the refrigerator, turned off the kitchen light, and left Mayo alone, finishing his dinner in the dark.

In the bedroom, Ellie put her food on the bedside table, turned on the lamp, pulled down the covers, piled the pillows up, and climbed into bed in her bathrobe. She lay there, her plate on her lap, took a bite of the sandwich, popped open the soft drink, and thought about the day.

It was the first time, in almost two years working with him, that she had seen Tommy let any serious perp take a walk. That was one thing . . . and not the worst thing. She had let people go before . . . was sure Tommy had, too, if it wasn't serious. But this, today, *was* serious. And the worst thing was, it hurt Tommy so much to do it.

Ellie cleaned peanut butter from the roof of her mouth with her tongue. Blackberry seeds.

Donaher . . . that fucking old thief. The young one even creepier. —It was the shittiest luck. The worst luck they could have had. Poor Tommy. —He'd looked scared to death while that thief was begging him. Known he was going to let them go, was what that was. . . .

The Puerto Rican up in the Bronx had looked asleep. It didn't seem like an awful death—go flying through the air like that. She thought about Sally Gaither. —Sally would rather have died that way; that was for sure. And Tommy up there, giving those old farts a hard time . . . making up, Ellie supposed, for letting Donaher go. Poor, quiet Classman. —To be killed by some morons like that—just by accident. His mother, too. —Just as well, though, she went with him, if she was as far gone as Serrano said. No one to take care of her anymore. . . .

Ellie finished her sandwich, drank the last of the Sprite, and thought of calling Clara in Chicago . . . maybe read a little, then call later. Or not. If Clara wanted to talk to her, she could call. She hadn't called earlier, hadn't left any message. . . . Susan Margolies could probably tell them both all about it. Probably had lots of dykes and queers paying her for advice—coming around trying to get cured. Or coming to her to get talked into being happy about it. —The old bag probably showed them around her apartment.

Ellie got out of bed, went out to the hall, took her revolver from her purse, and brought it back to the bedside table.

Why the hell she hadn't thought of asking Margolies about Audrey What's-His-Face . . . needed to do that, needed to get some kind of print report from Fingerprints, needed to call the M.I.'s office for the stuff from the autopsy, needed to call those people in Detroit—just in case Mr. and Mrs. Crowell were cuter than they seemed. Just in case Mrs. Crowell, for example, had decided to do something drastic about her husband's two-hundred-dollar visits. —And then the both of them showing up with that lawyer . . . playing it very cute.

So—they had to call Detroit; maybe Tommy could call tomorrow evening.

She heard Mayo scratching in his litter box in the bathroom, got up to take her sandwich plate and soft-drink can to the kitchen, wash the plate and put it away, and found the Siamese lying alongside her pillow when she came back to the bedroom. When she got into bed, Ellie leaned over, resting on her elbow, and gently stroked Mayo's small, taut, rounded belly—cream-furred, soft as a breast.

"Did you have enough to eat?"

Mayo stared away across the room as she stroked him. In profile, his muzzle was unexpectedly pointed, almost fox-like—the jeweled eye set like radiate-streaked topaz, split by the black vacancy of his narrow pupil—a funnel down which the world of light fell into the mazes of his brain. Ellie thought of painting cat's eyes as huge structures . . . light eaters . . . beneath which a dying mouse, bleeding at the ear, fenced by small, damp, white stakes of fangs, was minor.

"You're a fucking monster," she said to Mayo, and bent to put her ear to his belly to see if she could hear digestion—Puss 'n Boots liver. Instead, she heard only the neat, slight, rub-a-dub of his small heart. Smelled from his fur his faint, bestial odor.

Ellie wondered whether she was glad that Tommy had done what he had . . . was not as strong as he'd seemed. She lay back on her pillows, and wondered whether things would be different working with him, as time went on. . . .

Her reading glasses on, now—never worn on the job, not admitted to—Ellie was reading a Regency romance when the phone rang, and was annoyed. It would be Clara.—It was almost the end of the fifth chapter, and she'd meant to turn out the light and get to sleep. Now, it would be time on the phone.

"El?"

"Hi."

"I'm sorry to call so late. —I just got in from the most

monstrous dinner . . . every single legal jackass in Chicago was there, and each one blew cigar smoke in my face."

"How's the conference going?"

"Oh, they're just cutting up territory—they haven't agreed to any indictment pattern, grand jury scheduling, jurisdictions, nothing. It's been bullshit, bullshit, all the way."

"I'm sorry," Ellie said. "I know you really hoped there'd be something for you. . . ."

"Oh, there will be, sweetheart. —I'll get a piece of the action. If there *is* any action. Brave Henry has assured me of that. Said he would definitely talk to Halevy about our task force."

"And you're going to head it. . . ."

"So Brave Henry says. It's not easy to believe that guy."

"You'll get it, Clara—you're just a natural at that."

"I regret to say, you may be right. —A natural nasty-bitch prosecutor type, is what you mean."

"No—I don't mean that. I mean you're good. You're very good at what you do, Clara."

"Well . . . what this natural prosecutor would like to do right now, is to commit various offenses against several state codes with you."

"I know. . . ."

"But do you care . . . ? Improper question—let me rephrase. I hope you do care, because I certainly do care for you. . . . You know, darling, two extremely unpleasant realizations have been clarifying for me, lately—no pun intended. Am I—do you need to get to sleep, sweetheart?"

"No," Ellie said. "—I'm fine."

"Well . . . how's that major case going? The homicide."

"It's tough," Ellie said. "Nobody wants to come forward in a prostitute's killing—everybody's ducking and dodging—and we're getting shit for support from the Department. . . ."

"Just the same," Clara said, "—I'd bet on you and your attendant beast. You make a formidable team."

"Well . . . we may work it out."

"I think so. . . . Are you sure you wouldn't like to go to sleep?"

"No. Really."

"Well . . . two extremely uncomfortable things. . . . I hope you'll forgive me—this telephone thing is not . . . it's strictly the coward's way. First, I'm really terrified to admit that I think I'm in love with you. Not just loving you—I've always loved you. And—let me get this over with fast—a little bird tells me that you are feeling no such thing about yours truly."

Ellie didn't say anything.

"I see," Clara said.

After a few moments more, she said, "Well—then I won't trouble you with it."

Ellie's heart was beating thump-a-thump, as fast as Mayo's had.

"Were you watching TV?" Clara said. "Reading?—I know that brute of a job wears you out. —Would you just like me to hang up? We can talk another time."

"No . . . no; we can talk."

"A safer subject, then," Clara said. "What were you watching . . . ?"

"I was reading."

"O.K. —one of those god-awful Regency things?"

"That's right," Ellie said. Her heart was beating more slowly.

"Tell me about it," Clara said. "—Do you need to go to sleep? —If you do, just tell me—"

"I don't . . . I don't."

"O.K. —If you don't mind, just tell me about the book."

"Well, it takes place in 1814."

"Right."

"In the western part of England, near the sea."

"Right."

"I'm only about halfway through."

"That's O.K.," Clara said. "—Go ahead."

"Well, an American from Kentucky—a frontiersman—"

"Um-hmm."

"He was the grand-nephew of a rich English squire in the West of England; and in America, he heard—a lawyer from New Orleans came and told him he had inherited this estate in England. —And it was good news, because he had gambled all his land away. He was upset by the war."

"What war?"

"The war of 1812, with the British."

"Right. I got it."

"He'd been a big hero, a cavalry officer in that war. He fought at the battle of New Orleans with Andrew Jackson."

"Right. —Cotton bales. I got it."

"So, now, he's in England with this old trapper friend of his, and they're riding through the West Country to go claim his estate—and the English are still angry about the war."

"Um-hmm."

"Do you really want to hear this?"

"Damned right I do," Clara said. "—Just go on."

"Well—he and his friend go to an inn to get some food, and to have some ale—they have a little dog with them, and the dog gets into a fight with another man's dog. And then there's some trouble with one of the other men—the American has a fight with this young gentleman, and beats him up. And the man challenges him to a duel—"

"Does this young gentleman have a beautiful sister?" Clara said.

"Yes."

"She lives next to the estate the American guy is inheriting?"

"Did you read this . . . ?"

"No, sweetheart, but it's sort of a classic kind of situation. . . . I'm going to let you go to sleep."

"That's O.K."

"No—go on. Go to sleep. I'll call you in a couple of days. And, listen—when I said I loved you, I meant it. —I just get the feeling, sometimes . . . well, I get the feeling I'm supposed to be the dark, evil one in this relationship—you know, seducing little Miss White Bread . . . and, if it wasn't for me, she wouldn't do that kind of stuff. Is that true . . . ? That isn't the way you feel about me, is it, El? Just a sort of creep, who's handy when you want to do something dirty?"

"No," Ellie said. "—Never. I don't feel that way about you. I really don't."

"I hope to God you don't," Clara said. "Please, please don't feel that way about me."

"I don't. I really don't."

"Well—I apologize for running on here, begging for a word of love. —It is goddamn humiliating, I can tell you that."

Ellie heard Clara start to cry. She'd never heard Clara cry before, and it was frightening. Clara was a hard crier.—She would try to stop and say something, but the sounds seemed to force their way out of her, as if her mouth were made of rusty iron, forced apart so she could cry.

"Give me a minute," Clara said, sounding like someone else. "Give me a minute. . . . Jesus *Christ*!" The sobbing, the gasping for air began again. "Oh, my God, oh, my God," she said, "I'm so *sorry*. . . ."

"Clara," Ellie said, "—please don't do that. Please don't!" and began to cry, herself.

They wept together over the phone for a little while, then Clara blew her nose, said, "I just blew my nose on the sheet," and began to laugh. She stopped laughing, said, "Gee whiz . . ." and started laughing again. She caught her breath. "—Sophisticated gay woman, hard as nails." She blew her nose again. "A two-hundred-dollar-a-night handkerchief," she said.

Neither of them said anything for a few moments, then Clara said, "Stormy weather . . . I love you. I'll do anything you want . . ." and hung up.

"I love you, too," Ellie said. Late.

CHAPTER 8

Maureen Lacey almost never went with blacks. Brucie had given her that little lesson in spades—and he was black as the ace, himself.

"Usually—they got no bread. Jus' bullshit. Usually, they nothin' special with white chicks anyway—got too much ridin' to get it up. An' usually, they so pissed off they got to beat on somethin'—an' honey, you goin' be the somethin'!"

Sweet Brucie was upstate right now, doing three—and hadn't run Maureen anyway, not for a long time—but his advice was out and free and right on the street.

Maureen, who didn't like to, was working the tunnel entrance with a black girl named Rosalie; lady cops were staking their regular block for a couple days, playing pussy, and had asked the girls to give them room.

This evening, Maureen had turned two before ten o'clock, then had been flashed over by this black guy in a Dodge with rental plates. Big dude—bigger than Brucie, even—and wore glasses. Maureen took one look, and motioned him off on Rosalie; Rosalie would go with anything—had to go with anything because she had a coke hole through the middle of her nose, inside, that whistled when she breathed with her mouth closed. Except for that, though, she was nice-looking. But this big guy smiled and shook his head, and gestured Maureen over.—Maybe a cop, after all, Maureen thought.

"Listen," he said to her across the car seat, "I'm not a creep, I'm not a pervert—and I'd never hurt a nice working girl. —What I am, is a decent guy just in town from Cleveland looking for a little sugar-pussy for an hour. —What do you charge, darling?"

Probably he reminded her of Brucie, a little. A real

intelligent nigger. Big dude. Nice clothes. Rosalie was making a face at her—*my meat.*

What the fuck. "—It'll cost you a hundred."

Big laugh out of the guy on that one. "—And I bet you're worth every penny," he said, "but fifty's all I got. Tell you this, honey—you'll be safe with me. I won't hassle you—and nobody else will, either."

What the fuck . . . Maureen gave Rosalie the finger, and jumped in the guy's car. When they were in the tunnel, the guy dug in his jacket pocket, brought out money, thumbed through it while he drove and handed it over. Seventy-five bucks. "Split the difference—O.K.? I don't like to see women worried about money."

He took her over to Jersey, drove down to one of the container docks over there, then took her out of the car and over to some crates, under the lights. Maureen said she didn't want to do anything out there like that, because they have guards there, but the guy just said, "It would be a sad sucker would interfere with me," and right there pulled this real big boner out of his pants, balls and all—and she thought what the fuck, and got on it, right there. She couldn't take it all, but she took what she could, and got it as wet as she could, so it wouldn't hurt her.

He was really nice—but it sure as shit was no short time. She was lying on a crate under those bright lights for an hour, it felt like, this big nigger on her just humping away like he paid a thousand. He had a gun on him; she felt the butt against her right breast, sometimes. —A cop after all, or a runner or something. "Ooohh," he said—and about time. "Ooohh-*ooh*!" and came in her about a quart, it felt like. That stuff went all over. Ran down her legs when he got up off her and let her off the crate and she stood up, still blinking from looking up at those lights.

"Clean me up, please, honey," he said, and she got down on her knees to get that done—licked some stuff off his pants, too—and when she got up, he gave her another twenty-five bucks, and said, "You are a special little lady—a professional. You're a *person*. Don't ever let anybody treat you like shit, just because they call you a name."

Drove her back to New York, no problem—she'd had to blow her way back in some truck more than once—shook her hand and wished her luck when he dropped her off.

"Well, motherfucker . . ." Rosalie said, looking a little pissed (she was supposed to get all the niggers), "I thought you didn't go with bloods!"

"He was the exception makes the rule," Maureen told her. "—More tricks like him, this would be a good business to be in."

"I hope you don't want to be talking to the kids—because I'm sure as hell not waking them up at this hour. And Kameesha's got a cold and doesn't need to be awake this late."

"Don't wake them up," Tucker said, holding the phone in his right, a roast-beef sandwich in his left hand. He lay in bed in great comfort, wrapped in his terry-cloth robe. "—I know it's late." He'd gotten banana cream pie, ginger ale, and the roast-beef sandwich sent up, and was chewing the sandwich, swallowing his bites before speaking. "I didn't think they'd be up this late—couldn't help it; I was working."

"More of that snooping-around stuff. —I got to call that hotel for a 'Mr. Robbins.' My friends ask me what duty you drew, I'm ashamed to say. I really do not know why my husband, a full master sergeant with five years in grade—could be warrant with no trouble at all—can't get some troop-command duty overseas!"

"Too much chicken, sweet thing," Tucker said, and took another bite of his sandwich. "You may think I look cute in that uniform—"

"Who said I did?" his wife said.

"Well, you know you do. —But butter-pat, *you* don't have to take that morning-report shit that goes with it. —You don't mind, I'll just keep on spookin'."

"Fine—you go ahead. You see what those people are going to do for you for staying out of straight duty. —They don't give a damn about your career. . . ."

"Honey," Tucker said, "—will you continue my career counseling another time? I just called to see how you and the girls were doing."

"The girls are fine—except that Kameesha can't shake that cold and got an ear infection from it as usual—"

"Take her to the hospital?"

"No—I didn't take her to the hospital, I just let her suffer—"

"I was just asking."

"Eddie—you are not the only one who loves those girls! I am their mother—and I am very fond of them, too. Yes, I did take her to the hospital—and I took Kimana, too, because she likes to see her big sister suffer."

"What a couple of monsters . . ."

"Very much like their father—who is probably lying in bed with some white whore this very moment, while he's talking to the mother of his children."

"I am not. Honey—I told you; I do not step out on you these trips. I haven't got the time, even if I did have the inclination, which I don't. —And you know I don't like the way white women smell! Smell like sardines . . ."

"—'Stead of tuna, right? Eddie, you are full of it—and you always have been. I believe you would do it to any lady of any color that couldn't get up and run away."

"That's a lie. I've had the best—don't want the rest."

"If I ever catch you—you won't have any use for any."

"Listen, honey—I don't fool around. And I trust you not to fool around."

"You trust me because I'm a damn fool woman loves you and got two little girls to look after. —And I trust you, too—just as long as I can see you and you're on post, same as I'd trust any man."

"O.K. Mama . . . What did the doctor say?"

"He said Kameesha had an ear infection the way she always gets an ear infection—and he gave me some antibiotics, and he said she ought to have a drain put in that ear like he always says she ought to have a drain put in that ear."

"No drain. You can forget that shit—you hear me?"

"No drain."

"That procedure does no damn good. —It's dangerous. No drain or anything else in that ear—you understand me? I mean it, now!"

"All right . . . all right. He's not doing it."

"That's Captain Kirby, isn't it?"

"That's right."

"Well, you see that asshole doesn't do it. I mean that, Jacklyn; don't let me come home and find that shit sticking out of my little girl's ear."

"I won't let him do it—I promise. Now, sugar, calm *down*. Nobody's going to do anything you don't want."

"He can pull that quack shit on somebody else's child. . . ."

"O.K. He's not going to do it."

"All right."

"All right . . ."

"I miss you, sweetie. . . ."

"I miss you, too, my big man. . . . I miss you a lot. . . ."

"I wish you were right here, right now."

"You do . . . ?"

"Damn right."

"What would you do if I was?"

"I'd suck that sweet thing till it cried. . . ."

"That's a nice way to talk to your wife over the phone."

"That's what I'd do, just the same."

"Well . . ."

"That's just what I'd be doing."

"And I'd lie there and let you do it, too. —I don't give a damn who's listening on that hotel switchboard."

"You'd do something for me, too, wouldn't you?"

"Yes," his wife said.

"You would . . ."

"Yes, I would. I'd do anything you wanted me to do."

"You know what I'm doing now . . . ?"

". . . I guess I do."

"I'm doing it just for you, honey." He took another two bites of the sandwich, had some ginger ale.

"Go ahead, then," she said. "Do it—because I'm doing . . . the same thing."

"Oh, I love you," Sergeant Tucker said, and poured himself more ginger ale. "Oh . . . you *sweet* thing . . . oh, that feels *nice*. . . ." He finished his sandwich, and reached for the plate of pie. He leaned to the bedside table for the fork, and said, "*Jesus* . . . Oh, that feels so fine. . . ."

"Oh, Eddie . . . oh, my Eddie . . ."

"Damn," Sergeant Tucker said, "—I got jissom all *over* me!" He took a bite of the banana cream. It was very good—little chunks of fresh banana in it—but it wasn't quite as good as the coconut cream had been. "Did you come, baby . . . ? Did my sweetheart get her pretty gun?"

"You are a bad man," his wife said, out of breath. "—And never mind if I did. Oh, I do love you, Eddie."

"We have a mutual admiration society. . . ."

"Yes, we do."

"You have to be tired, darlin'—with Kameesha and all. You go on to sleep, now."

"O.K. You go to sleep, too."

"I'm going to have to take a shower—you got slick all over me, you pretty thing."

"Eddie . . . stop talking that trash!"

"You love it."

"It's the damn hotel operator that loves it!—You go on to sleep, now."

"Talk to you tomorrow night."

"Tomorrow night. Call earlier—call by nine, and I'll keep the girls up."

"O.K. And no—"

"Drain in her ear. O.K.?"

"Good night, sweetheart."

"Good night."

Sergeant Tucker hung up the phone, said, "Love and the ladies . . ." and sighed. He ate the last of the banana cream pie, recalling the bearing grunts of the skinny-legged little whore as she took his weight—took all his tool, too, up into that small box. —Black hair on that, black as the hair on her head. Not a bad-looking girl, maybe nineteen, eighteen . . . bad acne scars. Little tits. But she looked O.K. . . . very nice over there spread for it with her dress pulled up to her armpits . . . looking this way and that way to see if somebody was coming. —That skin they had—even the least of them, the trashiest. Creamy pearly white stuff, like an angel's skin. You see some black pussy hair on that whiteness, you know you're seeing something . . . Blond pussy hair, too. More than once, with officers absent, he and Briscoe had watched while filming Gaither and the other white whores at their work. With officers absent . . . It had made the Colonel and his then lieutenant—Canfield—uncomfortable to have Tucker sitting watching the white women at their exercise. Briscoe, a New York cop, hadn't given a damn.

Gaither had been memorable; it had saddened Tucker to hear of her death. That little woman had had skin white as a peeled apple. —It was the kind of thought that made him feel sorry. Talking that shit to Jacklyn . . . Was there anything wrong with her soft brown skin . . . his babies' skins? Anything wrong with their pretty, soft brown skins . . . brown as toast?

"Fallible man," he said aloud to the dresser opposite, "—and suffering woman. *Le coq a ses raisons, que la coeur ne connaît pas.*"

Tucker got up off the bed, and walked to the bathroom, his left ankle (injured parachuting long before) clicking softly the first few steps. The green carpet felt good under his bare feet—the whole hotel room was a pleasure, it was such a private public place, so cut off from other things, other people, by nothing except brief curtains of time . . . check-ins, check-outs. Tucker had always liked motels and hotels better than houses.—They seemed less artificial to him than the pretended, false permanence of homes.

He dropped his robe, took off his glasses and put them on the top of the toilet tank, then stepped into the shower—turning it on to fairly hot—and, revolving slowly under the steaming fall, reviewed the morning, its difficulties, their resolutions.

The Colonel had seemed calmer today. Resigned. Must have gotten his pale ass reamed over that telephone line to Washington. Only sign of upset was the setups. —The Colonel had been drinking for two, and early in the afternoon. "Right as rain on the Hispanic, Sergeant," he'd said, looking good, tie tied right. He'd had his jacket on, watching TV when Tucker came in to report.

Tucker, alone as requested (likely for the convenience of later denial), with Budreau ordering lunch at the bar downstairs, Mason up in his room taking a shower—had shorthanded for the Colonel their staking of the methadone clinic on West Ninety-seventh Street (Tucker suitably attired in dirty jeans, blue running shoes, and a dirty gray sweatshirt)—his conversation with two black men out on the sidewalk, followed by a more productive one with a junkie named Jesús, who agreed, after considerable persuasion, to go uptown with Tucker to check out a small package of shit there—with the possibility, then, of getting up enough bread with friends to buy it.

"I'm no fuckin' thief, man," Tucker had said. "—An' if I was, I sure as shit wouldn't be hangin' round this fuckin' hole, talkin' to dudes ain't got their shit together for a dime bag. I ain't fuckin' with you, man. —You check it out, you get the bread, that's fine. I ain't fuckin' with you, man. —You can't, then fuck you."

Reassured, Jesús had walked with Tucker—on promises to bring him right back downtown to the clinic—around the corner to the car. Seeing Mason and Budreau in it, the Puerto Rican had tried to part company, but Tucker had his arm, now claimed to be a cop—opened the right rear door, and shoved Jesús into Budreau's arms.

"Took him up to the Bronx, into an empty building up there—shot him through the lower right side with Budreau's weapon into a brick wall. Retrieved the slug, put a rough bandage on, took him up to the roof, and threw him off. We left the TV from the police officer's apartment up there as well, with Budreau's prints on it, to match."

"All right," the Colonel had said. "—O.K." He had nodded faster and faster during the recital, as if there were less and less he wanted to hear. "All right. —That's done," he said. "Poor guy's probably no loss. —Can't they tell he wasn't shot last night?"

"Probably not," Tucker had said, "—after a day in the sun."

To be told, Tucker thought then—no matter how accurately—is to be lied to.

The Colonel had, in receiving the report, avoided hearing the terrified clickity-clack Puerto Rican Spanish—an ugly Spanish at best—that Jesús began to chatter as they hauled him across the lot and up into the wrecked building that had seemed, and proved, ideal as they drove past it heading uptown.

Several people watched from a distance as they buckoed

him along—he not struggling, but hanging back, dragging, complaining, begging for explanations in Spanish, then English, then Spanish again.

"You wouldn't understand," Budreau had said to him. "Why don't you just relax . . . ?"

This had been seen by two or three people, at a distance of a block or two, gazing down long streets, or over the countless small bunkers of rubble. None of these people, experts in non-witness, had seemed inclined to interfere—not even to linger in the bright morning sunlight to see more. —They had paused, stood, stared, then moved along.

Jesús noticed none of them. Sagging between Mason and Budreau, depending from them, leaning against first one and then the other over the uneven ground, the busted bricks, chunks of concrete, shallow drifts of sun-bleached garbage, this short, soft-bellied man kept up a constant conversation of questions, as if a single answer might free him. Tucker had competent Spanish; so did Mason.—Budreau, though a two-year veteran of Central, none but the limited requirements for ordering beer or sugar-cane rum, or asking the short-time price of a brown Indian twelve-year-old with legs like bruised sticks and eyes bruised darker (but merry enough a dancer when drunk). Jesús' questions were directed to each of them in turn, as if he expected one of them, at least, to produce a reason—and all this as they hustled him hard toward the ruined building, satisfactorily deserted, its toasted windows bashed out or in, its door, boarded and plywooded over more than once, kicked wide open, split planks left swinging, plywood sheets torn like tar-paper.

They hustled him in over a wide, cracked concrete sill, swung right together as if familiar with the premises, trotted, dragged him to the stairs, and lifted him up by his armpits while he kept talking, requiring explanation.

On the second floor, Mason said, in Spanish, *"We're going to kill your ass, man,"* and Jesús appeared relieved to hear it, to be able to continue his line of questions on a new track. "Why, why, why, why, why? *¿Porqué, porqué, porqué porqué porqué?"*

On the second floor, and down a long hall, they found an empty, shattered room, the plaster ripped out of the walls as if by searches for treasure, the floor planking gouged and splintered. The window wall was bare brick, contused—and Tucker motioned his men to put the Puerto Rican up against it, stepped in to accept the short-barreled Ruger .38 that Budreau, one arm free, handed over, then stood well back as they spread-eagled the man, who was still calling questions.

It seemed unfair to Tucker that a person so accidentally involved should die in ignorance—if there were any kind of an afterlife, that would be the most restless sort of spirit. . . .

"We are killing you," he said in fairly good Spanish—and Jesús, not struggling, seemed appreciatively silent, listening at last to his answer. *"—We are killing you to confuse the police in the matter of the murder of one of their own. It is all an accident, for you."*

"An accident . . ."

"Correct. —Now, Jesús—be a man."

However, Jesús, having his answer, didn't care for it, and far from acting like a man, began to act like a baby—weeping, struggling weakly between Mason and Budreau, calling on a brother of his, apparently a dangerous man, to come and save him, and finally bending forward, his arms still held, to vomit a breakfast of what appeared to have been Cuban sweet rolls and lots of coffee.

When, trembling, weak, silent at last, he slowly straightened up from this purging, Tucker shot him through his lower right side, carefully clear of any bones or major arteries—the two men let him go—and he fell forward, and lay stretched out on the floor.

"I am killed?" he said, hugging his injured side, which, though struck a terrible blow, felt numb, as after a dentist's injection.

"Not yet." Tucker said, handing Budreau's weapon back to him, "—but soon." He took a long, folded strip of dirty cotton from his jeans, knelt, and bandaged the man's soft belly as Mason and Budreau turned him to accommodate. The wound's entrance and exit were only slightly different—the entrance puckered in, bleeding sluggishly, the exit wound more lively, colorful, slightly larger.

. . . "Switch to Silvertips from here on out," Tucker said to Budreau while bandaging, observing this not too impressive injury. "You're getting zip for expansion with that Teflon shit."

"O.K.," Budreau said, and rolled a softly protesting Jesús off his sore belly and onto his sore back—the dentist's shot wearing off—as Tucker wrapped his long bandage round.

"Am I not killed . . . ?" the Puerto Rican said, dreamy with shock.

"In a minute," Tucker told him, trying to get the bandage ends tied.

That accomplished, he motioned his men to pick the man up—and Mason and Budreau, now familiar with that sagging burden, hoisted it easily while it protested, held it up while Tucker pulled his Swiss Army knife from his jeans, went to the wall, located the bullet's entry almost between two bricks, dug the round free, folded the blade of his knife, and put both into the same pants pocket. —Then his men dragged their burden after him as he walked from the room, strode back down the hall to the stairs, and led on the four-story climb to the roof.

It was a hard climb on a warm morning, with such a plaintively murmuring load slung between them, and Mason and Budreau were panting when they reached the roof—where, in happier and still recent times, some celebration must have occurred, broken beer bottles, a torn pair of turquoise woman's slacks, and a stained Kotex testifying to it.

When they were up, and had him near the low brick parapet overlooking the building's back lot, Tucker, careful of staining his sweatshirt, came and gathered Jesús in his arms, cradling him pretty gently, and said—head bent, speaking Spanish to a sweaty big-eyed face, *"Now is your time, Señor. —Vaya con Dios. . . ."* Swung him back in his arms just once, as a man might a child he was to toss into a children's pool, then swung him out over the parapet and loosed him into the air.

After a long, short time and one slow somersault, Jesús landed on his back in the rubble below with a heavy thump, dust flying up around him.

"That's a good greaser, now," Mason said.

"Mason," Tucker said, "—you take off your T-shirt and your Fruit of the Looms, go back down to that room, and I want you to mop up every bit of that sad turkey's vomit. —And I mean every *little* bit."

"Why?" Mason said, surprised, and failed to get his hands up in time when Tucker stepped in and hit him once, very hard, in the belly.

Then Mason bowed slowly, his too-late hands stroking and playing at his middle, as if to coax in a little air.

"Budreau," Tucker said, "—go down to the car, get that TV out of the trunk, bring it here, and put it in the end room on the first-floor corridor. —You can leave prints on it, give them a match with some we left in the apartment."

"Yes, sir," Budreau said.

"'Yes, Sergeant' will do."

"Yes, Sergeant," Budreau said, and went.

"Mason," Tucker said, looking out from the roof as he spoke, looking over the ruins around them for signs of any particular activity, any interested witnesses—listening for any hint of sirens, of police response to a citizen's report of shots fired. "—It would certainly oppress my spirits, if I thought *you* thought that little demonstration you gave last night in the police officer's apartment had gone unnoticed. —That would certainly oppress my spirits."

Mason, still slightly bent, catching his breath, had nothing to say.

"I have been waiting all morning—all *morning*—for an attempted explanation. You have offered me none."

"He had me cold." Muttered.

"What? —What did you say?"

"He was right on me . . . Sergeant. He had my ass cold—I was fuckin' cold *meat* up there!"

"You certainly were," Tucker said. "—You were ducking and dodging behind that poor crazy old woman like Chicken Little. —And whose fault was that?"

"Wasn't mine. . . ! He killed the Lieutenant!"

"We aren't talking about *officers,* here, Mason. We are talking about troops—combat personnel—*men*!"

"He had me cold. . . ."

"I'll tell you what, Mason—you listening up?"

"Yes, sir . . . Sergeant."

"I'll tell you what, Mason—the very next time a man points a weapon at you in a firefight, you will—you *will* instantly take a long step to the left while drawing your weapon, and you will fire rounds into that opponent commencing with hits low middle. —That sound familiar to you, Mason?"

"Yes . . . Sergeant."

"And you will do it—oh, yes you will! Because if you don't—no matter what else is happening, no matter what shit is hitting what fan—I am *personally* going to put a round through your intestines. I'm going to blow those yellow guts right out of your belly onto the floor. —Do you believe me?"

"Yes, Sergeant."

"Then you're smarter than you look. Now, you come on down to that room with me, and you're going to clean every bit of that vomit up with your undershirt and your underpants. —Then, you're going to put that underwear back on, and wear it, just so you remember our little talk. —And you remember something else. When you kill a man, you show him decent respect—you don't call him a greaser or a kike or a nigger. —Have I gotten through to you?"

. . . Apparently, he had.

Tucker, having lathered and rinsed, now turned the water to cooler, worked some Essence des Pins shampoo into his hair, and began to sing "I Heard It Through the Grape Vine," upbeat, in a soft, accurate falsetto.

Ellie drove north in whizzing traffic through a cool and glittering morning just past Greenwich on Interstate 95, looking for the next exit. —She'd felt fine when she got up, though her breasts were a little tender, but a soft, gripping cramp had set itself into her on Bruckner, and wasn't getting better. There was no oily, tickling feeling of flow yet, but certainly would be, and pretty soon. She was a little early this month, and didn't mind it, except for the inconvenience now. She always enjoyed her periods, though not the cramps, and was pleased to bleed in secret while men went their noisy, dry, public way. —She was sometimes afraid they could smell her, though, and then was uneasy, and would prepare herself with patted clouds of powder, tug barely damp Tampax out, and insert fresh.

An exit came and went, and caught her still in a left lane. Ellie dropped down to fourth for more acceleration, let a tractor-trailer get past her on the right (a thundering, trembling wall, painted white, long black letters slanting up it), signaled, and steered the old Civic into that lane—and quickly over one more to exit without signaling. In her rearview mirror, she saw a man in a tan car just behind her, glimpsed his face as he shook his head, then wheeled the Honda down onto the exit ramp for Stamford, down and half around, the little car's engine buzzing to keep up with the larger others bowling along beside.

Ellie drove five blocks along a west-east access road, stopped for two red lights, then saw a Standard station on her right, and pulled into it.

She got the ladies' room key (lightly chained to a wooden paddle) from a handsome young black man with a goatee, who sat perched on a steel-legged stool behind his cash register, lean and lazy in neatly ironed jeans.

In the rest room, Ellie took off her suit jacket and skirt, folded them carefully, and hung them over the doorless partition between the grimy toilet and drip-rusted sink. She spooled some toilet paper off a diminished roll, tore it, and laid strips along the seat, then pulled her panty hose down to her ankles, sat, and searched for a Tampax in her purse. She unwrapped it, spread her knees, lifted her right knee slightly, then reached down, gently held herself open with the fingers of her right hand, and inserted the Tampax with her left. Slightly uncomfortable, and comforting.

An hour later, she was past Norwich, looking for the exit to 97 for Baltic and South Windham, enjoying the humming vibration of speed through the steering wheel, enjoying being alone among so many, hurrying, speeding. She thought of painting busy highways, thruways, beltways, parkways, expressways: wide black rivers of pavement—endless, immobile stages for millions of momentary dramas, movies, short stories, romances, horrors . . . rolling, rolling, day and night—missing each other, striking each other, passing, catching up and leaving behind in gorgeous glaring colors at night, subdued, sunburned tones of acceleration through the day. And all trembling as the big truck had trembled, passing her. Beautiful . . . so beautiful . . . full of life and intention. —Worlds traveling together, the metal working, cracking back and forth faster than a human hand could imitate, laboring in tight, black, snoring steel to make the hot wheels spin.

Light, thin paints, spread fine as water—carefully, carefully drawn—that would be so much work, so much work—so her colors wouldn't be betrayed. Sheets of gray buried in chrome and fire-engine red, divided up and down the picture with necklaces of cream and custard and dusty blue. The cars' big blind eyes glittering in sunshine.

And all their people a foot or two from dying . . . talking, arguing, listening, steering a few feet from their deaths. Death running alongside each car, galloping along, handsome, odd, long-haired, inhuman, its paw on the handle of the front passenger door, listening, bored with the conversation, the music on the radio—lifting the handle a little, ready to swing it open, reach in in a thunder of smashing metal, the second thunder of exploding gas—to reach in and snatch a person out and hug them, until, in much less than a second, they broke.

The cars well drawn—she would have to take her time and draw the cars really well (anybody seeing the picture would know she could draw, seeing how fine the cars were)—and then tell the people and death mainly in color, moving shades from dark to light and back again. Tint-rose to violet, mauve to purple to bruise. It would be wonderful to do, if she could do it. After the river painting. Maybe before.

Someone, a woman with a baby in her arms, goes out the car door to death in the first of a triptych, in realistic colors, as much like a color photograph as possible, and then—in the second panel—she understands, struggles, tries to save her baby—throwing the baby through the air as the cars begin to collide, racing side by side, shedding bright metal, glass, thermos bottles, magazines fluttering through the air like birds—but another death with different-colored hair is waiting for her baby in this picture, and catches it in midair across the traffic in the fury of the crash, stoops, handsome, inhuman, bored, and rolls the baby under the right front wheel of a bus racing by—the passengers not yet seeing anything. —One of the passengers, a sailor, beginning to see through the next to last window . . . his mouth and eyes opening together.

The third picture, the third picture, the third picture . . . the explosion of the gas—blast and fire, the tangled wreck (the woman's husband trapped in the folded car, already dreaming of another woman he loved more than her, writing the woman's name in his blood on the frosted splintered windshield). *Helen.*

The mother now doesn't care. Knows too much to know that anymore. Now she doesn't care about anything. She only is—is like a tall slight shaft of stone. Now, she is standing in the fire and blast above the torrent of traffic, her hand on death's odd shoulder as if to comfort him. Her dead baby is racing away with the traffic. The other death is carrying him piggyback, leaping from car top to car top, as the cars, trucks begin to swerve, collide, turn aside and skid to avoid the wreck.

The woman doesn't look back at the baby, but the baby looks back at her.

Three big pictures set among mirrors, so that people see many pictures of the same picture, and see their faces as they see. . . . Call them . . . *Traveling*—One, Two, and Three.

Maybe buy stretched canvas . . . maybe just do sketches, try to get it right. Maybe start with the river painting . . . or the one of Clara.—Finish that one, first. . . .

"Can I tell you something?" Clara had said. "—You won't get mad? . . . You won't be hurt?"

"No," Ellie had said, "—I won't get mad."

"There's nothing the matter with your drawing," Clara said. "Plenty of painters can't draw any better than you can. It's not your drawing. It's your nerve. —O.K., now, you said you wouldn't be hurt."

"I didn't," Ellie had said. "—I said I wouldn't get mad."

Ellie saw the sign for the 97 exit, glanced over her right shoulder and slowed a little, waiting for a break in the traffic over on the exit lane. A dark blue van, two . . .

three cars behind that. There was a break then, and she signaled and steered in behind the last car of the three, a station wagon, painted coffee and cream.

A blond little boy in a blue-striped T-shirt sat in the back of the wagon looking out at her. There was a dog in there with him, a big retriever—Golden, or yellow Labrador. Ellie nodded and smiled at the little boy, and he nodded and smiled in return as the station wagon drifted farther right, then swiftly down, sweeping farther and farther to the right along the exit ramp, Ellie's car buzzing along behind.

She lost the little boy at the interchange—the station wagon turning south on 12, Ellie rolling north on 97 for Baltic, the little Honda relieved to be moving slower, off the interstate, its small engine less noisy, now.

Some suburbs here . . . a sort of strip. Ellie turned off the vent fan and opened her window. Cool air came muttering, puffing in, patting her arm, fingering her hair. The air smelled of exhaust and earth, mixed like a dog's breath in sour and sweetness.

After a few miles, she passed a big shopping center on the left, then some construction scattered along the highway—huge yellow trucks and caterpillar tractors parked, the bulldozers still wearing jaunty summer umbrellas over their driver seats. Men in hard hats—looking frail beside these patient brutes, the raw heaped ramps of earth the great machines had piled—stood in small groups, talking.

Ellie drove into Baltic thinking what she might say to Sally Gaither's daughter, missed the turn onto 207, and had to go on through for four blocks past a big brick building before she could pull into an Exxon station, turn around past the pumps and pull out onto the main street, drive back to the intersection, and take the turn she'd missed for South Windham.

She thought it would be easiest on the girl if she was just businesslike—if she didn't hang around too long, a cop who'd come to ask about a murdered mother—a murdered whore. Just ask her questions . . . say she was sorry . . . and go.

Highway 207 was a pleasanter road, narrower, a plain two-lane blacktop unrolling up into low hills, past wooded suburban roads, houses here and there just showing as the Honda passed—a flash of white clapboard . . . dark roof. There was a pretty rust-red plant growing along the ditches. Ellie, driving slower, watched a split-rail fence stilt along beside her for a quarter mile. A green pasture past it—and a little more than a mile farther on, a white wooden fence that traveled almost as far, and five horses scattered, grazing. The two close enough to see well were small, dark, fine-legged, big-eyed horses with nostrils that flared like the Arab horses that Rosa Bonheur painted. *Feu de joie.*

She drove by a small house on the right just after that, a house back from the road, a yellow Chevy van parked in the driveway. —A person wouldn't have to be rich to own that house. It had been very small. A cottage . . . three or four rooms. She could live in that house, walk from sunny room to sunny room . . . find north light for a studio. . . .

South Windham was a handsome village with two antique shops. —If Clara had been with her, they would have had to stop, poke around . . . ask the price of a cherry-wood piecrust table, moderately distressed. "—For God's sake, Clar—that thing was made in Bridgeport yesterday and beaten with chains!" Clara was a sucker for age. Show Ms. Yale a piece of furniture with ten layers of liquid shoe polish on it, some work with a propane torch—and out would come the checkbook. The genuine piecrust table would of course wind up with Bekins in Brooklyn, along with a lot of other pieces, each one tried in her apartment for a month.

"Man," Ellie had said once, when they'd gone up to Providence for the weekend—one of the few entire weekends they'd both happened to have off, the only long trip they'd taken together, "—these people see you coming all the way from Seventy-first Street."

"It's my money," Clara had said, "—and lies are my profession."

That had been a nice trip. They'd been like friends on that trip; Clara hadn't always been after Ellie about love this and love that. They'd just had a good time. Stayed up for hours in that inn room, talking, smoking a joint, giggling like girls. . . .

A pretty dark-haired woman at a grocery store told Ellie how to get out to St. Christopher's. —Four miles out on the road to Willimantic . . . a little more than four miles. Then look for a road on the left, Spring Farm Road, and take that for maybe a mile and a half, and the sign for the school is right there.

The road out of South Windham, wooded along both sides, roller-coastered slowly up and down low hills. —There'd been no clouds at all when Ellie left New York, but now the sky was full of mountainous white clouds—clouds out of a book of fairy tales, like some book Ellie remembered from childhood, where a young girl in a long old-fashioned dress was standing on a steep, grassy hillside, holding her straw hat on to keep it from blowing away in the breeze—and beyond her, up into the sky, great soft clouds towering high as you could see. Beyond that hill was a wonderful world, like this one—but better . . . surprising. . . .

Maybe there'd been other children on the hillside. Flying kites . . .

Ellie saw the narrow green sign for Spring Farm Road, slowed, waited for a black VW bug to pass her, then turned left. She drove by two houses—one of them, the second one, had a swimming pool in its side yard—then passed a farm on her left, thinking it might be Spring Farm when she first saw it, and was pleased to read *Spring Farm* painted in white above the barn door. The barn was right on the road. *Spring Farm—1803.*

It looked more like an estate than a farm. The barn had been painted perfect dusty brick-red, the drive to the house paved in crushed white stone. —Cows in the field, though.

The sign for St. Christopher's was on the right, a small wooden sign painted coffee brown, the lettering of the school's name in white block. Brown and white . . . the school's colors, probably.

The driveway was fresh blacktop, swung in a sharp half-circle left as Ellie drove in, then straightened beyond a stand of big trees, and ran across a wide, mowed lawn. Some boys were playing something out there, running around in shorts, kicking a ball. Soccer. *Co-ed.* The school was co-ed. Ellie'd been thinking of it as a girl's school—with that sort of softness, secrecies.

Beyond this wide lawn . . . playing field, Ellie drove through an aisle of trees with houses on each side of the driveway—looked like housing for the teachers. Nice houses . . . very comfortable-looking. A beat-up play-set in a side yard. . . .

She drove through to a big turnaround (some cars and a brown-and-white van parked there) with two-story white clapboard buildings standing at the end of long walks around it—three or four of them, with big trees on their front lawns. The leaves at the treetops, shifting in a breeze, were already starting to turn dull gold along their edges.

Ellie had expected the place to look like a private school in England in the movies—cut gray stone, and cloisters—but this was very nice. The buildings looked fresh-painted; their walls under the trees were printed with moving patterns of leaf shadow, light gray-blue over perfect white.

Ellie parked beside the brown-and-white van (there was a stencil on the passenger-side door, a muscular man in a loincloth carrying a child)—got out of the Honda, reached back in to get her purse, then locked the car and walked up a flagstone path to the nearest building. Flowers were planted along the path . . . yellow and red-gold. Marigolds, maybe.

Sally Gaither might have been tight, buying new clothes, but not when it came to her daughter. Ellie supposed tuition at this school had to be at least ten thousand a year. —Hard on the girl, maybe. The whore's daughter at prep school . . . Not as hard, though, as it would be now.

An elderly woman with light blue hair and matching glasses frames was sitting at a desk in a group of desks to the left of the entrance hall.

Ellie went over and told her who she was.

"My, you are an unusual police officer, aren't you?" the elderly woman said, looking Ellie up and down. "Yes," she said, and got up out of her chair, "the doctor's expecting you. . . ."

"Expecting who . . . ?" A plump young man in a priest's black suit and white collar walked up to the desk behind Ellie, and held out his hand as she turned. He was Ellie's age, maybe younger, and was rapidly losing very fine blond hair. What hair he still had was fine as floss.

"This is the police officer—Mrs. Klein," the elderly woman said. "—Though you wouldn't think it to look at her. She looks like one of our mothers, doesn't she?"

"Yes, she does, Edna," the young priest said. His handshake was soft and dry, as if his palm had been powdered. "—I'm Dr. Peschek, Officer Klein." He turned to lead her away. "Why don't we go into my office. —Edna, do you think we could have some coffee?"

"Do you want your Danish, now?" The elderly woman seemed to disapprove.

"Yes—and one for Officer Klein. . . . Edna and Mrs. Pierce are trying to keep me from getting any fatter," the priest said as they walked up the corridor. The floor was bare, polished hardwood. "They use subtle indicators of tone. *'—Do you want your Danish, now?'* "

"Everybody has a weight problem," Ellie said.

The priest glanced at her. "—Not you, I should think. I, on the other hand, *am* a weight problem."

Two girls in identical dark-brown pleated skirts and white middy blouses came down the hall toward them and said, together, "Good morning, Dr. Peschek."

"Good morning," he said. "—Behave yourselves," and they went giggling by.

"Uniforms," Dr. Peschek said. "Not terribly attractive, but they solve the competition-in-new-clothes problem. We have scholarship students here who wouldn't be able to keep up." He opened a dark, paneled door, and stood back for Ellie to precede him. "I hope you like instant; it's all the ladies make."

Peschek's office was a large room, bare and sunny—no rugs, no pictures on the white plaster walls. The only furniture was a big oak desk and swivel chair, two oak armchairs facing them. Two oak file cabinets fitted side by side into the near corner.

"It's a little stark, isn't it?" Peschek said, "—but it's useful to impress parents with my priestly asceticism and dedication.—Please . . . sit down. They're more comfortable than they look." He sat down behind his big desk. "O.K.?"

The oak armchair wasn't more comfortable than it looked. "They are comfortable," Ellie said.

"Now . . . this thing. You'll want to talk with Sonia, of course. . . . And you may have some questions for me?" The priest had light brown eyes, almost taffy-colored.

"I will need to talk to Sonia," Ellie said. "—I guess I should thank you for breaking the news to her. That's something I was glad not to have to do."

"That sort of thing is one of the few dues priests pay," Peschek said, and smiled. "Particularly Episcopal priests—the poor Catholic guys give up more."

"It was very bad for her . . . ?"

Peschek stared at her. "—Officer, we are talking about a major disaster . . . a tragedy. I've had to tell a child his father was dead, here. Man died of a heart attack. —And you can believe me that was nothing at all, compared to telling Sonia Gaither—who has no one else in the whole world—that her mother had been dreadfully murdered." Peschek bowed his head a little, apparently remembering. The sunlight from the nearest window shone through his fine, sparse hair; he looked almost bald in that light. "I will be very happy," he said, "—not to witness anything that severe again. She went mad, is what happened. Shock and grief. The child simply went mad—raced through the building screaming for her mother. . . . We had to call Dr. Safir. He sedated her. . . . My wife and I have kept Sonia at our house until this morning. We have a baby, and I think that helping take care of Michael helped her a little."

"What did the doctor say . . . ?"

"Well—he said to me what I'm going to say to you. —Take it easy with her."

"I will . . . I only have a few questions."

"I thought it might be more . . . relaxing, for both of you, if you spoke outdoors. We have a place we call the Sanctuary—it's a small garden—and you could talk with her there without a hundred students looking on; most of them are in class."

"Good," Ellie said, "—that would be fine."

Someone tapped on Peschek's door, it swung open, and a sharp-nosed red-haired woman in a good beige wool dress came in carrying a tray.

"Thank you, May," the priest said, "—just set it down here on the desk." He moved some papers out of her way. "—May, this is Officer Klein of the New York City police. She's here to talk with Sonia about her mother's death. —Why don't you go over to Spilling's and ask John Fusco to let Sonia leave her class? Tell Sonia that a lady, the police officer from New York, wishes to speak with her in Sanctuary—that she'll be with her there in a few minutes."

"Yes, Doctor," the woman said. "—Edna put a prune Danish for you. —A cherry Danish for the lady." She nodded to Ellie, confirming the cherry Danish was hers.

"Thank you," Ellie said, and the woman nodded again, and left, closing the door softly behind her.

"Edna saw you, so then May had to come in and see you," Peschek said. "I hope I wasn't out of line, telling her why you were here—but I've found it's much better to let this little community know exactly what's going on. It's easier, in the long run, than trying to squelch rumors."

"I understand . . . it's no problem."

"May I ask—do you have any idea who murdered Ms. Gaither?"

"No."

"I ask . . . because it's difficult to understand why anyone *would* do such a thing."

"When we know why—we'll probably know who."

Peschek stood up and leaned over his desk to examine the tray. "Well, the cherry's yours," he said, came around the desk, picked up one of the plates and a coffee cup, saucer, and spoon, and started to bring them to her.

"I'll take the prune," Ellie said.

"No, no . . ."

"Yes—really. I like it."

"Well . . . really?"

"Yes. I do like it. You take the cherry."

"Well . . . all right." He turned back to the desk, exchanged Danishes, and brought hers and her coffee to her. "God bless you," he said. "Edna feels I'll eat less of what I don't like." He went back to the desk for a creamer and sugar bowl, brought them over to her, and when she'd taken some of each, went back to his desk, sat down, and arranged his cherry Danish and coffee in front of him. "What sin," he said, "compares in frequency of pleasure, to gluttony. . . ."

"Pride," Ellie said, and Peschek chewed and swallowed his first bite, nodded, and said, "I suppose so."

"Did you ever meet Sally Gaither?" Ellie didn't know whether to call him Father, or not. The Danish was terrible; the coffee, very good.

"Oh, yes—oh, yes. We met many times. And I was very impressed by her. She was a pretty woman—though I don't suppose you could say she was a great beauty. She was pretty . . . very small, you know. A small woman. She was charming—very intelligent, I would say—and quite seductive, though not in the way that one might think. She didn't act at all *like* a prostitute—none of that sort of thing.—And that, of course, was what was so seductive about her. You were faced with a lovely, intelligent, *merry* woman, a lady—who was a whore. I imagine—I did imagine—that going to bed with her, and paying, would still be to go to bed with a *person*—a woman, not a commercial instrument."

"Still . . . Father, she *was* a prostitute. Did the kids here know that Sonia's mother . . . ?"

"Oh, yes. Yes, indeed. Sonia told them—and, I think, on her mother's advice. At least she let her friends know—which is the same as letting everyone know." He ate more of his cherry Danish, drank some coffee. "Our kids are a little more sophisticated than most—some of them come from families whose social and sexual histories would make your hair curl. So—if anything—I believe it gave Sonia some cachet, to have a New York courtesan for a mother. And many of the kids had met Sally; she came up every third or fourth Sunday to take Sonia into town . . . spent the afternoon with her, and often took some of Sonia's friends as well."

"Parents didn't object?"

"To their credit—or discredit—no. I believe it to be to their credit." He finished his cherry Danish. "How's the prune?"

"Very good," Ellie said, and took another bite.

"Now, that's not true," said Father Peschek.

"It is. —It's really all right."

"Are you kidding?"

"No—it's not bad!"

"That's not true at all. —The prunes are terrible." He sipped his coffee.

"Tell me, did Sally pay full tuition for Sonia—or was it a scholarship thing . . . ?"

"Full tuition. —The school *has* an endowment, and about fifty of the students are here on some sort of assistance, but Ms. Gaither made no inquiries about it—didn't seem troubled by the full tuition amount."

"Which is?"

"Twelve thousand, four hundred dollars. That's full room and board; we do have a few day students whose parents pay less. —I see you're impressed by the sum. It isn't peanuts, is it?"

"No—it's a lot of money."

"Yes, but you might keep two things in mind. First—those students not on scholarship have parents very well able to pay that amount. And, second, for that money their children receive one of the finest junior and high school educations available anywhere in the country. —And I *mean* anywhere in the country. Almost sixty percent of St. Christopher graduates go into the Ivy League universities, or Stanford or M.I.T. —And those who don't go to those schools, make do nicely at Reed, or Chicago, or Berkeley."

"I'm sure it's a very good school."

"One of the best—if you'll forgive all that salesmanship. I get carried away."

"No—it was interesting to hear." Ellie stood up. "I think I should go out and see her, now."

"I'll show you the path." Father Peschek got up and came around his desk to open the office door. He motioned her to go through ahead of him, caught up, and walked with her down the corridor. "—Listen, I have to leave for a meeting in town before lunch—but I would very much like it if you could stay, once you've spoken with Sonia, and eat at the faculty table. —If you feel that Sonia wouldn't mind. The teachers would like to meet you, I'm sure—and I know our girls would. Who knows—you might recruit some future Officer Klein!" They passed blue-haired Edna at her desk, but she was busy typing, and only glanced up and nodded.

"I wish I could," Ellie said, "—but I have to get back to the city."

"Ah . . . I'm sorry. It would have been nice." He held the outer door open for her.

"Maybe I could come out another time."

Father Peschek took Ellie gently by the elbow, and guided her down the steps and to the right, onto a flagstone walk running back along the building's side. "Could you? —And bring a male counterpart for the boys? They'd love it. And I think a talk about real police work might be a useful antidote to that crap the children see on television."

"I know just the male counterpart," Ellie said. "—I'd have to persuade him. . . ."

Behind the building, the path curved up across a lawn, and on into a cluster of small, light green trees. There were flowers planted along this path, too. —Marigolds, Ellie thought, like the others . . . hanging on through early fall. Now, there was no breeze, no movement of the air at all. Perfect sunny late-morning stillness. The priest stopped walking as Ellie stopped.

"You're thinking we have a little paradise here, aren't you?"

"Yes," Ellie said.

"The garden—the students call it Sanctuary because it's their private place, and faculty isn't supposed to go there—the garden is right up through those maples."

"I was wondering," Ellie said, "what'll happen to Sonia, now."

"Nothing further grim," Peschek said, "—if we can help it. We aren't *entirely* at the service of the thoughtless rich, you know. We—or I, anyway—take St. Christopher's very seriously, even if some no longer regard our patron as a serious saint." The priest's scalp was bright pink in the sunshine, his fine hair no protection at all. "I've spoken to some of the parents about it, and we hope that Sonia will stay right here with us, will go to school here until she graduates, and then—hopefully with some scholarship assistance—will go on to college. She'll be spending her summers with her friends."

"Lucky."

"Maybe," the priest said. "—We won't know that for a long time."

"We found fourteen thousand dollars in Sally's apartment," Ellie said. "It'll be tied up for a while—but you could check with the Manhattan D.A., the District Attorney's office. If you have a lawyer, he could check with them. The probate court might release some of that. . . ."

"Well, thank you very much. That could be helpful. —What's your first name?"

"Eleanor. —Ellie."

"Thank you very much, Ellie. We'll check." He held out his soft hand to shake. "Will you come up and visit us again? —Bring your reluctant male counterpart?"

"I'll try, Father."

"Bye-bye," Peschek said, turned, and walked back down the flagstone path. He waddled slightly.

Ellie walked up into the maples, saw a low darker-green line of hedge ahead, then came into a small brick-paved garden circle, walled with the hedge, waist-high. The girl was waiting on a redwood bench to the left, sitting in her school uniform, her legs crossed, a green book bag in her lap, reading a textbook—pretending to read it, Ellie thought.

"Hi . . ." Ellie walked over to her. "You're Sonia, aren't you?"

The girl looked up from her book. "Yes . . ." She was not as pretty as her mother had been. Slightly stocky, with straight light-brown hair, almost blond, worn long. Blue-gray eyes, though, that looked a little like her mother's in her pictures. A long elegant nose—very like her mother's.

"My name's Ellie Klein. I'm a police officer, which I guess you know. —May I sit down?"

"O.K." Sonia closed her book—a small book with a red cover—and held it in her lap, on her book bag. "—Did you find out who did it?"

"No, not yet," Ellie said, and sat down beside her. "Well . . . the first thing I want to say is I'm sorry I had to come up and bother you—"

"You're not bothering me."

"Well . . . I took you out of class."

"I don't care about that," Sonia said. "It was just algebra. That stuff's a waste of time, anyway."

"Well, I had to come up. There're a few questions I need to ask you. . . ."

"So . . . ? Go ahead. Ask me."

The girl had beautiful skin, so smooth and light-attracting that Ellie could see the separate fine hairs of down along her forearm, could see shifting delicate pinks and pearls and silvers in it. —I'm sitting next to Sally Gaither's child, she thought. This is as close now as anybody can ever be to Sally. . . .

"Did you ever meet any of your mom's friends?"

"Mother. My mother."

"Did you ever meet any of your mother's friends?"

"I met Susan Margolies, once. She wasn't very smart."

"Why not?"

"She let all mother's plants die when we were in New Mexico—said she forgot."

"You meet any other of your mother's friends?"

"No—I didn't. It wasn't appropriate."

"Did your mother ever mention anybody to you . . . anybody she was close to, or afraid of? Any man she knew . . . who was kind of tough—or a little weird?"

Sonia Gaither smiled. "My mother knew lots of men who were tough—and a little weird. It was her profession, you know. Don't you know lots of guys who're tough and a little weird? —That wasn't a very good question."

"I mean somebody special, Sonia. You know . . . somebody who was bothering her. Somebody she mentioned recently."

The girl turned to face Ellie, and showed shadows on the skin under her eyes. It made her face look odd—a young girl's face, with a woman's shadows under her eyes. "—She didn't tell me about anybody like that. —Nobody bothered my mother. She told me, if anybody bothered you—either pick them up and set them aside, or if they're too heavy to lift, then walk around them and keep going. She wasn't afraid. —You can't be a professional prostitute, and be afraid of people. You need to like people, to be good at that."

"But there must have been somebody, Sonia—because somebody killed her."

Sonia stared at Ellie, reminded. Ellie, watching the change of light in the girl's eyes, the shifting shades of blue and gray, saw at their centers the round black pupils barely expand. "I don't understand it," the girl said. "—I don't understand it at all." Sonia smelled of vanilla and clean cloth.

"I want you to think about it. Please, Sonia. See if you can think of anyone your mom—your mother talked about."

"Mother didn't talk about her clients. —Well, she did, sometimes. But she didn't tell me their names or anything."

"Did she describe a man to you? —Maybe someone who was really close to her—maybe someone she really liked?"

"She liked George Soseby."

"And she told you his name."

"I *know* George. George wasn't a client. —He's my mother's lover. That's a whole different kind of relationship. —You know how they met? He was a date—and then afterward, he asked for his money back. And my mother asked why, and he said he didn't want money standing between them, and asked for his money back. She gave it to him, too. —He's really nice."

Ellie felt a little short of breath. "Where does George live, honey? —Has he talked to you since your mother died?"

"George lives in New York; he's a factor. You know what that is?"

"No—I don't think so. . . ."

"I think it's a trader who is kind of a middleman between other traders—importing things."

"Oh. —Where does George live? What's his address?"

"I don't know—but he's in Europe, now. He's in Brussels, Belgium. I don't think he knows what happened. . . ."

"In Belgium . . . He hasn't called you . . . written to you?"

"He sent me some postcards."

"Did you keep them?"

"No—the pictures weren't that great. I guess he knew something was wrong. He said something in the last one about mother not answering her phone . . . just kind of joking. I threw all those cards away. I didn't want to keep them."

"How does Mr. Soseby spell his name, Sonia?"

"S-O-S-E-B-Y."

Ellie took her notebook from her purse, and wrote that down. Then, they sat together without saying anything for a while.

"Is it true," Ellie said, "—that the teachers can't come here?"

"Masters."

"But they can't come here?"

"They're not supposed to," Sonia said. "—But if kids started smoking pot and stuff here, they would."

"I guess this is the prettiest school I ever saw," Ellie said. "Is it nice as it looks?"

"It's O.K. They don't bug you too much."

"Hard classes?"

"The classes are *very* hard."

"What do you do in the summer? —Stay with friends, or what?"

"I stay with my mother. —We went to New Mexico this summer to see the pueblos and watch the Pueblo indians make sand paintings and katchinas. —It's part of their religion."

"Did you stay with her in town, too? In her apartment?"

"That place was for business. When I came to New York, we stayed at a hotel. Any hotel I wanted to . . ." Sonia bowed her head, looking down at her textbook, her book bag.

"Well, I need to ask you one more thing. Then, I'll leave you alone."

"That's all right. . . ."

A sparrow flew down onto the brick pavement in front of the bench, and began to hop and peck at things in the cracks of the bricks.

"Did your mom—did your mother leave any notebook or diary with you? An appointment book, anything like that?"

"No."

"You don't have anything like that?"

"No. She wrote me some letters when we came back from vacation. . . ."

"A lot of letters?"

"My mother came up here all the time—she didn't have to write me a lot of letters."

Another sparrow came and joined the first, and they fluttered into the air, then landed again in the same place, and pecked between the bricks.

"O.K.," Ellie said. "Listen, I know it's a private thing. But it could be important. Could I just look at the letters—to see if there might be something important in them?"

"No."

"Even if there might be something important in them? —Something you wouldn't know about?"

"I know about what's in my letters," Sonia Gaither said, put her textbook in her book bag, zipped it shut, and stood up. She had narrow ankles, round, strong calves. "—I have to go and get some stuff for gym in my room. I have gym right after lunch."

Ellie stood up, too. "Can I walk with you?"

"Sure. That's all right."

They walked out of the garden, and down the path between the pines. Sonia was shorter than Ellie, by a good bit.

"Are these marigolds?"

"Mums."

They walked down to the building where Peschek had his office, then on across the turnaround and back down the drive Ellie had come up. Near the first faculty house, Sonia went to the left, and they walked down another flagstone path toward a long, two-story building—white clapboard, like the others.

A Hispanic-looking girl came walking up the path toward them—the school uniform looking better on her than on the others—glanced at Ellie, and said, "Hi, Sonia."

"Juana," Sonia said.

"You know," Ellie said, after the girl had passed, "—when I was nine, I came home from school one day, and my mom had left a note for me on the kitchen table. It said, 'There's a tuna-fish sandwich in the refrigerator, and pour yourself a glass of milk. —Good luck, honey.' She had left me and my dad—and I didn't see her again for four years."

Sonia didn't say anything.

"When I did see her again, it was like she wasn't my mother at all. I think, in a kind of way, my mother died that afternoon when I was nine. —You were lucky, Sonia. Your mom loved you. —That's one thing I already found out. Your mom loved you more than anything."

Sonia said nothing until they got to the building steps, then she stopped, and held out her hand. "It was nice meeting you," she said. "—I'm sorry I didn't know any of that stuff you wanted to know."

"That's O.K.," Ellie said, shaking her hand. "—It was nice meeting you, Sonia." She wanted to hug the girl, but Sonia didn't seem to want anything like that. Ellie searched in her purse, found her wallet, and took out her card; then she found her pen and wrote her home phone number on the back. "—Here, it's my home phone." She handed the card to Sonia. "If you remember anything, or . . . or if you just want to talk to somebody, call me. I have an answering machine."

"O.K.," Sonia said, "—bye-bye," and turned and went up the building steps.

Ellie closed her purse, stood and watched until Sonia went in through the entrance and was gone, then started back up the long walk to the turnaround. It was a big school. —Spread out, anyway. She thought the kids must get a lot of exercise, just getting around.

She walked up to the turnaround, went to the Honda, and leaned on its roof to write "Factor" and "Belgium" in her notebook. If Soseby had really been in Belgium—then that was likely that. Ellie supposed he didn't even know Sally was dead. —Unless he'd had someone kill her.

She unlocked the car, got in—it was warm inside, even though the day was cool—started it, backed out of her parking space (the brown-and-white van was gone), and drove around and down to the driveway, then past the faculty houses and out across the big lawn. The boys weren't playing on it, now. Probably gone to lunch.

As she pulled around the grove of trees at the end of the drive, Ellie saw a girl. —Sonia. She was standing beside the school sign at the side of the road, waiting.

Ellie pulled up beside her.

Sonia's hair was tangled from running. Ellie thought her face was sweaty—then saw she was crying. Ellie turned the engine off, got out of the car, and went to the girl and hugged her.

"I'm sorry," Ellie said. "Oh, Sonia—it's so terrible for you. I'm so *sorry*."

"Oh . . . oh, Mrs. Klein," the girl said, and held on to Ellie hard.

Ellie kissed her cheek, and tasted tears. "Poor, poor baby," she said. "—There . . . there."

"Why did he hurt her so *much*?" The girl's arms were locked around Ellie like chains. "—He could have just killed her. —He didn't have to hurt her so *much*!"

"Here," Ellie said, reached down for her purse for Kleenex, then realized it was in the car. "Oh, my God . . . come on, now. There, there, sweetheart . . ."

Sonia Gaither sagged against her, and wept the front of Ellie's white blouse wet, her body convulsing as she cried.

"Ah, darling," Ellie said, and held the girl to her. "There, there . . ." Ellie thought that Sonia, a little younger, could have been her daughter. She held the girl, and rocked her in her arms. "Now, now . . ." she said. "Now, now . . ." And, after a while, Sonia wept less, and then not at all, but sniffled.

"Come on," Ellie said, "—that's enough crying. Time to blow our noses. After tears—snot." And Sonia almost laughed. Ellie patted the girl's back and let her go. When Sonia let go, too, Ellie went back to the car, got her Kleenex, and both of them blew their noses. Then Sonia picked up two envelopes she'd dropped on the grass.

"Here's the letters my mother sent me. She just sent two of them, a couple of weeks ago. We used to talk on the phone, mostly." She used a wadded Kleenex and blew her nose again. "—She called them Truth Letters. She said that was the most important thing of all. . . ." Sonia handed the envelopes to Ellie. "—They're kind of dirty, I guess. People would think they're dirty."

"I won't," Ellie said.

"You promise nobody else will read them? —I haven't even let Joanna read them."

"I won't let anybody read them," Ellie said, "—except

maybe my partner. He's a very nice man, and he has a little girl of his own. I promise we won't let anybody else read them, not unless we have to, to catch whoever killed your mom. —I promise you, Sonia."

"Well," Sonia said, "—I guess that's all right."

"Here . . ." Ellie gave her another Kleenex.

"I ruined your blouse. . . ."

"Oh, this thing's polyester; it'll dry."

"Well," Sonia said, "—I'm sorry I was such a kid."

"I think your mom was worth a lot of tears," Ellie said, "—and I didn't even know her."

They hugged, and Ellie went back to the Honda, got in, and started the engine, while Sonia stood by the car, watching her.

"I'll come up and see you again, if that's all right," Ellie said.

"O.K."

"—and Sonia, my friend and I are going to find out who did that to your mother. We're going to destroy the son-of-a-bitch."

"Good," Sonia said, and blew her nose. "—Good."

CHAPTER 9

"Mother of God, would you look at that line-up. . . ." Lieutenant Eastman—still and likely forever a lieutenant, still and likely forever the assistant to the Assistant Deputy Commissioner for Community Affairs—was observing the civilian mourners at Woodlawn, gathered beneath a mild early autumn sun, but dressed in drab for deep winter. His new boss—a pleasant, but not particularly simpatico ex-reporter for *The Washington Post*—agreed. "The Dawn of the Dead," he said.

Old Mrs. Classman's friends, veterans of the Ladies' Garment Worker's Union, were few and drearily aged in aspect, and they made a poor showing for the TV cameras—facing, across the two caskets (best bright bronze), ranks of uniformed young patrolmen—and, in a loose semicircle to the right of these ranks, standing beside Rabbi Solwitz, the brass.

The Rabbi, a tall, handsome man with grizzled, curly hair—he'd grown up being told he looked like the late Jeff Chandler—was completing a soporific address on the indissoluble bonds linking mother and son, *"—that even death. . . ."* This speech, or sermon, had reduced the press corps and other hangers-on to standing sleep, though the police officers present appeared genuinely affected, and some grimly veteran eyes were wet.

"They are shooting nothing but those *hags. . . !"* Lieutenant Eastman slid out of place in a sinuous effacing maneuver, drifted back . . . turned, trotted to the right, and arrived at the small aluminum platform from which ABC Local News was covering the affair.

"For Christ's sake,"—to an assistant cameraman standing near. "Get some shots of the Commissioner! Get the *Mayor,* for Christ's sake!"

"He's gettin' everybody."

"Bullshit," Lieutenant Eastman said, and reached up to tug at the cameraman's trouser leg. "Hey," he said. "Hey!"

The cameraman glanced down.

"Is your mother over there or something?" Lieutenant Eastman said. "You've been shooting over there for ten minutes! —The Commissioner's here—if you haven't noticed. The Mayor's here!"

"You got any complaints," the cameraman said, and returned to his eyepiece, "—talk to the L.D.," and gestured with his thumb at the location van parked fifty yards behind them.

"I'm talking to you, motherfucker!" said Lieutenant Eastman, gay, but a policeman after all. "You turn that camera—you turn that fucking camera right *now.*"

The cameraman held his position, and his view—but only for a few more seconds, for self-respect. Then he swung to the right, found and focused, and videod the Mayor, the Commissioner, the handsome Deputy Commissioner for Public Affairs (his lower lip still slightly swollen), and almost two dozen other persons of importance.

"That's better," said Lieutenant Eastman. "This is a Departmental funeral. —You forget that, I'll come back and remind you."

"Pretty fierce, Sammy."

The Lieutenant turned, and seized Ellie in a hug. "You sweetheart," he said, "—have you been being good?"

"I've been trying."

"You—are late."

"I know. I was out of town. I just got back."

"Sweetheart, have you ever heard of gray? —It is absolutely not necessary to wear banker blue to every formal event."

"It's what I've got, Sammy. I'm not going out and buy a second funeral suit. —How are things going?"

"Oh, it's running along. Shomrin people set it up.—We can do these damn things in our sleep"—a glance up at the undoubtedly overhearing cameraman—"as long as we get cooperation."

"How's Fred?"

"Ancient history. —Handsome wasn't as handsome did."

"Maybe you need to try the ladies, Sammy."

Lieutenant Eastman almost said, "—That working for you . . . ?" but didn't, for fear of hurting and frightening her. A friend of a friend was a friend of Clara Kersh's in the Federal Task Force, and Eastman had been careful to see that *that* information went no further.

He said, instead, "Oh, I have—but that's just sex."

Ellie laughed, and tiptoed to kiss him on the cheek. Eastman had been very good to her the days after she'd been hurt in the fire. He'd stayed in her hospital room all one night, reading E. F. Benson to her, after—during an evening makeup session before an interview—she had begun to weep, and call for her ex-husband.

"Where are 'de boys'?" Ellie said, and flattened the end of her nose with her forefinger.

"You'll find them down there," Eastman said, pointing to the far end of the uniformed police ranks. "—Behaving themselves, I hope."

Ellie, her medium heels sinking slightly into the grass and soft earth, walked along behind a line of blue-coated backs, hearing the Rabbi's voice slow . . . deepen, under a thrumming mutter of traffic passing on the Parkway. "*Together now—as they were in their very beginning. Together now, once and for all. Together now, in the arms of their God. . . . Amen.*" A murmur of appreciation, almost applause. Rabbi Solwitz and the Department's Catholic chaplain, Father Gruenwald, had a long-standing disagreement in the matter of religious rhetoric, the Priest preferring a manly, laconic style—suited, he felt, to a paramilitary organization, while the Rabbi favored, for that very circumstance, a romantic, even thrilling approach, to match the sacrifice and aspirations of soldiers in the Army of the Just. Sophisticates in the Department, and those in a hurry, preferred Father Gruenwald's sermons—a considerable minority of romantics, this rabbinical music.

The detectives and plainclothesmen, male and female—here off duty—were gathered in bunches among the trees and tombstones, huddled in groups of a few to a hundred, representing squads, precincts, divisions, this or that side of town, but all—except for a few undercover oddities grown stuck to their tie-dyed T-shirts and leather goods, their Indian pajamas, their short shorts, sneakers, and snakeskin vests—wore Sunday suits, and, though they had been fairly silent during the Rabbi's number, now erupted in humming conversation concerning scandals, promotions, demotions, and Departmental politics. They did not, by and large, talk cases, since talking shop at funerals was considered no class.

Ellie was greeted by some of these as she wandered through, glanced at by more, and identified as a cop at once, even by men and women who had not met her—identifications that would have pleased her very much. She had gradually acquired—after years, and all unknowing—purposefulness in posture and directness in eye contact foreign to sidling civilians.

She saw Keneally in a blue suit, talking to some Homicide people standing beside a thicket of tombstones. He saw her, and waved. —A few yards farther on, Samuelson's massive head rose above a peninsula of people (past a white stone angel, mourning). Ellie cut through to there, and found the Squad up front in pride of place—the killed cop being one of theirs. Nardone, Serrano, and a sergeant named Seguin were still on their knees in the grass, completing prayers, slender strands of beads gripped in heavy hands. The other officers were quietly gossiping.

Ellie could just see one of the caskets past the end file of uniformed people. She didn't know if it was Classman or his mother in there. That gentle, quiet man . . . Dead meat. Pumped full of chemicals to keep it from rotting. —It was disgusting.

"You're late, Klein," Leahy said.

"Couldn't be helped," Ellie said, and went to Nardone. —He looked up, smiled, murmured ". . . and the fruit of thy womb, Jesus," and stood up with the other two officers as the mayor began to speak. The mayor's theme was Sacrifice.

Ellie and Nardone found a quiet place among the monuments—one, very massive, was carved only GREENHUT—a place behind a silent group of Stake-out people. These dangerous, active men, awkward in their Sunday suits, stood in the shade of a single large tree, listening to the mayor's amplified voice—bored wolves hearing a bullfrog's comments on the hunt. Samuelson had been one of these, once, and according to Nardone, gravely missed that precarious life—those long hours squatting in feral silence behind a liquor store's back counter, or in its storeroom among the crates and cartons, cradling like a baby a Remington twelve-gauge loaded alternately with double-ought buckshot and slugs thick as a man's thumb.

Those long, long hours, climaxed only rarely by an entrance of desired prey—two men, sometimes three, come with pistols to rob the place. Commencing as usual, to avoid later difficulty, by beating the man who clerked in or owned the store, by beating customers, these hoodlums might enjoy that part, or do it only out of duty—and were occasionally allowed to do so, the stake-out commander waiting, wanting them positioned more fruitfully. Those positions, fairly soon, they would assume—one man at the register, one man a lookout at the door—the third controlling sight lines across the center of the store. The clerk, and any customers, prone on linoleum under faintly buzzing fluorescents.

Pleased as a little boy with a present, the commander would then step out with a heavy handgun, make his announcement—and, at any motion but surrender, even the slightest, would produce his myrmidons in a sudden smashing storm.

Early in the funeral, while the crowd was gathering, the uniformed ranks forming up near the shining caskets, Samuelson had looked over at these men, nodded to them and been nodded to in return, but hadn't walked over the graves to visit.

"How's the kid?" Nardone said. "—She takin' it O.K.?" There were grass stains on the knees of his blue suit-trousers.

"I think she'll be all right. The principal up there is a priest—he said the school is going to look after her. Keep her in school, and send her to college, too."

"O.K. Then she's a lucky girl—right?"

"Maybe. I hope so."

"She have anything?"

"Two really long letters from her mom. I pulled over and glanced at them on the way down, and it looks personal, you know . . . mother-daughter stuff—what she learned being a prostitute, that kind of thing. . . . But there could be something there. I'll start reading them tonight, see what's what. —And Sally had a boyfriend, a guy called Soseby—George Soseby."

"Hey—that's somethin'! Where is this boyfriend? —Don't tell me . . . you got that look the guy's up at Ossining, been there a year."

"Belgium." Ellie had a cramp. She felt it tighten into her.

"Belgium?"

"And been there a few weeks, it looks like. Sent Sonia postcards. . . ."

"That doesn't mean shit. The guy could have come flyin' in and out. . . ."

"Brussels, Belgium. He's a factor, a financial guy."

"Well, we'll check . . . see if he stayed put, see if he got cute on the airlines. —An' that's it?"

One of the Stake-out men had turned to look at them, a tall, stoop-shouldered man in a gray suit.

"That's it," Ellie said. "—What have you got?"

"Somethin', anyway," Nardone said. "The load came in this mornin'. The M. E.'s preliminary report—nothin' new there. Lady was cooked. —Period. Nothin' under her nails. No semen. Nothin'. Fingerprints came in, too, long last.—You ready for this? Some funny stuff, but it doesn't amount to much."

"Who . . . ?" The cramp was easing.

"To start with, four cops—includin' you. Prints was really pissed off, 'unprofessional behavior' and all that shit. . . . Then, your buddy Margolies—"

"No surprise. —Where?"

"Under the toilet handle."

"Under the toilet handle . . . Got to be pretty recent."

"Could be. Ready for this? —Birnbaum."

"The mayor's man . . . ?" As if he'd overheard, the mayor commenced a loudspeakered statement concerning readiness to sacrifice what might be personally dear—even life, itself—for the greater good.

"*Used* to be the mayor's man. —An' guess who else?"

"I give up."

"A guy named Audrey."

"You're kidding me. —The black guy?" Ellie felt another cramp, and then a sharp twinge that made her slightly sick. Felt her flow coming down. It seemed so heavy she imagined herself walking in front of all these men with blood running down her legs, so they could think anything about her they wanted.

"That's him. But probably not recent. Birnbaum's an' Walker's prints were on a couple of wineglasses." He mimed turning on a faucet, swirled his fingers. "—They had some wine, washed the glasses . . . an' put 'em away. Didn't use the washin' machine."

"Who else . . . ?"

"The super—Correa, an' two sets no ID—those were on the back of the refrigerator . . . living-room couch. Probably movin' guys."

"That's it?"

"That's it. —That's it, but they still got to get a result for prints on the money."

"Mine'll be on it."

"Note on there, on the report. —Apartment had to take at least a one-hour wipe, get it that clean."

"That motherfucker was walking around dusting, while Sally was dying in there. . . ." She had another cramp, but this one wasn't so bad.

"That's probably right."

"God . . . Tommy . . . I told her daughter we'd get whoever did it. —Jesus, I'd hate for that fucker to walk away from this. . . !"

Nardone patted her shoulder. "Come on, come on . . . it'll just take us more time, that's all. We don't have a team . . . it'll take us more time. —No statute of limitations on this."

"Excuse me—am I interrupting something?" The tall Stake-out man. He was holding a black porkpie hat in his left hand. "I know you, don't I?" he said to Nardone. "—I know you from Sacred Heart."

"That's right," Nardone said.

"Phil Shea." He put out his hand to shake.

"Tom Nardone."

"Right." Shea was very tall—taller than Classman had been—and appeared to stoop slightly to minimize it. He had a raw, weather-burned face, like a farmer's. The Stake-out people usually hunted and fished, went out on cold, dark winter mornings to duck blinds on Long Island to wait for geese flying in high from the Arctic. Years of that had left weather marks on his face. He had a country person's pale eyes, as well.

"Am I interrupting something?"

"Nothin' can't wait," Nardone said.

The Stake-out man looked at Ellie.

"This is Detective Klein," Nardone said, and Shea held out his hand to shake again. He had a big, long-fingered hand, and held Ellie's very lightly, as if he might hurt her. She saw him glance down at her left hand for a wedding ring.

"Phil Shea," he said. "I'm very sorry about you people losing your guy like this. He must have been all right, put a slug in that fucker, anyway. —Excuse me, that guy."

"He was a good officer," Ellie said, "—he was a very nice man."

"Took care of his mother, didn't he?" Shea said.

"That's right."

"Nice of you to come over," Nardone said.

"Well," the Stake-out man said, "I came over to tell you we were sorry you lost your man. —And . . . I know it's a bad time"—he looked down at Ellie from a considerable height—"I also wanted to ask this officer . . . if she's free, you know . . . if she'd care to have dinner with me some evening. Some evening she's off duty."

Nardone laughed. "Man," he said, "—if you don't have some nerve. The nerve of this guy! You got some nerve, buddy. We're at a friggin' funeral to start with—an' how do you know she's not with me. How do you know we don't have somethin' goin'?"

Shea smiled. " 'Cause I know you're a happy married man, for one thing. You got a wife and a little girl—right? I saw the three of you with Father—right? And for another thing, I wouldn't care. anyway." He looked at Ellie. "I'm asking you to dinner, miss. —And this is not something I planned, let me tell you. But I saw you, and I couldn't not come over and ask could I see you again."

"Do you believe this?" Nardone said.

"No," Ellie said. "I think you're a wise guy, Mr. Shea."

"No," Shea said. "—I'm not. I'm just the only man out here with eyes in his head."

"This is embarrassin'," Nardone said. "—We got an Irish guy makin' love, here. It's a first."

Shea laughed. "I guess I'm not much of a lover boy," he said to Ellie. "Please, come out and have dinner with me, and if you don't like it, I swear I'll never bother you again."

"I can't—really," Ellie said. "I just don't have the time."

"Think again. —I'm a widower; I'm fair game."

"Jesus," Nardone said. "—Will you get serious? We got a friggin' *funeral* here."

"Say yes," Shea said.

"Maybe," Ellie said. "—We really are very busy right now."

"O.K.," Shea said. "I'll call you downtown, and we'll have dinner some night this week—whenever you have an hour free. You have to eat."

"Oh . . . all right."

"We have a date?"

"I suppose so."

"Really bad taste," Nardone said. "This is really what I call bad taste—an Irish guy, supposed to be a good Catholic, makin' this kind of pass in a cemetery."

"O.K., Tommy," Ellie said, "—quit it."

"I'll be calling you," Shea said to Ellie, and bent and kissed her on the cheek as if he knew her. "Take it easy," he said to Nardone, and walked away, swinging his porkpie hat in his hand.

The mayor had just finished his speech. The loudspeaker was humming a single high thin note.

"What in the world was that all about?" Ellie said, pleased. . . . It was such an odd thing to have happened.

"Guess he liked your looks," Nardone said. "—I don't know why he came over."

"Is he one of your friends, Tommy? Is this something—did you and Connie put him up to this?"

"No, no." Nardone shook his head and one hand. "—No way. I don't know anythin' about that guy."

"Who is he—does he usually pull stuff like this?"

"Oh . . . I don't know the guy except to see him

sometimes in church. The guy's on Stake-out, and he's a lieutenant; that's all I know."

"He's got a lot of nerve."

"Probably been drinkin'," Nardone said. "—Those Irish guys talk to a lady—they got to be drinkin'."

The commissioner began to speak. His theme soon appeared, and was Duty.

A satisfactory occasion, was the opinion of the brass after Solwitz's closing prayer, and handsome Jorge Molina, Deputy Commissioner for Community Affairs, received nods from several of his companions. A good funeral.

John Cherusco, whose proper place was lower down, pushed his way through the crowd as discipline dissolved, the mayor's and commissioner's cars swung slowly around the near access road to pick them up, their satellites gathered to escort them. A uniformed inspector, not liking the pushing, shoved back—but Cherusco ignored him, slid away, and pushed some more until he reached the Chief, just as Delgado bent to get into his limousine, third in line behind the commissioner's.

"Do we just let those assholes walk on this?" Cherusco said, his hand on Delgado's arm.

"You bet," said the Chief of the Department.

Nardone followed Ellie over the Queensboro and onto Roosevelt Island, waited while she parked the Honda in the community garage, then drove her to her building, and went in with her.

"I got an idea about this afternoon, if you're up for it. —An' I got some news—we're on the job this evenin'."

"Shit," Ellie said. "Just a minute . . ." She walked back to the bathroom, went in, closed the door, and took off her suit jacket and skirt. She took a Tampax from the cabinet, pulled her panty hose down, and sat on the toilet to take the other Tampax out. It was soaked, but she hadn't stained anything. She put the used tampon in a plastic produce bag from the grocery, twisted it closed, and put it in the wastebasket—then inserted the fresh one. It had been new blood; it didn't smell at all. She dressed, and washed her hands.

Nardone was sitting on the living-room couch when she

came out, reading *Newsweek*. "Another shitty theater season," he said, and put the magazine down. "—They're sayin' these so-called playwrights they got now are a joke."

"What about this afternoon?" Ellie said. "It's pretty late. —You want something to eat?"

"Well, I'll tell you what I figured—"

"You figured Birnbaum," Ellie said. "Get to him before some old buddy downtown tips him—right?"

"I called the man's office—he'll be in till five-thirty."

"What do you want to eat, Tommy?"

"Nothin'. I had lunch."

"You're not hungry?"

"I had a hamburger."

Ellie started back to the kitchen. "I'm going to have a tuna-fish sandwich." She went into the kitchen and called to him. "—You want lettuce on yours, or not?"

"O.K."

Mayo patrolled her ankles while she made the sandwiches—using whole wheat, though Nardone didn't care for it. It was the only bread she had. Ellie bent with a pinch of tuna in her palm for the Siamese, felt the quick needle nibble as he took it from her, the small wet rasp of his tongue.

She brought the sandwiches out with two root beers, and set them on the coffee table.

"I only had whole wheat."

"That's O.K."

"Why this evening? —We're not scheduled for night."

"Our idea—we got stuck with it," Nardone said, and started on his sandwich.

"What idea . . . ? You want some salt?"

"No. This is great. —Leahy wants us to take Bostwick down to Port Authority."

"You are kidding me! He's going to *do* it?"

"Bostwick's goin' up to Albany. —State guys are sendin' a car for him." He didn't seem to mind the whole wheat.

"Where is he—where are we supposed to find the guy?"

"Twentieth is holdin' him for us. Guy's supposed to be in bad shape."

"I'll bet" Ellie said. "That's O.K. for Leahy. —There's more to him than you thought, Tommy."

"He's O.K.," Nardone said, and took another big bite. "—There's worse guys."

Todd Birnbaum's office was on the eighth floor of a huge, fat, white-brick office building off Madison near Fifty-third. Office workers were already trooping out—done for the day at four-thirty—spinning the revolving center door, shoving the swinging side doors continuously open as Ellie and Nardone bucked the current to work their way in. They'd left the Ford parked in yellow around the corner, its slap light stuck on the roof. —It was not unheard of for particularly stupid tow truckers to snatch unmarked Department cars.

The elevator going up was empty. —Stayed empty all the way to the eighth floor.

Birnbaum's office—a small suite, glass partitions all the way through—was fronted at a reception desk by a tall, plain girl in an ivory blouse, black skirt, and soft black tie. There was a short sofa, stainless steel with pebble-finish black plastic cushions. Two chairs to match, and a glass and steel coffee table. —No one was waiting.

Ellie could see Birnbaum—in his shirtsleeves, sleeves rolled up—two offices over, talking with three men in dark suits. The intervening office was empty—bookshelves empty, desk bare.

"We're police officers," Nardone said to the tall girl, and showed her his ID. "We'd like to see Mr. Birnbaum."

"It's very late," she said, gestured his ID to be held closer, read it, and made a note on a long legal pad. "If this isn't terribly important, Officer, tomorrow afternoon might be better." The tall girl had a big nose, dark, direct eyes. If her complexion had been better, she might have been striking. She'd had acne, and been scarred by it.

"It's important," Nardone said. "We'll wait." He and Ellie went over and sat side by side on the sofa, leaned forward together to leaf through the magazines on the coffee table, picked two out, sat back, and looked through them.

The receptionist picked up her phone, pressed a button, and said something. Ellie saw Birnbaum on the phone in the back office. He glanced up, the phone to his ear, and looked out at them through the glass partitions. Then he put the phone down, and she saw him say something to the three men.

"What do you think about those guys?" Nardone said; he was looking at an article in *Forbes* on discount rate-setting. "They look like wise guys or what?"

One of the men talking with Birnbaum turned to look at them through the partitions.

"I can't tell if they're sorry to see us here, or not," Ellie said.

Ellie was looking at an issue of *Consumer Reports*. It was the August issue; there was an article on thin TV's. Only a little more than an inch thick, and you could hang them on your wall.—The sound was good, too. Turn them off, and there was a painting on them—in the illustration, it was The Raft of the *Méduse*. Still expensive, but coming down. Coming down . . . but not enough.

She looked at an article on car insurance, and then one on canned soup. The soup one was discouraging. She was still reading about chicken noodle when Nardone looked up, and she looked up and saw the three men coming out to reception.

They were businessmen, not O.C. people, a very elderly man, a younger man who looked like his son. And another man—handsome, nice blue eyes. The two younger men glanced at Ellie as they walked by.

"Garment guys," Nardone said, and he and Ellie put down their magazines and went in.

"It's a little late, Officers," Birnbaum said, "let's make this quick—O.K.?" He had not gotten up to greet them. Todd Birnbaum was a stocky young man—younger than Ellie—beard-shadowed though clean shaven, his curly black hair cut short. He had his feet up on a pulled-out desk drawer, and retained, from his important service at City Hall, a brisk and decided air. He didn't seem impressed by their ID's, though he read them both carefully. He had small, dark-brown eyes.

"Where are you people from?" he said.

"Commissioner's Squad," Ellie said, and Birnbaum smiled.

"So—you have an errand. What is it?"

"We have a homicide investigation," Nardone said. He

sat down in an office chair, and Ellie sat down, too. "We're investigating the Gaither killing."

"Really . . . ? Now, I wonder why they put you people on that, instead of Division Homicide. —Worried about who Sally might have shtupped?"

"How well did you know her?" Ellie said. "—When did you see her last?"

"No Miranda?"

Ellie dug in her purse, got the card out and read it to him.

Birnbaum smiled, and said he understood his rights.

"You want to talk to us," Nardone said, "—or not?"

"Let's save some time here," Birnbaum said. "I knew Sally Gaither for several years, and went to bed with her on a number of occasions—before I met my wife. I—"

"You paid to sleep with her?" Ellie said.

"I reserve my answer on that," Birnbaum said. "—We became friends. My wife was an old acquaintance of hers and very fond of her. —Sally introduced us, in fact. The last time we saw Sally, we went up to her apartment for dinner. . . . I believe that was four or five weeks ago—when she got back from New Mexico." He spoke as rapidly and smoothly as a rehearsed actor, and looked off to the right as he spoke, not at Ellie, not at Nardone. "—My secretary will have that appointment, if you want to check it. Neither my wife nor I saw Sally after that dinner. Neither my wife nor I had any reason to hurt Sally—or anything to gain by hurting her. We think the animal that did, deserves the worst." He looked back at Ellie and Nardone when he finished talking.

"You know nobody who'd have reason to kill her?"

"No, Ms. Klein—I don't."

"But you knew she was a prostitute. . . ."

"I'll reserve on that."

"You meet a George Soseby?" Nardone said.

"No—I never met George. My wife did. Her impression was that he was a nice guy—very solid—and in love with Sally."

"We'll need to talk with your wife, Counselor," Ellie said.

Birnbaum looked at Ellie for a moment, then said,

"You'll talk with Audrey, Ms. Klein—if she wishes to talk with you. —And if her doctor agrees."

"Audrey . . ." Ellie said.

"That isn't Audrey *Walker* you're talkin' about, Counselor?" Nardone said.

"My wife's name was Walker," Birnbaum said.

"She's sick . . . ?" Ellie said.

"Jumpin' Jesus, Counselor—you got to be kiddin'! You can't marry a guy in this state!"

"My wife is very much a woman," Birnbaum said to Nardone, "—and legally so in several states. We were married two months ago—and not in New York. Now, if I may, I'd like to cut short any further ignorant and insulting questions and comments. —O.K.?"

"Is she sick . . . ?"

"Yes," Birnbaum said to Ellie. "—My wife has been ill for some time. She's now hospitalized. She's dying."

None of them said anything for a few moments. Birnbaum had on his desk one of the small glass-enclosed ornaments of dark green fluid that propagated into a small ocean wave, a cresting roller, when disturbed. Ellie noticed that some slight, continuous vibration—from the building's ventilation system, or the constant running of the elevators—kept this novelty in moderate, stirring motion. A tiny deep-green sea, in rip tide.

"I didn't mean to insult your wife," Nardone said. "I'm sorry. —Came as a surprise, that's all. I should have watched my mouth."

Birnbaum said nothing.

"If she doesn't want to talk with us," Ellie said, "—she's that sick, then we won't bother her."

Birnbaum put his feet down and sat up. "You're a strange couple of cops," he said. "My wife is at New York Hospital. She has cancer—AIDS first, now cancer from that. If you want to talk with her, I'll ask her and leave a message with your Squad. —You're still under Anderson down there, right?"

"That's right," Ellie said.

"I'll call you tomorrow morning, either way." He stood up, and they stood up to go.

"Holy shit . . ." Nardone said, in the elevator.

They walked around the corner of Fifty-third to the Ford, and saw that someone had stolen the slap light off the roof. "—Goddamnit. We're going to have to pay for that!" Ellie looked around as if she might see someone, some kid, hurrying away with the light half hidden under his jacket.

"Bullshit," Nardone said. "—We lost that fucker in a chase. Patrol car—no number read—went past us on a chase, an' unit assisted until traffic obstruction proved too hazardous, an' unit desisted. Flasher lost in chase." He unlocked the Ford, and got in.

When they were moving, and in crosstown rush-hour traffic heading for the Twentieth Precinct Station House, Nardone said, "This is some job. —What a job this is." He speeded up a little to block a cab from forcing into the lane. "Had no business sayin' that up there, but the guy caught me by surprise."

"Caught both of us by surprise."

"I mean, the guy—we got a guy there could have been a congressman . . . could have been a senator.—We're talkin' about a guy could have been *big.*"

"That's right."

"An' the man *marries* a black faggot. —That's the truth of the situation—right?"

"Gotta be love, Tommy."

"That's right. —That's gotta be love."

"And now she's dying."

"Don't remind me."

"I'll go see her if you want, tomorrow. —If she'll see me."

"O.K. I'll get goin' on the paperwork. —And we got a ton of it."

"We've got to check the airlines on Soseby. Maybe the business people in Brussels, if we can find out who he was there to see."

"Right. —By the way, forget about Crowell. I called the people in Detroit. —Crowell was around there; he was in Southampton all the time. He didn't go into New York."

"Well—that was a long shot."

"That guy wasn't goin' to kill anybody. —He was goin' to kill somebody, he'd kill his wife."

The traffic had come to a stop; they were stuck mid-block, surrounded by tired people, dented machines. After a few moments, the horns began.

"Oh—hey, listen, you're still comin' to dinner Sunday, right?"

"Yes."

"Well, listen—Connie's gettin' everything for the dinner. A woman we know from the clinic, May Fazenda, sent up the whole thing from the food section in *The Washington Post,* an' it's got everythin' in there you need from A to Z. Wine, too. Tells you the best wine to serve . . . the whole thing. She's doin' that dinner A to Z, except she's doin' her mother's sauce for the pasta."

"It's going to be delicious."

"Well—we were talkin', an' she said she was worried you were goin' to bring some wine or somethin', some food—and then you'd be hurt if we didn't serve it.—So I told her, 'Serve it, anyway. Extra wine never hurts; it isn't goin' to spoil a dinner to have extra wine. Red—white—who gives a damn?' But she was worried."

"What about liqueur for after dinner?"

"She got it. It said hazelnut liqueur."

"Tommy—I'm bringing flowers. Is Connie using her white plates with the gold edges?"

"She's usin' the best dishes."

"Those are her white ones—the pretty ones with the gold scrolling around the edges."

"O.K. I guess so."

"Well, you tell Connie I'm bringing flowers for her table—white and gold. —If she isn't using those dishes, you tell her to call me."

"O.K."

"I hope to God this friend of hers—this Patty Daley from Chicago—shows up, after all this."

"Jesus—bite your tongue," Nardone said.

The traffic began to move, but only a few yards at a time—an accordion surge beginning on green far up the block, traveling to them, allowing them some travel, then closing down as the distant light went to red again.

"O.K.," Nardone said, and gave Ellie a boy's glance through a man's face. "—You want to hear somethin' wild . . . ?"

"What?"

"Want to hear what a certain detective detected this mornin'?"

"Tommy, did you mess around up in the Bronx? —*Did* you?"

"I didn't 'mess around' up in the Bronx. I just checked some methadone places this mornin'—"

"Jesus Christ, Tommy! —Just because those guys up there thought you were off base on that? Come *on*! Classman's not our case—we *have* a case. And we're not doing very well with it!"

"I got an idea, and I just went around to check."

"Sure. You did it because those old men up in the Bronx didn't listen to you. —And you did *that* because you were pissed off about Donaher."

"Right. —You know everything. I don't know what the fuck I'm doin'."

"I didn't say that, Tommy. I'm just saying we have enough to do. —They're loading us with shit to do."

"Look—I'm not tryin' to stick my nose in the Classman thing. But I had an idea—and I'm tellin' you, there could be somethin' to it!"

The traffic—trumpeting, enraged—began to move again. They could hear police whistles up ahead.

"All right," Ellie said. "—All right. What is it?"

"Started at nine this mornin'—checked four clinics. Our guy Chávez was registered at Ninety-sixth Street. O.K.? Jesús—right?"

"O.K."

"So—I hang around there, shmooze with the staff people, not makin' any noise, right?"

"Ummm."

"I'm just noticin' who's hanging out—what guys are out front in the mornin'. And I see some guys out there for a couple hours, lookin' to make deals and so forth. And one of 'em—I know. I used to know him. Nice guy, a junkie—Manuel Soto. Nice old guy. So I talk to Manuel a little bit—poor guy doesn't have a tooth left in his head; he's got to gum everything—and he tells me these brothers are always hangin' around. Young black guys, part-time junkies. An' he points 'em out to me, you know—and there they are." Nardone made the turn onto Broadway.

"Who are they?"

"Right. A couple of jerks, Maurice and Clayton. Last name's Garrison. —I go out to have a little talk with Maurice and Clayton. But Clayton's real shy and he takes off runnin' like a deer."

"So, you chased him."

"I did not chase him. The guy was runnin' like a deer, I'm tellin' you—he had the runnin' shoes and everything."

"So . . . ?"

"But Maurice wasn't so smart. Maurice runs into the clinic. He's goin' to hide in there, right?"

"O.K."

"I go in after him—and he isn't there. Guy's vanished. He's not in the waitin' room; he's not in the office. Nobody knows where Maurice is, and the lady runs the place is tellin' me to get the hell out. . . ." Nardone blew the Ford's horn to get a man on a racing bicycle out of his way. As they passed him, Ellie saw that the man was very well equipped. He had on a helmet with a little rearview mirror, like a dentist's mirror, sticking out the side, and he had a whistle in his mouth and was wearing bicycling gloves.

"So," Nardone said, "—on the way out, I figured I'd try the can. Sure enough, there's three guys sittin' in there—but one of them, his pants legs aren't wrinkled. That guy is sittin' there, but he isn't doin' anythin'. I said, 'Maurice—if you don't come out of there, I'm goin' to pull you out under the door.' Guy stands up, flushes the toilet like he did somethin'—force of habit—and comes out and right there we have this talk. He doesn't care the other guys are listenin'; I don't care; they don't care.. . ." Nardone made the turn into the side street. Policemen's private cars were illegally parked along the two blocks either side of the station house. Some were parked on the sidewalk. Nardone pulled the Ford in alongside two motorcycles chained to a fire hydrant, turned off the ignition, looked at Ellie, and said, "Guess what Maurice had to say."

"Tommy—I have no idea what Maurice had to say."

"Listen to this. —Yesterday mornin', right in front of that methadone clinic, a guy tried to lay a deal on Maurice, an' when Clayton came up, on both of 'em—wanted one of 'em to go with him, sample some shit, see if they wanted to buy. —See if they could get enough buddies together to get the bread to buy."

"O.K."

"Guy was convincin'. Acted O.K., talked O.K. Big black dude, wore glasses."

"O.K."

"Well, they would have bought it, except one thing—Clayton had been around the corner pissin' behind a parked car, an' saw that mother drive up in a rented Dodge, with two big white guys, looked like cops."

"You think the black guy was the same one the man saw in the project—saw through his door-peep."

"Wait a minute; let me finish. So—Clayton, who's the smart one, gives his brother the *Fuck this* sign, and they say no. Big Mr. Four-eyes goes right over to Jesús Chávez, is standin' in the doorway digestin' his methadone, talks to him for a minute—and leads that sad turkey away."

"Are you bullshitting me?"

"No."

"My God, Tommy—that's a big break. But you know, Homicide was probably going to get it, anyway."

"I know it. They were already there a couple of times before me, an' they'll come back there, too. They could get it—but we got it now."

"Two white guys . . ."

"Now you got it. Now you're puttin' your finger on it! What's a black street dealer doin', hangin' out with two white guys look like cops? —Can you figure that?"

"Wise guys . . . ?"

"Hangin' around some methadone clinic with a spade dealer? —Never happen."

A young man with a mustache tapped on Nardone's closed window, and when Nardone put it down, said, "You're blockin' my bike, pal."

Nardone nodded, started the car, backed it out into the street, and waited while the young cop unchained his motorcycle, put on his helmet, mounted, started the bike, and rode past them and down the street with a tremendous blatting roar.

"Wait'll he gets married," Nardone said. "—That'll put an end to that motorcycle shit."

"Go ahead," Ellie said. "What were you saying?"

"What I was sayin' was—figure it out—here's Classman lookin' to see if some downtown madam is connected up with Department people, if that's gettin' covered by Internal Affairs guys. —Next thing happens, Classman gets shot. An' we got a guy here—Classman—who's a nut case. That's just the fact of the matter. I know you liked the guy—but it's a fact. Classman is real good with a pistol—an' he's jumpy with it, too."

"What does that have to do with it?"

"Listen. —What do you think would have happened to two or three fucked-up junkies push into the old lady's apartment to grab a TV? What do you think would have happened to guys like that when Classman comes in?"

"I don't know."

"I'll tell you. Classman would have shot the livin' shit out of 'em. You'd have a bunch of dead junkies, real quick."

"That isn't what happened, though, Tommy."

"Right. That isn't what happened. What happened—maybe—is, Classman ran into cops. Trained guys waitin' for him. He hits one—then maybe they're yellin' *'Cops, cops!'* or one of 'em's got his badge out—and Classman stops shootin' to think it over—and gets nailed."

"That couldn't be."

"Oh, the hell it couldn't! Happened more than once in the Department, let me tell you. —That black guy maybe was a dealer, maybe another cop. An' him an' his buddies came out of Classman's with two problems. —One—they got a guy hurt or dead, and two—they killed a cop an' they got to cover. What happened to the guy got hit, I don't know, but I bet if he was a cop, you're goin' to find out he got a leave or a detached assignment real quick, the next day. —An' for cover on the killin', make it look like a junkie B an' E—they went and took Jesús Chávez up to the Bronx, an' they put a slug clean through him, look like Classman's shot—then they haul the poor guy up, an' did him a Brody off that roof."

"Jesus H. Christ, Tommy . . ."

"How do you like that one?"

"I think it's very farfetched."

"Listen, honey—there are three *witnesses* saw that black

son-of-a-bitch's face! We got one witness—old Clayton there—saw the two white guys. Saw that rented Dodge. . . . What do you bet—one million bucks if Homicide checks every car rental, just on Dodges, last couple of weeks—they're goin' to find a piece of fake ID, car rented by a guy don't exist. They start checkin' around all over town—the precincts, bars, restaurants, everythin', put the word out on the street lookin' for somebody remembers seein' a big black guy with glasses hangin' out with two big white guys look like cops. —They don't bust somethin' loose in a week, maybe two weeks, I'll be damn surprised."

"O.K., Tommy, what are you going to do? —We don't have the time to screw around with this—even if you're right."

"I'm not goin' to do a goddamn thing. What I'm goin' to do is tell Leahy, let him tell Anderson—an' that jerk can call Division an' let 'em know we aren't all assholes down there, after all. I mean, I could be wrong—right? It makes sense to me—but, O.K., I could be dead wrong."

"You certainly could."

"But it's a lead—right? It's witnesses saw that same guy takin' Chávez away. I didn't make that up."

"I guess you could be right, Tommy. But I hope you're wrong, and it wasn't cops."

"I know," Nardone said, opened his door and climbed out of the car. "I know what you mean."

A tiny woman, almost a midget, was talking to the only sergeant on desk duty when Ellie and Nardone went in. The woman had a high-pitched voice, and she was speaking a very rapid Spanish. The desk sergeant was black.

The woman finished what she was saying, and the sergeant said, "I want to know if he threatened you, physically. Did he say he was goin' to hurt you, you didn't let him do what he wanted?"

The tiny woman shook her head, and answered rat-a-tat-tat in Spanish.

"Look," the sergeant said. "How about just payin' your rent?"

More Spanish. When she spoke with such speed and force, the little woman rose on her toes with the effort.

"He said he doesn't want your money. . . ."

Spanish.

"He's makin' sexual blackmail on you—right?"

The little lady nodded.

"I was you, I'd move," the desk sergeant said.

The woman said nothing to that.

"How many kids you got?"

"Cuatro."

They looked at each other for a moment—the sergeant looking down, the small woman, up.

"Get a lawyer," the desk sergeant said. "—Tell that asshole you're gonna take him to court."

Sad, slower Spanish, then, which Ellie understood pretty well.

"The landlord *is* a lawyer . . . ?" The desk sergeant considered that. "—I was you, I'd move." He turned in his chair, and beckoned Ellie and Nardone over.

"What do you need?"

"You got a drunk named Bostwick," Nardone said.

"I don't know," the sergeant said, swiveled his chair and called behind him. "Hey, Morty? —We got a Bostwick holdin'?"

A patrolman clerk at the back of the room called, "We got him—he's down in three."

"Go get him—do these officers a favor." And to Nardone as Morty got up and left the desk room, "—Let me see some ID" as he pulled a blue form out of his desk drawer. "Fill this out."

Bostwick was able to stand, but only at a slant. He was a very slender man in his fifties or sixties, with a thick white stubble of beard. His top front teeth were missing, and he'd formed the habit of sticking his tongue partway out through that gap, and leaving it protruding. He was wearing a torn shirt, black with dirt, and a pair of baggy chinos stained darker brown here and there. There was a powerful smell of shit about him.

"You're going on a ride upstate, Carl," Ellie said. "An officer up there wants to talk to you. —You know? You remember that fight in the bar? The two state troopers?"

Carl didn't seem to remember it.

"We need a blanket for this one," Nardone said to the

sergeant. "—We can't take the guy in the car like this. Guy's got a load in his pants right now."

"We're supposed to give you guys an emergency blanket? —How we goin' to get that blanket back? You guys goin' dry clean that blanket?"

"Has he had something to eat?" Ellie said.

"Two Big Macs," the patrolman clerk called from his desk.

"Don't give us a hard time—O.K.?" Nardone said to the sergeant. "I'll pay you for the fuckin' blanket—you can get your captain somethin' for Christmas."

"—Anything else?" Ellie said.

"That's it," the patrolman clerk called. "—He kept it down."

"All right," the sergeant said. "We'll give you a blanket—you sign for it."

The drive to Port Authority was a slow drive in early evening traffic. Carl Bostwick's odor, issuing from the back seat, was severe, and seemed only strengthened by their opening the car's windows. Bostwick, after the first two or three blocks, began to make a sort of tooting sound, lips rounded, his tongue still slightly protruding. The sound would begin as a soft, almost humming note, swell slowly to a hornlike toot—pretty loud—and end in soft tongue-flapping farting noises.

"Will you give us a break back there, Carl?" Nardone said. "—It's kinda late in the day."

"Carl—do you need a drink?" Ellie said.

"Yes," Bostwick said.

"Let's stop and get him something."

"Jesus . . ."

"Come on, Tommy. . . ."

A block farther crosstown, Nardone pulled over to the left, and double-parked in front of Palace Liquors. A cabbie behind them started on his horn right away, and Nardone got out of the Ford, walked back to the cab, bent down to the driver's side window, and spoke to the man. Then he walked across the sidewalk to the liquor store, and in a couple of minutes came out with a small paper bag and got back into the Ford. A lot of horns were sounding behind them by that time—though not from the cab—and that had encouraged Bostwick, who'd tooted louder and louder in competition.

"Christ, Carl—will you cut that shit out!" Nardone took a half-pint of St. George's rum from the paper bag, twisted the top off, and handed the bottle back to Bostwick, who completed a last long tooting sound before he reached out and took it.

Ellie turned to watch, and saw Bostwick, wrapped like an Indian in his dark blue blanket, tilt the small bottle up to his toothless upper gums, and empty it. "That's more like it," he said when he was finished. "—That's the ticket, man," grew swiftly red in the face, and apparently moved his bowels. "I did doody," he said.

"Why don't they show *this* shit on TV, those fuckin' cop shows?" Nardone said. "You don't ever see this shit. —What's so funny?"

"Nothing," Ellie said, but couldn't stop laughing.

Nardone tried to keep his face straight, but couldn't, and began to laugh. "Carl," he said, when he caught his breath. "Carl—you got what it takes to be President."

"Look—this man doesn't go on this bus. That's all there is to it." The dispatcher, called down by the Trailways driver, was a short tough-looking elderly man, bald but for a silvery fringe. He had a nameplate pinned to his shirt pocket: *Mr. Konjelewski.* Mr. Konjelewski was standing beside a large bus parked in a row of other giants in the long, gray, thundering garage. He was blocking the bus door.

"Well—you're wrong about that, pal," Nardone said. "Carl, here, is an important witness—and the State Police want him up in Albany. This bus gets into Albany nine-fifteen—right? There's goin' to be a trooper waitin' right at the station for him."

"O.K.," Bostwick said. He was leaning against the side of the bus, wrapped in his blanket, gazing into the ground floor of the terminal through thick plate glass. There, a line of men, women, and children—none prosperous—waited with suitcases, duffel bags, backpacks and paper bags to board.

"This man," said Mr. Konjelewski, "is simply not in condition to travel safely. Beside which, there is an odor that would disturb other passengers."

"Put him in the back," Nardone said. "—You don't always have daisies ridin' these buses, do you?"

"No," Konjelewski said, "we don't." He had a habit of poking his right cheek out slightly with his tongue, after he'd said something—a tongue person, apparently, like Bostwick, pleased with an organ most ignored. "But this is an extreme odor situation, here."

"This is a special case, Mr. Konjelewski, really very important," Ellie said, "—and the Department would appreciate your cooperation."

"Well, the Department is not going to get my cooperation, miss."

"Detective Klein."

"Detective Klein . . . I'm not going to *cooperate,* and put an obviously incompetent and foul-smelling person on board one of our buses. Period."

"Oh, I think you're goin' to," Nardone said.

"Sure you will, Mr. Konjelewski," Ellie said, "—because if you give us any more of this crap—and we've had a very long day—we're going to have our captain call the State Police right now, and have their Vehicle Safety people come in here in the morning and hold every fucking bus you have coming in or going out, and check their brakes, steering, transmission—every fucking thing they've got. Take those motherfuckers right apart! —*Period.*" She beckoned Bostwick with a finger. "Carl," she said, "—come here and get on this bus. Come on—I'll get on with you, and we'll find a nice seat in the back."

They had stayed to watch the bus pull out—Bostwick, in pretty good shape, waving from a back window. He was excited, Ellie having told him he might see deer along the thruway farther upstate, if there was enough light.

"Will he be able to see any deer?" She and Nardone were on the escalator going up to street level. "I didn't want to lie to him, but he looked scared being on that bus."

"If he wants to see 'em," Nardone said, "—he'll see 'em."

On the main concourse, they walked toward the Eighth

Avenue entrance; they'd left the car two blocks south, at a construction site. The evening rush hour was still on for people trying to get out of the city; the long concourse was streaming with them—walking fast, half-trotting, one or two running for the escalators. Still, planted, immobile amid the hurry, a few bag ladies—establishing presence in shelter for the night—stood along the walls and store display-windows, fat, short, filthy mountains, glowering, muttering in multiple layers of sweaters and skirts, dirt-streaked down their necks, swollen legs stippled with small, furious ulcers as they stood guard on broken-wire supermarket carts packed with shopping bags and clear plastic laundry bags and brown plastic garbage bags—all stuffed with treasure half forgotten (and occasionally tugged out, examined, recalled, and repacked to threats and promises heard by any passerby).

Ellie thought what pictures they would make. A series of portraits—this one with a worried grandmother's face . . . round and gentle as a pillow, but dirty as a child's would be from playing in the yard. Ellie caught that woman's eye, and the woman made a grotesque face at her, puffing out her cheeks, rolling her eyes first to one side, then the other. Some of these women were mad—and those who weren't took pains to appear so, to be left alone. After years, Ellie supposed, of living on Manhattan's winter streets for out-of-wind, and summer avenues for just those north-south breezes, on guard perpetual, caked in stink and dirt as further armor, it would become an easier and easier part to play . . . until one blazing summer day, taunted by young Puerto Rican boys, there remained only madness, and no pretending. Then, after that richest afternoon of all, a woman might spend the rest of her days in girlhood, in her girlhood room, her skin as clean and smooth and white as girlhood sheets—and only dream she was a monster in the streets.

The bag lady in a haze of fiery light, the slender handsome circling boys—dressed in bright orange, yellows, greens, reds—dancing around her, screaming in chorus. Screaming in celebration of the birth their presence has occasioned. The bag lady going perfectly mad—her face, her head exploding silently in pale, pale blue . . . the quietest color. Her face dissolving in the blue.

Under her, as she rises in pleasure on her toes, out from under the layers of dirty skirt, crawling out from between the woman's thick and rotting legs, coming out . . . still wet, still with a rope of red attached, the girl crawls newborn across the pavement.

First picture.

Second picture. The boys gather around the girl, so very pleased—and wipe her clean with their bright shirts, lick a spot of blood from her naked shoulder—pick her up, fondle her, tug gently at her nipples, squeeze her pale buttocks, tickle her until she laughs, while the smallest, most thoughtful boy bites the red cord in half. —Hold her high on their shoulders in the burning sunlight, and she now white as powdered crystal. They hold their madness girl up higher on thin brown strong arms, with delicate brown hands. Hold her up as high as they can, so that a crowd of people across the very wide street can see her.

Third picture. The celebration—the dancing and singing—is moving away down the street. The naked girl, so very young, lies sleeping high on the crowd's uplifted hands. Their cheering makes her silence, their activity her peace. Here—left behind, the bag woman crouches at the curb, her head a rich and royal blue—folding the afterbirth like a small red sweater, tucking it into a Macy's shopping bag. She's calling out her warnings, shouting out her threats to people running by to join in singing, screaming, dancing under the sleeping girl. They pay no attention. She's only what the girl is dreaming. . . .

Just before they reached the entrance doors, Ellie saw three men standing with their backs turned in the recessed doorway of the Hoffritz store. Knives glittered beside them through the glass. She saw they were facing someone standing against the door. The store was closed for the day.

"Look at that," she said, but Nardone, having noticed her turned head and attention, had seen them and started that way, cutting across the stream of people passing by. Ellie hurried and caught up, and as they got closer, saw between two of the men a slender soldier in uniform standing against the store door, a girl standing beside him with her hand up to her mouth. Their suitcases were at their feet. The soldier looked young, and frightened as the girl.

One of the men—the biggest, with a Rasta dreadlock "do" and wearing a long brown leather jacket, was leaning on the store window's glass with an outstretched hand. He was leaning down, saying something to the soldier. The other two men, one wearing a dirty white sweater, were standing almost side by side, fencing the doorway in.

Ellie heard the big Rasta say, "—both goin' suck my cock"—and stepped up behind him and kicked him in the ass as hard as she could.

He spun around like a top—handsome black, big nose like a blade, and was reaching under the back of his leather jacket when Ellie said, "Police," and put her hand in her purse, feeling for the Smith & Wesson. She heard a light sound, *whack,* and saw Nardone had cracked the other two men's heads together.

"What are you goin' to do, motherfucker?" Nardone said, apparently feeling some resistance from the man on the right, the one in the white sweater—and shoved the other man away to seize the struggling one more firmly, gripped him by the back of his neck (the man was young, bulky, a Puerto Rican with a pleasant face—contorted now), and shoved his head against the steel framing dividing the store's display windows. That made a solid sound.

"Have you got anything back there?" Ellie said to the big man, and nodded at where his hand was still reaching behind his back. She had the revolver in her hand, now, in the purse.

"No." He let that hand fall to his side.

"That's good," Ellie said, stepped a little closer to him, and stomped down on his right foot with her left high heel. He grunted with the pain of that. "You're not a bad guy," Ellie said, "—are you?"

"Where you goin'?" Nardone, talking to the man he'd shoved away. Gripping the other by the back of the neck. "Don't be in such a hurry. —Stick around."

The soldier and his girl were still standing against the store door.

"What was going on, here?" Ellie said to them.

"They was lookin' to buy some grass," the Rasta said. "Man—we don't know nothin' 'bout that shit . . . an' they tried an' give us some shit about the bread—you understan'?"

"Is that so?" Ellie said to the soldier, and saw Nardone shake the Puerto Rican and let him go. "—Is that so?"

The soldier had nothing to say.

Nardone looked at Ellie, and shrugged.

"You smart enough to get out of here?" Ellie said to the Rasta.

"You fuckin'-a."

"Then go," Ellie said, "—and take your girlfriends with you."

"You got it," the Rasta said, and turned and walked away, favoring his injured foot a little.

"You hurt my head, man," the Puerto Rican said to Nardone, lightly stroking at his hair where it hurt. As he walked past Ellie on his way, the other Hispanic, smaller, slighter, circled to join his friends.

A number of commuters, stopping to see what was happening, had blocked the flow of people at those spots. Now, these moved on, and the crowd flowed with them.

"You try to buy something from those people?" Ellie said to the soldier. "—Did you?"

"I guess so," the soldier said. The voice was from out of town. The girl said nothing.

"Where the fuck are you from?" Nardone said.

"Wisconsin."

"Are you kiddin' me?"

"No, sir," the soldier said. He looked to be about eighteen.

"We're from Green Bay," the girl said—her first words. She looked younger than eighteen. There was a wedding ring on her finger.

"Well—you're not in Green Bay, now, are you?" Ellie said.

"No, ma'am," the soldier said.

"So—use your fuckin' head," Nardone said. "Wake up—watch out who you're talkin' to."

"Yes, sir," the soldier said.

"You have someplace to stay?"

"Yes, ma'am," the girl said. "We have a reservation at the Mansfield Hotel."

"All right," Ellie said. "You go out those doors, and turn left, and walk up two blocks to Forty-fourth Street. —O.K.?"

The soldier and girl both nodded.

"Then you turn right, and walk down Forty-fourth Street for three blocks, across Seventh Avenue and Broadway, and just before you get to Fifth Avenue, you'll see the Mansfield. —O.K.?"

"O.K.," the soldier said.

"If you stop at a newsstand," Ellie said, "—you can buy a map, a guide to the city. That's a good thing to have."

"Thank you very much," the girl said, and held out her hand to Ellie to shake. "Thanks for helping us."

"Thanks," the soldier said to Nardone, and shook his hand.

"They're just babies," Ellie said, as she and Nardone walked to the entrance.

"There's another one," Nardone said, and veered over to the center door, where a young Transit patrolman, blond and mustached, stood amid the crowd hurrying in. "—You're doin' a real shitty job, pal," Nardone said to him as they went by.

The sun had almost set—bands of black cloud a mile above swung slowly east between the borders of the building tops, barred with ribs of purple, lighter reds, and gold. It was a cool evening, a gusting breeze driving trash and paper down the gutters now and then as they walked to the car. People on the street went with their heads slightly lowered before the wind.

"That's it for summer," Nardone said. He disliked the cold. "You can kiss summer good-bye."

"I like the fall," Ellie said. "—It doesn't bother me."

A gust sent a paper cup tapping down the sidewalk alongside them for a few steps, then rolled it into the street.

No one had disturbed the Ford, though they'd left it parked up on the dirt back-hoed out of a pipeline ditch beside the site.

"What's going up here?"

"Hotel," Nardone said. "—One of those weirdo's got a jungle in the lobby. Two hundred a night, birds shit on your head in the restaurant." He unlocked the car, climbed in, and leaned over to unlock her side.

"You remember?" he said, waiting to pull out into the traffic. "—You remember we got court appearances day after tomorrow?"

"Oh, crap."

"You and me both in the mornin', then me in the afternoon. You got Prescott; I got Siniscola."

"I forgot it came up this week. . . ."

"Well, it did."

Edgar Prescott, two months before, had publicly threatened the life of Samuel Prinz—Comptroller of the City—during an open session of the City Council. Ellie, escorting the visiting mayor of Delft, Netherlands—a pale, plump, tough woman with very good English—had unfortunately been standing close to Prescott, and heard his shouted threat, which had been "to get a fucking gun and put a bullet through your head, you fucking thief!" —Prescott at the time being involved in litigation over payments due from the City to his firm. He hauled garbage, privately.

Nardone's case was more serious, a patrolman named Siniscola being accused of entering into conversation with a thirteen-year-old boy outside Joan of Arc Junior High School, then escorting the boy behind two Dumpsters alongside the school yard to compare penises. —The case complicated by Siniscola's older brother, a division commander for Manhattan South in Internal Affairs—who might or might not have attempted to cover the matter up.

"An' tomorrow," Nardone said, driving out into a space in traffic vacated by a delivery van swinging in to double-park, "—tomorrow, we got to spend some time goin' over that Gaither stuff. All the papers, her bills—the print reports, the whole damn thing. Leahy's goin' to see if we can't get a copy of her state tax return, an' her will out of probate court. —You know she had a will?"

"No."

"Well, she did. —Guess who was attorney of record."

"Birnbaum."

"Good guesser. So, we gotta go through all that shit. We could still get lucky talkin' to people—but if we don't . . . You want to solve that case, we're goin' to have to dig for it."

The light changed, and Nardone took the right onto Forty-second.

"I know it," Ellie said. "I'll read those letters tonight, and if there's anything there, I'll bring them in."

"Could be evidence, you know, honey."

"I won't lose them."

As they drove east, the cars in traffic, the pedestrians' clothes—all colored objects in bright or muted shades took up tints from the sunset's yellows and reds. The same sunset colors were reflected in car windows and this and that plate glass along their way.

"I'm not sayin' we can't get lucky—maybe bust it in a week," Nardone said, stopped for the light at Madison. "Better be diggin' just in case, though."

"O.K., but if I can see Audrey Birnbaum, I think I should."

"Oh, yeah—if she'll talk to you, that's great. That lady—whatever you want to call her—could be she knows a lot about a lot, if she wants to say somethin'." Nardone reached into his right-side jacket pocket for a box of Tic Tacs, and thumbed one out as the light changed and he drove on. "By the way, Leahy talked to me up at the funeral—before you showed? He's got another crappy checkout for us. Do you believe this? —This Internal guy is partners with his brother-in-law in a sailboat out in Patchogue. —An' we're supposed to drop everything, go out there an' hang around the friggin' dock, find out who paid for the anchor, who paid for the sails, who paid for the ropes. . . . Came right down from Anderson."

"Well, fuck that," Ellie said.

Nardone took his hand from the wheel and reached over to pat hers. "That's exactly what I said to him. —I said, 'Fuck that.' "

"What did he say?—Did he say where we're supposed to get time for the Gaither thing?"

"Nope. He gives me a look, that's all."

"And the UN session's coming up."

"That's right. —We're goin' to get buried in a sea of

shit." He drove across Lexington. "—I'll drop you up at the tram; you got no need to come downtown."

As they stopped behind a florist's delivery truck for the red light at Forty-second and Third, Ellie saw a young woman walking, holding hands with her little boy. The little boy had light brown hair, and was wearing a green wool sweater with a smiling chipmunk's face knitted into the front in yellow. Brown corduroy trousers. He was saying something as they walked along, his mother's head bent to listen. His mother was pale and pretty, with long, straight light-brown hair falling free. She was wearing jeans, and her legs were short—not long and slender, as Ellie had thought they would be, glancing at her face. There had been a time, Ellie supposed, that Classman and his mother had walked like that, one young, one younger, pleased to be together.

"Tommy—you don't think Morris was happy, do you?"

"Happy? —Hell no, I think the poor son-of-a-bitch was miserable. Always mopin' around there, callin' his mother. How could the guy be happy? —An' he was a nut case, to boot!"

"You don't think he got the slows up there? You know . . . on purpose. Sort of a way to go?"

Nardone looked over at her, astonished. "Are you kiddin' me? Jesus—I didn't say the guy wanted to die, did I . . . ? He was just a miserable guy. You can be a sad person without wantin' to be a corpse! He tried. . . . He gave it a good try!"

"I guess so," Ellie said. "He was so quiet. . . ."

"Well . . . he was a troubled guy, but he wasn't fuckin' crazy; he wasn't goin' to stand there and *let* some asshole shoot him. —Besides, I told you what could have happened up there to Classman. . . ."

"You *are* going to butt out of that, aren't you, Tommy? —No fucking around with that case . . . *please.* It could get us into real trouble. . . ."

"I'm not goin' to mess with it," Nardone said, caught the green, and made his left turn up First. "—I did all I'm goin' to do. I'll let Leahy know what I got, and if those assholes can't grab the brothers and get a description on those guys—then fuck 'em. Let 'em explain to the papers they haven't caught anybody on that killin'."

"—And I need to know what dishes Connie is using for Sunday. If it isn't the white and gold, be sure and have her call me—O.K.?"

"O.K."

A half block south of the tram station, just short of the ramp up to the Queensboro Bridge, Nardone pulled the car over, double-parked.

"Listen," he said. "Don't worry about Classman. Did you know Morris liked you? He liked you; he told Serrano you were a nice girl. —What about that?"

"It doesn't make me feel better, Tommy. I never even said anything nice to him. —I could have asked about his mother. . . ."

"You did ask about his mother.—You asked plenty of times." Nardone leaned over and kissed Ellie on the cheek. Spearmint Tic Tacs. "Now—get out of here, an' forget all this shit. Go shoppin', get yourself somethin'. —What's over with, is over with. Morris isn't worried about nothin' anymore."

CHAPTER 10

Dear Sonny,

It hasn't escaped my notice, and probably not yours either, that your nickname is a boy's, and has been since you were a baby. I thought I'd mention that here to assure you it doesn't mean a thing. It was just the easiest nickname out of Sonia, unless you wanted to advertise TV sets.

When we were in Albuquerque, we talked about my sending you a letter or two about stuff you wanted to know about my not-very-exciting youth, complete with boo-boos, and some things about my work, and what I've learned from it. Truth letters about stuff that was too boring or embarrassing for us to talk about.

I think that was a good idea, because the one great thing about my profession is that sometimes you can deal with people without using any lies at all. That means that sometimes, at least where sex is concerned, it's real life, and not pretend life. People call it The Life, because of that. So here goes.

I've found—I guess it's no big secret!—that people lie all the time, they lie to themselves even more than they lie to other people, and they lie about sex and love most of all. Of course that's not all there is to life, either, but it's a big chunk, and it's the part I know about.

Let me say, right up front, that there was a time a few years ago I was as dishonest a whore as you could find, and didn't mind betraying the people who came to me for pleasure, or out of desperation. But I caught myself turning into what I didn't want to turn into, one of those shits that abuses pussy power, and I've never done that again.

Now, I don't lie to people about those things, and they usually don't lie to me about them, either, so I know a few truths about sex and so forth that most people don't know, or are scared to find out. This doesn't make me any better than they are, or any happier either. It's just my profession, and it means that my life is as different from most people's as if I was living on another planet entirely. But it wasn't always, because I, like everybody else, started my life doing a lot of lying to myself about sex and love and related subjects like friendship and money, until being a whore—which is exactly what I am—taught me to lie as little as possible to other people, and not at all to myself. I don't recommend that you try to do the same, because it's a hard road, and you're not suited for it, and you don't wind up any happier, darling, without these lies, except there's an enormous load of shit off your back forever.

It's a lonely life, too, because everybody else, or almost everybody else, is pretending about those things, and if you don't pretend with them, they get upset. And that's where what risks there are in my business come in. So, in my life, true friends are the most important thing, except for you.

Take a very intelligent, sensitive man in his forties, a really important person in his business, or a doctor, a complicated human being with a wonderful education, married to a charming woman for a lot of years, still loves her very much, some nice kids doing very well. When a man like that is sitting on the side of my bed, naked, making silly noises, his head thrown back, the veins in his neck standing out, out of his mind with pleasure just because yours truly is kneeling on the rug in her blue bathrobe sucking on his penis, when you see that, you see something about people that has to do with their not admitting what they are. And don't get the notion that only goes for men. Some women come to me, too, some that have the courage to do it, or are so lonely they're just about out of their minds, poor things. And they talk to me for hours, and pay me a great deal of money to sit and listen to them. They talk about their children and their husbands, they talk about everything—and then sometimes they'll get up the nerve to ask for sex, but often not.

"Well," you're saying, "Mother's just saying that people are animals, that's all. And she's taking a long time to do it." But you're wrong. People aren't *just* animals. People are *wonderful* animals, sweetheart, but they pretend not to *be* antimals, and that's what causes a great deal of trouble! That's the lie that makes all the other lies necessary, and about death and other things, too, not just sex. That's the big lie that's the foundation of the house of lies, but I try not to live in it.

People come to me and pay me to spend a little while in the house of truth. In my house, they can tell me anything they want to about anything they want. They can talk about what they really like and what they don't like. Or they can talk about how much they really love other people, or how much they hate them. For example, I spend a lot more time listening to people talk about their parents than I do getting spanked or screwed in the butt, which is the kind of thing people like to think prostitutes spend most of their time doing.

So, as an outsider who is paid to listen to people tell the truth about what they really want, and paid to do with them what they really want to do, I found some truths that might save you trouble. The fact is, though, even after many years working, I know very little about people. They are all mysteries. But what little I've learned, I'll tell you, and I'll start with my boring biography, because that's where *you* start, too!

First thing is, keep in mind that for better or worse—and because of my profession many people would say it was for the better—you are an entirely separate person. You couldn't be me if you tried, any more than I could be you. You popped out of my belly, and I loved you because I couldn't help it by instinct or chemicals or whatever, but I don't know if we would even have liked each other if we just met somewhere. Lucky for our relationship we didn't just meet somewhere! But I've found in my work that a lot of people never realize they are entirely separate people from their parents, and go through life mooning over them and whining about them as if they were unfaithful lovers. And of course, the reverse is even worse. A lot of parents, mothers particularly, have nothing to do but be mothers, so they stick to that forever, until their children are sick of it and sick of them.

I was an ordinary little girl—skinnier and smaller than most of the girls I knew. I didn't get breasts until I was thirteen, and then they weren't much. I was crazy about the Cats-an'-Jammers and I was in love with Tony Creski, who was lead guitar for Infirmary, and I suppose you never heard of any of them. There were a couple of months when I would have been happy to die for Tony Creski, if I could have died in his arms with him crying and looking down at me. I used to spend a lot of time daydreaming, and I would use the mirror from my brush-and-mirror set to look at my vagina, especially after I got hair down there. I masturbated, you bet, as I hope you have been enjoying doing; I also occasionally picked my nose and occasionally I would eat the result, which, as you probably know, is nothing much in the good-taste department, either way you take that.

I never read anything I didn't have to for school, and Chicago schools were not great then, anyway. Reading is something wonderful I found when I got sick of television.

Your grandparents were very nice people. They weren't drunks and they didn't beat me up, and my dad didn't try to get in my pants. You would like them a lot if they were still around.

My dad was a pipe fitter in the union, and we owned half a house with a family named Quinn. Quinn worked for a specialty tire company. The Quinns were O.K., and I did play doctor with their boy, Sean, but he was too young to know what to do when we tried it, and got to be such a wimp later I didn't want to try it again.

You will be relieved to know, sweetheart, that your supposedly sexy mother finally did sleep with a boy when she was sixteen. He was a basketball jock named Norm Witt, and he was very, *very* cute, and I was crazy about him. We had first sex on his brother's bed upstairs while his parents were out somewhere and we were supposed to be sitting for his little sister, who thank god went to sleep early that time.

The sex was good for me, and didn't hurt me any more than getting my ears pierced. I didn't come all over the place, but it felt very nice. The nicest thing, though, was having Norm Witt naked in my arms. I guess I just about hugged that honey to death. He was much too skinny, and while he was working away on top of me, puffing like The Little Engine That Could, I was imagining us married and me feeding him these wonderful meals to make him stronger and show him how much I loved him. There was no lie about any of that; that was all truth to me. When they say men and women are different, that's no lie, either, though it's a troublesome truth, especially to women. But it's the truth just the same, so if you love a man, you better love men, or you're in for a bad time.

I'll get into that later, how they are different from us, being really different animals in some ways.

My dad died of a stroke on the job, and they called my mom at home and came and told me in school. Then, two years later, after I graduated, my mom married a salesman named Mark Shuski, a Polish guy, and a nice man. He was very nice to me, and I guess it was the best thing that could have happened to her.

Now, I know what you want to know. You want to know what happened with Norm Witt. Right? Well, I'll tell you, and it'll be no surprise. That brown-eyed sweetie betrayed yours truly with Trudy Pavlich. "What?" you're saying. "My mother aced out by a Trudy?!" But it happened, and I'm damned to this day if I know why. It certainly was not anything I did. I was that tall asshole's slave. I gave him the answers in geometry. I did everything!

Let me tell you about Trudy. She was one of those girls who look great for a couple of years. Lots of baby fat, and goldfish cheeks and big blue eyes. Then, after a couple of years, the baby fat turns to lady fat. At least I hope it did in her case. If you want to know what I think really happened, I think what really happened is whatever chemical Norm and I were breathing or farting at each other simply changed by a molecule or two.

It makes most people very uncomfortable to think that way, though. They'd rather believe that something complicated is wrong with them and can be fixed. Whereas I've found that if something complicated is wrong with a person, it can never be fixed, and just has to be lived with. (Did you notice the use of *whereas,* there, Sonny? Isn't that nice?) Men and women like to think they can be repaired like cars and be their own mechanics, and that's what keeps my professional rivals and colleagues, the psychiatrists, in business.

O.K. Almost over the where-I-came-from bit. You've been very patient, and you better have been very patient, because I'm getting a severe case of typewriter fingers.

I graduated from high school with good grades; I was fifth in the class, and it was a big school. Then I decided to become a career woman, and went to the Great Lakes Secretarial School, since regular college wasn't a big idea on Tremaine Street at the time. My mom and Mr. Shuski helped me out with the tuition, and I worked part time at a hairdresser's, where I got my first lessons in how tough it is to keep a lie styled.

Now, here comes some news that will upset you, but a wise man once said: If you chew, and chip a tooth, you've bitten truth. Actually, it was I who said that, just now.

You have a brother, darling, three years older than you, and I don't know where he is. He was adopted away, and I named him Tony, probably after Tony Creski the lead guitar, although I hate to admit it. Which is another lesson, which is that we never grow up. Anybody who tries to act like a real grown-up is the biggest baby of all.

It's a shock, isn't it? And you can blame it on the cowardice of a woman who has known better than to keep that kind of secret. There are a few lies, you see, still surviving in my life. They live on the fear that if you know too much, you won't love me anymore. Well, you have a brother.

I had a love affair, my second one after Norm, with a man who was the brother of the man I worked for on my first job. His name was Rudy Kraft, and he was a nice sort of guy, middle-aged, who was divorced and going crazy drinking. He used to want to play house more than anything. He'd pretend we were married. I suppose that was the first time I saw so clearly how much pretending people have to do. He'd call me dear and honey, but not the way you call somebody that when you're hot for them and having a wonderful affair (Speaking of which, I got a call last night from George. He said to apologize to you for the crummy postcards, but the only other thing worth sending were the fried potatoes, and he didn't think they'd travel). Anyway, Rudy dealt with me as if I was his wife, and always wanted me to sleep over, cook him breakfast in the morning, that kind of thing.

I don't know why women learn so much from men, and men usually don't learn a thing from women, except to be more careful next time. Anyway, Rudy asked me to marry him after we'd been going together about two weeks, and he kept asking. I thought that probably any man who wanted to get married that much was going to be a problem; it's not a natural state for men. So, I said no, and I wouldn't marry him even after I was pregnant. And by the way, I got pregnant using that so-called spermicidal foam. Don't you be a dope. If you're having sex with one of those cute spoiled boys up there, then make him use those condoms I gave you. In another year, if the doctor says O.K., we'll get you a prescription for the pill, one of the low estrogen ones. In the meantime, if you have gotten up your nerve or fallen in love, make the kid wear that condom! Of course, if you're playing kissy with some girl, it's not a problem.

There was a tremendous drama in Chicago that summer, let me tell you. I went to the Catholic Unwed Mothers, and told them I was Catholic, which I wasn't. One of the nicest things about my parents was they didn't load me down with that religious nonsense, flying carpenters and camel drivers and volcano gods and so forth that help so many scared people get through their days. I had plenty of time to read the Bible waiting for Tony to be born, Old and New Testaments—which would be sad if they weren't so funny—centuries and centuries of wishful thinking adding up to a big pile of horse manure.

You don't, by the way, have to tell Tubby my opinion on the subject. As priests go, he's a nice guy. Of course, these days, priests don't have any choice but to be nice guys. As Ms. Batten probably has already taught you in European history, there was a time they didn't have to be so nice. And they weren't.

Anyway, the Mothers Home could have been worse, and they got a good Catholic baby for a good Catholic family. Now, I suppose, Tony is trying to be a cop or a fireman or a ward heeler, and is watching out for blacks moving in.

And who's to blame for leaving him high and dry? Me. I did it because I didn't want to be bothered with a kid, then. Not so nice, myself, was I? Am I?

I guess you want to know if I loved him. I did love him. He had an odd-shaped head; it came to sort of a point. At least it still did when I saw him, although the other girls told me it would squash back down and be O.K.

Do I love him now? No way. I don't give a damn about him one way or the other. He didn't have the chance to hook into my heart the way you did. I've got you stuck in my heart.

All this time, Rudy Kraft was hanging around the Home, yelling up at the windows and so forth. The police came twice to take him away. I guess he saw little Tony keeping him company, so he wouldn't be so alone without Edie. That was his wife's name.

Now you're thinking, "I don't give a damn about this ancient history. All I care about is where I came from. I want to know about my *daddy!*"

Your father was Fred Pascoe. He was a short, bald man, and he was an insurance executive. I met him at the company I was working for after Tony was born and gone, and, of course, after I left the Kraft brothers' printing business, and we dated and I didn't particularly care for him. After we dated some more, and really to my surprise, and I'm still surprised thinking about it, I fell in love with him. If you're ever foolish enough to go to Chicago and meet him, you will think I was out of my mind. What I loved about Fred was that he did whatever he wanted, whenever he wanted. And if he did want to do something, and was scared to try it, he admitted that, too. I must have gone to a dozen motorcycle showrooms with Fred, and he would stand there in front of some mechanical beast, and really wring his hands because he knew he'd kill himself if he bought it. "I don't want to die," he'd say, "but I'm dying to ride." He was thirty-five when I met him, and was married and had a little girl. So that you won't think your glamorous courtesan of a mother was also a nasty little shit, let me tell you that the first I heard about it was when his wife called me on the phone.

I suppose, because it is very hard for a woman to live a free and honest life, that I loved him because I envied him. He had told his wife all about us, by the way, because she asked him what he was up to, and all hell broke loose, and kept breaking loose. She was a very ladylike person and kept calling me up and telling me she was going to get some gangsters to kill me. She'd say that, then I'd say please get them to kill Fred instead, so I'd be rid of him, too. It's tiring to be with a man like that.

Women like to talk about excitement, or read about it, a lot more than they like to live it. She'd talk and I'd talk, and we'd wind up talking two hours on the phone about Fred. And finally and at long last I got sick of it, got pregnant again three years after I gave up pointy-headed Tony, and I got out of Chicago and had you in Binghamton. And if there was a God, I'd thank it for your company ever since, my darling, because it would be hard to live alone without lots of lying.

All right, that's about it for the biography, except that I became a prostitute for two good reasons. The first was five years spent nine-to-five sitting on my butt, word-processing in offices and watching my life drain away. The second was, the money was great. I didn't know then what a wonderfully strange world it was going to be, where people share the secret of no secrets.

You asked me once, by the way, if there were a lot of criminals around my work. I think you were worried about it. Well, I've met a few hoods, of course, sweetheart, but nothing for you to worry about. They talk more business than businessmen do, but with a lot of nicknames, so unless you know what's going on, you never know what's going on, and I suspect that most of the time nothing is going on. They love for people to know they're connected up, though, and if they take you out to dinner, sometimes they'll talk about Joey or Frankie Jumps so the maître d' can hear them. They're like spoiled children, greedy, like advertising people. But I've never met one that was bored or boring.

They're always up to something, always very energetic. I think square living is just too slow, too dull for them, and that restlessness becomes dangerous.

Well, I had you, and I moved to the city, and I posed for some stills showing my everything, and I worked in two different massage parlors, which showed me some of the other side, and I found that I liked it. I liked masturbating a man more than obeying a man's orders in an office, and he liked it better, too. We were two human beings, then, you see, sweetheart? We were two wonderful animals exchanging close favors of money and pleasure, and I enjoyed it.

Love,
Your Weird Mother

P.S. I couldn't find a copy of *Green Horses*. Find out who published it, and we'll write to the company and see if we can find a copy that way.

And please, *please* don't hand this aging prostitute any more bullshit about not being able to do intermediate algebra. What you mean is, it's hard for you. O.K., it's *very* hard for you. All the more reason to bear down and do it, so that difficult things won't frighten you later on. It's just another language, you know, and a lot simpler than French. Just take it slow, step by step, and if you find that it starts slipping out of your head, then *talk* to Mr. Manning, tell him you're losing it, and ask for help. When I come up, week after next, you poor, sad, abused child, I'm going to go over quadratics with you, and if you can't do them, you get zip for dessert at the Ferry Tavern. You can watch Joanna make a pig of herself while you sit there with tears in your ears.

Ellie folded the letter, slid it back into its envelope, and lay back on her pillows to think about it. Mayo, full of Cat Snax, was stretched beside her, asleep.

Ellie had doctored up a can of Gebhardt's chili and eaten that. It wasn't settling in very well. She yawned, took the other letter out of its envelope, and leafed through it. Like the first. Several first names. No last names, except for Sally's lovers of years ago. No thorough physical descriptions. No mention of present trouble . . . motives. . . . She reached up and turned off the bedside lamp, and lay still in the faint light shining from the hall through the half-open bedroom door. Fred Pascoe in the motorcycle showroom . . . and what was the small Chicago girl beside him thinking . . . loving him while he loved the beautiful, dangerous machines. Short, bald Fred Pascoe. That's why Sonia was stocky, would be heavy if she weren't careful. Sonia would never call Fred Pascoe—if Fred Pascoe was alive now, fifteen years after his little blond office girl had left him and left Chicago forever.

Supposing Pascoe was rich. Supposing his wife was dead, or was a nice woman . . . "a lady" Sally had called her, perhaps nice enough to take some slight care of Sonia, so she wouldn't be so alone.

Sally had been a brave whore, Ellie thought, and she was trying in her letter to make Sonia strong, too. Trying too hard, maybe. Now, Sonia was as strong as she'd ever be.

"I'll take care of her, if I can," Ellie said to the shaded room, the sleeping cat. Then, she felt cheerful enough to get up and go to the kitchen for some ice cream, and poked Mayo with her finger in his soft white belly until he woke. "Come on, you lazy little fart," she said, "—and I'll give you some."

Ellie was standing naked, leaning against the refrigerator, eating Häagen-Dazs chocolate from the carton with a grapefruit spoon—the spoon's serrations helping scoop the frozen ice cream out—when the phone rang. She stepped over Mayo, who was grunting small rapid grunts of pleasure as he lapped and bit gingerly at his chill portion softening slowly in a small saucer.

The machine had answered, "This is Eleanor Klein's answering machine . . ." when she got to the phone in the hall, and Ellie listened for the caller's voice before she picked up.

"Hello, Eleanor Klein's answering machine," Clara said, "—tell your mistress that her mistress called from this toddlin' town to say the conferencing continues, nothing is decided—and that said mistress will be back in a few days, and loves her."

Ellie listened, but didn't pick up. Then she went back to the kitchen to have some more ice cream.

It took her a long while to get to sleep, afterward, and

she only managed it by going into the bathroom for a towel, spreading that on the sheet under her hips, tugging her Tampax out, then gently toying with the vibrator. Relaxed, her knees wide as if she were giving birth—Mayo observing, bored—Ellie thought of Clara, replaced her with the tall Stakeout man standing in his gray suit, watching her now . . . and hummed, groaned, cramped her feet, and came.

She slept, and dreamed she was shopping for a new car in a showroom that had every kind of vehicle in it. "—I want a plane," she said, but the salesman, a pleasant man, said she must be kidding. Then she dreamed something else, but forgot it.

Ellie woke because she was sleeping on her side, her left breast pressed against her upper arm, and it was hurting her. She woke, or almost, and rolled onto her back. Just that movement made her breasts hurt a little; they were very tender. —Big ones must hurt worse, she thought, and went to sleep again.

Toward morning, when the traffic sounds across the river rose from whispers to conversation, Ellie dreamed she was taking a shower, and soaping herself with English lavender soap in the steam and hiss of falling water. She heard a soft, clicking sound behind her, turned under the spray, and saw Sally Gaither wired to her folding chair, staring up at her with cooked eyes, her lips drawn back like a snarling dog's, her small bared teeth clicking softly together as she stared up at Ellie. Oh, don't be angry, Ellie said, and Sally put her spoiling head to one side, like a wet dog's, and still watched Ellie. Then her tongue came lolling out.

"You're runnin' a half hour late, today," Serrano said. "Listen—would you like to have some lunch around here? You know, go out for just a bite?"

The black girl said, "How many coffees?"

"You got to have a little time, middle of the day. We could go over to Jerry's, maybe have a sandwich and one beer. That wouldn't hurt."

"You want five coffees?" the black girl said. She still wore her long hair sculpted and stiffly set down to her shoulders. When he was a boy, Serrano had had to do with a black prostitute, once, who'd warned him harshly not to touch her hair.

"Five coffees. Right. Listen—I'm not tryin' to make a cheap pass or somethin'. I just want to be friendly. You look like a nice girl, and I'm not a bad guy."

"What you want?" the girl said, and seemed annoyed.

"Five coffees, one tea, and I'm gettin' two prune Danish, one cherry, one cheese, and a buttered bagel."

"Listen, man, I said what you *want*!"—really annoyed.

"Oh—I don't want anything. I just thought we could go over to Jerry's . . . have a sandwich, a beer. You know. No funny stuff."

The girl snorted and shook her head, a black and slender mare. She finished filling the coffee containers, filled the tea container with hot water, and said, "You want cream, there it is," indicating the tiny cream cups heaped beside the box of wooden stirrers. Then she looked straight ahead into the coffee urn's sliding reflections, and said no more.

"Look," Serrano said, "you can't not like me—you don't even know me! I'm not a bad guy"—dug around among the pastry, and finally found a cherry Danish.

The girl waited until he had his cardboard tray filled, had paid his money, then shoved the heavy cart into motion, starting past him down the corridor toward Personnel.

"Is it because I'm a cop?" Serrano said, as she went by.

"You had a call," Medina said, when Ellie came back from the rest room. It had been threatening to rain when she'd left the island, and she'd worn a hat with her raincoat and mussed her hair. She'd been wanting to take the time to fix it all morning.

"Who?"

"Guy named Birnbaum, said it was O.K. for anytime this afternoon. New York Hospital. —And listen, do me a favor; tell the guy you're not extension one-four-seven, O.K.?"

"Thanks . . . O.K.," Ellie said, and went back to her chair at Nardone's desk. Their new case board was up on the wall, and almost covered with stapled Action Report copies, fingerprint reports, scene-of-crime diagrams, Major Crimes S.R.'s, witness lists, P.S. lists, a calendar page, a seventy-two-hour time sheet, and photographs of the victim—private snapshots previous to the homicide, police photographs after. Ellie had stapled a light blue file cover over the police photographs after a detective sergeant named Sutton had made a remark about steamed pussy, in passing.

"Shea?" Nardone said, leafing through a thick sheaf of canceled checks, making occasional notes as he went. He'd come in this morning in his brown winter suit. —The summer was over.

"No. —Not that it's any of your business, Tommy. Birnbaum. It's O.K. to see her."

"That Irishman's never goin' to show. —It was strictly funeral talk."

"Where were we?"

"Here you go . . ." Serrano said, pausing in the aisle with his tray. "You get one coffee, one tea, one buttered bagel. You owe me a buck-eighty."

"I'll get this one," Ellie said, got up, went to her desk for her purse, and counted out the amount in change for Serrano.

"No bills?"

"I have a ten. . . ."

"No, forget it, this'll be O.K."

She sat down at Nardone's desk again. "All right, where were we?"

"You been through the property inventory?" He took a closer look at one of the checks, then kept leafing through.

"I read that, and I checked for insurance policies, traffic violations—she got four parkings in the last three years, rental cars—and any outstanding liens or repossessions. —Nothing."

"No insurance?"

"Nothing. She couldn't fill in a false occupation without nullifying the coverage. —She couldn't fill in a true occupation and *get* coverage."

"So, she went cash."

"Right. That was the fourteen thousand."

"Insurance money—an' not much insurance money.

An' two bank accounts?" Nardone held up one of the canceled checks and raised an eyebrow, or tried to. Whenever he raised one eyebrow, both went up.

"—That one's regular checking at Manufacturers. And she had savings at City. —Seventeen hundred in checking. Nine thousand, two hundred in savings."

"We got a lazy prosty, here," Nardone said, "—even figurin' she owned the apartment. She had to be slowin' down, be that short."

"I think she spent a lot on Sonia."

"Got to be a hell of a lot."

"So—what's next?"

"M.E.'s follow-up," Nardone said, and set the checks aside. "—An' there's only one thing we didn't already know. 'Shock and systemic collapse due to prolonged exposure to excessive heat, additional steamburn trauma. Multiple cincture depressions, wrists and ankles . . . two small puncture wounds anterior lower left mandible.' "

"We never saw them." Ellie put sugar and cream in her coffee, and stirred it.

"Nobody saw 'em. You couldn't tell anythin' with that skin that way. —Take a look at those pictures. You tell me you could see any little puncture wounds in there."

"A knife." She poured half a sugar into his tea, and stirred it for him.

"You bet. —And that, we should have figured. He'd need somethin' to keep her quiet, keep her from yellin' or somethin' while he was wirin' her up. Probably stuck her a couple times, show he was serious, then he puts the knife to one side where he can get it, an' wraps her up. —Then he shoves that rubber ball in her mouth, an' she's a goner. He's got her any way he wants."

"I guess so . . ."

"You notice that 'multiple cincture' stuff? Means he wired her up first, left her in the bathtub—out of the way—then, later, he gets the bright idea to put her in the chair. Somewhere in there he has some fun with the bananas."

"I'd yell, anyway, if somebody had me tied up, was trying to shove a rubber ball in my mouth. —I'd scream my head off."

"Go ahead," Samuelson said, passing by. "—Won't do you any good."

"So would I," Nardone said, "—unless the guy picks up that knife again, got the point stickin' in my throat. Then I'm goin' to be quiet as a mouse—an' hope the guy's not a nut case."

"Well, it's something new, anyway." Ellie unwrapped her bagel and took a bite; it was a little stale.

"It's nothin'. It's somethin' we already should have figured. Five'll get you ten he used one of the kitchen knives, then wiped it like everythin' else, an' put it back."

"Doesn't sound all that passionate to me," Ellie said. "—Sounds like a goddamned cool son-of-a-bitch."

"That's a point. You got a point, there. —If that lady had been pimped up, I'd say it was a pimp killing."

"But she wasn't. There isn't a smell of anything like that, Tommy. At least the last few years, Gaither was independent as they come."

"O.K. Right." Nardone took a sip of his tea. "So—that leaves love. And, I'll tell you one thing"—he set the M.E.'s report aside on a thick stack of fingerprint folders—"Kenny was right about the answerin' service. We can forget about calls incomin'. We got the numbers of a thousand people called in there every couple of days—but we got no way to tell which ones got forwarded to Gaither. All we got on calls are the numbers on her phone bills, and Leahy had to talk to the asshole at the phone company a half hour, tell him to get us the names and addresses to go with 'em. —That'll take a day or two, right there." He drank some more tea, and went back to the canceled checks.

"That's still a lot," Ellie said. "That's not bad at all—that's a lot of people."

"Yeah. —Sounds good, right? But you want to bet somethin'? —You can bet those calls went to Gristede's for deliveries; they went to Connecticut to her daughter; they went to a few girl friends, a few fag friends around town. Period."

"Maybe to Belgium."

"O.K. Probably to Belgium. It'll give us the guy's phone over there, anyway. —But that doesn't help us. That hurts us; means the guy stayed over there." He stopped and looked at a canceled check, then made a note in his notebook.

"What's that?" The bagel was so stale it spoiled the taste, even with the butter.

"Liquor store. Let's see if their delivery guy's had any problems gettin' along with ladies."

"You know, I don't think Soseby has any way to know what happened. He must think she's still alive. . . ." Ellie reached down to the floor for another shoe box of receipted bills.

"Probably," Nardone said, "—that's right. Unless he's the one arranged to have her put away. It occurred to me, you know . . . maybe he's doin' her a favor, investin' her money for her. —It's part of his business—right? Could be he decided to just hang on to the bundle. —Speakin' of which guy, I did some sharp detective work at home this mornin', and looked the guy up in the phone book. He's right in town, and I already asked Leahy to get us an E an' S on his place. Supposed to come through tomorrow—if you believe that—and we'll go over there and take a look. Find out who he works for, and they'll have that Belgium address."

"O.K. But then, *you* call and tell him," Ellie said. "I went up and saw the daughter—and I'm seeing that dying lady this afternoon." She finished going through a bundle of paid bills, took a rubber band from the side drawer of Nardone's desk, and snapped it around them. The bill receipts so far had been for electricity, phone, groceries, dry cleaners, answering service, laundry, and a carpet cleaner.

"O.K.," Nardone said, "—that's fair. I'll tell the poor son-of-a-bitch she's dead." He held up a canceled check. "Hairdresser. —Those guys got a good business."

"—And how she went?" The coffee was all right, but the bagel wasn't worth finishing.

"Only if he asks. —Reminds me; what about the kid's letters?"

"I read one last night—they're long letters—and it was strictly mother-daughter stuff. She was something, though. You know, you can hear her voice there. . . . She mentions some guys she knew years ago, and that's about it."

"I don't care. You're talkin' about evidence. —You

can't hold that stuff out." He finished his tea and threw the cup into the wastebasket.

"Well, I promised, and I'm going to—unless there's real evidence in there. And so far there isn't."

"Evidence?" Leahy said, coming down the aisle. "—Don't tell me you two actually came up with evidence? I thought this team operated strictly on bullshit—like, for example, that astronomer up in the Bronx. That kind of bullshit." Leahy was wearing a new double-breasted blue trench coat; it had epaulets, and there were grenade rings on the belt.

"It's just a couple of letters, Lieutenant—the Gaither woman sent them to her daughter. Personal stuff. No suspects, no trouble, no nothing. I promised the daughter I wouldn't show them around."

"I'm not runnin' that case, Klein," Leahy said. "You two are runnin' it. —An' you're sure gettin' great results."

"We'll get results," Nardone said, "—if we got time between runnin' out to Long Island lookin' at rudders an' anchors and shit."

"Job too tough for you, Tommy?" Leahy said. "We keepin' you too busy? —Well, you come on in my office, because Anderson's comin' down about the peeper up in the Bronx you handed that bullshit AR in"—and went on his way. The trench coat looked to be a size fifty, short.

"Well, partner," Nardone said, "—was that guy a legitimate astronomer, or not?"

"Damn right, he was," Ellie said. "—It was a comet he was looking for. It's his dream to get a new comet named after him. The comet Gershon."

"That's pretty good. —That's a good one," Nardone said, getting up. "I'm goin' to use that one. See how they handle that fuckin' fast ball. —While I'm in there with the Inquisition, keep goin' through those bill payments—electric bills, that friggin' answerin'-service bill, repairs, paint jobs, furniture—any plumbers come callin', anything. We got a year's receipts in there, separated pretty good, courtesy of Kenny Keneally. —Look out for somethin' doesn't jibe."

"Tommy, if you tell them about the Classman thing—go easy. It's not our case."

"Oh, I'm goin' to tell 'em. Right after I explain about

the comet Gershon—then, if they're interested, I'm goin' to tell 'em I got two private eyewitness junkies stashed, the minute they want to get serious with the Classman thing. —Nothin' to do with you; you're out of it."

"I don't have to be out of it," Ellie said, but he was heading down the aisle.

Sally Gaither had kept her receipted bills for exactly a year—discarded all of them past that date. Noted considerable increases, too. Underlined, question-marked them. She'd been very careful with her money. The answering-service bills stayed within a fifty-dollar range per month—but it was a steady high range. Cost of business. Like the tips to the doormen, which probably could have been noted and written off her taxes—if she'd entered her occupation as prostitute on those forms. Probably had called herself a consultant, or therapist. The fourteen thousand from her closet wouldn't appear there, for sure.

Truth House . . . but occasional lies, still, to use in conversation with the House of Lies.

"Klein . . ." Captain Anderson, smiling down, changed for autumn into a light gray wool worsted. "How are things going for you two with that Gaither case? —No client records at all . . . ? You haven't sent anything upstairs." He leaned over the desk to get a better look at the case board.

And how would the handsome Captain have behaved in Sally's bed? Would he have touched her so gently at the start, stroked her cheek . . . or having paid so much, not cared to waste the time . . . ?

"No, sir. —Case is going a little slowly." She started to stand up, but he gestured her down.

"Um-hmm. You were with your partner on the Gershon thing, weren't you?"

"Yes, I was."

Anderson looked the board over for a few moments more, then lifted the blue file-cover and looked at the photograph of Sally Gaither, naked and ruined in her folding chair.

"There's an Internal Affairs officer who seems to have become quite a yachtsman, in the last few years. . . . You people should have the paperwork on that."

"I think the Lieutenant has it."

Anderson let the file-cover fall back over the picture. "Hope you two have better luck with that, than with those officers up in Spanish Harlem, yesterday, at Cruz's book. —That was a mess." He smiled at her, then turned and walked down the aisle to Leahy's office.

Ellie set the rubber-banded bill receipts aside, and started on the others, watching as carefully as she could for some oddity, some bill higher than the others. A bigger electric bill in the middle of a season might mean Sally had somebody living with her for a few days—a lower one, and maybe she was staying for a while with someone else . . . a man. Perhaps a little possessive. Maybe more than a little.

It seemed to Ellie it would be difficult for a man to be in love with a prostitute. —Soseby supposedly was. . . . A very gentle guy, maybe. Another kind of man, though, not so easily, so gently in love, would be full of imaginings of her . . . of her taking money, and putting it in her top dresser drawer, then going back to the bed, and arranging herself to do what she'd agreed to. —Sweating, grunting, saying things as it was done. The lover growing angrier the more clearly he imagined it, remembered her, the richer his recall of all her details, her body, her odors, her sounds—angrier with every reminiscence. A picture in that . . . his picture. The slight, small blond whore standing on her bed in her blue bathrobe, holding a bare foot up to be seen, and her naked clients—naked except that each wore one thing, a single shoe, a necktie, a T-shirt, a gold butterfly pinned through a pinch of skin on a woman's ordinary breast—some of these people disgusting; several beautiful. The shriveled old sprinkling their urine on her carpet, ivory adolescents in a perfect, grinning pack, the girls giggling, the boys glancing at each other's erections. At the corner, in the back, the top dresser drawer is half open, choked with sheaves of money green as leaves. . . .

"*Klein, you got another call!*" Medina, from up the aisle, over the sounds of talking, and other phones. "—Come here an' get it, an' for Christ sake will you tell *this* one you're not one-four-seven!"

Ellie hurried up the aisle. "Thanks, Bobby—I'm really sorry. . . ."

"Don't be sorry. Just tell him. —O.K.?"

"O.K., I will." She cleared her throat. "Yes . . . ?"

"Hi . . . What's all the yelling about?"

"Oh . . . nothing."

"Well, I know it's rushing it; you're probably not going to be free . . . but I thought I'd better call you and apologize for that routine out at Woodlawn. I mean I think I carried it off O.K., and you were very nice about it. But let's face it—it was not a class move. And I want to apologize to you for getting so cute, an occasion where it wasn't called for."

"Well . . . that's all right."

"I just didn't want you to think I was usually such a jackass."

"Oh, I didn't think you were usually a jackass."

Shea laughed. "Just at the time—right?"

"No . . . really."

Neither of them said anything for a moment.

"Well . . . I'm calling to see if you'd like to come down and have some lunch."

"Down . . . ?"

"I'm downstairs. I had to come down and see Inspector Manugian about some evidence, and since I was here . . . Now, that's a lot of crap. I came downtown to see if you could come out and have lunch. That's the fact of the matter. I don't give a damn if I never see that Armenian."

"I don't know . . . I'm really busy—and this afternoon I have to go see a someone."

"I won't keep you long. Quick lunch. It's noon on the dot. —You have time for a quick lunch?"

Anderson walked up the aisle past Ellie as she listened. He glanced at her, but gave her no more smiles.

"Yes. Yes, I think I can."

"Good. I'm at the front desk."

"O.K. I'll be down in a couple of minutes."

"O.K. Good-bye."

"Good-bye."

Ellie hung up, and Medina looked up from his keyboard. "You didn't tell him you weren't one-four-seven."

"Bobby, I'm sorry. I'm going to meet him right now, and I'll tell him." She saw Nardone standing in the doorway to Leahy's office, his back half turned, saying something to the Lieutenant. She walked across the room to Classman's desk, which Samuelson had appropriated as being farther from Leahy's office, and found Samuelson sitting, leaning on the dented gray metal like a hillside, reading the racing page of the *Post.* The two young black detectives, making a rare appearance, were at their desks deeper in the short leg of the squad room's L, each on his phone, each looking bored, listening.

"Max . . ."

Samuelson turned his massive crew-cut head, and stared at her.

"I'm sorry to bother you—" Samuelson always read the various racing articles and racing forms at noon, so as to be able to place advantageous bets on afternoon and evening races, and disliked being disturbed at his studies. "—But I'd like to ask you something."

Samuelson sighed and put down his article, which concerned track conditions as they affected the performance of Proof Positive, now a four-year-old.

"What?"

"Do you know a cop named Shea?"

"I know half a dozen cops named Shea."

"No, I mean he's in Stake-out."

"There's two of 'em in Stake-out."

"This one's tall; he looks like a farmer. Phil Shea."

" 'Cookie.' "

"What?"

"Cookie Shea. Call him Tough Cookie, 'cause he knocked over two at once, once. Got a third one, too, couple of years ago. —Sergeant."

"Well, he's a lieutenant, now."

Samuelson didn't seem surprised. "O.K. He's a good cop. Real hardnose. —Why? What do you want to know for?"

"Oh . . . no particular reason," Ellie said.

"Yeah . . . ? O.K." Samuelson turned from her, and picked up his *Post.*

Nardone was back at the desk, studying the canceled checks.

Ellie pulled out her chair and sat down. "What happened?"

Nardone looked up from the checks. "—Good news

an' bad news," he said. "Good news is they buy that Gershon was gazin' stars. —Reason they buy that, is they can't prove he wasn't. That 'comet' shit helped there, too. That one set 'em back a little."

"Bad news?"

"The bad news is, we're goin' out to Long Island an' look at that friggin' boat day after tomorrow. Anderson wanted us out there tomorrow—I told him we had to be in court."

"What the hell are they so hot for these chicken-shit cases for? —These aren't serious investigations!"

Nardone took a look at another canceled check, then leafed past it.

"I got no idea," he said. "—They want us to waste the time, we waste the time. —Tell you this, I'm not findin' one fuckin' thing wrong with that boat."

"Right. —What did they say about the Classman thing?"

"Well—thing on that was, Leahy liked it better than Anderson. Anderson said it sounded like junkie shit to him—tryin' to get gravy for the next time they fall. He was pissed off I even went askin'; I told him you were out of it."

"Oh, bullshit, Tommy. Everything you're in, I'm in. —Don't say anything like that again."

"O.K., O.K. . . . Anyway, he said he'd pass it on to Division, give 'em everythin'—and 'thanks a lot an' in future mind your own fuckin' business.' "

"Well . . . what did you expect? A citation?"

Nardone did his gay impression. "*Well . . . !* He *could* have shaken my *hand!*"—from which Ellie gathered his methadone junkies had put a minor block to the brass after all, in the Classman thing, and had possibly increased the honor of the Squad.

"I'm going to go to lunch early. . . ."

"You're goin' . . . ?" Nardone gave her a look. "—Did that Irishman call, or what?"

"Yes. He called."

"Well, well, well . . . at least that Harp's got some follow-through."

"Tommy . . ."

"I'm not sayin' nothin'. Guy's O.K. apparently—supposed to be a good cop. . . . I hope you know the guy's a killer. Killed three guys like he was shootin' ducks—which is another thing the guy does all the time."

"How do you know all this?" Ellie got up to go. "—You check up on him, or what?"

"I happened to hear, that's all."

"What a liar . . ."

"Hey—there's plenty of creeps in the Department, too, you know. You gotta be careful."

"What a liar you are," Ellie said, and bent and kissed Nardone on the forehead. LaPlace and Seguin whistled and made kissing noises from their desks. "I'll be back in an hour, then you go—O.K.?"

Nardone heaved a heavy sigh. "—That's O.K.; I'll just be up here doin' the work." Ellie started up the aisle to get her raincoat. "—An' look out for that guy. He's probably been drinkin', get his courage up!"

Ellie gave Nardone the finger, over her shoulder—more whistles from LaPlace and Seguin—took her raincoat from the coat rack, went out to the corridor, and down to the fire-stair door.

At quarter to one, Captain Anderson left his office, took the elevator to the basement, and hitched a ride with the Chief of the Department's relief driver, a patrolman named Futterman, five blocks east to Flowers'.

At that corner, the Captain went to the phone booths beside the restaurant entrance, found the first phone wrecked but the second one working, and made a call.

The place was already crowded for lunch when Anderson walked down the short flight to the open door, went in, nodded to Buddy Flowers at the cash register, and walked on into the back room—but Captain García-Bueno had a table for four to himself, and no one pressing to join him.

Anderson eased his way through the tables—mouthing hellos to Department and City people he knew over the waterfall noise of conversation echoing off the low stamped-tin ceiling—got to the table for four, nodded to the Captain just as the waiter put a plate of boiled potatoes and lamb stew in front of him, and sat down opposite.

"I'll have the same."

The waiter, an old man with large, pale hands, scribbled on a new check-blank, then walked away.

Though Captain and Commander, and genuine hero-cop, García-Bueno didn't look the part at all. Twenty-two years before, he'd faced three dealers in a small room on the Lower East Side, placed them under arrest, and been shot through his left knee with a twelve-gauge for his pains. On the floor, his lower left leg only tenuously attached to him, García-Bueno had shot and killed his assailant—forced one of his living prisoners to apply his belt as tourniquet to García-Bueno's thigh—then had read these men their rights, and held them and consciousness until aid arrived.

This small, scrawny man, unpleasantly bald, brown as a cigar and slightly walleyed to boot, had then and thereafter exhibited ferocity and determination sufficient to insure his steady promotion, and the cautious respect of anyone required to associate with him. He lived, and had lived for decades, in a small apartment building, a tenement in Spanish Harlem that stood in the center of a side block buzzing with addicts, thieves, whores, muggers and murderers. In this row of buildings, where desperate trouble and awful sounds were commonplace, the tenement where the Captain lived was a neat oasis of calm, quiet, and perfect safety—and had been for some years, following an episode in which three men (apparently the Captain's magic number) chased a screaming woman, who owed a certain sum, into that building and up its stairs.

These men were not fooling, and were armed—two with knives, one with a small, inexpensive West German revolver—and no doubt considered themselves all-conquering. When, roused from his after-dinner nap by jungle cries, the then Lieutenant García-Bueno came out of his apartment—shared with his sister, brother-in-law, and a fat old cat named Jorge—his slight brown body was nude except for a pair of clean white boxer shorts. He had his service revolver in his left hand.

Continuing his apparently established pattern of dealing with such threes, the Lieutenant placed two of the men under arrest, ordered them to remain absolutely still on the staircase (with the now silent and subdued lady they'd been chasing), and followed the third—the perp with the revolver—up onto the roof, and shot him through the head.

When he came back down the stairs, the Lieutenant found his prisoners and their intended victim docilely waiting for him, nor did their friends ever make fun of them for not trying to run their separate ways.

From that, and the previous incident, and many incidents in the Department's bureaucracy thereafter, García-Bueno earned a reputation as a man with no sense of humor whatsoever—a man who, if he hadn't been so ugly, would have been a serious candidate, someday, for Chief of the Department.

This slight, small brown man now sat opposite Captain Anderson, and looked at him with blank brown eyes—the right eye slightly walled. He was smoking a cigarette, holding it pinched between his left thumb and forefinger. He hadn't unrolled his napkin and silver, and didn't seem interested in the plate of food in front of him.

Anderson got the notion the Captain was waiting for him to talk, and so he did, beginning with a graceful salutation from Chief Delgado—and, when García-Bueno nodded in acknowledgment, got to the point.

Two years before, the Hispanic Captain had been given a precinct—an appointment somewhat overdue on merit, but delayed because of the Captain's unbecoming personality. It was felt he might be a public relations deficit.

Wrong.

The precinct—in a largely black area of Brooklyn—had, after the first few months, embraced their sour, dangerous little Captain, and grown fond of him. Fond of him because he dealt mighty strokes against the murderous young men and boys who hunted through their streets. The Captain kicked ass—and kicking, made two groups of enemies beside the hoodlums: the patrolmen in his precinct, ordered to stand foot-patrol one shift out of three (against assignment agreements negotiated with the PBA)—and several local black politicians and churchmen with no leverage on a Puerto Rican police captain interested only in police work.

It had begun to make for difficulties, downtown—the difficulties compounded by some Departmental and a great deal of press approval of the excellent job García-Bueno was doing. —Compounded further by the man's adamantine character.

Chief Delgado had two methods of dealing with difficult men—too bad or too good at their work. He had decided, quite correctly, that subtlety was wasted on the Captain.

"—The Chief wants you to take those men off foot-patrol, except for specific posts that he personally approves. You will also set up a civilian advisory committee. We'll supply the names of the people you'll request to serve on that."

This bluntness had come at the end of a very reasonable summary of the problems the precinct presented, and congratulations, as well, for the fine job done so far. In the course of these, Anderson's lamb stew lunch had arrived, and he'd begun to eat it before realizing that García-Bueno—having said not a single word—had still not unwrapped his silver, apparently didn't intend to, and was sitting opposite, silent, smoking another cigarette and staring in that blank way. He was listening to Anderson talk, watching him eat, his own plate of food growing gelid before him.

Anderson, choosing between not eating at all, or gobbling and swilling while the little Captain sat watching him, decided on a middle course—ate an occasional spoonful of stew, very neatly, and began to speak more and more laconically. It became a long lunch.

"The Chief would like," Anderson finally said, "your undertaking to obey those orders—and no bullshit about it, Captain." Anderson's temper had frayed.

As if he'd waited just for that, García-Bueno nodded, said, "O.K.," and added, "—this time." Then he leaned forward, and reached over to drop his cigarette into Anderson's stew.

"Where's Tucker?" the Colonel said, having encountered Mason at the Algonquin's newsstand. "—Where the hell is he?"

"Out shopping, sir—over at that fancy toy store across town." Mason had just bought two body-building magazines, and was suddenly concerned that viewing the tanned, oiled, and strenuously muscled men adorning the covers, the officer might think him queer. "—Getting something for his kids." He folded the magazines—covers in—and held them down along his right leg, tapping his thigh with them, casually.

"You're checking out of here," the Colonel said, "—at once, if not sooner. Pack up and check out, pay your bill with your issue card. . . ." He took a small, folded piece of paper out of his jacket pocket. A door key was Scotch-taped to it. "Go to this address—it's down in Greenwich Village—and stay there. Budreau's already on his way."

"Could I ask what's up, sir?"

"Just do as you're told," the Colonel said, and stood looking up at him till Mason got the idea, and went on his way to the elevators. —Not the best material for a crisis situation, the Colonel thought. And maybe a fruit, too.

He bought a pack of Wrigley's Cinnamon, and opened it while he walked out of the hotel to the sidewalk, to get a cab.

"O.K. —How'd it go?" Nardone closed a Gaither shoe box, and sat waiting to hear.

"It's raining out there," Ellie said, sat on the edge of his desk, and brushed raindrops off her skirt, which was a blue fall tweed, and probably wouldn't water-stain in any case.

"I don't care about that. —I'm askin' for gossip! Did the guy have somethin' to contribute, or what?"

"Phil's very nice," Ellie said.

"'Phil,' huh?"

"That's right."

"Any bum can be 'very nice' for one meal."

"We're going out again. . . ."

Nardone leaned forward and patted Ellie's knee. "That's better. That's more like it. —Now, we're talkin' a relationship."

"Tommy, why don't you get going—have some lunch?"

Nardone stood up, and began to stack the shoe boxes and reports to the side of his desk. "O.K. . . . O.K. I'm not goin' to bother you about it. It's strictly your business."

"Thank you."

"I got some news. —I got lucky. They put Siniscola forward to this afternoon, so I can go get that over with—three o'clock, an' then they'll break for dinner, then till whenever the hell they get to it—an' we'll just have the mornin' in court tomorrow. We could go out an' get that boat shit done in the afternoon."

"Good," Ellie said, and sat down in his chair. "—What did you get done, here?"

"I finished the whole year's worth of bills—you got the ones I pulled out there on the long sheet. Take a look at 'em, see what you think."

"O.K."

"Thing left to do, is go through all the rest of the papers—an' that's plenty. I looked through 'em, but I didn't *go* through 'em. —They're back here. . . ." He leaned down behind the desk, picked up a cardboard carton so she could see it, and put it back down. "More there than you're goin' to get done this afternoon—an' you got to get everythin' back down to Torres before six. —Don't forget the pinks on this stuff."

"O.K."

"I got to be back here this evenin', anyway, make some calls, get some stuff done. I can take it down . . .."

"No, Tommy—I'll take care of it. Who's got watch?"

"Murray."

"O.K. I'll give him the pinks; he can lock them in Leahy's desk."

"O.K.," Nardone said. "Well . . . I'm goin'. See you in the mornin'."

"You didn't bring a raincoat?"

"I'll buy an umbrella," Nardone said, halfway up the aisle, then turned around and came back. "You know," he said, "the guy's got two kids—little boys."

"I know; he told me. Tommy—will you get the fuck out of here?"

"Hey, watch that language," Graham said, on his way past to Leahy's office. "—This is City property, here."

The train was a freight—a long transcontinental with collected cars from half a dozen lines linked for the pull east, a mountainous red-and-white double diesel on the haul. This locomotive, which had worked so hard to pull the load up into and through the hills, now worked nearly as hard to control the train, to keep the tons of rolling stock from wheeling free down shelving slopes to the narrow valley floor, where an evening town and an evening station waited, lights glowing yellow through the gloaming.

"Just what the hell do you think you're *doing,* Tucker —on some vacation here, playing with some goddamn trains?" The Colonel's breath—his voice's volume damped, its pitch quite high—smelled of scotch and cinnamon. Having introduced himself, the Colonel's own attention was momentarily claimed as the great diesel whistled, and rumbled slowly, then slower still, into the station—switching, at the last moment, from track two to track three, to ease away from the passenger platform and into freight loading.

The Colonel hadn't startled Tucker, but he'd surprised him unpleasantly, and the sergeant straightened up from his concentration on the electric train and felt with his left hand to be certain of his FAO Schwarz shopping bag—set at his feet when he'd first fallen into the evening world spread out under lamp-lit cotton clouds on a great table weighted with hills, tunnels, the small town, and miles and miles of shining track. It was only, or almost only at such times, when confronted with a marvelous toy of this sort, or a boy's more particular article of play . . . a mitt, or bat, or BB gun . . . that Tucker felt some pang considering his house of women.

The shopping bag was full. —He'd bought Jacklyn a small gold pin at Tiffany; it was shaped like a honey bee, and, for eyes, had tiny pearls. Then, at this store, he'd bought a complete nurse's outfit for Kameesha—plastic thermometer (oral), stethoscope, fake IV setup with tube and stick-on plastic needle, and a white uniform dress and cap. He'd bought Kimana a Green Berette kit—fatigues, rubber combat-knife, two gray plastic grenades, and a plastic assault rifle that clucked rapidly when its trigger was pulled.

"Sergeant," the Colonel keeping his voice down as two adults and three small children circulated past, heading for airplane models. "—I really do not appreciate having to chase across town on that fool Mason's say-so, tracking you down. We have a crisis situation!" The Colonel was wearing his British Warm. Rain had wet the wool, and it smelled.

"Sorry, sir," Tucker said.

"—Do you have to wear those goddamn glasses?"

"No, sir. I have contacts."

"Well—take the fucking things off!" A breeze of scotch. "For your information, Sergeant, you have provided a *portrait parlant* for every stupid flatfoot in the city. Gold-rimmed glasses! —You're supposed to be a professional!"

Two of the small children who had just passed them, now wandered back, bored by airplanes, to watch the red-and-white locomotive pulling out of the station—and the Colonel, tugging at Tucker's sleeve, steered him away toward a wall of small robots, each standing before its empty, stacked box, glittering, peering with bright eyes—red, green, or amber.

Tucker took his glasses off and put them in his raincoat pocket.

"—I've just been informed that you, Budreau, and Mason have been made. —Budreau and Mason are already down in the safe in Greenwich Village, and that's where you're heading, pronto. Two junkies at that methadone clinic can supposedly identify all three of you—that great idea!—you, by those damn glasses, just like at the Classman thing."

"Those two people should be no problem, sir," Tucker said, and picked up a robot, a small, stocky, bright gold machine with fat, articulated legs, green eyes, and a car-grill grin. It was dressed like a boxer, in shorts and high-lace athletic shoes. Tucker shifted a silver lever at the robot's chest, and the machine, batteried for display, squawked a sentence in what sounded like French, put up its small, gloved fists, and began to pat irregularly at Tucker's chest.

"The junkies aren't the problem, Sergeant. The investigating officer running them is the problem. Pursuing the investigation. —Pursuing it! The New York City Police Department is the problem."

Tucker put the little robot back in front of its box, and it spoke, and sparred busily with a larger, murderous blue machine, horn-headed and armed with a small ax, but silent and still.

"Let's move . . . let's move," the Colonel said, took Tucker's sleeve again, and towed him away down the wall of robots to the second floor's central aisle.

"It seems to me, sir," Tucker said, "—that this would be a really good time to get our asses out of this town."

"And I might agree with you, Sergeant," the Colonel said, and walked to the left around a cashier's station to avoid a young woman, dressed as a clown, handing out balloons to children passing by. "—However, Washington does *not* agree with you. —They think these assholes in blue have been handing us nothing but bullshit since this mission came up. Beginning with steering us to try and recruit that goddamn maniac that murdered Bob. —They think our police friends are being very cute, pushing us to see how far we'll push—playing politics, sticking their big New York Democratic noses into a very delicate matter of national security."

The young woman dressed as a clown—red fright-wig, white polka-dotted costume, an enormous lipstick smile—had, full of initiative, trotted around the cashier's station to intercept them, now performed a giant-shoe shuffle, and handed them each a balloon. Tucker, a blue. The Colonel's, orange.

"Let's get the hell out of here. . . ." The Colonel, gripping the string of his balloon, headed for the escalator, and Tucker—pausing to give the blue to a young man with a baby in his arms—followed after, catching up to the Colonel halfway down. "—We have orders," the Colonel said, "—to call these people's bluff. Raise and call."

On their way to the front door, walking against a tide of children and patient parents, eddies and whirlpools of toddlers around the stuffed animals, Tucker said, "Sir, we're not fooling with a bunch of Centrals here, don't know better than shit in their breakfast. —We already lost one man, just screwing around."

"Tell me about it," the Colonel said, and had difficulty getting his balloon through the revolving door.

The walk was windswept, the air still damp and cool, remembering rain.

"Ours not to reason why, Tuck," the Colonel said, and released his balloon to ride the weather.

At just after four, Ellie left Headquarters, walked over to the Lexington line through slight, wayward breezes, the tiger-stripe shadows of traveling overcast, and took the train up to Sixty-eighth.

She walked east toward the hospital from there, the wind, blowing a little harder as she neared the river, tugging at the hem of her raincoat, opening the coat below its last button, toying with that flap and letting it fall. Ellie thought of Audrey Birnbaum as she walked, and hoped the woman wouldn't look too dreadful. A vision of a huge black plumber's assistant lying swollen, dying, massive new breasts with milking nipples exposed by the down-turned sheet as he stared up at the ceiling TV. —Pro football . . . opening game of the season. A yellow, murderous rolling eye when Ellie walked into the room. . . .

Tired of imagining this, standing on an uptown corner on First, waiting for the light, Ellie began to review her day instead, saving until last her lunch with the Stake-out man—who'd been as tall as she'd remembered, but harsher-faced, not as handsome. He was wearing brown slacks, white shirt, a dark brown sports jacket, tan raincoat. Loafers. They'd eaten lunch at Chow-Chow's, and at Shea's prompting, "Let's get sick—make it memorable," they'd ordered four chili dogs, fat fries, and black-and-white shakes.

"I hear your partner's a damn good cop," Shea had said when they found a side booth beneath a wall-sized photograph of Lou Gehrig saying good-bye to Yankee Stadium.

"He checked on you, too," Ellie said.

Shea had talked of this and that, then mentioned his young boys. "—About a year after Celeste died, every lady in Sheepshead Bay was looking for a mother type for me. I was the target of the year."

"No longer?"

"They gave up. —I wasn't looking for a mother for the boys. I figured if I was lucky enough to find a woman I loved—loved me, well, she'd *be* a mother to the boys if she felt like it—and if she didn't . . . that would just be their bad luck. Kids have to take their chances getting loved, just the way we do."

The chili dogs had been awful. They each ate their two, then ordered one more and split it.

Shea had done two years at Fordham law before joining the Force, and was still being pressured to go back and finish. "—But I just can't get it done. That's a profession is either boring or disgusting—it's even worse than police work."

"But you like police work."

"I love police work."

He talked about a case two of his men were handling—a heartbreaker. A plainclothesman named Taubman, on stake-out with two others at a gas station on Staten Island, had, last spring, shot and permanently paralyzed a fifteen-year-old boy who tried to rob the place with his grandfather's revolver. The attempted robbery had been a bluff, the revolver unloaded. The grandfather, who'd raised the boy, was a retired Suffolk County cop—and in August, at the boy's request, had procured another pistol, gone to the hospital, and shot his grandson to death.

"I read about it," Ellie said.

"My people are trying to prove it was a temporary insanity thing—depositions from the old guy's doctor and his friends—keep the poor bastard out of prison . . . not that they'd put him away for long. —Well, let me be honest. My people *will* prove it was a temporary insanity thing. Period. There's enough tragedy, without making it worse. Harry Taubman's a basket case, as it is. Kid gave him no time to say maybe."

Ellie had mentioned the Gaither case and its circumstances, and Shea found it odd. "—All kind of cold and careful, wasn't it? —Even if she died hard. Man kills a beautiful woman, it's usually kind of sudden, sloppy. Not so careful. Not so neat."

While they were finishing their milk shakes, Ellie mentioned her painting, her old art classes—comparing that to his two years at law school.

"No comparison," Shea'd said, abruptly. "—Painting's more worthwhile. You sound like you're ashamed of not staying with it—right?"

"No, I'm not," Ellie said.

He'd picked up his metal milk-shake container, and poured the last into her glass. "I'll tell you what—you come out hunting with me this year—you don't have to shoot any birds. You come out and look at the colors on the Sound just before the sun comes up. Everything out there looks like silver, you know, with some tarnish on it? —You come out there and paint that. You give that a try. You don't freeze, you'll get some damn good work done."

He'd kissed her on the cheek, when they parted after lunch, and said he'd call her. "Not tomorrow," he'd said. "—You'll need time to digest me and the chili dogs. . . ."

Ellie turned at the hospital's gate, at the entrance drive, then went up the curved concrete walk—only three or four early autumn leaves scudding across the pavement—climbed the wide steps into the building's lobby, stopped at reception-information, and asked an elderly oriental woman for Audrey Birnbaum's room number. The woman asked for the spelling of Birnbaum, then looked up the name on her Rolodex.

"Mrs. Birnbaum is on Communicable, seventh floor, room seven-fourteen. You'll need to check with the station nurse before you go in." The elderly woman had a girl's thick, gleaming black hair. The rich tarry fall looked odd framing her round, soft, crumpled face . . . as if a Chinese princess had been cursed by a witch to suddenly suffer age.

Ellie shared the elevator going up with a young couple and their little boy. The husband was slim, snub-nosed and handsome . . . he smiled at Ellie as the elevator rose. His wife was pretty, in an angular auburn way. She had freckles on her wrists, just below the cuffs of her green sweater. Ellie supposed she had freckles on her face, too, under her makeup.

The little boy—about eight years old, Ellie thought—in dark blue corduroy pants and a blue-checked flannel shirt, had hands as thin and white as bone, but his face was fat, his cheeks puffed out as if he were holding his breath, filling them with air. He was wearing a white knit watch cap pulled down to his ears, and no hair appeared from under it.

He noticed Ellie looking at him, and glanced sideways to look back at her. He had light blue eyes; the pupil of his left eye was bigger than the right's.

These people got off at the fourth floor, and a tall, stooped, balding doctor in a wonderfully cut dark blue suit with real button cuffs on the jacket, got on and rode one floor up. He had his cuffs unbuttoned and folded back—to examine a patient, or, Ellie thought, show what a wonderful suit it was. His stethoscope was stuffed into the jacket's right side pocket.

On the fifth floor, no one else got on, and Ellie rode up alone to seven.

On seven, she stepped out onto shining, waxed white flooring, streaked with patterns of black, and immediately felt guilty satisfaction at just visiting, at being all right, and not sick at all. Seven-fourteen was down the long leg to the left, past the nurses' station, and Ellie stopped at the station as the oriental woman downstairs had said she should. A nurse—very pretty, blond, with cheekbones like a Ukrainian girl's—was sitting at the station counter, making some sort of notes on a page in a small black loose-leaf notebook. There was very faint blond down on her upper lip.

Ellie said, "Excuse me . . ." and the nurse looked up and said, "Be with you in a second . . ." looked down, and went on entering her notes. She hadn't been as pretty, full-face, as she'd seemed with her head bent. Ellie heard a soft announcement on a speaker above and behind her. They were asking for a Mr. Carlson . . . or Dr. Carlson. It was hard to tell.

"Yes?" The nurse put her notebook away in a drawer.

"I'm here to see Mrs. Audrey Birnbaum."

"Are you a relative?"

"I'm a friend."

"Well . . . you'll have to sign a disclaimer, Miss . . . ?"

"Klein."

"You'll have to sign a disclaimer, Miss Klein, since Mrs. Birnbaum has a serious communicable disease." She tugged a small gray form out of a slot below the counter, and reached up to put it in front of Ellie to sign. And reached up again with a black Bic pen.

"I thought Mrs. Birnbaum had cancer," Ellie said, and signed the form.

"Well, she does. But she's suffering from AIDS as well, and the hospital's been sued by a few people who claim they caught it visiting patients—which is a lot of nonsense, but this is to protect us against that."

Ellie pushed the form back over the counter. "O.K.?"

"O.K. Just go down the hall; her room is fourth on the left. —And you probably don't want to stay too long. She tires kind of easily."

Ellie walked past three doors on her left, and paused at the fourth; it was open a few inches, and a small white cardboard sign reading *Communicable Disease* in red letters, was thumbtacked to it.

Ellie took a breath—floor wax, food (smelled like sweet potatoes), and some sharper, chemical odor—and pushed the door gently open to go in.

"Toddy . . . ?"

"No . . . I'm sorry," Ellie said to lustrous gray-black eyes set in an elegant dark brown skull. The skull rested propped on a blue satin pillowcase, and beneath it a narrow rack of shoulders was draped in a bed jacket of lighter blue satin, bordered with cream lace. The arms were long, brown, nobbed sticks, blackly bruised—the hands, large, skeletal, an IV needle taped onto the back of the left one. A white open-weave cotton blanket mounded down over more bones in a long, slight, irregular ridge, almost to the bed's foot rail.

"The lady cop." Mrs. Birnbaum had a Southern woman's husky voice and complicated vowels, not yet ruined to match her. She wore a pale cream turban, the same shade as her jacket's lace.

"That's right," Ellie said. "My name's Ellie Klein. —O.K. if I come in?"

"I'd be plenty P.O.'d if you didn't," Audrey Birnbaum said. "—Except for Toddy, an' a gay friend who's too insane to fear anythin' I have found myself resoundin'ly short of visitors."

Ellie walked in, and hesitated about taking off her raincoat.

"Take it off, sugar, and hang it over there in the closet. —Where'd you get that?"

"Tabouri's."

"That shit costs a fortune. —Have you been a naughty little cop?"

"No," Ellie said, hanging the raincoat up, "—it was a birthday present from me to me." She came back to the bed, and sat to the right of it in a small armless chair upholstered in maroon plastic. She put her purse down on the floor beside her.

"Toddy told me about you," Audrey Birnbaum said, "—but it got so late, I thought you just decided to skip it." A small black machine, a white tube coiled and clipped to its top, rested on a steel bedside table. Kleenex, paperback books, and a six-ounce bottle of Fleurs Fauves were lined up in front of it.

"No," Ellie said. "—I had a lot of work to get done before I came over." The walls of the room were covered with pictures. All pictures of flowers. Reproductions of Van Goghs, Eugene Tillerys, Redon and de Heem. Some, Ellie didn't know. —There were no real flowers in the room.

Slowly, carefully, the skull finished turning on its blue satin to face her. "—See all these pretty paintin's? I told Toddy I didn't want to be seein' cut flowers die, so he's buyin' me these. Every few days I get a new one.

"They're beautiful."

"Which one you like the best?"

Ellie looked at them, looked over her shoulder to see the ones on the opposite wall.

"I like the de Heem. —That one." The picture was between the far window and the door to the bathroom.

"You know who painted that paintin'?"

"I just happened to recognize it," Ellie said. "—I like that one because he makes the whole vase of flowers seem to be still growing. As if the flowers were still alive."

"That's right," Audrey Birnbaum said. "—It does look like that. Either he was real good, or those flowers were real fresh."

"Which is your favorite?"

"Depends how I feel. If I feel good, I look at the bright ones, where it really looks like summertime. If I don't feel so good, I just pick one of the dark ones doesn't hurt my eyes. —Listen . . . how much did you pay for that raincoat?"

"A hundred and ninety-two dollars," Ellie said.

"I had my eye," Audrey said, "—I had my eye on a light brown leather coat over there—you know, light cocoa? But it was a trench-coat style, and honey, at the time—I had not yet had my pecker removed—I just couldn't afford to be dressin' so butch."

"I think I know the one you mean," Ellie said. "Did it have a sort of woven belt . . . ? Light and dark kind of ropes of leather?"

"That was it! Did you see the price tag on that mother?"

"No."

"Six hundred and sixty-one dollars. —I mean, give a girl a break!"

"It was very pretty."

"Oh, honey—it was beautiful. . . . It was Italian or Brazilian, some place where those people know *leather.*" Having said so much, Audrey appeared to tire. Lids curtained down over anthracite eyes. She'd been made up carefully; a tongue tip, very pale, almost white, came out to touch lips tinted tropic coral.

Ellie sat quiet, thinking the woman might be drifting off, sleeping. . . . She was surprised to find the small room—sunlit, as clouds drifted away over the river—restful after all. The dying woman's silence restful as well. Ellie sat at ease in the maroon chair, relaxing, looking at the pictures on the walls.

After two or three minutes, Audrey said, "Well? —What's the news?" She didn't open her eyes.

"We don't know who killed her. We're still digging."

"Well, sugar, you are goin' to have to dig deep—because there was no one, as far as I know, who disliked Sally, let alone hated her enough to do that. —To do what they did." Audrey opened her eyes, and they shone with such luster it seemed impossible they were soon to rot. She appeared to put all she had left of beauty into them. "—Only person I know who had any motive for that, was me."

"How so?"

"Well—you want to hear a confession?"

"You bet."

"Well, here it is. I loved Sally Gaither like a sister, and better'n a sister. An' if I had a choice whether I was goin' to be the one lyin' here, or she was, I honest-to-God don't know which I would choose. —However, an' here's the confession . . . I'm happy she died before me, an' died even harder than I'm goin' to. —And that, sugar, is how lonely dyin' is, how desperate a dyin' person gets for company. I'd take the whole damn world with me if I could—except for children, and my Toddy. An' I was raised in the Church an' a Christian, too."

"We'll all feel like that," Ellie said.

"But I feel like it now. Do you mind if I tell you somethin'?"

"No," Ellie said.

"—Because you're a woman, I suppose. Lance is a real easy crier—but there's not much else *to* Lance. An' Toddy . . . well, I'd never hurt Toddy by tellin' him some things I feel."

"You can tell me anything you want," Ellie said. She felt tired, the backs of her knees ached, but in other ways she was quite at ease, rested. She sat back, her head turned as the dying woman's head was turned, so they could look into each other's eyes.

"Well, like that song—I'm sorry to be goin', but I'm pleased with where I been. —It's not nothin' for a little sissy nigger boy from Birmin'ham, didn't know beans when the bag was open, only thing different he was suckin' dicks when his friends were suckin' pussy, turn out to be a wife to a fine, *fine* brave man, went to Harvard College. It's not nothin' get all that done when you're twenty-six years old, 'cause that's all I am. An' I had two, three other very important men in love with me. —An' I'm not jus' talkin' about sex, either."

"It never is just about sex, is it?"

The skull smiled and showed wonderful teeth. "Now that," Audrey Birnbaum said, "—that's somethin' sounds like Sally."

"You have no idea at all who might have killed her?"

"Not one. An' not for lack of tryin'. —There was a Greek man liked to beat up ladies, a few years ago. He beat up Sally, just once. —She didn't mind a paid-for spankin' sometimes. You know what she said to me? She said, 'It's a pleasure, once a year or so, to lie across some silly man's lap an' get what we all have comin', with kisses to follow.' —Isn't that nice?"

"What was his name?" Ellie thought of Clara, her strong, smarting little hand, her busy fingers.

"Oh, hell—Mike somethin'-or-other. He didn't bother her any after that. Sally told him, 'Man, you rented—you didn't buy.' She told him she was goin' talk to some people, he didn't stay away. So he stayed away."

"Who was she going to talk to?"

"Oh, you know—some guys. She wasn't out there on a limb, sugar. Not back then. She had people watchin' out for her—more ways than one.

"Not a pimp, though."

"Not the way you mean it," Audrey said, and lay looking at Ellie, silent. After a while, she said, "You're a pretty woman. Isn't it weird to have people always after your ass? Tryin' an' put their hands on you? —That was the worst thing I found out about bein' a woman. Everybody wants to be touchin' you all the time, and whether they do or they don't, that's always in the air. —Isn't that so?"

"As long as women look good, I suppose that's true," Ellie said.

"Well, ain't nobody wants to touch my ass now, you better believe that," Audrey said. "—That's somethin' I don't have to worry about, a-tall."

"Who were those people watching out for her?"

"Same folks watchin' out for everybody," Audrey said, smiled, and closed her eyes. After a few moments, with her eyes still closed, she said, "Listen, you find some money at Sally's?"

"Yes. We found a lot—in the closet."

"She was scared of taxes. 'Bout the only thing that lady *was* scared of. . . . But you didn't find nothin' in no closet. Ain't nobody hide shit in a closet. —That's the first place any fool's goin' to look."

"That's where we found it."

"How much money you find in that closet?" Her eyes still closed.

"We found fourteen thousand dollars," Ellie said.

Audrey Birnbaum's large, brown, skeleton's hands

stirred on the cotton blanket. "I know it's time for my shot," she said, "—an' I'm not even hurtin' too bad. But it's stirrin'. It's like I had a little dog or somethin' in my insides, an' he wakes up hungry and starts eatin' on me in there—in my hips? You see how a dog breaks a bone . . . ?"

"Yes . . ." Ellie said.

"Breakin' live bones . . . eatin' on me like he hates me. Just hates me in there. . . ." She slowly turned her face from Ellie.

Audrey Birnbaum was quiet for several minutes after that, though her hands were restless.

"That Sally," she said, finally. "—She put that in the closet, make some jackass think he got it all."

"There was more money in the apartment?"

"You go look in her big coffee maker . . . She didn't drink any coffee. Sally just drank tea. Anybody wanted coffee, she had a little Melitta. —Just you remember that's for Sonny. Don't you go stealin' that child's money. . . ."

"We looked in the coffee maker, Audrey. We looked in there."

"You motherfuckers," Audrey Birnbaum said, her eyes still closed, her hands, raised slightly off the cotton blanket, playing some instrument of air. "—You stole Sonny's money."

Ellie got up and put her hand on Audrey's arm. She felt two cool narrow bones wrapped in skin. "—Audrey. There was no money in the kitchen when the police were there. —How much money did Sally keep?"

"It's almost time for my shot."

"Audrey—how much money did Sally keep?"

"Are you touchin' my arm?"

"Yes. I'm sorry." Ellie took her hand away.

Audrey opened her eyes. "I didn't mean to hurt your feelin's. But that's my bad arm. —I didn't mean anythin' personal."

"Oh, Audrey . . . I'm sorry. But, please tell me how much cash Sally kept."

"All right . . . all right. Jus' give me a minute. It gets time for my shot I can't think of anythin' else. You'll understand that, sometime. Give me a minute . . . an' I'll tell you. . . . I'll tell you she had more 'n a hundred thousand in there in hundreds an' a *bunch* of old one-thousands, a couple months ago. . . . You ever see a thousand-dollar bill? You can't get 'em any more. She had a hundred an' thirty-seven thousand dollars in there, all counted out. An' she gave me ten thousand dollars to pay my bone man, 'cause he wouldn't wait, an' I couldn't bear to tell Toddy. He doesn't have a bit of money left. I hope . . . oh, I hope I haven't ruined my Toddy. . . ."

"No, no. He loves you, Audrey. He's very proud of you."

Audrey Birnbaum's large right hand—a drawn hand, all lines—searched like a chill spider for one of Ellie's. Audrey's eyes opened, were brighter than before. "Don't tell him I need my shot," she said. "—Don't you dare tell him I said anythin' about it. I tell him this cancer makes me sleepy, an' that's all he needs to know."

"I won't tell him," Ellie said, and Audrey's hand loosed hers and wandered away. Audrey's eyes closed again, as if the light in the room were much too bright.

"Listen, Audrey," Ellie said. "—Who else knew about that money?" She was afraid to sit on the side of the bed, afraid that would hurt the woman, so she stayed standing.

"Shit, honey—Sally was no goddamn fool. Nobody knew that shit. You know how I found out?"

"No."

Ellie waited, but Audrey said nothing more.

"Audrey . . . Audrey, could you just tell me how you found out about that money?"

The skull opened elegant coral lips, and breathed in a deep, sighing breath. "—That was a good one. I had my shot I'd be laughin'." Another deep, deep breath. "—I tried makin' some coffee in that fucker when she had a party a couple years ago—got it out from under the counter—an' Sally came walkin' in the kitchen while I was pourin' water in the top, an' had a shit fit. She was scared I'd spoiled all that money."

"And nobody else ever knew?"

"No way. Toddy an' I used to laugh about that—an' we were over there once an' he say he was goin' out an' make some coffee, just for fun, see Sally jump. . . ." The skull smiled. "I tell you one thing," Audrey said. "—It sure is time for my shot."

"Audrey," Ellie said. "I have to go, now—but I'd like to come see you again.

"What . . . ?"

"I'd like to come and see you again."

Audrey lay still, a shrunken brown study except for her shifting hands, and didn't answer for a moment. Then she said, "O.K. That'd be nice. You go by Tabouri's an' see if they still have that trench coat in stock. I ever do get out of here, I'm goin' to buy that motherfucker. I earned it."

Ellie leaned over and kissed her as lightly as she could on the cheek, imagining the little dog eating at the bones. "Bye-bye," she said to Audrey Birnbaum, as though they were friends.

At the nurses' station, when Ellie mentioned Audrey's shot, the blond nurse—not so pretty, full-face—smiled, shook her head, and said, "Not yet."

CHAPTER 11

In the lobby, Ellie waited at a row of phone booths, all busy, until a short man in a tan raincoat came out of the third one, his face red, frowning, tears in his eyes behind bifocal glasses. —Ellie supposed he'd been upstairs to see someone.

She called Nardone's number at the Squad, and the phone rang several times before it was picked up. Ellie recognized LaPlace's voice.

"Frank—it's Ellie. Is Tommy there?"

"He's over at court. He didn't come back yet."

"Well . . . do me a favor. Leave a message for him—O.K.?"

"Right."

"Tell him we got a break on the Gaither thing."

"Right."

"Leave a message for him.—Tell him it was a robbery."

"No shit? —Hold on while I get a piece of paper. . . . O.K."

"It was a robbery. Sally had a hundred thousand dollars in her apartment. A hundred and twenty-seven thousand, maybe more, some hundreds, some thousand-dollar bills. —We have a witness."

"All right! Nice goin'. —Wasn't there fourteen thou still in there?"

"No—this is beside the fourteen thousand. —Tell him Audrey came through for us."

" 'Audrey . . .' O.K., I got it. I'll give it to him when he comes in."

"If you leave before then, let Murray have it, O.K.? —I'm going shopping, so tell Tommy he can give me a call tonight, when he gets home. —And I need to know about the plates."

"Will do. —What plates?"

"Never mind, he can tell me when he calls."

"O.K. I'll see he gets it."

It was darker outside, and close to raining, but no wind blew to shove the few early-fallen leaves along.

Ellie went down the drive to the street, and reached over to grip her left forearm as she walked, reassured by sturdy muscle, by roundness, thickness more than only bones wrapped in cold, slipping skin. She took several deep breaths, deep enough so her lungs ached slightly, expanding with them. The air . . . cool, heavy, damp. Leaf smelling. Smelling of car exhausts. Smelling slightly dark from the river running along the hospital's other side.

She walked up to the corner, pleased with the swing of her arms, her legs' steps and strides, the motion of her hips provoking touches of her clothes, cloth stroking her as she moved. Ellie thought that someday, in a hospital, she was going to wish to be just as she now was—healthy, walking, breathing cool air. Not sick, not old. —I'll wish that then, she thought, but too late. Now, is when that wish is granted. I have my wish, if I wish it now. . . .

Day after tomorrow—tomorrow being wasted in court and out on Long Island—day after tomorrow, she and Tommy would see Todd Birnbaum again, and ask him how he was paying his wife's medical bills, and with what money.

It would be time for Tommy to call George Soseby—to give him sad news, and ask him how his business went. —Ask him where a factor found cash to leverage out his deals.

They'd have to check the bank accounts, debts, spending habits of every name and address referenced by the phone company on Sally's bills for the last year. —It would take weeks to get that done. Bank accounts, debts, spending—by that super, Correa, and the doormen, delivery men, the people from the laundry, dry cleaners, groceries, liquor store.

Go back to Margolies, twist her arm a little for something better than first names. —No more apartment tours. Soseby—if he was clean—had to have something on Sally's johns. Something more than first names. He wouldn't be a man at all, if he didn't know a little more than that. . . .

They would have to start over, thinking about money this time. —Shea had been right. Too cool a killing, too neat, too patiently dreadful to be for love. They'd have to start over—and do the Long Island thing as well, and any other bullshit handed to them. —Then, in another week, they'd be over at the U.N. at least half their time for a month, listening to Evelyn Costello's crap on behalf of U.N. Security, listening to security lectures by clowns from a dozen countries, most of whom knew zip about security or police work of any kind. —The classic being the Sec. Rep. from Upper Volta last year who was afraid of witchcraft, and wouldn't be separated from his magic bag containing god-knew-what, which he carried around in his briefcase with his papers on interrogation modules and crowd control.

Tommy and Ed Graham had bought a tarantula at a pet shop and put it on the seat of the yo-yo's limo. —Everybody getting into real trouble for that, Costello almost having a baby. . . .

Ellie waited for the light on the corner of Second Avenue. The cool, damp air was making her cheek ache a little, where the bone had been broken.

All for money, after all . . . not for Sally's beauty, or sex, or a loss of love. For money. Unless Audrey'd been lying . . . had some reason to lie. —Pictures, Ellie thought, should come in threes: expectation; the thing itself; the memory of it. There should be a second picture of the whore. A picture of questions . . . all lines, all colors left unfinished. No final definitions. What flowed from between Sally's slender spraddled legs as she lay on her open bathrobe, now, posed on the field of blue, her thighs wide-spread to her fork, where tendons rose at last to show the way—all approaches polished, pumiced, waxed, perfumed—to the damp, small socket enjoyed by a thousand men (a mist over her slight white belly, a haze of mother-of-pearl made of ghost semen, ghost smiles, ghost cries, gratitudes of those thousand ghosts)? —Did a green fountain flow from there, that wound permanent, spurting, squirting at first, then gushing a narrow river, all currency (folds and leaves and sheaves of printed light green bills) rushing out to those who loved her, who had said they loved her—each running those verdant rapids in a small planked boat? And one of whom had lied?

The liar, the surest sailor, rowed a ruby oar.

Ellie walked two blocks uptown to Market Garden, went in and took a cart. It was more expensive than the supermarket on the island, but had delicacies, and was richly decorated with flowered wicker arches, and, high along the walls, intricate floral abstracts worked out of overlapping sheets of sawn and painted plywood. Leaves, petals, stamens. Whites, creams, mauve. She thought of Phil Shea while she shopped, as, she supposed, a number of women were doing as they shopped—considering men they had, had had, wished to have. Might have. Considering their children, too, of course. Their parents . . . Or sometimes, in the aisles, simply summing up the day. —She could consider Clara. Probably one or two of the women were considering Claras as they picked out their oranges—the Valencias, as usual, a little green.

Ellie'd never been sure if that small area of green at the end of the orange meant it was really unripe, could make you sick. —Though if two and a half chili dogs, half a pound of fat fries and the shake hadn't, she didn't suppose a green orange would.

Having so far to walk, she shopped light, and bought a can of skinless-boneless sardines in olive oil, a jar of Greek olives in herb oil, a pound of corn bread—her rye and pumpernickel were still in Leahy's little refrigerator—a head of cauliflower, a half pound of Land O' Lakes sweet butter, and a single-stack box of Cracked Wheat crackers.

She got into line, paid—the girl asked for coupons, and Ellie remembered she had coupons for the butter, but not in this purse—carried her plastic shopping bag out into the street, and headed downtown to the tram.

It began to rain as the tram car rose, murmuring along the roof, spangling the windows first, then sheeting them. The river lay flat charcoal-gray below—the gray the superficial ruction of rain across its surface, the charcoal all beneath.

The men and women crowded in the car smelled of wet wool, the duller sweat smell of wet synthetics. The dampness drew out the odors of the women's scents, as well—

deodorants, powders, perfumes—deepening them, darkening them so they partitioned the car. Here Tea-rose, there Choise—then Shalimar.

At the apartment door, Mayo performed (unusual for him) a small curvet of welcome—and didn't bolt out to the hall. Ellie switched on the light with her elbow, put her purse on the hall table, then bent to pick him up one-handed, and carry him pleased and limp into the kitchen to feed, a light balance-weight for the grocery bag.

She opened a can of 9-Lives liver, emptied it into a saucer, and slid the dish under the table for him; then went back to the hall to check her answering machine. A message from her mother. A message from Mary Gands. *"Engaged at last—engaged at last! —Call me!"* Ellie supposed Joseph had agreed to stop drinking. Or at least try to stop drinking.

Ellie undressed in the bedroom, hung up her jacket, skirt, and blouse, and went into the bathroom to change her tampon. She sat on the toilet for a few moments afterward, peeing. —And what would Mary say if Ellie left a message on *her* machine. *Engaged at last—again!* Am going out to Sheepshead Bay to live the rest of my life with a cop named Shea . . . and take care of his little boys. And probably love them—to his satisfaction, no matter how tough he talks. And have Sonia Gaither come and visit us, and consider us her family . . . get some rest from sorrow and loneliness, be safe behind Phil Shea. "Tough Cookie." Ellie supposed, if anything ever did happen, which it probably wouldn't since she didn't even know the man, that she would bake him cookies on his birthday, make gentle fun of the nickname—not wanting to picture too clearly the places, circumstances, the portions of seconds in which he'd earned it. That was another house for Sally to have written about—the house of terror. —But she'd only visited there once, and then it was too late.

Ellie couldn't imagine herself making love to Phil Shea. She supposed she could imagine him making love to her! Fucking the daylights out of her, to be precise. . . . He'd screw a baby into her in no time flat. A Catholic baby, like Sonia's lost brother. —And Tommy would be very pleased. He'd liked Shea right away at the cemetery, been worried Shea wouldn't call after all. . . . would hurt her. —Then, he and Connie would come out and visit the mama-to-be, very happy for her, and Tommy would go fishing with Phil—and there'd be Tommy's ex-partner, left behind on the dock with Connie for health reasons, the baby coming soon. There she'd be, with her belly stuck out a mile, advertising it to everybody at the grocery, all the waiters in the seafood restaurants out there. —This lady has spent some time on her back with her legs in the air, getting laid but good, and it's turned her into something different from what she was.

If it came to a choice at St. Margaret's emergency, between her and the baby—which would Phil Shea choose? Ellie thought of his big-knuckled hands, his face's coarse, weather-scraped skin, his chill gray eyes when she'd compared her painting to the practice of law. . . . She supposed he'd choose her, after all.

She put on her bathrobe, and went out to the kitchen to put the groceries away . . . decide about dinner. After dinner, she thought she'd do a load of laundry. Maybe do sheets, too, make an evening of it. Read Sally's second letter carefully.

There was a Swanson's Macaroni-and-Cheese Dinner and a Bird's Eye Spinach Lasagne in the freezer. Ellie took out the Swanson's, peeled the foil top off, and put it in for power medium, six minutes. Mayo's saucer was still sliding, clinking under the table. It took him longer to eat liver.

Nardone had bought an umbrella on his way to court in the afternoon—and that evening, on the courthouse steps, a gust had broken one of the ribs of the thing so it flapped like a black half-broken wing. It was still better than nothing, and he held it up over his head now, walking out of Headquarters into the rainy night, then along the wet red bricks of the Mall, through the Municipal Building's high arches, and across Centre Street to the Lexington's City Hall stop. The rain was slanting down through the streetlamps' yellow light pretty hard, hissing across the pavement, then letting up. In the dark beyond the streetlights, you couldn't see the stuff coming down, but you could hear it. His shoes were wet. Water poured off the broken fold of the umbrella about right to wash his hands in out of a faucet.

Curtis had offered him a lift over to Clinton, but getting home from there was more trouble than just taking the train right across. Most times, the train was fine. —This late, this kind of weather, not so good.

Nardone crossed the street, jumped an overflowing gutter, and trotted down the subway steps, trying to shake some of the water off the umbrella without breaking it any more. Wound up stroking the water off, furling the thing very gently. It had one of those thin little tie strips on it, about halfway down, with a snap—or supposed to have a snap. Nardone fumbled for it, found the little metal thing supposed to snap in, but couldn't find, farther down, any place to snap it into.

He looked, felt around the base of the strip, the umbrella's cloth there, while he went down the second flight of steps. Nothing. The thing had half a snap, and that was it.

You get what you pay for. Four bucks and fifty cents, you get half a snap. He tried to wrap the tie around the umbrella, get some sort of knot there. —No dice. Let the frigging thing flap. Nothing to eat for dinner, either, thanks to that asshole of a judge—and poor Marty, bending his ear for an hour on the phone with nothing but complaints and promises. Scared to death, convinced old Vinnie knew it all, was going to have a blow torch put on his face. . . . No dinner. Connie'd make him a bacon and tomato when he got home. Marie could come sit with them.

The man in the change booth was a man Nardone knew, an old black man named Broughton, and Broughton waved Tommy through while he was still reaching in his jacket for the tin.

Nardone, sporting his broken umbrella, walked across the long ramp over the IRT trains, and was passed by some kids coming up the other way. White kids—high school jocks from Queens, they looked like, red-and-white varsity jackets and so forth—probably walk over to the Village, see if they can find some excitement in town.

Had girls with them; the girls would keep it all cooler than otherwise.

Nardone remembered being just such a jerk, a Brooklyn jerk in his case, coming over to town—looking for what, he didn't know. Trouble . . . start trouble, duke some guy out. Maybe get laid. Some different kind of girl . . . Manhattan girl. —He didn't even know what the hell he wanted. Then Connie wised him up, grew him up, and he stopped coming over, stopped being such a jerk.

"I was a beauty," Nardone said to himself, walking through the long yellow-tiled tunnel for the J train for Newkirk Avenue. "—I saw me like I was, I'd kick my ass." He'd developed the habit of talking to himself when he was alone. Company. And he could tell if something he was thinking of saying to somebody sounded stupid.

Plates . . . second time Ellie said to find out. First thing he got home, before he called . . . that was the first thing he had to ask Connie. Then the Gaither thing. It was a break—and it wasn't. Ellie'd be going nuts; she'd figure they had the case solved or something with just a little more work, and the truth was they just had a shitload more suspects dumped on them. Now, the guy did it didn't have to be a john, didn't have to be a lover boy, didn't have to give a damn about Sally Gaither. Just wanted some bucks. —Could even be some ordinary junkie cruising the building while the back was open, walked in—jackpot. Scares her, ties her up—maybe she gives him some shit—he scares her worse, plays with the bananas, sticks her with the knife. She tells him about the money, he takes it—and leaves her to cook.

So, then, we got a rich junkie somewhere—and we wait till a buddy of his turns him, or he OD's and we never know about it at all. The money blows away. —None of it what El' would like to hear. . . .

"I'll pass on that with her," Nardone said to himself, "—too discouragin'." A young black woman walking toward him grinned and rolled her eyes at her boyfriend as they went by. —Heard him talking to himself, thought he was a nut case. . . . For one thing, he'd like to know when that transvesto plumber went into New York Hospital. Could be the guy had had enough strength to do in his old buddy—her old buddy—and grab a hundred thousand bucks for himself. Herself. Plenty of sick people can get up and walk if they want to. —There was an old movie on TV about that very thing. Jose Ferrer gets up out of a hospital bed and goes and kills somebody. Not an unheard-of thing.

Ellie could tell him how sick that lady was. "—If she's that sick, then that's a different matter. . . ." he said to himself, and walked out of the tunnel, across the upper level, and down the long flight of stairs to the southbound platform just as the J pulled in.

There were only a few people waiting for the train in that vaulted, grimy, two-story space, and two men came trotting down the long platform when the train doors opened. One of them called, "Hold it . . . !" as Tommy, stepping into the doorway of the second car from the front—noticing an old Hispanic man asleep on the bench opposite—reached behind him with his right hand to hold his side of the sliding door open, careful of the umbrella in his left. —Anybody step on that piece of crap, kick it, that would be the end of it.

A short, black-haired guy with wide shoulders reached in and held the other half of the door open as both sides jolted, tried to close. He glanced at Nardone, said "O.K." to somebody out on the platform, and Tommy felt right then a hard push, more like a very hard punch in the middle of his back. Somebody—some asshole had really hit him hard . . . and punched him again!

Nardone hit out behind him with the umbrella, turned in the doorway and saw a guy, then stepped out onto the platform and saw the motherfucker had a knife—a goddamn dagger with blood on it. A tall white son-of-a-bitch with red hair.

Guy came at him too quick for Tommy to reach for his .38, so he dropped the umbrella, put out his left hand, took the guy by the wrist and pulled him in and hit him in the face twice. He held the tall man's knife-hand up as if they were dancing together, then pulled him in again—the man a pretty strong guy, which didn't make a bit of difference—and stomped down on his foot and felt some little bones break in there—and he was slugging and he smacked the guy a good one, doing just fine except for his back.

Behind him, Nardone heard the doors shut, the train jolt, starting up, and another guy came jumping right in—maybe a cop, Nardone thought—came jumping right in and grappled and grabbed Nardone, giving him a bear hug or some shit, so Nardone couldn't get to his gun.

"I'm a fuckin' cop . . . !" Everything seemed to be moving slowly . . . underwater. Tommy'd noticed that before, on other violent occasions.

Guy still hanging on—another strong guy. Both in it. Nardone got a look at his face; it was the short, black-haired man who'd held the other door.

Big close-up fight now, lots of slugging. Somewhere in there, Tommy lost sight of the knife, didn't know if the asshole still had it or not. He hit out left and right as hard as he could, shook the short, black-haired guy loose and hit him in the mouth—tooth went flying out of that—then turned and stooped down when the tall man came in again and swung up from the platform and hit him in the balls—and that was it for the tall guy. Busted foot, busted nuts.

The tall man doubled up all the way, and even when the black-haired one came in again and was hanging on hard, Tommy managed to get room enough to kick the tall one somewhere when he was bent over—then drag the short guy along to get closer, and kick the tall man again (this time hard in the head) and send him over the edge of the platform onto the tracks.

The short guy was a strong motherfucker. He was hanging on to Tommy's right arm, to keep it away from the gun—and with his free hand, trying to stick fingers in Tommy's eyes. Tommy hit the guy hard along the side of his head, hit him again and knocked him loose, just for a breather, just to get his breath, get the .38 out—but the man came for him again right away—a stocky guy, big shoulders on him. Tommy caught his fingers when he went for the eyes this time, got two of them gripped in his left hand, bent them back and broke them. —And if his back hadn't been so bad, he would have killed the guy right there, gone after him and busted his fucking skull, because the man didn't like those broken fingers. —But give the guy credit, he made a sound when the fingers went, but stayed right in hanging on to Tommy's arm with his good hand, so he couldn't reach for the gun.

"You want some more?" Tommy said, out of breath from his back, gripped the broken-fingered hand and leaned into the short man, kneed him, butted him, nuzzled in close, took a nice bite into the guy's cheek there, and tore at it, trying to rip out a chunk. Man was yelling, then. "—Go on an' yell," Tommy tried to say, chewing. "I'm goin' to kill you!" Losing his temper. Blood all over the place . . . all over the place. Man yanked his face out of Tommy's jaws, left some meat—still got you by the arm, motherfucker! Still got your arm! You can go—the fuckin' arm *stays . . . !* Tommy hauled the black-haired man in again, and tried to break the arm across his knee. Too tired to get it done right away. Things were moving so fast and seeming so slow.

Blood coming out all over, spitting it out all over. from that guy's face and coming up from inside, too. The short man kicked and kicked and struggled free, and Tommy let him go. Time for a breather . . . That back was taking the strength out of him. He reached down for the .38, but the jacket was in his way—and the short guy was on him again, hangin' on to that arm. A stubborn guy . . .

They wrestled, the short man snorting blood and snot, and Tommy was turned to the left and saw the tall one down there between the tracks, just now getting up on his hands and knees, shaking his head. Tommy, turned again, slugging hard, hit the short guy three times with his left, felt a bone or something break in the man's face, and saw a big black guy standing a way away. Black guy nodded to him. —Called out something.

"Pretty damn good . . ."

That's what he called—and came running. The short man sounded like he was crying, out of gas—blood down his face, just hanging on—but still holding that right arm. That fucking .38 could be on the moon all the good it was doing! —And the big black guy was there and had Tommy's left arm. The black guy held the same kind of knife the tall jerk had, holding it in his right hand, looking for a place to stick it—and Tommy lifted his left leg, kicked out, and caught the black guy in the gut and backed him off—and kicked and kicked at the short man's knees, hit him good in the neck with the left and almost pulled away. The short man was sagging, stumbling.

It was the black guy Tommy wanted. —This is that Classman thing, he thought, I'm fighting cops. . . . And reached out with his left as the black man came in again and hit that fucker alongside the head so hard that Tommy felt a bone in his wrist break. The black man staggered back, tripped, and sat down on the platform, looking surprised, but the short man, drawing wailing breaths, still grappled and gripped and Tommy couldn't get him loose. They spun half around as they fought to the platform's edge, and Tommy saw the tall man on the tracks try to scramble up—and his back foot slip on the cinders into the third rail with a *BANG* and bright blue flash and sizzle as the black man came back up and drove into Tommy hard—a very, very strong guy, and Tommy spit blood in his face, try and blind him. Plenty of blood all over the place, and there goes the suit. Never get that out. As much wind left as blood, he'd be O.K.

First guy, tall guy, put that knife into him, but good. —That was for sure.

Tommy reached down to grab the black guy's nuts—tear 'em right off the motherfucker—but that hand wouldn't work because of the wrist. That hand wouldn't close. Tommy butted the black man in the face to get some room, then raised his left leg, kicked, and again knocked the man back, but not so much this time. Blood on that guy's knife, too. These motherfuckers all had knives. Would like to see a good cop, right now, coming running down the platform. Not Ellie, though . . . thank you Holy Mother. . . . Never around when you need 'em.

"I can't get the black one," Nardone said out loud, noticing he was gargling with all the blood. He was talking to the short man as they fought, and heard a horn blaring as the next train came thundering in. —Its brakes began to scream and scream. He wrestled and kneed and butted at the short man, and beat at his head—the wrist broken all the way now, the hand flapping and not much use—and Tommy felt the black guy there doing something at his other side, and elbowed him in the face, snapped his head back hard. "Lucky you brought your buddies, pal," he tried to say, but it didn't sound like him at all, and he and the short man—the short man sobbing, drooping, barely hanging on—waltzed and turned and toppled over in each other's arms down into the noise of a world beneath the world, where great wheels came measuring over the tall man, to measure them.

Dear Sonny,

Mothers are good for something. I found a copy of *Green Horses.* I just finished reading it, and I'll send it up to you so you won't have to wait until I come up. I thought it was a beautiful book, but sort of sad. A child shouldn't have to wait for death to reunite her parents, even in a jungle paradise. You know me. I'm a life nut. Life is everything, and death is nothing, and that's the truth. And I know that because like everything alive, I've been dead, zero, nothing, up to just thirty-seven years ago, when I was conceived. Before that, back to the beginning of the universe, I was dead as dead can be, and so were you, and so was everybody else. And it wasn't interesting at all.

But there's one thing about death that is interesting, and that is it's in the back of most people's minds all the time. Men, women, and kids, too. They know they're going to die. It's there all the time in a little place in their heads, and a lot of what they do—work, sex, you name it (including, I suppose, civilization)—is just something to take their minds off it. That's what I think, anyway.

I'm glad you called, and we were able to talk about my first letter. I know you think I treated it all too lightly—your father and so forth—but I treat most things lightly, and I didn't want to make the whole thing a tragedy for you when actually it was more like a farce. Hell—it *was* a farce. And I didn't mean to underrate your father. He wasn't an ordinary man. He was much braver than ordinary. Most people are afraid to admit to half the things they want, or want to do. He wasn't. And I suppose if you really want to visit him in Chicago, and he hasn't moved and is still alive, you won't be too disappointed. I wouldn't be in a big rush about it, though.

I'm glad you don't miss your brother, Tony, but you better keep in mind that the Tony I wrote you about was the easiest kind of Tony for me to think of without regrets. The real Tony might be a boy I'd love. Ah, the geometry of the heart!

I'm embarrassed that you noticed your oh-so-truthful mother skipped a part of the truth in discussing her profession. Two questions. One: Does selling sex lower its value to me, personally? Answer: It doesn't affect it either way. Two: Doesn't it make me feel crummy to go to bed with ugly, nasty, weird, disgusting people? Answer: It makes me feel crummy to go to bed with nasty and disgusting people, but not with weird or ugly people. And, as far as the nasties and disgustings go, unlike a wage slave—a teacher, or a waitress or a nurse, for example—I never deal with such people twice.

Now, what's this? Is your mother suggesting it would be a great career for you? Your mother is not. Why not, if there's nothing wrong with screwing for a living? Well, the "Why not?" is simple. You don't have enough of a sense of humor.

"Yes I do, yes I do, yes I do!"

No, you don't, no, you don't, no, you don't.

Now, on to a really touchy subject. A *really* touchy subject. There are a lot of secrets between parents and kids that should stay secret. It isn't true that parents need to know everything about their children, and it's even truer that kids don't need to know everything about their parents. In the first place, everything is never everything. In the second place, it's none of their damn business. However. However. It does seem to me that a kid's schoolwork *is* their parents' business. And it also seems to me that the parents' work is their *kid's* business, because that's how the kid is getting fed. I think kids should grow up understanding very clearly what their parents have to do to keep them safe and fed and educated.

However, my profession is an odd one, is an illegal one, is loaded with all sorts of fears. So, I'll leave it to you. You decide how much you want to know about my business.

If I sold cars or insurance, I'd be a little ashamed for you to see some of the stuff I'd be pulling on people in the course of a day's work. As it is, however, although I'm nothing special in other departments, I am a good, honest whore, and wouldn't be ashamed for you to see me practice my trade, though it might embarrass me.

Now, you're saying, "Gross, gross, *GROSS!*"—but I think that what you're *feeling* is scared, scared, SCARED! Isn't that interesting? Why is everybody so frightened about such a usual thing? Why do they find it so terrifying, so disgusting, so secret, when they don't mind eating pizza in front of everybody— wiggling their tongues while they stuff the toothed end of their tube like mad? (Isn't that great? I stole that "toothed end of their tube" part from a woman poet named Misrahi. If you want, I'll send you the book.) But I mean it. It's a serious question.

As far as my profession goes, it's just business-and-sex, and the only thing weird about it is that both parties are getting exactly what they want, and aren't wearing suits. Anyway, you decide. And if you ever do want to see this mysterious, gross, terrifying, disgusting, criminal stuff that keeps you supplied with yucky school uniforms, Delius tapes, and strawberry floats, just tell me. I have a client named David, who's sweet, intelligent, great-looking, four years younger than yours truly—in fact you'd probably fall in love with him—who'd think it was very funny to have a disapproving schoolgirl solemnly observe her aging mother earn an honest dollar.

Anyway, think about it. If it's all just too much, and the most nauseating thing a mother ever proposed to her innocent daughter—then forget it. Though the truth is, sweetheart, let's face it, you've been having your period now for a lot longer than a year, which means that nature considers you a grown-up. But it is a scary notion—scares me, too— and if you feel it's too scary, then forget it. Whatever you feel is probably right for you, although I do believe all kids would be better off if they knew that sex was angel food cake—not dog shit.

"Well," you're saying, now that you're over the shock, "Well, I notice she didn't want me to watch her and George!" And you're right. That's love. It's just between him and me.

I told you when I started these long, *long* letters that I would try and tell you some truths I've noticed maybe more clearly than some people might who are in different professions. Now, these are my truths, and some of them may not turn out to be true for you. But I've worked hard to learn them, so don't be too quick to say your freaky mother doesn't know what she's talking about.

But before I get to people, let me tell you a truth about money. Money and love, love and money. Add health, and you have the three great worries. Money. You will probably have a great advantage over me. You will probably earn legal money. When you do—put as much as you can aside every *month* into some government-insured investment. Start when you're *young*. When you're in college. *Do it.* That money will compound into a fortune, and you will someday thank your old mother for letting you in on a fact that most people are too dumb to figure out: Time, plus interest, equals big bucks.

Money and people. Old folks use money in place of sex, dealing with other people. If they haven't got money—unless they're very lovable—they're in trouble. Men use money to push other people around. Women use money to try to stay safe. Here's my advice on money: Earn as much as you can without devoting your life to it. Start saving early. Spend the rest and have a ball.

O.K. Human beings. Let me start with women. Sigmund Freud wanted to know what women really want. Well, here's what I've noticed most women want, but not many get. One: A man to love them who's a little smarter and stronger than they are, but not smart enough or strong enough not to love them. Two: Something important to do. Three: To take care of people they love. Four: The admiration and envy of other women. Five: Children. Six: Money. Seven: A maid. Eight: To stay young forever. Nine: To be a perfect size eight. Ten: Not to get cancer. Eleven: To suffer, but not too much.

I better add fast that I know some women who don't want any of the above, except not to get cancer. But these are the exceptions that prove the rule. And I better add just as fast that young girls have slightly different "wants" than the above, and you know more about that than I do. Still, when you deal with women, you might keep this little list in mind. The reason we're such great complainers is that these are hard needs to satisfy, and it is definitely not a good idea to stand between a woman and the satisfying of even one of them.

What else about women? Well, they're pretty and soft. They smell good almost all the time. They're fun to have sex with, if you keep in mind it isn't the big obsession for most of them that it is for a man. And they were designed to be baby buckets, like it or not, do it or not, be it or not.

Anything else your wise mother has noticed about women? Yes. They're wonderful company, for a while.

Now—men. A good friend of mine says that men can be satisfied by a blow job, kids by a peanut-butter sandwich. And, in a way, she's right. Men, like kids, enjoy specific pleasures very, very much. Physical pleasures. Atmosphere doesn't mean much to them, although admiration does. O.K.—so, what do men really want?

One: A woman who's not quite as smart and not quite as strong but who's smart enough and strong enough to love them anyway. Two: To be brave. Three: To have something important to do that everybody knows is important to do. Four: The admiration of women, the envy of other men. Five: To be able to screw every good-looking woman they see. Six: Money. Seven: To take care of people they love, or people they don't love who are grateful. Eight: To be able to screw every good-looking woman they hear about. Nine: Not to get a heart attack. Ten: To want something else, something they can never have.

Well, you suspected as much, and grown-ups are always going after these shitty things, or those silly things, right? Wrong. Most grown-ups don't go after what they want, at all. They do what their parents and friends think they should do; they do what *they* think they should do; they do what most other people they know are doing, and they hope that somehow something special will come to them. It's my experience that waiting and dreaming like that tends to make most people sad. They make their own disappointments that way.

Don't misunderstand me, sweetheart, when I talk about things like women wanting to be a size eight—not that they don't. And speaking of which, I would like to see you lose a couple of pounds. Nothing gigantic, just a couple of pounds. Look out for food; it's the most addicting drug of all. Of course I don't mean women yearn only for the dress size. I mean they yearn to be all right. To look nice. Not to be fat, or ugly, or too thin, or anything that people are going to laugh at or pity.

And the same is true of all those other silly and not so silly things people want. Behind each want are a lot of other wants, a lot of other fears that pop out now and then in weird ways. One person wants number Three most of all, and another one decides he'd die for number Six. People's wants are like combinations to a lock, but the combinations keep changing.

Which brings me to love. Being in love, being loved, makes people feel good about themselves, as you well know (or should, since your mother loves you like crazy), and since that's what most people lack, they need love a lot. Let me tell you a whore's secret: People come to me the first time, to come. The second time, they want some love.

I try my best to give them their money's worth both ways, but with affection for the second part, not real love.

I knew a man . . . Wait a minute, let me tell you a story. I knew a man who was very special to me. His name was Larry; he was in the shipping business, and he claimed he used to play semipro baseball, which could be true. He was a sweet, sweet man, not very smart, though I suppose he was good at business. He would tell these awful jokes, not funny at all, and start breaking up in the middle of telling them and not be able to finish, he was laughing so hard. Well, here was a darling man, really handsome and physically just perfect—which you will discover is a mighty rare thing—and one of those really unusual men who are naturals in bed. He wasn't ashamed to do anything, he never worried about anything—he just loved it. He lived in bed with a woman as if she were a brand-new duplex apartment and he was crazy about it and was checking upstairs and downstairs and into every cabinet. Most men are a little worried about women's bodies, their vulvas, vaginas, their assholes, and so forth. They're a little worried about some surprise here or there. Not this Larry.

Well, I fell in love with him. In love with a john.

And the moment I did that—fearless Larry fled. He hadn't been afraid of my body, but he was scared to death of Sally Gaither. Well, maybe I'm lying to myself. Maybe he just didn't like Sally Gaither. Whenever a man runs like hell, we like to think he just wasn't mature enough to appreciate us.

So, I got a lesson that hurt. As far as men are concerned, a woman is a two-part person. The body, and the rest. For example, a woman meets a man, and thinks, "Does he like me? He has nice eyes. What a wonderful voice. . . . He looks in really great shape . . . so strong! He would come home to me flying in from Europe to our place in Connecticut, and I'd be there with the kids, and that wonderful smile as he came in the door. . . ."

Right?

A man meets a woman, looks at her face, her legs, her butt, then starts trying to imagine her pussy, in detail. What she's like with her panties down. What she's like with her panties off. What sounds she makes during sex. Then, after that, while they talk, he decides if he likes her. If she's nice. If she's good company . . . intelligent.

It's the two-part problem. If a woman is lucky, she has a man who loves both parts of her. If she's unlucky, he doesn't. Men are always being blamed for this, but that's like blaming the grass for growing. And of course the reason men divide women into fuck and friend, is that they are divided just that way themselves; their cocks are semi-independent —a fact of life that women have never accepted, to their sorrow and my profit.

"Well," you're saying, "if a prostitute doesn't know what men are really interested in, she's a pretty dumb prostitute."

I was a dumb prostitute, and a young one, too, and of course I knew what men were interested in. I just didn't realize how separate it was for them.

So, I'd suggest when you deal with boys and men, especially if you like them a lot, that you remember the two-part person problem. You can remember it as tee-pee pee-pee. You might also remember the significance of this synthesis, as they say at NYU (at least they say it in the Continuing Ed. courses). If a boy or a man isn't your friend, as well as your lover, he'll never last.

Anyway, that wised yours truly up, and I started to realize I'd been way out of line with Larry. That the Life wasn't just a game, get-fucked-and-paid, or at least it shouldn't be. It was a profession, and one that's done a lot less harm than most of them. So, I got professional, and stopped looking for my personal satisfaction with clients who were paying for theirs. I don't mean to say that I don't enjoy sex with them. I do and I always have; it's the extra that makes the work worthwhile, like a travel agent's being able to travel cheap. I mean I stopped leaning on them for love, stopped romancing them, stopped trying to take advantage of them. For a prostitute to get a client to love her is like a psychiatrist getting a patient to screw. It's unfair. The odd thing is, when I stopped trying, I began getting a lot of them falling in love with me. Some people like hopeless love a lot better than the other kind. And also, people are full of surprises. It's safer to bet on horses.

"Well," you're saying, "what about George?"

George refused to be a client. He asked for his money back. Once I handed that honey back his cash, he was fair game.

Now, one more quick story. The man with the tiny dick.

A friend of mine named Gloria, who used to be in the Life and has since retired to married happiness and three kids with a vice cop—which is quite a story in itself, since he blackmailed her to have sex with him, and then fell in love with her—anyway, Gloria had a friend on Long Island who was crazy in love with a man named Carl who owned a Buick dealership out there. This Carl was something special, apparently. But there was a problem.

"What was the problem, Mother?"

Thank you, dear. The problem was the man had a tiny penis, and was so ashamed of it that Gloria's friend had to practically force him into bed with her. And that wasn't much use, either. We walk around and pass people on the street, and some of them are in agony, have been living in agony all their lives. This poor man had lived like that. Short of serious illness, I don't suppose there's much worse suffering than a boy's with that deformity. Their cocks are a big deal for men. If you put all our worries about our hair and our weight, and how big our breasts should be all together, they still don't balance a man's concern for his penis.

Anyway, Gloria's friend, who was a very nice woman, and who was dying for love of this man, made as light of the matter as she could—"It was not important . . . women don't care about that sort of thing" . . . and so on and so on. And of course since the man was no fool, he didn't believe a word of it. He stopped seeing her. Of *course* he stopped seeing her; she just reminded him of another humiliation. Men are great brooders. That's what they do instead of complaining.

I told Joey—that was the jerk policeman redeemed by love—to send Carl to town, Joey and Gloria and Gloria's friend all being in on it together, since Carl was a friend of theirs. Of course the man didn't want to come and see me—Joey presenting it as a sneaky thing the girls didn't know about and so on, but Joey told the man I was very small and big ones hurt me and so forth, so the poor devil called me, had a few drinks, and came over one summer evening.

Well, he was a very nice man. He was pretty tall, was starting to lose his hair, wore nice clothes, and wasn't handsome at all. But to look at with his clothes on, nothing wrong with him.

I guess it took me almost an hour, talking, fixing very light drinks for him, talking some more, to get him into the bedroom. Well, sweetheart, yours truly has cooed over and coddled many an inadequate penis—and the truth is most of them will get the job done if the man enjoys doing. But not this one. Your mother stripped and strolled around in her birthday suit, and told of her adventures the week before and so forth, since men enjoy listening as well as looking, and then finally got down to business. No good. The man was just too frightened. And he had reason to be. His penis was bigger than a finger, but not by much.

I suppose Carl had been told by every woman he'd tried to go to bed with, that it didn't matter. And hadn't believed any of them, of course. I could have continued that lie, but it was killing poor Carl, so I didn't.

"Holy shit!" said yours truly. "That one's nice for tickling, Carl, but it's too damn small for heavy duty." Well, the poor guy sat on the side of the bed staring at me like I'd shot him. Couldn't believe I'd said that to him. The truth is your know-it-all mother was also scared this was only going to hurt him worse and not accomplish anything. "Carl, you have a handicap," I said, "just like being deaf, or missing a hand or a leg. Why in hell haven't you done something about it? You must have left a bunch of pissed-off ladies in your life."

No response. Carl can't believe someone is *saying* it to him.

"You better get on the ball," says the Big Mouth, "and learn to dance around that dingus, or you're not going to make any lady happy. Ever."

"What?" Carl says. "What in hell . . . can I *dooo?*" The ice is broken, and I, as a lewd, down whore, spend the next half hour with the Buick dealer crying in my arms, begging for this and that, help me, help me, help me . . . blowing his nose in my handkerchief, wiping his eyes. Sob, sob, sob. Yours truly sobbing along (anybody cries, I cry too) and at the same time breathing a big sigh of relief that more good had been done than harm.

Next two and a half hours: anatomy, funny stories, more anatomy, more funny stories, instruction in the arts of love talk, lovemaking, caressing, kissing, more love talk, more lovemaking, the use of the hand, fingers, tongue, and last and not least, vibrator one, two, and three.

It all cost Carl the price of a microwave oven with limited features. And, if I may be permitted to boast, made a new man out of him. I will hasten to add, after blowing my own horn this way, that that was an unusual session. With most of my clients, it's fairly routine. . . .

"Hi," he says. "How're you doin'? How's it goin'? My partner is the asshole of the world and is ruining the business. Ruining it! How much this time? . . . That's a lot of money. Let's do this. Let's do that. Oh, that's fabulous. Oh, that's great. You're fantastic. . . . Not bad myself? Thanks; I try to stay in shape. My wife's crazy about me. And I love her, too. She's a wonderful, wonderful woman and we still have great sex. What do you hear about the market? You must have guys in the market up here. . . . Running fairly stable, but be careful? Guy must know his stuff. Listen, before I go; this friend of mine is having a relationship with a girl at his office. It's a very casual thing, but it could be getting serious, and you know, this guy, this friend of mine is a lot older. Keeps himself in shape; he's really in great shape, but he is older. You got a lot of experience; what do you think? This could be a serious thing. What do you think? . . . You think my friend is about to make a fuckin' fool of himself. I think you're right. You know, you're quite a woman. You ask me, you're too good a woman to be in this business. Listen, you want to go and have a drink? Just go somewhere and have a drink and talk? No. You don't. You find me dangerously attractive. You're scared I'll ruin you for other guys. Very funny. I'm fallin' in love here and you're makin' me laugh. Listen, take care of yourself; you're a sweet girl. Now I'll get the hell out of here and leave you in peace. . . ."

A typical hour for a typical working mother.

Oh, and a footnote on the Carl thing. Carl did get together with Gloria's friend, they got married, everything fine, and a couple of years later he left her for a lady customer that bought a spruce-green Regal with power sun roof and adjustable lumbar support in both front seats. (I made the part about the car up.)

Poor women . . . Poor men. And what does your mother find so fascinating about these clumsy, cocked creatures? Sweetheart, there's a world in every one of them. Get them in bed, get them close to you, and you can tear the "man" right off them like an animal's hide, the lawyer, doctor, businessman, the brother, father, husband, or son; you can tear all that away, fuck, lick, and suck it away, listen it away, talk it away, nag, cry, scream it away . . . and then deal with the tender truthful animal that comes crawling out, stark naked. It's a game no woman ever gets tired of.

Every good two-hour trick is like being introduced, going together, getting pregnant, having the child, raising it, kissing it goodbye, then getting a friendly divorce . . . but moving faster. In fact—and get ready to be grossed out entirely!—I've suspected for some time that mothers and fathers should screw their children farewell when the kids are old enough to leave home. Maybe the lack of that kind of loving good-bye to their children's childhood is what keeps both parents and their sons and daughters permanently unsatisfied, unseparated, dealing with each other like disappointed lovers.

What do you think? Yes? No? Scare you?

Anyway, I don't have a son to screw, and your father lives in Chicago.

Of course, just for example, a really adventurous young woman might go out to Chicago in a few years, find that old dreamer, and seduce him as, say, a friendly young waitress . . . or a new girl hired into the office . . . or a local college girl getting a business interview for the school paper. A girl like that might get to bed with Fred Pascoe, who I'd guess could still get it up for a new young piece, and learn more about her father in half an hour than most women ever know. Maybe enough to make up a little for not having a daddy as she was growing.

"Mother! Will you please cut that shit OUT?"

Well, darling, if you don't want to do it, then don't. People talk a lot about knowing other people, but usually they don't want to know that much, after all. What they really mean is, they'd like to find out something that will comfort and please them. Of course, you don't have to do any such thing; it just occurred to me it might be an exciting exploration, a way to come to terms with what's been missing for you. Something to make you richer, more interesting to yourself. Otherwise, you know, you're not talking about a father at all, are you? You're dreaming about a daddy, and there's a lot less to a daddy, and less to learn from him, and less to learn about yourself. It's true that most women are content to have only daddies. Then they wonder why they don't understand men.

And of course, concerning the above, exactly the same is true of men and their mothers.

How well do you want to know people? How well do you want to know yourself? Sex is one of the great can openers, if you're sure you want to know what's in the can. Most people don't want to know, and are scared to death of the opener.

And don't think I don't know how nutty some of my

ideas sound. Sometimes I think I'm like someone who can see, where everybody else is blind. And sometimes I just think I'm a weirded-out hooker, and I must be the blind one. I suppose everybody feels like that about something, think they know something that nobody else has noticed.

O.K. *Men.* How do you handle these fragile beasts, practically? How do you get them? How do you keep them? When do you get rid of them? And I'm aware I have much less long-term experience with a single sample than most women have. Well, a good friend of mine, a man, always says riding is the best way for girls to learn about dealing with men. It's practice controlling a big, strong, dumb, smelly, hairy animal between your legs. So, concentrate on those riding lessons with Ms. Strickland; maybe they'll be useful. Seriously? O.K. Here's what I think, seriously.

To get them. To get a man . . . And it's amazing how many women still want one around. Women you wouldn't think need anything or anybody still want one, even if he can't hit the toilet when he pees. All that trouble; they still want one. It's instinct, and it gets us by the belly button and won't let go.

O.K. How to get one. *Want* one. Look into their eyes just a little longer, then look away and get out of the room. Let them think about it. Let them catch you looking at them, then a quick shy smile and turn away. Never cling, not even with a look. Walk slowly, talk slowly, move slowly when you're near a man or a boy you want. Don't jump around, don't be perky, don't be a pal. Let them look at you, even if you're dressed in a snowsuit. Let them look. Say to yourself, "Here it is, here's what you want to see. Here's what you can see all naked, soft and smooth. Here's what you can kiss. You can lick it. You can put your fingers there. If you're gentle . . . if you're gentle, you can slide a finger in, and find out where I hide. Then, if you want, you can hurt me a little . . . and please me a lot."

In other words—get hot. A man who can't smell wet panties is one you can do without.

Handling them. The best way to handle them is to enjoy them. Love them all out. Open yourself up like a book. Open those legs till your hips ache, and show them everything you've got. Open up your mouth, open up your memories, open up everything. Let them settle down and live inside you. Hold them up like a plant stake, comfort, praise, cook, and clean—scratch those little specks of shit off the toilet bowl with your fingernail.

And if they don't do the same for you at first, if they're slow learners, then teach them and give them more time. . . . But if they won't ever do the same for you, if they won't ever learn, then close your legs, close your mouth, store your memories, stop cooking, stop cleaning, get up from the bathroom floor, and kick that asshole out the door.

Clean shit forever. Eat shit, never.

Love,
Mother

P.S. You're the pleasure and triumph of my life, sweetheart.

Ellie put the letter back in its envelope, and lay thinking about it for a moment. . . . It seemed to her that Sally had loaded a lot of her own problems onto her daughter. A young girl like Sonia didn't need to have that sex stuff thrown at her that way. —And, there was something else . . . Ellie took the letter out of its envelope again, leafed through it, and found the page. Then she got up to get her purse, and looked up Susan Margolies' number in her notebook—came back, sat on the edge of the bed, and called her.

"Hello?"

"This is Ellie Klein. NYPD? I spoke with you last week."

Silence.

"My partner and I are coming over to see you tomorrow morning. I don't know what time. —I think it would be a good idea if you were there all morning . . . didn't make us come looking for you. Understand?"

"What did you say your name was?"

"Klein. You know my name."

Silence.

"You be there, O.K.? You be there waiting from seven o'clock on," Ellie said, and hung up. Then she tried calling Tommy in Brooklyn, but the line was busy.

Delgado got several calls on his limo phone, coming

into town fast—no siren on, but slap light revolving to ease him swiftly down boulevards washed medium yellow by tall stooping streetlights. The fourth call was Cherusco's.

"Well . . . ?"

The Chief sighed. "John," he said, "—I shouldn't have to tell you these things . . . John, when people with the power to embarrass and severely damage the Department commence a course of action that lowers their balls deeper and deeper into our pocket, it seems reasonable to encourage, rather than discourage. —Besides, we're one up."

"For the time being," Cherusco said. "And I've got some advice for you, Chief. —It might be a good idea to tell your boy Anderson we've had a cover tap on that corner phone near Flowers' for three months. We got it for the Pisano thing, and it's still in place."

"I'll certainly pass that on, John," the Chief of the Department said, pushed a button, and took his fifth call. Father Gruenwald, and arrangements.

The Counter Intelligence people had left no comforts in the Village apartment when they'd gone, and Tucker had been lucky to find a half-melted bar of soap with two curly brown hairs sticking to it for his shower. The shower did him good, though—the soap didn't offend; he was in that rare tender mood when he felt grateful for other people's insignia. He took his shower, dried with a small dirty towel, and looked at his face in the mirror over the sink. The right side was very swollen, right eye almost closed, black skin mottled blacker. There was still a buzzing in that ear. He walked into the bedroom, lifted his suitcase onto the bed—his belly and side were sore, too, from the kicks—and took fresh chinos, socks, Fruit of the Looms, and a white shirt from his suitcase, and put them on. Put on his running shoes, too. —Felt better on his feet.

At the closet—he'd stacked Budreau's and Mason's suitcases in there, out of the way—he took his Italian pistol in its shoulder harness down from a hook and strapped it on, then went back to his suitcase for a tan windbreaker.

He walked to the apartment door and out, doublelocked the door behind him, went down the hall and one flight of stairs, and out the building's front door and stoop into Thompson Street. A line from *Camino Real* occurred to him. "—The streets are brilliant, tonight." Thompson Street, shadowy, quiet on a cool autumn night, opened into Bleecker, blazing in yellow and red, decorated in series with cross-street arches of light bulbs reflecting in pavement still wet from rain and thick with traffic, foot and vehicular—ambulating oddities (rarer now than they had been), tired tourists doing their last round before going uptown to their hotels, and ethnic kids in from the boroughs for adventure, all drifting toward or away from Mulberry Street and the last night of San Gennaro, the festival late this year, delayed by the death and funeral of the parish priest.

Tucker walked a block east on Bleecker, crossed the street, walked down a flight of steps into a drugstore, and bought a pair of large-lensed dark glasses for twelve dollars and seventy-three cents. He climbed up again to a shadier, green-tinted street, all lights dimmed, the night enhanced, even sounds seeming subdued.

Tucker walked back down Bleecker to MacDougal, then up a block to a coffee house called the Olive Tree, went in, and up some steps into a large room, busy, dimly-lit and Levantine, and saw the Colonel sitting in a booth against the opposite wall.

A girl came to seat him, but Tucker said, "My buddy's over there," nodded to the Colonel, and sidled through the crowded tables to him. The Colonel had taken off his British Warm; it was folded on the seat beside him. Tucker slid into the booth and sat opposite.

"That's a bad face, Tuck," the Colonel said. His breath was sweet with alcohol.

"Feels just the way it looks."

"Well," the Colonel said, "—the thing's all over TV."

"I'll bet," Tucker said. A Chaplin film, a silent, was being projected on a large screen at the back of the room. Charlie was having trouble with a big man with thick black eyebrows.

"I've heard of jinxed operations," the Colonel said. "—I suppose this one takes the cake."

" 'Jinxed' doesn't really describe it, does it, Colonel? —A fucking disaster, would be somewhat more accurate."

The Colonel looked away, out across the room to the bar. "I already ordered. . . ."

"—First we had that nut with the groceries; now, tonight, we had this animal. Let me tell you, that cop chewed Mason up and spit him out real quick. —And Mason had already stuck him in the back twice. Seven inches of steel, double-edged."

"Bizarre," the Colonel said, still gazing over at the bar. The Colonel was looking old; his face seemed to Tucker to have been cut out of light green paper by someone very skillful. An artist.

"Sir, this operation has been bizarre for some time. . . ." Tucker took off his dark glasses for a moment to wipe his right eye with a napkin; it was tearing. With his glasses off, the Colonel's face turned to white paper. "—We are also losing the body count on this one."

"Tell me about it," the Colonel said, green again, and smiled as a thin gray-eyed girl with long light-brown hair came to the booth carrying a tray. "—Just in time to save my life," the Colonel said, smiling up at her, and the girl smiled back and served the Colonel a drink, and Tucker the other.

"Your dinners will be coming in a minute," she said, lifted the tray, and left.

"Bourbon," the Colonel said. "Doubles. —I think we need them."

Tucker took a long drink. "—Kicked Mason's ass down on those tracks—where that moron proceeded to fry himself—and commenced to tear Budreau *up*. We are talking here, about one tough motherfucker. We should have just shot him in the back of the head."

"No, no, *no!*" the Colonel murmured on a high note, trying to keep his voice down. "—You can't pee in these people's faces, Sergeant. I told you! There has to be at least the *possibility* it was muggers, some thugs picking on the wrong man. You can kill a cop in a robbery or a brawl, but you can't assassinate one without *The New York Times* sticking its nose in!"

"We should have assassinated this mother; that's for shit sure," Tucker said, and had more of his drink. "—You know how many times in my life, since I was grown, I have been knocked on my ass?" He held up two fingers. "Tonight was the second. And if that man had been able to get hold of me, I'd be right down there on those tracks with them. —Mason had stuck him twice, and I stuck him twice."

"What about Budreau?"

"Budreau did O.K. He was fighting for his life, is what he was doing. —And he didn't make it."

"Those boys," the Colonel said, mournful. "Those boys . . ." and took a drink. "Well," he said, "—I called Washington. They are very pleased, feel a useful lesson has been administered. Not so happy about the casualties. Upset about that; said they were excessive. Gave me some goddamn . . . nonsense. . . ."

The girl came back to their booth with their dinners on her tray, and served them out.

"I ordered shish kebab," the Colonel said to Tucker, "—supposed to be very good here."

It was good, but Tucker had trouble chewing on the right side of his mouth. He tried chewing on the left side, and that was better.

After a few bites, Tucker said, "What next . . . ?"

"They didn't say we could leave," the Colonel said, finished his drink, and looked around the room for their waitress. "—But I don't think there'll *be* anything next. Washington thinks we've made our point . . . they doubt there'll be any more police activity on the Gaither thing, or in our direction either." Their waitress started to walk past the booth, heading back toward the kitchen, but the Colonel held up his empty glass.

"*Miss* . . . I'll have a refill on this, I think."

When she'd gone, the Colonel, flushed, livelier, said, "I think the boys in blue understand us, now. . . ."

" 'Another such victory . . .' " Tucker said, took a bite of shish kebab, and chewed it carefully.

"Pyrrhus . . . yes," the Colonel said, looking toward the bar.

Ellie made herself a small ice-cream soda with ginger ale and Häagen-Dazs, vanilla, finished it in the kitchen—ignoring Mayo's begging—then went to the hall phone and tried Nardone again. Still busy. She thought of calling Clara, and decided to do it, rather than wait for Clara to call her. It was getting late.

She had to go and get her purse for the number, then called the Palmer House and asked for Clara's room. Clara picked up on the second ring.

"Yes?" Very businesslike.

"Very businesslike, Clar."

"Oh, you bitch . . . I'm glad you called."

"What's happening? Is Henry coming through for you?"

"Darling, I don't think Henry *can* come through for me. These Midwest guys scare him to death. Very, very earnest. Very, very ex-FBI. I think they still carry cuffs on the back of their belts, just in case."

"You really think they won't appoint you?"

"Oh, not to worry. I'll get something. Tomorrow's probably going to be the last day of the conference, coming down to the wire. —I'm playing it very ladylike, very quietly competent, very eager to learn from men with such *experience.* They ask me out for dinner; I go to dinner, I shake my butt a little, I laugh at their jokes a lot, and when asked to dance, I gracefully take the hard-on on my hip. —I think I'll get something."

"It sounds like a pain in the ass to me, Clar."

"That, I won't let them do. —And if they do give me assistant fed pros, they have a big surprise coming, because little Clara is going to bust their chops. I'll kick ass from Cicero to Chevy Chase."

"Well . . . I think you'll get it."

"And if I do—and I have to move out here in January . . . ? I'll be out here for a year, anyway, on this Teamster thing—which will come to nothing, by the way, courtesy of the present administration—I'll be out here for a year, anyway. . . ."

"I know . . ."

"Well, little Clara has learned her lesson. —Begging don't help. So, little Clara ain't a goin' to beg."

"I do love you, Clar—"

"But not 'that way'? Not forever and a day?"

"I don't think so."

"I didn't think so, either. . . . Well, what's new with the Gaither thing? How the hell's that big case going . . . ?

And how's that little rat of a cat?—I almost said 'our little rat of a cat,' but I suppose that's no longer accurate."

"I think the case has started to give—"

"No shit?—That's great!"

"First place, she was robbed. We think that was the motive."

"How much?"

"Over a hundred thousand, cash."

"Then I think you're right. —What does the Male Principal think?"

"I don't know yet. —But I think Tommy'll agree."

"Well, go to it, tear 'em up. —And Mayo's been missing me?"

Ellie jumped a little when her door buzzer sounded. —The night man usually called on the intercom if anybody asked for her.

"Clar, somebody's at the door—"

"O.K, O.K—signing off. I should be back in town in a couple of days. I'll call you."

"O.K. Bye-bye . . ."

The buzzer sounded again as Ellie hung up, and she tied her robe tighter and went to look through the peep. At first, she saw only the shoulder of a raincoat, then she saw Anderson's face and somebody standing behind him—and unlocked the door.

Anderson was standing there in a damp tan gabardine raincoat. Leahy behind him in his epauleted blue. A woman detective Ellie knew named Terri Reise was with them. And Samuelson coming hulking down the hall.

"What is it?" Ellie said . . . and felt rising from her bare feet a slow wave of cold. Anderson made an odd face, then started to say something.

"Don't tell me," Ellie said. "—Don't tell me. It's bad." She backed into the apartment, and Anderson led them in after her with Terri Reise saying, "Honey . . . honey, please. Come on, now . . ."

"Is it Tommy?" Ellie said to the woman detective. "It's not Tommy. —Is he dead?"

"Oh, honey," Terri Reise said, and put her arm around Ellie's shoulders to stop her from backing up any more. "—I'm afraid so."

"Well . . . why didn't you just say so?" Ellie said,

hearing her words oddly low-pitched and long-drawn-out. Everything moved in the slowest motion. "Come in the living room and sit down," she said to them in the new voice, and tried to shrug Terri Reise's arm off her shoulders. —This is the worst dream I ever had, she thought, and must have said it out loud, because Anderson made his face again.

"He was killed in a fight in the subway," Anderson said.

"Tommy wasn't killed in a fight," Ellie said. "—Do you know anybody that could kill Tommy in a fight?" She had goose bumps all over, it was such a ridiculous idea.

"Come here and sit down, dear," Terri Reise said.

"Why don't you just leave me alone," Ellie said. "—If you want to take care of somebody, why don't you go and take care of somebody else?"

"Hey . . . come on, now," Leahy said. "Come on, now, sweetheart." Fat face sagging. Ellie felt sorry for him.

Samuelson was standing over by the bookcase. He had taken a paperback book out, and was looking at it. "—Two, three guys jumped him with knives on the J platform," he said. "—Little after nine. A lady other end of the platform saw 'em fightin'. Tommy took two with him, down under a train." Samuelson closed the book and put it back.

"Let's go. I want to go down there!" Ellie said. "—I'll get dressed." She started out of the living room, but Terri Reise kept hold of her arm and said "No, no, honey . . ."

"No, you don't," Leahy said. "You don't want to go down there. —There's nothin' to see. CSIU's just finishin' up."

"Well . . ." Ellie said, and sat down on the couch. "Well . . . who would have done that to Tommy?" She looked up at them as if they'd brought an answer for her.

"We don't know," Anderson said. "—But two of them are out of the picture now, anyway. Homicide and Major Crimes are all over town—no time off. We'll get the third man, too." He stood almost at ease in his handsome raincoat, looked only a little tired.

"I have to go see Connie," Ellie said. "—I'll get dressed."

"You don't have to, not right now," Terri Reise said, and sat down beside her. "Father Gruenwald's over there, and people from the Commissioner and everything. —You just take it easy."

"Was it an accident?" Ellie said. "—Some bums came by and that was that?"

"Another goddamn Classman thing," Leahy said. "—An' both from my Squad, an' both in less than two fuckin' weeks." He took a handkerchief out of his right-hand trench-coat pocket, and blew his nose.

"Guys fell with Tommy were white guys. Big. Good clothes," Samuelson said. "—Other guy was a black guy."

"A black guy . . ." Ellie said. "—Then Tommy was right all the time."

"—Right about what, El'?" Anderson said. He'd been looking around at her living room, the pictures on the walls. Homer and Hargrave prints. Copies of a Pissaro, a Vlaminck, an early Kandinsky (one of his fairytale pictures). Ellie was glad there was nothing there of hers. "—I'd like to know what you mean by that." Anderson stopped looking at the pictures, and looked at her.

"Never mind," Ellie said. "You'll see. —Some fucking people think they're getting away with something, and they're not going to. They're going to be sorry. . . ." She got up from the couch. "I really thank you for coming over. I want to thank all of you for coming over." She started out of the living room. "—I have to go to the bathroom," she said.

Ellie'd been in the bathroom for a little while, sitting on the toilet in her bathrobe, when Terri Reise knocked softly, spoke through the door, and asked if she was O.K.

"I'm O.K., Terri. Thanks a lot. I appreciate your coming over. —I really do."

Later, Terri came back and knocked again. "Honey," she said. "Would you rather we went . . . left you alone . . . ?"

"I suppose so," Ellie said, sitting on the toilet.

"Don't you want to come out . . . ?"

"I'll come out pretty soon."

Ellie heard Terri walk away, and then some people talking.

She was looking at the shower curtain. Beige fish with long, flowing tails. On lightly frosted plastic. The fish were bigger than she remembered. There weren't so many of them, either.

"El' . . . ?" It was Anderson. "El', we're going, now. You are not—repeat, not—to report tomorrow. That court thing . . . you had a court thing tomorrow, I believe. The District Attorney's people will get a postponement on that. We want you to take a few days off. Just get the hell out of town . . . whatever you want. —O.K.?"

"O.K."

"You come in after that, we'll have a little talk. All right?"

"O.K."

"All right. We're going, now. —You get to bed, get some sleep."

"O.K."

There was more soft talk out there. More talk. Silence . . . Then Ellie heard the front door close.

She sat on the toilet awhile longer, then stood up and took her bathrobe off, sat down again, took out her tampon and reached over to put it in the plastic bag in the wastebasket. She got up to get a fresh one from the counter beside the sink.

She looked at her reflection in the sink mirror, then reached down and put her left forefinger into herself a little way, took it out, and, watching herself in the glass, painted a faint rust-colored streak down her face from the inside corner of each eye. Once she'd done that, she saw tears, their trails broken, sliding down her face at last.

Weeping, she put her right foot up on the side of the tub, inserted a new tampon, then climbed in, slid the shower curtain shut, the beige fish swimming into place, and took a shower, the water dialed quite hot. She turned under the spray, breathing the warm mist, holding her face up so the innocent water might wash her tears and blood away. —It must have felt like this to Sally, if she cried at first, Ellie thought. Only the water was hotter, and she couldn't turn it off.

When Ellie came out of the bathroom tying her robe, she thought she heard someone say something, and walked into the living room and saw Samuelson sitting in the easy chair—filling it—with Mayo curled in his lap. He was reading to the cat from a paperback book.

He looked up and said, "O.K. —So, how ya doin'?" when Ellie came in.

"I feel better, Max," she said. She wasn't sorry he'd stayed.

"Well, you're not goin' to feel too good for a while," Samuelson said, "—'cause you just lost the best partner goin'."

"I know it." Ellie sat on the couch. Her hands were trembling, so she folded them together and held them in her lap. "—It wouldn't have happened if he just drove a car . . . if he hadn't taken that fucking subway."

"Maybe," Samuelson said. "—Listen, this is a good book. Me and the cat, we were enjoyin' it."

"What is it?"

Samuelson held the book up so she could see the cover. "*Wake of the Red Witch,*" he said. "—It starts pretty good."

"Yes, I liked it, too. I bought a lot of old paperbacks at Dog-Eared, over on the West side. —Why don't you take it? I finished it."

"You tryin' to kick me out?"

"No. —You hungry, want something to eat?"

"You got peanut butter and jelly? —What's so funny?"

"Nothing . . . Yes, I think I have. That's what you want?"

"Sure. —What kind of jelly you got?"

"Blackberry," Ellie said, "O.K.?" and got up from the couch.

"Oh . . . I guess that'll be O.K." He lifted Mayo gently down, and got up, too. "—Are we talkin' crunchy here, or smooth?" he said, following her into the kitchen.

"Crunchy."

"Oh . . . that'll be O.K., I guess."

"Max—do you want this sandwich? I don't have smooth, and all I have is blackberry jam. Is that going to be all right?"

"No—that's fine. That's fine."

Ellie got the peanut butter and jam out of the refrigerator, and two slices of whole-wheat bread, and started making the sandwich on the cutting board by the sink. The peanut butter was cold and hard to spread, and tore the piece of bread a little. Samuelson, watching, murmured.

"Jesus Christ—what is it now, Max?"

"Nothin'. That'll be great."

"How do you usually fix these things?" Ellie said. "—How did Harriet fix them?"

Samuelson gave her a reproachful glance. He was standing in front of the refrigerator, obscuring it entirely.

"You take white bread," he said, "—an' smooth, an' grape jelly, an' salt."

"Well, this is all I've got . . . and I'm crying on your sandwich," Ellie said, and was as she picked up the second slice of bread, put it on top, and pressed it down a little.

"Needed salt, anyway," Samuelson said, and took it from her.

When he was eating, standing, leaning against the counter, Ellie said, "I want to ask a favor, Max."

"Don't hurt to ask."

"I don't have time tomorrow to do it—I've got a couple of other things—and I want you to check up on Charley Ambrosio, fast, before he can get some bullshit story settled in."

Samuelson slowly chewed and swallowed his bite. "What do you think?" he said. "You think he had some guys kill Tommy—just 'cause they had a scrap?"

"Probably not—but I don't want to miss anything, Max. I don't want to take a chance. And I think Ambrosio is not a forgiver. —You want some milk?"

Samuelson slowly shook his head. "This is fine," he said.

"Will you do it, or not?"

"O.K.," Samuelson said, and took another bite of his sandwich.

"I notice you're eating that," Ellie said, "—crunchy or not."

"I'm not so choosy I got to have everythin' my way," Samuelson said.

* * *

The phone rang twice, just after Samuelson left, but Ellie didn't answer it. She was afraid it was Connie. About half an hour later, it rang again, and Ellie felt she had to answer it, that everything would be worse if she waited.

"Ellie?" A man. She didn't recognize his voice. "—It's Phil Shea."

"Hello . . ."

"You let me know if there's anything at all I can do for you. —Understand me? Anything at all."

"Yes. Thanks," Ellie said.

"Get some sleep," Shea said, and hung up.

Ellie put the phone down, then picked it up again, and called Connie.

"Hello? —Ellie?"

"Yes, sweetheart—it's me."

"Listen, don't be sad, now," Connie said. "I believe in heaven, an' that's where he is. —So, don't you be sad for a minute. Father said somethin' like this wipes purgatory right out."

"I'll bet it does," Ellie said. "I think you're right. But we're going to *miss* him so much. Marie . . ."

"Oh, no," Connie said. "Absolutely not. He's here with us all the time. —I don't miss my Tommy; he's right here."

"I hope so. Boy, I hope so."

"He'll look out for us the rest of our lives," Connie said. "He won't ever leave the house unless we go out, too. —I told Marie that, and she's fine."

"That's good."

"It's too bad about that dinner, though. I'll tell you, Tommy would have loved that dinner. —Everythin' was goin' to be perfect."

"I was going to bring flowers."

"You were? Well—I knew you were goin' to bring somethin'. I told Tommy, 'Ellie isn't comin' over without somethin' in her hands.' "

"I was going to bring flowers to match your plates. . . ."

"Gold—to match my china?"

"Yellow and gold," Ellie said. "Chrysanthemums. I saw some like that in Connecticut. They were beautiful. . . ."

"Perfect. That would have been perfect. . . ."

"Well, give Marie a hug for me," Ellie said.

Silence.

"Connie . . . ?"

Silence.

"Connie . . . ? You O.K.?"

After listening for almost a minute, and calling Connie's name twice more, Ellie said good-bye, and put down the phone.

Ellie thought of trying to go to sleep, but she wasn't sleepy, so she went to the hall closet, got the vacuum out, plugged it into the outlet near the phone table, and started cleaning the hall with the floor-sweep attachment, moving the table aside to get at a small streak of dust under it. When the hall was done, she did the kitchen, too—then switched attachments to the carpet sweeper, did the bathroom and bedroom carpets very thoroughly—moving both bedside tables in the bedroom, getting under the bed as far as she could reach—and that done, towed the vacuum into the living room to finish up an hour's work, Mayo fleeing before her. He hated the machine's whine and roar.

When the vacuuming was done, Ellie carried the machine back to the hall closet, took off the carpet-sweeper attachment and hose, and put everything away. Then she reached up to the top shelf, and got her paints, palette, and medium mixes down, and reached behind her winter coat and parka to haul out a small stack of stretched canvases—most painted over. She took it all into the kitchen, separated the framed canvases until she found a sixteen-inch square single-primed linen, with nothing on it but a charcoal sketch of Clara, naked, kneeling. There was also a small scratch sketch of Mayo in the lower left corner that was better than the sketch of Clara. —Easier, less effort to it.

Ellie took her three shoe boxes with her brushes, knives, charcoal, paints, copal, linseed, varnish and turps out to the living room, brought her palette, cotton rags. cup and canvas out next, set up her easel by the lamp, and put the canvas on it. Then she went back to the kitchen for old newspaper to put the stuff on, so it wouldn't ruin the coffee table—to put under the easel, too.

When she was set up, Ellie tilted the shade on the floor lamp so the light fell over her left shoulder directly on the canvas. She'd have to paint a little hot throughout, to contradict that harsh yellow.

She went to the bedroom for her small radio, brought it out to the living room, plugged it in, tuned to WYNY for classic rock, and turned it low. Then she stood at her easel, closed her eyes, and imagined the walk at St. Christopher's. She remembered the flowers very well, but not the stems. She imagined the walk at St. Christopher's, then thought of a wind blowing—breezing down through the grove of little maples, combing across the grass . . . then hide-and-seeking through the flowers, separating them, tossing their bright heads, bronze, yolk, and gold, the small, rough-pointed palmate leaves—showing the slender stalks as smooth and fine a green as green glass rods.

She wiped the sketches almost away with a clean cotton rag, picked out a charcoal stick, sharpened it with a single-edge razor blade, and quickly drew three long stalks growing together up through the faint ghost of Clara, then a shorter, frailer stem to the left of the others. The leaves curling, clustering together into dusty green scrolls and tangles. She could see these would be special flowers, not quite chrysanthemums, but almost. Dream flowers. The blossoms held, and then exploding slowly from their small green cups. Still resting there, though, their soft bottoms still seated. Ellie saw she wouldn't have to draw each petal, each blossom even lightly. Instead, she could sketch a small resting place for the proper kind of color. Each place shaped for a dab of color, a reminder that color must come there. Many small sketches, not one big one.

She had, when she'd finished, seven flowers sketched and jotted, heavy-headed, rising, nodding out of a slow tornado of leaves. No single piece of draftsmanship was fine, but the slight, indicating lines seemed to work well enough together.

Ellie thought she would paint the flowers and their leaves full out, the few lengths of visible stem, and only mark the canvas around them with broad, scumbled drifts of lawn green. Painting background didn't interest her.

She felt she wouldn't see the flowers as clearly, if there was solid color behind them. She didn't want to pretend the flowers hadn't been painted.

She decided to do the scumbling in a dark yellow green, but didn't bother with it, now. She was too busy.

She mixed her medium, with more copal than she usually used, set the cup aside, then squeezed out a blob of flake white, smaller turds of cadmium red, alizarin, yellow ochre, viridian, venetian red, cobalt, Prussian blue, French ultramarine, burnt sienna, ivory black, cadmium yellow, lemon yellow and burnt umber—most of which, she wouldn't need. She used a small springy-bladed palette knife to mix a dab of black with the viridian, one to four, mashed and mixed it to a shade of light pine, thinned it only slightly with a few drops of medium, dipped in a sable filbert number three, and painted the rare appearances of stem, very pleased with such a soft, smooth, creamy green, almost asparagus. Very pleased. She painted the lengths of stem to be visible only here and there through the small thicket of leaves, the weighty blossoms, but still, she felt, important as slender pillars to support the plants, to keep her from making leaves and blooms where no stems could support them.

These stems painted, slim and stalky, rising in divergent angles up the canvas, Ellie squeezed a long fat worm of more viridian across the palette, over an old dry smear of tangerine. Squeezed out more black alongside that, and mixed it in with her narrow knife—not wanting the mixture quite perfect, wanting slight streaks of forest. Streaks of black.

She painted her leaves this dark, thick, smooth and solemn green with a sable five, and felt it was now their natural color.

She'd sketched the places for the paint to go so well, the paint no longer had to go there, but could fall to this side and that side, wherever it wanted. Where one leaf joined another, Ellie joined them, and painted them together with a stroke, smearing here and there to show their motion in the wind. She thought her weakness might become her strength, and what she found difficult to draw separately, she might find easier if drawn together in a mass meant to be moving.

It took half the night for her to paint her leaves, remembering to accent the darker green with lighter green and occasional narrow edges of butter yellow, because of the lamp she painted by. The painting would live under cooler light.

At almost quarter to three, Ellie stopped painting, left her brushes in turpentine, then went to the bathroom, sat on the toilet, peed, and shat small. After she washed her hands, she went back to the kitchen, and ate the rest of the Häagen-Dazs, except for a small bite. She put that in a saucer for Mayo.

Then she painted the blossoms.

Cadmium yellow and lemon, mixed and slightly thinned, painted with a sable four. Ellie twisted her wrist slightly to the left finishing every swift, small stroke, so the yellow barely folded back on itself at the paint's upper edge—brighter yellow left to rise up through this color less lustrous. Each petal was made in one short stroke, and she was pleased for any imperfection to become the petal's. She mixed venetian red with cadmium for a duller, deeper orange-yellow at the blossom's outer edges, where the petals had been soaked in sunlight, beaten by weather. Ellie painted petals from flower top to flower top as her hand moved across the canvas, favoring no blossom over the others. She painted left to right, then started left to right again, lower, painting in the yellow where it was needed, shifting to a thinner brush for delicate radiant lines of sienna, borders of flake white marked with umber, sometimes, on blossoms' bottom edges. Several times, she thought of stopping and standing back to look, to rest, and decided not to. She was afraid to lose what she had.

She finished her flowers a little before seven, and erased what sketch marks she still could see—Mayo, Clara's arm and knee—then used her palette knife with lemon-viridian, to describe on the primed canvas where no flowers were, broad bands of deep yellow-green—dark grass's color when late sun shone on it. She scumbled those edges with her big brush, clouding the color away into the primer dun.

Then she walked back around the couch to take a look from fifteen feet away.

They were flowers, rich in yellow, greens and gold. They were plants even more than flowers, untidy, odd, and gorgeous, the blossoms sagging slightly to the right, unbalanced with the green, but beautiful, the heavy blossoms weighting the leaves like rough medallions hammered out of brass and thrown down among them.

Ellie stood and looked for a few minutes, then said to Mayo, asleep in the easy chair, "I've seen worse than that growing in the ground," and went to the bedroom to get dressed, fairly pleased with herself. She thought she'd give the picture to Audrey Birnbaum. She was afraid if she gave it to Connie, it would only remind her of the dinner never served.

CHAPTER 12

Ellie felt fresh and fine on the tram, as if she'd slept all night. Her breasts were less swollen, no longer sore, and she had no cramps, only a mild tightness high in her pelvis sometimes, as she walked. The morning was cool, and clear as water, the mist and rain all done. She was wearing her old brown tweed suit, the skirt a little short for fashion, now, with a pumpkin silk blouse and foulard—all easy, warm, and comfortable, except for the shoes she was wearing, and they'd be O.K. if she didn't walk a lot. As the car swung up, paced its cables over the river—the river glittering, glistering, flashing in sunshine below—Ellie thought that she might have slept after all, and been dreaming Tommy was dead—or she'd gone crazy and imagined it, and was about to make a fool of herself meeting people from the Squad, going down there later, and talking about Tommy being dead—having Leahy look at her as if she were out of her mind, and glance over her right shoulder, and when she turned around, there would be Tommy. "What's goin' on?" he'd say. "Are you kiddin' me?—Is this supposed to be funny, or what?"

"I dreamed you were dead. Killed in the subway . . ."

"Listen," he'd say to Leahy. "—This isn't funny! You hear this shit . . . from my own partner? She's worn out! —You're worn out, honey. Besides, if I'm dead, I want a couple weeks off. We both want a couple weeks off, startin' with not goin' out to look at some friggin' boat, see if it has an anchor there. . . ."

There was no reason that couldn't happen. No good reason it couldn't be true. . . . Ellie reached out and put the palm of her right hand against the tram-car window. Cool and hard. Standing between her and the morning air. Between her and all the distance down to the river below. —This is real, she thought, even though it lets light through. It's much more real than Tommy. . . .

At the Manhattan station, Ellie trotted down the stairs, looked for a cab, then walked a block south and climbed into an empty waiting at the light. The cabbie, a tall Haitian woman, didn't want to go crosstown—said she was heading for Kennedy—and got snotty. Ellie showed her shield, and advised the woman to move her ass.

At Broadway and Eighty-seventh, Ellie stopped the cab, paid the woman but didn't tip her, got out, and walked down the two blocks west to Riverside, to the Donegal. She went up the steps, then through the door into the entrance hall. There were ranks of mailboxes and intercom buzzers on both side walls, and it took her a minute or two to find the one labeled *Superintendent,* on the far left of the bottom row, left-hand wall.

She pushed the buzzer, and waited. After a while, she pushed it again, but no one answered. She pushed it a third time, and while she was waiting, a very old man in a dark gray Chesterfield coat came out through the inner door with a dog on a leash. The dog was a puppy, looked like a Kerry Blue, and was very lively. It was dancing, excited to be going out.

Ellie smiled at the old man, managed to reach the door before it closed behind them, and walked into the building. There was a staircase on the right, and she went down one flight, saw a green steel door labeled *Furnace,* walked down the corridor past two doors with no labels, then saw one on the other side of the hall with a peep, and a small card with *Walsh* printed on it.

She rang the doorbell, waited, rang it again, and heard a chain lock rattle. The door swung open, and a short, muscular man in his sixties, with white, crew-cut hair, stood staring at her. He was wearing blue jeans, a blue workshirt. Eyes blue as well—washed out.

"You're not a tenant," he said.

"No." Ellie took her shield and ID from her purse, and showed them to him. "—I'm a police officer."

The white-haired man looked at her ID, started to step out into the hall, then changed his mind. "You want to come in?"

"That's right."

"O.K." He stepped back to make room for her. "I'm the super, here."

"Walsh?"

"Emmett Walsh—right."

Ellie walked into the apartment entranceway. It opened into a small, neat living room. Two windows across the room were open onto a redbrick air shaft.

"My name's Klein," Ellie said, and turned back to shake hands with him. He had small hands, and a thick, strong grip.

"Well . . . what's the problem? —Was that you buzzin' upstairs, by the way?"

"That's right."

"Well—I didn't answer. If I was to answer every time some joker buzzed up there, I'd be goin' nuts. —They have a problem, all they got to do is give a phone call down here, or put a note inside my mailbox. All the regulars know about that."

"That's all right," Ellie said. A toilet flushed in the back of the apartment. "—We need some information from you, Mr. Walsh."

Walsh shrugged. "Whatever . . . You name it." A young woman walked into the living room through a white-painted double door from the back. Ellie saw a dining-room table through the doorway. The young woman looked Puerto Rican, mid-twenties. She was very plain, with a big Indian nose and a bad complexion. She was pregnant.

"My wife," Walsh said. "Teresa—this lady's a cop. Detective Klein."

"Hi," Ellie said, and the girl smiled and nodded, apparently shy.

"We got some business here, honey," Walsh said. "Why don't you go watch TV, an' we'll go out an' go for a walk in Riverside in a while. O.K.?"

"O.K." The girl's voice was hoarse. She smiled at Ellie, made a sort of sketchy curtsy, went back into the dining room and closed the double doors behind her.

"Flu," Walsh said. "She had the flu, and that's no joke, her condition." He seemed very worried about the girl.

"No—that can be serious," Ellie said. "I just lost my partner." She didn't know why she'd said that, she hadn't even been thinking about it. "He was killed in the subway," she said. It was as if her mouth didn't care what she thought.

"Holy shit," Walsh said. "I saw that on TV. —That was your partner?"

"Yes," Ellie said.

"Why, you poor thing," Walsh said. "Jesus—you should be in church or restin' or somethin'. —You shouldn't be out on the job, should you?"

Ellie felt like a fool talking to a super about Tommy being dead. Now that she'd done it, she didn't like it. It made Tommy seem more dead. "—Well, I have some cases to work on."

"I don't care. They shouldn't have you out workin'." Next, he'd be telling her to go in and watch TV. They'd walk in the park, later. . . . Ellie imagined herself walking in the park with the old man and his young wife. She'd ask who owned the Kerry Blue, and hear the whole story—how the old man's cocker spaniel had died after fourteen years, the old man sad, lonely. . . . How the man's son, over his protests, had gone and gotten him the Kerry Blue puppy—younger than young, foolish and energetic. How the puppy loved the old man, but was wearing him out—killing him, really—with his constant leaping and playing, his need for long walks day and night in every weather. "Some things a man loses," Walsh would say as they walked, "are natural things to lose—an' it don't do to replace 'em in a hurry."

"It probably wouldn't have happened," Ellie said, "—if I'd been with him." She was suddenly embarrassed that the old man would think she was trying to act tough. "I don't mean that I'm so tough," she said. "—I just mean there would have been two of us."

"I see what you're sayin'," Walsh said, and seemed uneasy. He looked around as if he wished his wife would come back. "—But you know, it don't do no good to blame yourself for things you can't help."

Ellie didn't know what to say after that. She felt herself blushing. Making such a fool of herself in front of an old man who probably thought she was crazy. "I'm sorry," she said, "—I had no business bringing all that up."

"An' why the hell shouldn't you?" Walsh said, "—losin' somebody like that." He looked around for his wife again. "Listen, dear—miss—you want a cup of coffee?"

"No, thanks," Ellie said. "I need to use your phone. . . ."

"Go right ahead."

"And I need the name of the man who manages this building—who owns it. . . ."

"Well, now," Walsh said, "—the owner is Terrace Associates, but the man you'll probably be wantin' to talk to is Mr. Simons; he's vice president for residential properties."

"You have his number?"

"I have his number."

"I need his home number." She looked at her watch. "It isn't nine, yet. He won't be in his office."

"Well . . . all right. I have it for emergencies—would this be an emergency?"

"Emergency enough," Ellie said.

"I'll take your word for it." Walsh went to the double doors, then turned. "—Sure you don't want a cup of coffee? I just got some cinnamon rolls for Tessie. You could have one of those and a cup of coffee. . . ."

"No, thank you, Mr. Walsh," Ellie said, wishing he would stop offering her things.

"O.K." He opened the doors, and walked into the dining room and out of Ellie's sight, and in a moment she heard him saying something to somebody. His wife. —An odd pair. An old Irishman and a Puerto Rican girl. Maybe she'd been working as a maid for some people in the building, and Walsh had stopped and talked to her in the hall a few times, as she came and went from work. Fell in love with a skinny little Hispanic girl with a big nose, young enough to be his daughter. Very tender with her . . .

Walsh came out with a small business card in his hand. As he gave it to Ellie, his intercom buzzer sounded. "Go ahead," he said, and Ellie thought for a moment he was talking to her. "—buzz your goddamn head off."

"Can I use this phone?" Ellie said. There was a phone

on a little table with a yellow lamp, against the living-room wall.

"It's all yours," Walsh said.

"I guess I need some privacy."

"Oh—you bet," Walsh said, and walked back into his dining room and shut the double doors.

There was a number on the back of the card, with *Home* printed next to it. Ellie went to the phone and picked up the receiver, punched that number, and heard at least four rings before somebody answered. It was a woman, and when Ellie asked for Mr. Simons, the woman made an impatient clicking sound with her tongue, said, "All right," and put the phone down.

It was picked up quickly. "Yes?" A man's voice.

"Mr. Simons?"

"That's right. —Who is this?" A deep voice. Ellie had imagined a small thin man, but Simons sounded big. He sounded impatient, too, and Ellie supposed tenants sometimes got his home number, and called to complain about this or that.

"My name is Klein, Mr. Simons. I'm a police officer, a detective with the Commissioner's Squad, downtown."

"I see . . ." Different tone of voice. "What can I do for you, Officer? —If it's a matter of some information or other, it might be best to call me at my office later in the morning."

"I don't want to wait for that," Ellie said. "I need some business information on one of your tenants—a Ms. Susan Margolies."

"I know Dr. Margolies," Simons said. He had a very deep voice. "—Excuse me, but may I ask how you got my home number, Officer?"

"From the Bureau of Records, Mr. Simons."

"I see."

"I need some information regarding Susan Margolies' co-op payments to your firm, Mr. Simons. —I was informed she does intend to purchase her apartment?"

"I believe that's true, Officer—but I certainly wouldn't have any records of that here. —It would really be better for you to contact my office later in the morning. I don't know what interest the Police Department has in that transaction—there might, for example, be some legal complication in revealing those records and so forth. I would simply feel more comfortable dealing with the matter in a more conventional way. O.K.?"

Ellie felt suddenly tired, as if she'd already worked a long day. Her feet were starting to hurt. The brown shoes fit fine in the toe, but they'd always been a little too long and tended to slip down off her heels. She'd glued moleskin patches inside the backs, but the heels still slid a little, sometimes, when she walked, and it made her feet tired.

"I understand your concern, Mr. Simons," she said, "—and if I could wait, I would. Now, what I'd like you to do, is call your accountant or whoever at home—somebody has to be familiar with the transaction—and get me that information. I want to know the amount that's been paid for that apartment, and I want to know when it was paid. I'll call you back in twenty minutes."

"I'll tell you what, Miss Klein—why don't you put your superior on the line, and we'll make any arrangement that seems reasonable."

"I'll tell *you* what," Ellie said. "If you don't stop farting around—if you don't have that information when I call for it, I'll ask my *superior* to have the Commissioner's office call the Department of Inspections, and have them *really* go over the various properties of Terrace Associates for any violations they can find, payoffs or not. —And I'll be sure and let the 'associates' know who they have to thank!" She hung up.

Ellie had two cinnamon rolls, and two cups of coffee, and—Walsh having gone upstairs to replace light bulbs on the fourth-floor corridors—discussed marriage and motherhood with Teresa, who, though shy, had been raised in the barrio, and knew shit from Shinola.

"I bet you wonder what I'm doin' with this old man."

"No, I don't. He loves you."

"Oh, yeah," Teresa said. "He's a nice guy, too. —I had some guys love me, you know, want to live with me? Next thing I know, they come in an' beat me up. —You know, Emmett don't lay a hand on me unless he's bein' nice. Oh—when he's ballin' me, too."

"Then he's nice. . . ."

"Oh, yeah. —He keeps goin' good, too, for an old guy."

"Sounds great."

"Oh, you think I don't know I'm lucky? You should see some of the stuff I have to do before I met Emmett. Clean up old ladies . . . you don't believe some of the stuff I have to do."

"You meet him in the hall?"

"No. The laundry room. —What does it mean if the baby kicks all the time?"

"He's either a boy, or a tough girl."

"Like you—right? Like a cop."

"We're not tough," Ellie said. "—We're scared all the time."

Teresa took another cinnamon roll. "Emmett said that was your friend, got killed."

"That's right. He was killed last night. If I'd been there, you know, he probably wouldn't have been killed."

"Bullshit," Teresa said, sitting well back from the table for belly room as she ate. "He was goin' home, wasn't he? You wasn't supposed to be there. —An' you're a lady, anyway. They would just kill you, too."

Ellie called Simons back twenty minutes late.

"Very well, Officer. I have the information you requested. —I also intend, by the way, to report your rudeness. . . . We have received an overdue down payment of fifty-three thousand dollars from Dr. Margolies, on an amount for purchase totaling one hundred and ninety-three thousand dollars. The down payment of fifty-three thousand was paid by a check on Citibank, drawn Monday before last. Received by our office on Wednesday of that week."

"Received Monday?"

"Received *Wednesday*—drawn Monday, September the twenty-first."

"All right. All right. I want to thank you, Mr. Simons. That's good information."

"You may be sure I still intend to report your rudeness, Officer Klein." Click.

Ellie thanked Teresa, asked her to thank her husband—then left the apartment, climbed the stairs to the lobby, and went out into the street. She walked east to Broadway, and found three phone booths near a newsstand. She could see headlines reading *Hero Cop Slain* from the near booth, got out of it, and went to the one on the end. She deposited her quarter, asked Information for the number for Todd Birnbaum's office, got her quarter back, deposited it again, and made the call.

"Birnbaum and Sefton."

It sounded like the tall girl with the bad complexion. That girl and Teresa. Bad complexions. "Is Todd Birnbaum in?"

"No. Mr. Birnbaum is not in the office yet. —May I take a message?"

"This is Detective Klein. My partner and I spoke with Mr. Birnbaum—"

"Yes, I remember. Mr. Birnbaum won't be in the office until about eleven o'clock."

"I need to talk to him, now."

"Well, he's at New York Hospital. He's visiting his wife."

"Thank you." Ellie dug for another quarter, called Information, got the hospital switchboard number, then called that. The switchboard gave her the nurses' station on the seventh floor, and a nurse who answered agreed to go and bring Mr. Birnbaum to the station phone. —The phone in Mrs. Birnbaum's room had been disconnected. The ringing disturbed her.

"Birnbaum."

"This is Detective Klein, my partner and I spoke—"

"I remember you," Birnbaum said. "—I believe Officer Nardone was the policeman killed last night. —Is that so?"

"Yes, it is."

"Well, he seemed a decent man. I'm very sorry."

"How is Audrey?"

"She's not having too much pain," Birnbaum said. "—I think she enjoyed your visit, yesterday. My wife doesn't have many visitors."

"I need to ask you some questions, Counselor."

"You can ask. . . ."

"First, where were you on Sunday morning, a week and a half ago?"

"Ah—nitty-gritty time. I was here. —I'm here every day from six till about ten-thirty. I like to be here when she wakes up."

"How are you paying for your wife's treatment, Counselor?"

"A good question," Birnbaum said. "—And a good lawyer would advise me not to answer it. . . . We have major medical coverage to about eighty-five percent of expenses. I have, so far, had to borrow an additional forty-three thousand dollars."

"Would you have any objection to telling me who the lenders were?"

"No, no objection. —One was a friend of mine, Aaron Silber; the other was a Westchester bank, National Republic. —I've also been advised that an additional uncovered charge of approximately sixteen thousand dollars will probably be incurred within thirty to sixty days. I believe I can borrow that amount as well."

"And if you can't. . . ?"

"Then, Ms. Klein, I will do whatever I have to do to get that money. If I had to, I would commit murder for it. —Does that answer your question?"

"I'm sorry."

"Don't be silly. You have your work to do. —Anything else. . . ?"

"Were you ever in therapy, Mr. Birnbaum?"

"Yes. —And still am, occasionally. What about it?"

"You went to Susan Margolies, didn't you?" Ellie felt out of breath, as if she'd run a long way to ask the question.

"Yes, I did. And do."

"She sent you to Sally a long time ago?"

"Yes, she did. —That's how Sally and I met. I had some . . . dysfunction. Did Susan tell you about this?"

"No, Mr. Birnbaum, she didn't. I thought it might be possible, that's all."

"Is there anything else you need to know? This may sound absurd to you—probably does—but I find myself worrying that my wife might die when I'm not with her. Gone to the bathroom or something stupid. Not that there's any emergency now—but when I am here, I like to stay with her."

"I understand. I feel the same . . . I felt the same. Just one more question. —Sally's money, hidden in that coffee-maker? Did you ever mention that to Dr. Margolies?"

"I see. Of course. I should have thought of that one, myself. —So the money isn't there. I suppose I assumed you people had found it. . . . Oh, hell . . . let me think. I believe I may have joked with Susan about it. I guess I thought Susan knew all about that treasure trove. —Certainly didn't seem surprised, that I recall. . . . And I hope you don't think that Susan would murder a friend for money. You happen to be talking about a wonderful therapist, and one of the few real grown-ups around."

"I hope you're right, Counselor."

"Is that all?"

"Yes. Please tell Audrey I asked about her. —And tell her I have a present for her. If she feels well enough, I'll bring it to her tomorrow."

"All right," Birnbaum said, "I will. —And again, my regrets about that officer. It was a rotten thing to happen." He hung up, and Ellie stood for a few moments, still holding the phone, leaning against the inside wall of the booth.

"Tommy," she said into the mouthpiece, wishing there were a number by which the dead might be reached. "—Tommy, we're going to break it." She listened for an answer over the hum, just in case.

She spoke to the newsstand man—careful not to look down at the newspapers on the counter—then walked downtown five blocks, and crossed the street to the branch of Citibank. She went through the revolving door, and along the counter past the tellers to a narrow office space with four desks arranged in it among white waist-high partitions. She stood at the rail there for a minute or two, then caught the eye of a young black woman at one of the desks. This woman worked on some papers for a while after that, moving them from one part of her desk to the other. Then, she got up and came over. She wore a dark blue dress, and a string of light blue beads. She had a modest Afro, and wore button earrings that matched her beads. A set.

"Yes—you want somethin'?"

"I'm a police officer," Ellie said, and took her shield and ID from her purse. "I need some information concerning an account here—an account I believe to be here, anyway."

The woman looked at Ellie's ID. "Well," she said, "—we don't give out information on people's accounts."

"You're in charge of this branch?"

"Mr. Weygand is downtown. He's the manager of this branch. While he's gone—I'm in charge. And we do not release account information to anybody without authorization."

"What's your name?" Ellie said.

"My name's Ms. Luanna Harris."

"Ms. Harris," Ellie said, "—here's the situation. I can get some information from you on this particular account, which involves a possible deposit of felonious gains resultant from a homicide—or I can start pulling your tellers out of their cages for questioning right now, pull you out from behind that rail for questioning right now . . . and maybe take your ass downtown as a material witness with possible prior knowledge of this same felonious deposit I'm looking for. —In other words, Ms. Harris, I advise you not to play hardball with me."

"I'm just tryin' to tell you bank policy—"

"Don't tell me shit, Luanna. Just get your buns over to an account ledger and look up Susan Margolies. M-a-r-g-o-l-i-e-s. I don't have to see it, and I don't need a lot of details. Just a couple. —I don't think that's a problem, do you? It isn't as if I was one of your poor sad-ass customers."

The black woman bit her lip, turned away, and walked back behind the tellers' cages. In three or four minutes, she came back with a small white slip of paper.

"What did you want to know?"

"I want to know her last big deposit," Ellie said. "How much and when."

Ms. Harris looked at the slip of paper. "Seventeen thousand dollars. Eight thousand deposited September twenty-first. Nine thousand, September twenty-second."

"Twenty-first and twenty-second. Monday and Tuesday."

"That's right."

"O.K. One more question, and I'll get out of here and

leave you alone. I need to know how that deposit was made. Particularly if it was in large bills. . . . Hundreds, maybe even a few thousands."

"There's no way in the world to tell that on deposits under ten thousand," the black woman said. "—Not now."

"Sure there is," Ellie said. "Go back there and ask the tellers. One of them might remember a deposit—if it was twenty or thirty hundred-dollar bills—and some thousands. Go on. —Do it."

Ms. Harris pouted, looked mighty sullen, and went away to do it. Ellie saw her walk down the line, talking to each teller in turn. All the tellers had something to say; Ellie couldn't tell if it was yes or no.

Ms. Harris came back to the rail, and said, "Jennifer remembers those deposits. And there weren't any hundreds or thousands. She remembers it was all small bills and it took a very long time to count out. —What's all this about, anyway?"

"A robbery and a homicide," Ellie said. "I appreciate your help. . . . I'm sorry I had to push you." She walked to the revolving door, waited while a small, fat lady in a black wool coat struggled through with two shopping bags, then went outside.

The morning was getting brighter, warmer—sunlight glancing off the mica chips in the pavement. Sparkling. A man with a canvas shoulder bag walked by, glanced at Ellie, at her legs, then looked into her eyes for a moment before he passed. Not a bad-looking man. In his late thirties . . . short, a blunt, pleasant face. Brown eyes. —Warmer than Phil Shea's winter gray.

The cinnamon rolls had made Ellie hungry. There was a good hot-dog place on Seventy-second that Tommy loved. . . . That Tommy used to love.

Ellie stood on the corner for a minute or two, thinking, watching the people walk by. Then she walked back into the bank and stood at the rail again, until the black woman—Luanna—saw her and came over. Then Ellie asked for the closest branch of any other bank.

Ellie had two hot dogs and an orange drink for brunch at Seventy-second, then walked back all the way up to

Eighty-seventh Street—very uncomfortable in the brown shoes—because she didn't want to go down into the subway, and she wasn't able to get a cab until she'd walked too far to need one. At Eighty-seventh, she walked west to the Donegal. She went through the lobby to the elevator, rang for it, and when it came, took it up to the seventh floor.

"Who is it . . . ?" Susan Margolies' voice came muffled through the door.

Ellie stood in front of the peep. "Officer Klein," Ellie said, and after a few moments, heard the door locks begin to rattle.

"Good morning . . ."

"Good morning."

"You already had the grand tour, didn't you? I showed you the apartment?"

"Yes, you did. It's beautiful."

Susan Margolies, tall, big-boned, walked as she had walked before, leading Ellie down the fine, high-ceilinged hallway, past the small lamps, the German prints—or Austrian. The tall woman was better-dressed this time, in a long, black, pleated skirt and a fine long-sleeved white silk blouse. She had pinned her iron-gray hair up, held it with two tortoise-shell combs.

"Just a minute," Susan said, "—I think I have an appointment this morning. We may have to cut this short. . . ." She stopped at a door on the right, opened it, and walked into the small, perfect, blond-wood den. Ellie stood at the door.

The tall woman leaned over her desk, leafed through her appointment calendar. "No. O.K.—we're all right." She stood up, motioned Ellie out through the door ahead of her, and followed her down the hall. She stepped up close behind, and Ellie heard her sniff once or twice.

"One perfume, today," Susan said, so softly that Ellie supposed she was talking to herself.

There was something new in the living room, that grand and pleasant space, and Ellie saw that a harpsichord, slight, angular, and elegant, was standing in the far corner, under one of the wide, tall windows. The windows were open, and the soft waterfall sound of traffic from the West Side Highway drifted in with sunlight.

Ellie supposed the light was brightened by reflection off the Hudson. —The apartment was as special as she'd remembered it.

"What do you think?" Susan Margolies said. The fine white blouse blanched her long pale face even paler, softened soft wrinkles. Her blue eyes assumed a more definite blue.

"It's beautiful. They're such pretty-looking instruments."

"Pretty-sounding, too, if you know how to play them. —I know I'm a little long in the tooth for it, but I decided what-the-hell, and I got it, and I'm going to take lessons."

Ellie didn't know what to say to that.

"Would you like some coffee, or tea? I could make us some muffins . . . ?"

"No, thanks. I've had breakfast."

Susan Margolies sat down in an armchair, and gestured Ellie to the couch. "Well—what is it now? You know, I just decided that it's uncivilized for a person to live and die and not know how to play an instrument, at least a little. Most people today can do only one thing. —And they usually can't do that very well."

"I think that's right, Susan," Ellie said.

"All right—I canceled my appointments, and here I am at your disposal. Ms. Klein—right?"

"Right."

"Well—what do you want to know?"

"Well, the first thing I'd like to know"—heart going bump, bump, bump—"I'd like to know why in the world you lied to me? If you hadn't lied, it might have been weeks before we got back to you. —Maybe a couple of months."

The tall woman seemed surprised. "Well, you're going to have to explain that one. —I don't know what the hell you're talking about."

"You told me that Sally only met Rebecca Platt a couple of times, had nothing to do with her. That was a lie—and it was the same lie Rebecca told me. . . ."

"I didn't lie. . . ."

" 'Men, and kids. —A blow-job or a peanut-butter sandwich, and they're satisfied.' —Heard that before, Susan? Sally quoted that in a letter, quoted a 'good friend' of hers."

"That doesn't prove a thing. . . ."

"I'll bet Sally paid for two hundred lunches over the years. I don't think it'll be hard to find some restaurant people who remember them. —Rebecca only likes a few places."

"All right. —All right, Sherlock, you made your point. O.K. I did fib about that."

"Why?"

"Because Rebecca asked me to. She didn't think it would make the slightest difference, except she didn't want to be involved. —And considering her background, I didn't blame her. —Now, if that's caused a big stir down at Headquarters, I'm sorry." She reached behind her to shift a pillow on the couch. "All right . . . I suppose I *am* sorry. It was a stupid thing to do—and if it's made your job tougher, I'm sorry. O.K.? Now, is there any other crisis we have to deal with this morning?—I assume, by the way, from all the fuss, that you people are not getting very far with this case. . . ."

It was moments like this one, Ellie supposed, that spoiled police officers, sometimes made ugly bullies out of them. —To be able to step into people's lives, and change them as if you were God.

"I'm sorry, Susan," she said, "—but you're in trouble."

Susan Margolies put her head back, so slightly it was hardly noticeable. "Oh—I see," she said. "I'm in trouble—and I'm supposed to tremble. Just what sort of trouble am I in, Officer?"

"Susan—I'm going to have to ask you some questions. You are not under arrest right now, and you don't have to answer them if you don't want to . . . but if you don't, I'll have to place you under arrest, read you your rights, and have you taken downtown. —I know it's a pretty shitty choice."

"Oh, well—since you're being such a pussy cat about it, why the fuck don't you just ask your fucking questions?" Sitting up straight, now.

"Where were you that Sunday morning, Susan? —The morning Sally was killed."

"I was rght here. O.K.?"

"Was anyone else here? —Anybody who could testify to that?"

"No.—Next question."

"Do you know if Sally kept any money in her apartment?"

"No, I don't know if Sally kept any money in her apartment—but I wouldn't be surprised."

"In two days, week and a half ago, you deposited seventeen thousand dollars in the Citibank branch over here to help cover a check you wrote for a down payment on buying this place. That down payment was already overdue—"

"My, you've been a busy little bee!"

"Where did you get the money, Susan?"

"Out of my piggy bank. That was *my* money, honey! Singles and five-dollar bills and some tens I saved for more than thirty-five years—whenever I had a couple of bucks left over from groceries and rent, if you don't mind!"

"You made your deposits at Citibank in small bills, on Monday and Tuesday of that week. —But on that Monday, first thing in the morning, you went to the Bankers Trust branch on Broadway and changed eight thousand dollars—hundreds and six thousands—into smaller bills. On Tuesday morning, early, you went to Manufacturers Hanover, a few blocks downtown from Bankers Trust, and you changed nine thousand dollars—hundreds and thousands—for singles and fives. That teller remembered you very well, because you hurried her up and she lost her count and had to start over. People at these local branches remember large amounts. All those big bills. —You probably should have gone downtown."

Susan Margolies sat still, back straight, staring just over Ellie's right shoulder. She seemed wrapped in the bright, slow, liquid light of catastrophe. The air around her sang with it.

"Where did you get those big bills, Susan? Why did you change them?"

The tall woman relaxed a little, sat easier against the cushions. She put her hands together, and they each gripped their opposite. When they were bound together, fingers intertwined, she laid them down in her lap.

"Where are you keeping the rest of the money, Susan? Here in the apartment? In a safe-deposit box?"

Hunting. That's what this is, Ellie thought. Like Phil Shea, out on Long Island before daylight.

"I'm going to read you your rights, Susan. You're under arrest." Ellie was surprised to hear her voice shaking. She searched in her purse, found her badge case, got the Miranda card out, and read it. Her voice sounded better as she read.

When she finished, Ellie put the card away. "Now," she said, "—you don't have to say anything to me, Susan. But I'll tell you what I think happened, and if you want to, you can tell me if I'm right."

Silence, from a tower of silence. Susan Margolies sat on her couch, listening to distant traffic.

"I think you found out from Todd Birnbaum that Sally kept a very large amount of money in her apartment. —And Todd, assuming you already knew, mentioned where the money was kept. Then you did something very dumb—or maybe you needed her to give you the courage to do it; I don't know. You told Rebecca."

The apartment smelled faintly and finely of potpourri. Ellie remembered she'd wanted to ask what mixture Susan used for it. Now, she'd never know. . . .

"Rebecca took over right away, didn't she? The chance of a lifetime. More than one hundred thousand dollars just sitting there—and Sally couldn't call the cops. What could Sally say if that cash turned up missing? 'I'm a whore, and I was hiding a hundred twenty-seven thousand dollars from the IRS, and I think some friends of mine stole it from me. . . .' No, Sally couldn't call the cops."

Far below, at the edge of the Hudson, some impatient traveler caught in slow traffic was blowing his horn.

"And it was so easy! You were supposed to water her plants this summer. —You still have a key to the apartment, don't you, Susan? Sunday before last, Sally was going up to visit Sonia in Connecticut. So, I think you and Rebecca went in the back while the carpet cleaners were working over there. You took the elevator to her floor, unlocked the door, and went right in. —And everything would have been fine—but Sally'd gotten a late start. She was still in the apartment, maybe in the bathroom—so she didn't hear you in there at all, until she came out and caught you in the kitchen, with the lid off that coffee maker."

Susan had nothing to say. Her hands were no longer clenched together; they lay relaxed in the lap of her fine long black skirt, side by side. The nails were rounded, perfectly manicured, polished in clear. They looked as if they belonged on younger fingers.

"—Or, I suppose," Ellie said, "she might have gone out for something . . . come back, and walked in on you. Either way, she must have told you both to get the hell out of there—and that would be when Rebecca came out of the kitchen with the knife."

"I didn't hurt her," Susan said. "—I left."

"You didn't do what Rebecca told you? You didn't get some hangers from the closet when Rebecca told you to go get them? You didn't help hold Sally while Rebecca twisted those hangers around her wrists? —Just to keep her still, keep her quiet until she calmed down? Maybe she was angry enough to call the police, after all. . . ."

"I didn't hurt her," Susan said. "—I left."

Ellie stood up, the brown shoes hurting her insteps. "I need to use the phone," she said. "—You'll have to come with me, Susan."

Susan got up off the couch as if she were fine, as if everything was all right, and led Ellie down the short hall to the kitchen. Then she went to stand near the sink—her reflections, smeared, obscure, moving slightly on the stainless cabinets at either side.

Ellie called Leahy's number on the Squad, and the Lieutenant answered, caught just before lunch. "Lieutenant," Ellie said, "—this is Klein."

"Klein? —What is it, honey? You O.K.?"

"I'm fine, Ed. I'm working."

"What the hell you doin' working?"

"We have the Gaither thing, Lieutenant. It's broken."

"What? —Are you kiddin' me?"

"No. I'm up at the suspect's apartment. I have her under arrest."

"Are you serious?"

"Yes, I am."

"Jesus . . ."

"I need a car, and somebody to take her down and

book her—and I need somebody else to go with me for the accomplice."

"Who is this you got?"

"A lady named Margolies. Went over for the money."

"You got a good chain, I hope."

"More than good enough."

"You sure about that?"

"She had motive, access, and opportunity, and she can't explain seventeen thousand in very big bills. She's hiding more."

"O.K. . . . O.K. Murray's on the street. We'll call him over to you right away. Where is this place?"

"The Donegal, Eighty-seventh and Riverside. Apartment Seven D."

"O.K. Well—you aren't supposed to be workin', but looks like you got one for the Squad."

"Yes," Ellie said, "—we got one for the Squad." She hung up, and began to wait with silent Susan.

"Congratulations on this one," Murray said, following Ellie and Susan Margolies down the hall to the living room. "—Are you all right? Nobody down there can believe Tommy's gone. . . ."

"Tommy was the one," Ellie said, "—who wanted to come back and check her. Susan, this is Detective Murray. He'll be taking you downtown. . . ."

"Nice apartment," Murray said when they walked into the living room. "—Really nice." John Murray was a slender black man in his fifties, with a short, artful "do," and a mustache. Figured for a fag by most of his colleagues, but not despised on that account, he was regarded as a competent cop, patient and pleasant, if not much for rough stuff, no boon companion.

"I read Susan her rights," Ellie said, as Susan Margolies went back to her couch, sat down, and looked away out one of the tall windows. "—And we packed a big purse for her, toothbrush and a paperback and some things. She's got change for phone calls."

"All right," Murray said. "—Susan and I'll get along just fine."

"I wouldn't leave her alone."

"No," Murray said, "—I won't do that. We'll get along

just fine." He smiled at Susan Margolies, but she didn't notice. She was staring out through her tall window, as if a new, giant, and wonderfully pinioned bird swung high over the Hudson. "—Lieutenant's sending a woman officer up to come in with her, and somebody else from the Squad. —You want to wait for them? They'll be here pretty quick."

"No, I better not. Whoever the guy is, have him meet me at Bloomingdale's, O.K.? Lexington Avenue entrance. I'll wait as long as I can."

Susan sighed on her couch. She looked dreamy, as if the intrusion, the excitement and despair, had made her sleepy.

Ellie went to the couch and put her hand on Susan's shoulder . . . felt the white blouse's fine silk, a bone beneath. "I'm sorry," she said.

Susan reached up and patted her hand. "—What in the world for?" It was the first thing Susan had said in some time.

Ellie got out of the cab at the corner of Fifty-ninth and Lexington. The driver, a pleasant young man from Pakistan, hadn't known how to get to Bloomingdale's, and they'd gone several blocks out of their way before he admitted it. He said he knew the West Side very well.

Ellie crossed the street, trying to step lightly in the brown shoes, and stood on the downtown side of the store's entrance doors, waiting for whoever Leahy sent up. A lot of people were going in and out . . . a constant flow, almost all women. It was nearly noon, and more of these women, sleek, nervous, harried, up from their offices to shop over their lunch hour, now unfolded from their taxis, left small tips behind them, and strode past Ellie to strike the door handles hard, going in.

Ellie stood waiting for ten minutes—then couldn't wait any longer. She went in, took the stairs up to the mezzanine, and found a security guard—a thin, blond young man in a maroon blazer—standing beside a counter of Lancôme cosmetics with a small walkie-talkie in his left hand. He was talking to a young woman clerk wearing a purple sweater-and-skirt outfit and several large pieces of costume jewelry.

Ellie tapped him on the shoulder, and showed her ID when he turned.

"Is your chief in the store?"

"No, he isn't. Mr. Watson is, though. —He's exec under Mr. Delacroce."

"Fine," Ellie said. "—Please call Mr. Watson, and ask him to meet me in the female employees' locker room. —There is one, isn't there?"

"Yes, ma'am," the security guard said. "It's on the fifth floor, now. You can take the elevators up, then go left. —Anybody up there can tell you."

"O.K. —And he'll meet me up there?"

"Yes, ma'am," the young man said, lifted his small radio and began to talk into it.

Mr. Watson, also wearing a maroon blazer, was tall, thin, and black, and wore luxuriant sideburns. He'd met Ellie in Lingerie just off the fifth-floor elevators, and taken her back through a fire door into long green-painted corridors—complaining all the time about current disruptions and moves from floor to floor, the women's locker room being only an example. Then he took a right-hand turn to an open sliding metal door. There were mirrors lining the wall of the white-painted room beyond it.

"What's Commissioner's Squad doin' workin' on a homicide?" he said, taking his time now examining Ellie's ID. An ex-cop. Sergeant, probably.

"We were told to . . ." Three women walked past them and through the doorway, talking about somebody named Gary.

"And Platt's your pigeon?"

"I think so."

"Well—you got some backup comin'?"

"I have somebody coming. —But I don't want Rebecca leaving the store before we get to her."

"Well, I can station my people on the doors—report back to me. But they can't stop her if she tries to leave—we got no powers of arrest on some criminal charge comin' outside the store."

"She could be holding stolen cash on these premises," Ellie said.

Mr. Watson smiled. "O.K. That's a little better, now. —Now, you talkin' somethin' 'sides shit!" He took another look at Ellie. "Didn't you lose a man off your Squad, yesterday?"

"Yes."

"Well . . . I'll put my people on the doors. They all know her. —She tries to leave, they'll hold her, suspicion of usin' store premises for illicit storage."

"I appreciate it."

"O.K. —Let's go see what old Rebecca been hidin' in her locker. . . ." He took a small notebook from his back pocket, flipped it open, and leafed to find a page. Facing pages were filled with lists and numbers. —Lock combinations, Ellie supposed, and the names they went with.

A stack of Italian fashion magazines. A wide-mouth thermos—empty. A tan raincoat. —Ellie lifted that out of the locker to look into the pockets, smelled Rebecca's perfume. . . . A scarf, polyester—small green-and-white checks; a pair of transparent plastic galoshes; a folded Bloomingdale's shopping bag; a flowered makeup kit (Ellie opened that, then closed it and put it back); a small box of Tampax; a blue folding umbrella; a bar of Dove soap, unwrapped but not used, lying on a folded brown paper towel. And her purse.

Ellie went through the purse, then Rebecca's wallet. There, amid checks, a pen, her calculator, and small paper debris, were nineteen dollars—one ten and nine singles—a MasterCard, driver's license, bank card—Chemical—and two old photographs of Rebecca, years ago, at the beach with the same man—a smiling young man with a sharp-jawed face and long dark hair, neatly combed back. They were both in bathing suits—the young man slight, gangling, and pale—Rebecca, in a bikini, darker, small-breasted, round-bellied, rich-thighed. She and the young man had their arms around each other in both pictures, facing the camera smiling, squinting in the sunlight. —There was some change, a few tokens, and a book of stamps in Rebecca's change purse.

Watson said something into his radio, waited awhile—watching Ellie put things back into the wallet, the wallet into the purse, the purse into the locker—heard some response, and talked a little more.

Ellie closed the locker, and snapped the lock shut.

"Perry saw Rebecca on four," Watson said. "She did a big new display down there last week. Always checkin' it out. She was down there about a half hour ago."

"All right, I'll go down, see if I can find her," Ellie said. "—I'd appreciate it if you could have somebody check the Lexington Avenue entrance. See if there's a detective there waiting for me—send him up to four."

"All right. My guess is," Watson said, "she's headin' out for lunch. I'll make the rounds of my people, see they're on the ball. —You be surprised the shit a man'll say on the radio, an' him nowhere near where he supposed to be."

Watson left her back in Lingerie on five, and Ellie took the escalator down one floor with a companion group of women, all silent, staring out over a murmurous expanse of furniture, furnishings, whole rooms and separate suites entire, lamps, mirrors, and a thousand articles of decoration, the aisles sifting with shoppers as they descended. This section of the floor was Italianate, the pillars faced with what appeared creamy, swirled butterscotch marble, each surface fronting on mirrors that gave it back to passersby on every side. Lights—focused spots, unfocused floods—dazzled into the mirrors, gleamed on the cream and brown and yellow surfaces. Ellie got off the escalator and walked back, out of furniture.

Here, behind the escalators, lay another kingdom. Its pillars were deep blood red. Between and among these, low showcases lined the aisles. Strewn beneath their glass, or draped over small stands, lay costume jewelry, combs, handbags, gloves, scarves, hats, belts, long, thick mufflers, and all and every sort of accessory for the clothes gathered in their sheepfold racks, soft, rich islands of cashmere, shearling, and wool. Autumnal colors.

Ellie, walking down the center aisle, paused for a moment at a stand of long tweed overcoats with wide, draped sleeves. She looked at a light gray, stroked the material, which was heavy and soft as warm water, and checked the size . . . price tag. It was very expensive.

At the end of that long aisle, where a number of women stood alongside two counters of cosmetics lit from above by gold-filtered light—displaying toilet water, perfumes and lipsticks in gold containers, gold-flecked bottles, pomanders, compacts, and powders, all in boxes of gold—Ellie went down three steps to a lower level, and saw Rebecca's display in the center of the floor.

It was beautiful. A small carousel—a real one, turning slowly, the little horses real merry-go-round horses—and on each a perfect mannequin, a lovely woman dressed for autumn in tawny colors, thick, soft, warm fabrics in slacks and skirts, jackets and suits, boots (sheepskin, maroon leather and black), sweaters, mufflers, berets, fedoras and tams. The mannequins were riding into the new season, gliding gently up and down as they swept slowly around through a scattering of falling leaves, each leaf red and gold and brown—these hanging on long black silk threads, blowing gently here and there as the carousel turned. Above, at the carousel's peak, turning with it, a huge cornucopia lay on its side, spilling out more flaming leaves, great jewels of glass and gilt, small, fat pumpkins, and huge cartwheel wooden coins painted gold. A long, carved, white wooden sign hung from brass chains above the display. *Rushing the Season* it said, in crimson paint.

"Not bad . . . ?" Rebecca said, behind her.

"No. It's better than not bad, Rebecca. It's beautiful." Ellie slowly turned to face her. "—I was looking for you—where've you been?" Rebecca was wearing a dark green dress. Her black hair was drawn back into a soft French knot, held with a silver clip. She wore silver earrings.

"I had a bite in the cafeteria. —I was down in the shop all morning, and I have a feeling I'm going to be there all afternoon, too. They have a carpenter down there must be as bad at his job as Jesus. I've been trying to get a simple window display out of him—you know, sunny window, curtains, grass and flowers on a backboard? It's for a kitchen faucet. You'd think I was asking the asshole to build me a house in Connecticut." She looked over Ellie's left shoulder at the display. "—But this thing's pretty good."

"Better than good."

"Well . . . not bad, not bad. You notice I used that 'Rushing the Season' thing."

"It's just right."

"You see anything you'd want to wear? —You know, they just moved all this shit down here, last few weeks. They're always turning the fucking store upside down."

"There was a nice coat back there. . . ."

"Oh, yeah—they have some good ones. Tweed—right?"

"A light gray . . ."

"Umm-hmm . . . but you need something with a little more color, honey. You're too pale to wear light gray—you'll look like Dracula's daughter. Medium gray at least. Go for medium. —If you fell in love back there, I'll pick it up for you, employee price. What the hell—figure Christmas came early. . . . It still isn't going to be cheap."

"Rebecca . . . I need to talk to you."

"O.K.—So, come on down to the shop with me. I have to get going, anyway, or he'll make me a toilet seat instead of my window."

"I need to see you privately, Rebecca."

"We'll be in the basement. —How private do you need?"

They walked to the escalator, and stepped on behind a tall blond woman with three small children. The children clung to her, hung on her arms—and one of them, behind his mother's back, kicked another in the leg.

"There're some things," Rebecca said, watching, "—I don't regret. . . ." She cocked her head, looked sideways at Ellie. "—I'm sorry I never warmed up to that partner of yours. Is it killing you—what happened?"

Ellie didn't say anything.

"O.K.—It's killing you. I'm sorry. What was it—a friendship? Not just a partner, right?"

"Right."

"Well, I'm sorry—even though he treated me like shit, the times we met."

"Rebecca . . ." They stepped off the escalator, the blond woman towing her children away to the right.

"All right, don't be angry. I'm sorry the guy was killed. He was a man, anyway—not like the caterpillars around here."

They walked back toward the next escalator through an aisle of furs. —Coyote, Ellie thought. The jackets were deep, frosted gray, a soft wall close on either side of them.

Rebecca took a right turn past the jackets.

"These coyote?"

"Yeah," Rebecca said. "Everybody loves wolves—nobody gives a shit about coyotes. —What's new on Sally Gaither?"

"I just saw Susan, Rebecca." Rebecca stepped onto the escalator, Ellie behind her. Four Indian women—mothers and daughters, apparently—stood a few steps below them wrapped in brilliant silk, pearls in their ears.

"Saris," Rebecca said. "That's quality clothing—not like the crap those French faggots peddle over here. . . . So, what did Susan have to say for herself?"

Ellie was tired of pretending. It seemed more and more unfair. They were slowly sinking toward the second floor—bright, light, and spacious. Here, below cream-white walls, cream-white pillars, lay a shallow lake of woolen dresses, and polyester blends almost as fine as wool, and an acre—more than an acre—of wool slacks, designer jeans, corduroy trousers, corduroy knickers, artful windbreakers with their style names sewn across their breasts, and, here and there, bright showcases of pattern-knit clutches and shoulder bags, light leather gloves, striped woolen mittens, and stands of English wool driving caps, Irish tweed hats, American watch-caps, and baseball caps in black and blue felts.

"She's under arrest," Ellie said.

"That'll be the day."

"It is the day," Ellie said. "I mean it."

"Under arrest for fucking what?" said Rebecca. "—You're heading for a lawsuit for false arrest, is what it sounds like." She looked at Ellie with black eyes bright as a crow's. "—Not the Gaither thing?"

"That's right. She stole some money over there. —That's what happened to Sally. Robbed."

Rebecca stepped off the escalator, Ellie beside her, and they turned right, then right again, to walk toward the next escalator down—past yards of bras and panties, chemises, panty hose, and a few lacy garter belts (white, pink, and black) framing clear plastic groins on stands along the counters.

"Bullshit!" Rebecca said after a moment, walking faster. "You people have to be desperate . . . ! I thought you had some brains. I thought you were a smart cop. —Susan Margolies couldn't kill a cockroach! —And anyway, I don't think Sally *had* any money!" Rebecca stopped walking, and reached over a countertop to straighten a bra strap on a plastic torso. "You know," she said to the clerk, an elderly woman with an elaborately curled hairdo, "—you know, Annie, it wouldn't break your hand to straighten up stuff on your displays." Annie had nothing to say, and Rebecca walked on. "Did you catch that wig?" she said. "That old bag has been here for forty years. . . . And just guess who Susan's going to blame for getting her into this? —Three guesses, first two don't count. . . . Unless you're kidding me. Because if you are, *Officer*, it isn't funny."

"I'm not kidding you," Ellie said. They stepped onto the escalator. "—And I don't think Susan killed Sally. I think it was you, Rebecca."

"I want you to tell me something," Rebecca said. "I want you to please tell me why I should take this shit from you. —You think some lunches buy you the right to say stuff like this to me? Because if you think so, lady—you are dead wrong."

They were sinking toward a world of glittering glass, the perfume counters reaching away before them to the distant stairs from the mezzanine down to the last department, then the doors out to Lexington.

"You shouldn't have lied to me about being friends with Sally. . . . We have a case. Solid against Susan—and I think she'll tell us about you."

"Oh? —You do?" Rebecca smiled and glanced at Ellie in a friendly way.

"Yes. —I think you stayed behind after Susan left, and you had Sally there, in the bedroom or the bathroom, tied up with wire hangers. You used hangers on your little boy, didn't you? —I don't think you could stop yourself, once you had Sally like that. Helpless. I don't think you could stop yourself if you had anyone like that . . . and you must have resented her, hated her all those years . . . buying lunches for you . . . making all that money. She probably bought you a lot more lunches than I have."

"I've heard of horse-pecocky," Rebecca said, "—but this takes the cake." They stepped off the escalator together, and walked side by side along a counter of bright green glass under soft green lights.

"I think you had some fun with her," Ellie said, "—with the bananas. I don't know where you got that rubber ball you gagged her with. . . . Maybe you've used something like that before, and brought it along, just in case. —Maybe Susan was lucky she got out when she did."

Rebecca didn't seem very interested. She strolled along at Ellie's side, watching the shoppers, looking over the displays.

"You decided to put Sally on the chair under the shower after a while, after you'd had some fun. I suppose you knew she'd call the police, then. It had gone too far."

"Don't use any of this stuff. . . ." Rebecca indicated the ranks of green glass, their contained scents, deodorants, and sprays. "—It smells exactly, but exactly, like a wet dog. —And that's a good one, by the way, that 'fun with bananas' bit. You're the dyke, honey, not me. Did you think you were fooling anybody all this time? —I sure as hell hope you don't think you were *fooling* anybody. Susan called me when you first went over there. 'Your pretty friend must have had her head in it last night, Rebecca. . . .' She smelled that other perfume all over you." Rebecca stuck her tongue out and wiggled it. "—Who's the lucky girl?"

"You wiped everything down very well," Ellie said. "But you missed one of Susan's prints in the bathroom. —The toilet handle. She was nervous, I suppose, and had to pee. . . . And you wound up with at least sixty thousand dollars in your purse. Hundred-dollar bills and thousand-dollar bills. I'd guess you divided the cash right there, before Susan left. I don't think you trusted each other. . . ."

They were passing the Chanel counters, then. White boxes, white-gold perfume in clear square-cut glass, white powder in boxes with white-gold accents.

"Quality tells," Rebecca said, and nodded her approval of these displays. "That old bag knew her business. —I met her, you know. She came here on a trip a long time ago. Little ugly wrinkled old lady. I mean *tiny*. I was a kid—what the hell did I know? I thought I was shaking hands with God. —You know, honey, I can understand you're all excited, you think you made your case and so forth. People are strange . . . people are odd. Here I am, you're calling me a killer, you're all set to arrest me and everything—and I'm sorry to have to pop your balloon. Isn't that weird? You tell me people aren't weird. —You remember Evening In Paris?"

"Yes," Ellie said. "—My mother said that was her first perfume."

"I used to buy that in the drugstore when I was a little, little kid. Midnight-blue bottle with a tassel. —And not bad, either. Better than some of this shit a hundred times the price. —And I want to say something else to you, too. I shouldn't have made that remark about you being a dyke. Somebody gets lonely enough, they'll fuck a card table." She cocked her head, stared at Ellie with polished black eyes, the left pupil showing a tiny wedge of yellow. "—You forgive me?"

"Yes."

"O.K. —Look at that. Poursuivre. They try to make the bottles look like dicks. . . . Well, what I was going to say is that poor Susan's got Alzheimer's. —Didn't you notice? Poor lady. She doesn't have many patients left—a few old-timers. —*Their* names, she can remember. Now, if this ever does get serious—if you really want to make a fool of yourself—I have to tell you that by the time my lawyer lets this get to trial—months, at least—poor Susan won't even know her fingers from her toes. She got the diagnosis at St. Luke's beginning of the year. . . ."

Rebecca stopped walking, stepped into a small alcove beside the Lanvin display, a counter away from the mezzanine stairs, and looked into Ellie's face, smiling. "I don't want to embarrass you," she said. "—And, as far as Sally Gaither goes—O.K., I knew her. She let me hang around the same way you let me hang around. She was a very selfish person. —You know what her idea of a loan was? —Five hundred bucks. She thought that was a big deal, five hundred bucks sometimes. You know the most money she ever gave me? I'll tell you. Seven hundred and fifty to have some periodontal. That's exactly three fucks. Four fucks, tops. Big deal—right?"

"I'm arresting you, Rebecca," Ellie said. "—I'm going to read you your rights." She looked for the card in her purse.

"Will you cut this shit out? I told you—you don't have a case!"

"I think I'll have the money, Rebecca. You have those hundred-dollar bills. The thousands. And you know something? —You did a great job wiping Sally's apartment, but I'll bet you never thought to wipe the money . . . every single bill, front and back. If you didn't, it's got Sally's prints all over it. —I think I'll have that money. It wasn't in your locker—"

"Great—it wasn't in my locker . . ."

"You're too smart to put it in a bank—"

"I'm too smart to put it in a bank . . ."

"And you wouldn't leave it in your apartment. You know we'd search it."

"Oh, right. That's absolutely right."

"—And I don't think you have a friend, Rebecca, that you could trust with sixty thousand dollars."

Rebecca laughed. "—Except for you," she said. "Otherwise, you got that one right."

"It's in the store. —You hid it here."

"Find it, then," Rebecca said, "—or kiss my ass."

Ellie got out her Miranda card, and read Rebecca her rights, keeping her voice down. Rebecca listened, nodding. When Ellie was finished, she put the card away and took Rebecca by the arm.

"Come on—we'll go out the front."

Rebecca pulled her arm away.

"Don't cause trouble in here, now, Rebecca." Ellie took her arm again.

"Let go of me," Rebecca said. "—Just don't put your hand on me and you'll be all right." She reached up and pulled Ellie's hand away.

"Don't make me cuff you."

"Try it, and watch what happens."

Two women standing by the Lanvin counter were looking at them.

Ellie opened her purse, reached in for her cuffs, and Rebecca hit her in the face—then shoved her, hard, with both hands. Ellie stumbled back, her left shoe came off, and she fell down on one knee against the opposite counter, knocked a quart bottle of perfume off the countertop and broke it. —She kept her hand on the cuffs, and pulled them out of the purse.

Rebecca was shouting, "—You don't know who you're dealing with!—*You don't know who you're dealing with . . . !*" She lifted up a small decorative lamp from the Lanvin counter, raised it high over her head, and smashed it down into the glass countertop. A woman screamed softly, almost in inquiry, at the end of the aisle.

Ellie got up, pulled off her other shoe, and went for Rebecca barefoot, the cuffs clutched in her right hand—got a grip on Rebecca's dress with her left hand and tried to hold her, but Rebecca kicked out at her and hurt her hip—kicked again as Ellie tried to get close—fished down into the broken glass of the countertop until she found what she wanted, and turned to face Ellie with a foot-long splinter of break-frosted glass gripped in both hands. Her fingers were running red.

"—You don't know who you're dealing with," she said, not shouting any longer, and came at Ellie fast, hacking at her face, grunting with effort as she swung. Ellie ducked down and put up her left arm, embarrassed by what was happening, and Rebecca struck down with the glass and Ellie felt a sudden slicing intimacy, that realest thing of all, as she was cut. Now she wished she had the purse and gun, and as Rebecca came at her again, imagined the woman falling, shot to pieces.

Rebecca was making an odd face, as if she could barely keep from laughing—as if this were a joke, and she didn't realize she'd cut Ellie on the arm, was going to carve her face if she kept on. She rushed in and swung twice, hard as she could, and Ellie jumped back each time—falling to all fours, the last—then scrambling up to back away some more, into a chorus of screams (now rich, full-throated), the bright silver sounds of breaking glass as displays toppled over.

Women shoppers stampeded away as Ellie staggered, holding up her arm so that Rebecca would cut that again instead of slashing her face wide open so her teeth showed through a split, spurting cheek. Trapped behind their counters, the clerks stood still, eyes wide as painted dolls', mouths wider still, adding their sopranos to all the others.

Rebecca, hunched, stalking over smashed glass through fumes of many gardens, face red from not laughing, hands dripping bright drizzle on the moss-green carpet, came more slowly, tired of trying for the face—and, grunting with effort, swung her long, lovely glass knife around and up to get it into Ellie's stomach.

Ellie jumped just barely aside, and hit Rebecca with the handcuffs. —Then, it having felt so right to have done that, clenched her fist still harder through the double steel bracelet, drew back her arm, and hit Rebecca in the mouth, just as hard as she could.

Now, terrible Rebecca went tripping back to the screaming choir, the shouts of approaching men in maroon blazers, her lips bleeding to match her hands. Ellie went after her, struck out with the cuffs at the delicate knife when it struck at her—shattered it—and hitting Rebecca again, and then once more, broke teeth in her mouth and knocked her down the mezzanine stairs.

On her belly down there, kicking, writhing in smears of blood, Rebecca provided a lively pony as Ellie rode her, wrestling to get her wrists together behind her back, to get the cuffs on and locked. A number of shoppers had gathered around to watch.

Heavy footsteps, and people pushed away. A hand as big as a baseball glove came down and gathered Rebecca's wrists, suddenly frail, into its thick fingers so the cuffs could snap.

"How ya doin'?" Samuelson said. "—Talk about makin' a mess, here. . . ."

Watson and two other men in maroon blazers came trotting down the mezzanine stairs, Watson upset. "—I thought you were goin' to stay on the fuckin' fourth floor! —Jesus. You people need a doctor here!"

"Max," she said, as he helped her up off Rebecca. "—Would you call for a car to take her over to New York Hospital, let the emergency people look at her. She got hurt. I arrested her and I read her her rights—suspicion of accessory to murder. And resisting . . ."

"That resisting thing should stick, anyway," Samuelson said.

"Have you seen that mezzanine up there?" Watson said to him.

"I got your shoes," the blond young security man said, and held them out to her. The heel was broken on the left one.

"Throw them away," Ellie said. "—I don't want the damn things."

Rebecca lay at their feet, saying something softly through ruined lips, her pretty dark-green dress destroyed, her black hair, wrenched from its silver clasp, spilled like black water across her face.

"Mr. Watson—I'd like you to come with me back up to the fourth floor," Ellie said.

"You don't have any more suspects up there, do you?"

"No, I don't."

"Well, thank God for that. —Come on."

"You O.K.?" Samuelson said to her.

"I'm fine. She cut me a little."

"Looks like a lot to me. Come here . . ." He unbuttoned her blouse's soaked left sleeve, pushed the material up to expose the cut—which licked her arm with a bright red tongue of blood—took a handkerchief from the breast pocket of his jacket (dark gray wrinkled polyester in size fifty-two), tied it around Ellie's forearm and knotted it. "—You hurry up what you have to do. You're goin' to New York, like she is."

"Goddamnit," Watson said to his men, "—will you get these people movin' an' shoppin' here—and get Royceman, tell him we got a fuckin' humongous cleanup. He better get on it."

"You're bleedin' on the carpet," Watson said. They'd taken the elevator to four, were walking through a maze of slacks on racks. Ellie looked at her arm. "—Not the arm. Your feet. You must have stepped in some of that glass. . . ." Ellie looked back and saw a set of odd smudged footprints, brick-red on a sky-blue carpet. Her feet felt numb, but better than they had in her brown shoes. She supposed her panty hose were ruined.

"Goddamnit," Watson said, stooped a little, and picked Ellie up in his arms. He carried her out of the maze of slacks, and past three elderly women, each with her shopping bag, who stepped aside and stared.

"Took sick," Watson said to them.

At the carousel, he set her down. "I don't think the sucker turns off," he said, "—until the main lights go."

Ellie, soon surrounded by a casual drifting crowd, climbed up carefully onto the delicate, turning thing, eased her way between two of the small horses—their lovely riders staring past her—to the central steel post supporting it, and found a foothold on a short cross-strut. She reached up, stretching, to pull away the cornucopia's decorations, crumpled paper leaves, glass jewelry, the little pumpkins (they were plastic), some ears of Indian corn, fifty or more of the large wooden gold-painted coins. The big, curled horn was papier-mâché, painted amber-brown.

Ellie stretched higher and got her hand into it, tugged out a wad of paper leaves, some folded cardboard . . . reached deeper, and felt something smoother . . . got a grip on it, and pulled out a package the size of a hardcover book, wrapped in butcher's paper and strapping tape. She climbed down, wriggled back between the horses—getting dizzy from watching the fourth floor slowly revolve around her—then stepped off and tried to tear the package open. The strapping tape was very tough, and Mr. Watson had to take out a small pocket knife and cut it.

Then the butcher's paper folded out, and stacks of mild green money lay fat in Ellie's hands.

CHAPTER 13

Samuelson drove differently than Tommy. He drove with dash, rather than inexorably, his huge hands dancing around the wheel, sending the car darting here and there, challenging every car around him, looking for spaces, for cowards who might brake and let him through—driving as if making up for his ponderous pace afoot.

Ellie sat beside him in new sheepskin slippers—gifts from a Mr. Binder, of the store's management, and fitted over gauze bandages from the security people's first-aid kit. She wasn't feeling well. Her arm ached; her feet hurt too, now. "—I don't feel good, Max."

He looked over at her. "Hang on. Be there in a minute."

Ellie leaned forward and put her head in her hands. "I'm grown up. Now, I'm all grown up," she said. Her hands were tingling. "—I'm not going to make it," she said, and felt the car swerve right and suddenly slow.

Samuelson stopped the car, got out to a fanfare of horn blowing, ran around the back to Ellie's side, opened her door, reached in and lifted her out. She tried to get to a big steel-wire trash can, failed, and began to vomit on the sidewalk as Samuelson held her. She vomited Walsh's cinnamon rolls, her hot-dog brunch, and tried to vomit more. She retched until her stomach ached. "—Thank God for New York . . ." she tried to say, and stepped along lightly in her new slippers, Samuelson supporting her weight, to the trash can. She clutched its rim and found her balance. "—Nobody watches in the streets." And it was true that this cool and sunny day at least, very few people walking by—after a measuring glance at the two of them, at the obstructing car and angry Third Avenue—bothered to stay and see more.

Ellie clung to the trash can and retched again, trying to

bring up something more. —Then, after she got her breath, slowly began to feel better. "She scared me to death," she said. "—I was so frightened. . . ." When Ellie was able to straighten up, Samuelson let her go. She'd gotten a spatter of vomit on the front of her skirt. She limped back to the car, opened the passenger-side door, and searched in her purse for Kleenex.

"You O.K.?"

"O.K."

Samuelson looked at her for a moment, then walked around to the other side of the car, and got in.

Little butterfly bandages for the feet . . . and a slight surgical repair under local, then butterflies for the arm. Two shots—the tetanus painful.

"You're lucky," the doctor said. She was Chinese-American, fat, round-faced, and very young. "You're lucky," she said, while she was working. It was a very New York thing to say, and meant that Ellie wasn't dying. "—Your friend is very jolly," the doctor said, and Ellie didn't know what she was talking about. Later, Samuelson told her Rebecca had been in fine spirits three emergency rooms down, entertaining staff people with the tale of her arrest—using gestures when necessary while they sewed her lip, and when a dentist examined her broken teeth.

"I think she's insane."

"Could be," Samuelson said, "—but don't say it in court, or she'll be on release in a couple years, come an' look you up."

Leahy and Serrano had walked into emergency—Leahy sweating slightly in his tight blue trench coat, Serrano trotting along behind—and stuck their heads through the stiff white curtain while the doctor was doing the last butterflies on Ellie's arm.

"Hey—you finished?" Leahy said to the doctor, and bulked on in, rustling blue, to bend and kiss Ellie on the cheek. "—Only cop I can kiss," he said.

"How ya doin'?" Serrano, still behind the curtain, peeping in.

"I'm still treating," the doctor said.

"Great job, too," said Leahy, sat down on a tiny white metal stool, and said, "Kleinie—tell me about it."

A half hour later, Samuelson drove her home so Ellie could wash and change her clothes—waited outside, then drove her downtown (first to Central Booking, where Ellie made her statement, filed an arrest form, and had a short talk with a D.A.'s man named Carberry) and then to Headquarters.

"Sorry," Leahy had said, "—but you got A.R.'s to write; you got lots of stuff to fill out. D.A.'s people are goin' to want to talk to you more than just at Bookin', maybe tomorrow, if you feel O.K. But take it from me, a major case, the sooner you get that paperwork in, the better. Save us trouble all around. —And, by the way—next time you approach a serious suspect for an arrest, you have another officer right there. You understand me? Samuelson was walkin' around on Lexington waitin' for you, while you were gettin' chopped. —The store security jerk didn't make him for a cop for ten minutes."

"O.K.," Ellie said.

"—I know you didn't have a partner. But never again."

"O.K."

She and Samuelson—come from Central Booking—had then, at Headquarters, walked into an empty squad room, Ellie still in her Bloomingdale's slippers, but with clean white socks on. She'd changed to dark blue slacks, and a white shirt and white pullover sweater. There was a faint, high buzzing sound in her ears—some medication she'd been given (small, round pink pills, each marked across its center for dividing). Except for the buzzing sound, though, she was quite pleased. She felt fine, very calm. Her arm hardly hurt at all. The ache from the cuts on the soles of her feet didn't disturb her.

"Whatever that was she gave me," Ellie'd told Samuelson on their way downtown, "—it really works. I feel great." He had turned to look at her for a moment, then back to the road—they were running down the East River Drive in heavy late-afternoon traffic. Samuelson didn't talk as much as Tommy had. Didn't talk much at all. —Ellie had the feeling she amused him.

"Ambrosio," he said, as he turned off the drive, west.

"—He just got back from Pennsylvania—huntin' with some guys. I asked some people knew him a long time. Their opinion—guy's an asshole, but he'd never kill a cop."

"You think he's out of it."

"I think he's out of it."

They walked into an empty squad room, then down to the office to see if Leahy was back yet, opened the door—and found everyone in ambush. This small, jammed crowd cheered before expanding, relieved, out into the squad room, very pleased that Major Crimes had got one in the eye from a shit squad—and LaPlace then opened two bottles of Cold Duck sparkling wine, purchased out of Squad petty cash.

Anderson came down to have some wine and relay the appreciation of the brass, pleased by this headquarters contingent. "The Chief says, 'Good work,' " Anderson said.

Ellie, sitting on her desk, enthroned, her tender feet in fancy slippers propped on her chair seat, raised her paper cup and said, "To Tommy . . ." which all repeated as they drank, Serrano crossing himself before he swallowed.

While they finished the wine—and shared some potato chips Murray had provided—her colleagues asked Ellie questions as direct as those they might have asked poor Susan or fierce Rebecca, Graham asking the cleverest of these . . . asking about Sonia, about what yarn end Ellie had found, or Nardone had found to commence the unraveling. There was general humor about Audrey Birnbaum.

"O.K.," Leahy said, after a while. "—We had our fun. Let's get back to work."

"Congratulations," Anderson said, before he left to go upstairs. "—I understand, from Lieutenant Leahy, that the victim wrote a couple of letters. . . ."

"Yes," Ellie said, "—but no hard evidence for this case . . . just a hint in there. And there were some things that don't need to be read in court."

"Just the same," the Captain said, and started to say something more, but changed his mind, smiled at her, and walked away.

"*Klein . . . ?*" Leahy called her from his office door. "—You got some work in here."

"I need to go down to Personnel for a minute. . . ."

"Well . . . hurry it up."

When Ellie returned from asking Gloria Murillo, secretary to Captain Cahill of Personnel, for the home address of a certain officer and detective in good standing, Leahy had laid out seven several-page forms for Ellie on his desk.

"Close the door an' sit down," he said, "—an' let me run you through these. You're goin' to find out a nice juicy homicide case is real different from these Departmental trial things you're used to down here. A homicide case is a royal pain in the ass. Everybody's got a stake—right? The Department don't want to lose it; the D.A. don't want to lose it—and, above all, the defendants don't want to lose it. So—one mistake, one little booboo, and we're up shit creek. —Because this one, the lawyers really go to work. Understand me?"

"Yes."

"All right. First thing is, you're goin' to the arraignment—you already filled out your arrest form with the D.A.'s guy at Central Booking, right?"

"Yes—but how come I have to go to the arraignment? Why can't the officers over there handle it from my statement?"

"Ask the D.A.—don't ask me. Maybe they want to talk to you some more. . . . That's the first thing.—Second thing is, if you feel good enough' we're goin' through every form we got here. We're reviewin' arrest procedure; we're settin' up witness evaluations, reviewin' witness testimony. The whole thing. —You feel all right for this?"

"I'm fine."

"O.K. Because you don't have any team with you—an' now, you don't even have a partner knowledgeable on the case. —As it is, I'm goin' to have to send a couple people back to the store to get depositions an' everything. —That security guy saw you find that cash? He *saw* you?"

"He saw me—I think he's an ex-cop."

"What's his name?"

"Watson."

"Watson . . . I never heard of him. —But it doesn't make any difference; we're goin' to get a deposition from him, too. —Suppose he gets hit by a cab? Then, where's your case? And that wrappin' an' everything is down at Evaluation, right?"

"That's right."

"Be nice if she left her fingerprints on that. . . . So, the D.A.'s people are goin' to give you the same lecture I'm givin' you—but they're goin' to be too late, 'cause you and me are already goin' to have this shit done. An' done right."

"O.K.," Ellie said. It was probably the wine, but she wasn't feeling as well as she had driving down.

Leahy leaned back in his chair, and made it moan. "First, the A.R.—we're goin' to review Probable Cause, we're goin' to review Miranda, an' we're goin' to review Necessary Force. We slip on any of those, the case goes right down the tubes—an' the word from upstairs is, this case is goin' to be open and shut, an' shut quick."

"What have they found out about Tommy?" Ellie said.

"Were you listenin' to me? —Am I talkin' through my hat here, or what?"

"I'd just like to know." Her forearm was throbbing. It felt warm all the way down to her hand, as if her arm was in warm water.

"O.K. —What I know, they have two guys dead with Tommy, down on the tracks. White guys, in good shape. Chinos, windbreakers, regular stuff. They got nothin' on prints yet—but it's early days."

"What about ID?"

"They had ID. —Only got a checkout on one Pennsylvania driver's license, so far. A fake."

"A fake . . . ?"

"That's right. —Now, can we get back to work?" He picked up the A.R.

"O.K."

"Look . . . Klein. They're *workin'* on it. The commissioner is pushin' 'em, the mayor is pushin' 'em, the papers an' TV are pushin' 'em. . . . That is *the* case right now—O.K.?"

"I know. O.K."

"All right. Now, if we can get back to what we're doin', because we don't have all evenin' here—you feel all right?"

"I'm fine."

"O.K. By the way—somethin' I meant to mention, and I'm not sayin' you should have used a weapon on that woman. . . . However, I notice you're still carryin' in your purse."

"Right."

"Well, the summer's over. Take my advice—an' it's more than advice—an' put on your shoulder rig; wear a jacket or whatever you want to call it, an' carry your weapon that way. So it won't take you ten minutes to find it."

"All right."

"Now—can we get to work on this? Anything else we got to deal with?"

"No."

"Oh, one more thing—did Anderson talk to you about that upstate thing? —Bostwick goin' up there on the bus?"

"No."

"Well, some guy up there's got somethin' between his ears beside cow shit—got a sense of humor. He sent the commissioner a registered letter—a cleanin' bill for back-seat upholstery on a patrol car. So that's goin' back an' forth, but nobody's pissed off about it. They think it's funny. —I'm just lettin' you know."

"What happened to Bostwick?"

"Nothin'. They're feedin' him, keepin' him warm. I think they like him up there. . . . O.K. Now. What are you usin' for probable cause on this . . . ?"

"Probable Cause . . . I had two indicators for Probable Cause. . . ."

At five, Leahy put down the Summary of Physical Evidence, and asked if Ellie wanted to go home. "—How're you feelin'?"

"I'm fine, Lieutenant." And she did feel better—they'd ordered bacon-burgers in, and she'd finished hers. Leahy had had two, and a double fries. "—I feel fine; I'd like to finish these up." Ellie's feet didn't hurt much, but her arm did. The stitches or whatever they put inside the cut, into the muscle, seemed to be what was hurting . . . something they did in there.

"Medina's got watch," Leahy said. "We only got a couple more to go—maybe an hour. An' you can fill out Witness Evaluation yourself. You want to wait till tomorrow on that one?"

"No. I want to get it done. —Aren't they going to arraign tomorrow?"

"If the D.A. likes this stuff—you're damn right. Don't make any plans, tomorrow afternoon—but don't come in in the mornin'. I want you to rest. Give me a call about noon." Leahy farted, a soft, puffing sound. "—Excuse me. O.K., I'll go over this one with you; you fill out Witness Evaluation. You can stay if you want—but you don't have to. Either way, I want Medina to take you home when you're ready."

Ellie smelled, faintly, the Lieutenant's fart. Burned carrots.

"That's not necessary. . . ."

"He's goin' to do it. Period." Leahy got up, went to his office door, opened it and called, "Hector! You got watch—right?"

"Right."

"When Klein's ready to go home—you drive her up. O.K.?"

"O.K."

"It's settled," Leahy said, came back to his desk and sat down in his suffering chair. "—You don't look so hot."

At six-thirty, Medina still having some work of his own to key in, Ellie left her filled-out forms on Leahy's desk, closed the office door—making sure it was locked—went to her desk to pick up her purse, and walked out to the elevators. Downstairs, in the lobby, she saw Serrano, looking very pleased, standing by the phones with a thin young black girl—the girl laughing at something he'd said.

There was still plenty of traffic on Park Row. The evening was pleasant, cool and clear—cool enough so that Ellie wished she'd brought a jacket. She thought of walking to the corner, then down the block to wait for the light—but it seemed to stretch the walk too long for sore feet and sheepskin slippers, so she went down the Mall, through the Municipal Building's arches, waited for a lull, then jaywalked across Centre Street, watching for cars as she crossed—standing for a moment on the divider, waiting for a limousine, smoke-gray, to breeze by.

She went down into the Lexington Line entrance, feeling the warmer air well up as she descended. The soles of her feet hurt a little on the stairs, and Ellie was nervous that some of the people making faster time might jostle her sore arm in passing, so she kept close to the stair rail until she was down on the concourse. Her feet feeling better off the stairs, she took her shield wallet from her purse, showed it at the change-booth window, then walked on through the gate, and across the ramp to the tunnel. There was no one in the tunnel as she went through. She saw herself vaguely reflected in smudged yellow tile along the walls. . . . Heard people talking, the echoes of their voices. She realized she was used, in those circumstances, to hearing the sharp percussion of her heels; the slippers made no sound. Tommy had come this way just the evening before. Some of his breath must still be in the air. . . .

She left the tunnel, walked out onto the upper level, then carefully down the steep staircase, her feet hurting on the risers. At last descended to the long, long platform, the dark, vaulted space above it, she saw distant light, heard distant sound rumble into thunder as a train came surging in. Ellie closed her eyes, turned her head away, and reached up to put her forefingers in her ears—which she sometimes did anyway when she was alone, and the scream of steel on steel was too harsh to bear. Now, her eyes shut, her hearing muffled, she could think of something else than the train coming in. Of something else than Tommy on the tracks. —To help, she hummed to herself to obscure the noise of steel.

Even so, she heard the sighing doors, the chuckling of motors turning over . . . the long pause . . . the sighing again as the doors slid shut. Then the jolt, the slowly rising clearing of its throat as the tunnel rid itself of the train. The platform trembled.

She took her fingers from her ears, then opened her

eyes to find the train pulled out and gone—the passengers, too, except for two white boys. They were watching her, and drifting her way, one talking to the other. The one talking looked tough.

"Hey, lady! —What're you doin'?"

"C'mon," the other boy said to that one. This was a bigger kid. Softer. "—Leave her alone."

"Shit," the tough kid said, "I think she's a gooney." He walked over to Ellie. Glanced down at the sheepskin slippers. "—You O.K.? You were actin' a little weird. . . ." He was handsome, as so many tough boys were. He had a broad head, like a young bull's, and hair rich, dark, and oily as an animal's pelt. —The rest of him wasn't as fine. A poor diet, some other factors, had left him with a strong body, awkwardly shaped. He had handsome brown eyes, but avoiding.

"What are you—just out of the hospital . . . ? You been sick?" He glanced around the platform. There was no one but a potbellied man in a plaid suit ambling almost their way.

Ellie didn't feel like saying anything to these kids. She felt too tired to bother with them.

"C'mon, Chris . . . let's leave her alone." The bigger, softer boy.

The tough boy stepped closer to Ellie. "Listen," he said, "—you O.K.? You want to go someplace? Want to go someplace with us?"

"That'll be the day," Keneally said, strolling up beside him. "I'd be amazed she wanted to go with a faggot like you."

"C'mon, Kenny," Ellie said, sounding like the soft boy.

"Listen, fat-ass," the tough boy said, starting well—but getting no further because Keneally pushed him in the chest, the smacking percussive two-handed shove the old beat cops used to use.

The tough boy staggered back a couple of steps, and would have recovered himself if Keneally had given him the chance, but Kenny had stepped forward as the boy went back—and shoved again, the same pounding two-handed push.

"Beat it," Keneally said to the tough boy, "—or I'll bust your fuckin' head for you."

The tough boy—staggered, uncertain in the face of such surprising and confident aggression—recovered his balance and stood undecided, his face reflecting such an innocent confusion that Ellie felt sorry for him.

"We're police officers," Ellie said. "—I think you boys better get out of here." She spoke to the big, soft one. "—Is a creep like this the best you can do for a friend?"

"Move," Keneally said, his mottled face flushed rosily, and the two turned, drifted, sauntered away, their stiff backs knowing they were watched.

"I saw you come out of the buildin'," Keneally said. "—Figured you were comin' down for a look." He strolled over to the platform edge, then walked down along it. Looked back over his shoulder. "C'mon—don't be scared. There's nothin' bad to see. All cleaned up . . ."

Ellie walked after him, went to the edge and looked over. There was nothing to see she hadn't seen hundreds of times before. Gleaming tracks reaching along their dark, timbered, cinder bed. Concrete curved back up from the tracks, up and under and out to the edge of the platform. The concrete, here and on the platform, was cleaner than farther down, scrubbed almost white.

"By the way," Keneally said, "—congratulations on that Gaither thing. Pissed Maxfield off. . . ."

"Thank you. . . . What do you know about this, Kenny?"

Two young couples—Puerto Rican—had come down the stairs at the far end of the platform. Their voices echoed along the tile walls.

"I'm not on it," Keneally said, "—so I don't know all the shit they're doin'. —Oh, there's one weird thing. Those guys? They were armed."

"I know. They had knives."

"More than that. Guns. One guy had a thirty-eight; other guy had some bullshit German pistol."

"Guns."

"Right. —Try that one out. Guys are fightin' with Tommy—who never got his gun out either, by the way—they're fightin' with Tommy, who is likely kickin' the shit out of 'em—"

"And they didn't use the guns. The third man, either."

"Right. Knives, an' fist-fightin'."

"We're talking about trained men, Kenny. —Aren't we talking about trained men? Disciplined?"

Keneally sighed and shook his head. "How the hell do I know? Could be some O.C. people . . . wise guys. What I do know is, Homicide's pullin' the town apart. Everybody's after every friggin' source in town to come up with somethin'. —Nobody's doggin' it."

"I didn't say they were."

"You look like you had an attitude, people weren't doin' what they should be doin' here."

"No. I know they'll give it a good try."

"Don't forget, Tommy already took care of two of 'em. The nigger's the only guy left."

"But why . . . ? Don't you wonder what this was all about, Kenny? You're telling me three guys with guns just happened to come down here and try to kill Tommy— and beat him and use knives, when they're armed? —It doesn't make sense!"

" 'Sense,' huh? Who you kiddin'? How long you been on the cops?"

"They had to have a reason."

"Maybe they did, maybe they didn't," Keneally said, and strolled farther down the platform, looking down at the tracks. "One guy was fried. . . ."

"What?"

"Fried. —Guy must have hit the third rail, before the train hit him. They figure Tommy beat his ass for him, threw him over."

"The other man . . . ?"

"Couldn't tell.. Train probably killed him." Keneally stepped casually off the platform edge, and dropped the four feet to the tracks with a heavy grunt. He was down out of Ellie's sight for a moment, and she was afraid he'd hurt himself.

"Are you O.K.?" She trotted sore-footed over to see. . . .

"A button," Keneally said, still below, and held it up for her. —It was a button off a woman's blouse, she thought. Small, rounded, false pearl.

"It's a woman's."

"Yeah, an' probably too far down," Keneally said, and

suddenly and nearly gracefully heaved himself back up onto the platform and his feet. "—Tell you this," he said. "You go down there while you're fightin' a guy—you won't make it back up. I bet those guys wished they had four, five guys, they started waltzin' with Tommy."

"The button's nothing?" More people were on the platform, now. —Office workers who'd stayed downtown for a drink before heading home. "Dyin' of paper cancer," Tommy had said once, observing a group of Wall Street office people waiting on a corner for the light to change. Some of these people looked like that—as if they were being folded a little smaller every day.

"No, it's nothin'—but I'll turn it over to the guys anyway. Never know." He put the button in his jacket pocket, and stood, puffing slightly from his exertion, observing Ellie. "I hear you got hurt," he said. "—I saw the slippers, I figured you hurt your feet."

"Nothing bad," Ellie said. "I stepped on some glass."

"That was it . . . ? You got cut, I heard. She cut you."

"A little on the arm . . ." Ellie raised her arm, moved it up and down. "It wasn't serious."

"Umm-hmm . . ." Keneally stared at her for a moment, silent, rocking back and forth like a large toy plaid balloon on cardboard feet. Then he looked up over Ellie's head, at a fluorescent fixture. "I'm a Catholic," he said. "It isn't the time, or the place—but it's so fuckin' embarrassin' I want to get it over with."

"What is?" Ellie said. Keneally's face was red, his nose the reddest part.

"I'm a Catholic, an' I got a penance, you know." He was still staring up over her head.

Ellie didn't know what to say to that. She thought that maybe Keneally had been drinking. —He looked a little drunk.

"What is it, Kenny? —You O.K.?"

"This is somethin' I got no choice—an' I'm not sayin' it's wrong, either."

"Well," Ellie said, "—what is it?"

"What it comes down to," Keneally said, staring up at the fixture, keeping his voice low, "—is I got a penance from a priest. . . . I got to tell you I been committin' adultery with you in my heart. An' it's caused great sufferin' for my wife, and she didn't know why. —An' I'm sorry." His fat face was royal scarlet. *"Jesus Christ!"* he said, and did a sort of dance step to turn away from her, first to the right, then the left. "—That fuckin' priest must be out of his fuckin' *mind* make me do somethin' like this." There were tears of humiliation in his small blue eyes. "Fuckin' little *shit . . . !*"

He'd raised his voice then, and some people were looking at them.

"Kenny . . . come on, now. . . ." Ellie reached out to pat his shoulder, and he shrugged her hand off.

"I did what I was supposed to do—an' that's it," he said, and turned to walk away.

"Kenny—it's no big deal. —Everybody has thoughts like that!" Ellie had a terrible feeling she wouldn't be able to keep from laughing. It was like the urge to lean out over the edge of a roof—a disastrous temptation.

"Right . . ." He was on his way, and Ellie had to hurry to catch up.

"Kenny—this is hurting my feet. . . ." She thought as much as she could about her sore feet, to keep from thinking of laughing.

He slowed to a walk as they got to the stairs. "Great. —Don't you have any feelin's? What are you followin' me for? I said what I had to say"—and started climbing.

"We don't have to talk about it, if you don't want to."

"Look, I'm not *goin'* to talk about it." He glanced back at her over his shoulder. "—I said what I had to say, and I'm not goin' to talk about it, period."

"O.K." She was having trouble keeping up with him.

"O.K. Just forget I said anythin'. —I don't even know you, for Christ's sake. It's a completely private matter—it's a religious thing."

"O.K.," Ellie said. "—Slow down, you're going too fast."

"Where're you goin'?"

"Back up in Headquarters."

"O.K. I'll walk you over. You shouldn't be workin' in this kind of condition. —You should be home."

"I think you're right," Ellie said, "—but I've got one more thing to do."

They walked up out of the subway stop, across Centre

Street, and over to Headquarters, Kenny silent all the way. On the steps at Headquarters, he stopped and said, "Look out you don't get an infection with those cuts."

"They gave me a couple of shots," Ellie said. "—Tetanus, and something else."

"O.K.," Keneally said, nodded, turned and walked back down the steps. No good-bye.

Ellie was alone in the elevator going up, and laughed the first three floors—then said, out loud, "Tommy . . . you went a night too soon. You missed Kenny's confession. . . ." Then supposed she couldn't have told Tommy about it, anyway.

"Yes?"

Ellie held her badge up to the peep. "I'm a police officer, Mrs. Donaher." Gloria Murillo had given Washington Square Village as the sergeant's address, and Ellie hoped it was current, hoped the sergeant was home. She didn't feel like driving out to Suffolk. Didn't feel like driving anywhere.

She'd pretended to search for her keys downstairs, until another tenant—a thin young black man carrying an armload of books—had opened the security door. Then she'd walked in with him, and ridden up in the elevator with him to the fourth floor, where he'd gotten off—then on up to the sixth, alone.

A second lock clicked and clacked, and a pretty gray-haired woman in her fifties opened the door. Her hair was cut short, with low bangs, and brushed back clear of her ears. She would have been pretty, if she'd been thinner.

Ellie showed her shield and ID. "Mrs. Donaher? —I'm Detective Klein. I'm sorry to disturb you—"

"Oh, don't worry about that—come on in. We're used to being disturbed in this house." Grace Donaher stepped back and stood aside. "Paul! —There's a detective here to see you . . . ! You want some coffee? Would you like something to eat?"

"No, thank you."

The apartment reminded Ellie of her own—but bigger, a two-bedroom. The same flat white paint on the walls . . . same low ceilings. The entrance hall was narrow . . .

large family photographs on the walls. A young girl in some school uniform. Other photographs of her in graduation robes. College graduation, it looked like. The apartment smelled of pot roast.

Grace Donaher finished relocking the door, and Paul Donaher, in shirtsleeves, came into the hall, looked at Ellie, then looked at her again. He put his head back, just a little.

"Go on in," Mrs. Donaher said. Ellie noticed her noticing the Bloomingdale's slippers.

"I know they look weird," Ellie said. "—I stepped on some glass."

"Oh, that's terrible," Grace Donaher said, "—you shouldn't even be on your feet, should you? Go on in. . . ." She herded her husband and Ellie down the hall and into a large living room, one side all sliding glass doors looking down into the Village. It was a nice living room, with the dining area a part of it, just this side of the kitchen counter. The room had been done in blues and grays. There was a cut cake on the dining-area table. Looked like coconut.

"What do you want?" Donaher said. "—What's up?"

A girl and a young man were sitting on a couch at the other end of the room, talking—and they looked up as Ellie, Donaher, and his wife came in.

"Margie . . . Richard . . ." Mrs. Donaher said, "—this is Detective Klein. Miss Klein, my daughter and her friend, Richard . . ." The girl and young man said, "Hi . . ." Margie was the girl in the graduation pictures. She had long light-brown hair, and was as beautiful now as her mother had probably been.

"What is it?" Donaher said. "—What can I do for you?"

"Wouldn't you like some coffee . . . a piece of cake?" Mrs. Donaher said. "You should sit down, dear, get off those feet."

"No, thank you—I don't have the time. They're all right. —I just have some papers that Sergeant Donaher needs to sign, that's all."

"O.K.," Donaher said. "Come on—we'll go in the bedroom, get it done."

"It was nice meeting you," Ellie said to the Donaher girl and her boyfriend.

"Nice meeting you . . ."

"Sure you don't want some coffee?"

"Thanks, Mrs. Donaher—I really don't have the time."

Ellie followed Donaher back to the hall, and through a door on the right into a large bedroom. It was his and his wife's room; they had a queen-size bed with a dark-brown figured spread, and family pictures on the lowboy, under a wide mirror. Donaher closed the door.

"What in the fuck do you think you're doin'?" Keeping his voice low. "—Tommy's dead, and right away you're over here looking for what, some shakedown money—right?"

Ellie turned and hit him in the face with the back of her hand. It made a louder smacking sound than she expected, and both of them were still for a few moments, thinking it might have been heard in the living room. She'd hit him with her left hand, and her injured forearm started aching at once.

Donaher put his thumb and forefinger up to his nose, to pinch it, test for bleeding. He looked at his fingers to be sure.

"O.K.," he said. "—So I was out of line. O.K. Just don't try for seconds. . . ."

He hadn't done it. He wasn't frightened enough to have had any part in killing a cop. —Ellie tried, though, just to be sure.

"I came over to let you know Homicide's got your name as a possible for killing Tommy."

That scared him.

"Are you out of your fuckin' *mind?*" He was forgetting to keep his voice down, and Ellie glanced at the door to remind him. "—Are you *crazy?*" said much more softly. "You couldn't say anythin' like that! You're fuckin' crazy!"

"If you didn't do it—maybe your friends did. Maybe your thief friends didn't like Tommy giving them that trouble uptown."

"Oh, wait a minute. Wait . . . a . . . minute! There's nobody up there goin' to hurt Tommy. That's no big deal, for Christ's sake! They just move the pickup. What's the big deal? —They're not goin' to kill a cop 'cause he won't play. What do you think—there's a bunch of maniacs up there? Tommy didn't turn *me*—they know he's not goin' to turn *them*. Those guys aren't goin' to hurt Tommy!"

"Somebody hurt him."

"It wasn't *them*. Probably some fuckin' junkies . . ."

Ellie stood looking at him. —He hadn't done it, and his friends hadn't done it. . . . Her arm was hurting her worse.

Sergeant Donaher was sweating. He was handsome, with all that fine white hair. In the car, uptown that day, Ellie hadn't seen how really good-looking he was. He looked like a senior detective in a movie. He cleared his throat. "—What in God's name did you tell the Homicide guys?"

"Everything. —They'll be coming around."

"Oh, nooo . . . !" said Sergeant Donaher, his face reddening as it had in the car, uptown.

Ellie opened the door and walked out of the bedroom, pleased with imagining Donaher waiting through the next few days for that visit. At the living-room entrance, she waved to Gracie Donaher and the young couple on the couch. They were having coffee and cake.

"Bye-bye . . ."

"Oh, wait," said Mrs. Donaher, and she got up. "I'll let you out. . . . Where's Paul?"

"I think the sergeant's in the bathroom," Ellie said, and was ashamed, right after, of taking her pleasure at this decent woman's expense.

Ellie got off the island bus near the travel agency, and limped down the sidewalk to her building. The night was becoming colder than cool. A black sedan, a Chevy, was parked in front of the building entrance. —Its engine started as she came up, and a tall man in a tan raincoat got out of the back and stood in streetlight.

"Busy day . . ." said Phil Shea.

His face looked plainer every time she saw it—a long, raw, Irish face.

"Yes . . ." Ellie said. Shea seemed very relaxed, standing on the sidewalk talking to her—as if they had the whole night.

"You O.K.?"

"I'm fine . . . thanks."

"Your partner'd be proud of you," Shea said, bent and kissed her on the cheek, then kissed her mouth, turned and climbed into the car. There were three other men in the Chevy . . . stony, watchful faces. The car pulled away, and Ellie watched for Shea to look back, but he didn't.

Mayo greeted her at the apartment door with a long complaint, then marched before her down the hall. Ellie set her purse on the telephone table, and had intended to listen to her messages, but felt suddenly sick. She walked down the hall to the bedroom, called, "Will you shut up . . ." to Mayo—moaning in the kitchen, waiting for food—then limped to her bed and fell across it.

She lay there for several minutes, and slowly began to feel better. She had felt she was going to faint, or vomit again. She turned over, reached up and got a pillow under her head, and lay still a little longer.

"I shouldn't have gone downtown," she said, out loud. "—I should have stayed here when Max brought me. . . ." She turned her face to the pillow and began to cry, but didn't cry long. When she finished, she propped herself on her elbow, got a tissue from the bedside table, and blew her nose. Then she got up, and felt all right, but very tired. Her feet were hurting her, and her arm was hurting her more. —She should have hit Donaher with her right hand.

She walked out to the kitchen, took a can of Puss'n Boots Chicken n' Gravy down from the cabinet, opened it, emptied it into a saucer, and stooped to slide that under the kitchen table. Then she went out to the hall to listen to her messages.

There was a short one from Clara: "*—Hello, sweetheart. I'm fine and getting ready to get out of here. I miss the hell out of you, and will be sorry to leave none of the windy city except for some of its architecture—pure Howard Roark. See you soonest, your new friend, old lover—Clara.*"

Ellie didn't know who Howard Roark was—assumed he was modern. Clara hadn't heard about Tommy.

There was a longer message from Mary Gands. The engagement was definitely on, Joseph wasn't drinking at all—only a glass of wine at dinner—and why hadn't Ellie called her?

Charlie Corsaro had called, and had had to call back a second time for space on the tape to complete his message. *"Hi, El—I know this thing has hit you real hard, too. You an' Tommy were close. . . . I'm sorry for the pain you must be sufferin'. Doctor's put Connie to bed for a day or two. She's O.K. but she just stopped talkin' much. Truth is, I think it took a while to really hit her. Mrs. Donatto and Mrs. Evans are comin' in, takin' care of Marie. I don't think Marie realizes exactly what happened, and that's a blessing. Requiem Mass is set for day after tomorrow, Sunday, at St. Gregory's, two o'clock. You come a little early—O.K.? You're sittin' with the family. Love, Charlie."*

Ellie turned off the machine, listened to it rewind, then walked out to the living room. It was stuffy, smelled faintly of paint and thinner. She turned on the floor lamp, then went to open the windows wider, welcome in some of the cold night air. From the second window, near the far corner of the room, she could see the lights of the cars on the FDR Drive across the river—running along like bright beads of mercury. At this distance, whispering.

She tilted the shade of the floor lamp so its light fell directly on the painting—and stood for a few moments, trying to look at it like a stranger.

Ellie was relieved to see it wasn't too bad—especially for wet in wet. It was a good painting . . . not as pretty, maybe, as it should have been. The blossoms—bright yellow, dull orange, traces of brown—looked like blossoms . . . and seemed to burn like small fires in their clump of greenery. But it wasn't very pretty. Everything was off to the right a little—the leaves, the stems and blossoms leaning that way. If there'd been more of a wind blowing, it would be perfect.

Before she thought about it anymore, and got worried, Ellie picked up her tube of viridian from the newspaper on the coffee table, squeezed some onto her palette, a smaller blob of black beside that, took a clean brush, shook two drops of copal medium onto the paints, mixed them—then leaned over the picture and painted four curled leaves against the white canvas to the right of her bending flowers. —Three of the leaves flying, scattering away in the wind . . . one fluttering, its painted edges smeared, about to go. . . .

It worked pretty well.

Ellie walked around the couch to look at the picture from farther away.

It looked good.

She walked back, and touched the picture lightly, just with one finger on the edge of the biggest blossom. —Almost dry. Dry enough to carry, tomorrow, if she was careful. . . . She'd be able to put a coat of retouch over it, take it over in the morning. Ellie squeezed another very small dab of black onto the palette, dipped the brush, and signed the picture in the lower right corner. *Klein.*

She cleaned the brush in the kitchen, then went to the hall phone, looked up St. Christopher's number in her address book, and called. After several rings, a woman answered (elderly, perhaps Edna) and Ellie identified herself, and asked to speak with Sonia Gaither. There was a thoughtful pause at the other end of the line, then considerable clicking as the call was transferred to the dorm, and several more rings before a young girl answered the phone, then shouted for Sonia.

"Hello . . . ?"

"It's Ellie, Sonia. Officer Klein. Sorry to call so late."

"Oh . . . hello."

"I'm just calling to let you know we have the people who . . . did that to your mom, your mother. There were two of them."

"Two of them? —You got them . . . ?"

"Yes. They were arrested today. —Two women . . . Rebecca Platt and Susan Margolies. They robbed her. —They did it for money. . . ."

"But I met Mrs. Margolies. . . ." Sonia's voice had begun to wobble like a child's.

"I know . . . I know. Sweetheart, sometimes decent people do indecent things. I think Dr. Margolies is sick. The other lady, too, I think, in a different kind of way."

"That's why they hurt her . . . so much?"

"Yes. Probably the other lady did that. —But they won't hurt anybody else. They're in jail."

"Are they going to put them in the electric chair?"

"No. They'll lock them up until they're very old. —Don't spend a lot of time thinking about them, Sonia. They're not worth your spending a lot of time on them. I'm sure your mother would say you have better things to think about than that."

"I guess so. . . ."

"I'll come up in a day or two, if you want me to. I'll come see you, and tell you anything you want to know. —And I'll bring the letters, too."

"Nobody else read them?"

"Nobody else read them."

"I guess you think she was really weird . . . all that stuff she wrote about."

"No, I don't."

"Can you come up Sunday . . . ?"

"No, not Sunday. I have to go to a funeral. —What about Wednesday? You have classes all afternoon?"

"No. Wednesday'd be O.K. —Two o'clock is my last class. Latin."

"O.K. —Main building at three? We can go for a drive and have dinner, if it's all right with the people up there."

"Oh, it'll be O.K."

"All right. Three o'clock, Wednesday. —You take care, sweetheart."

"Ms. Klein—"

"Ellie."

"Ellie. —Did you catch them?"

"My partner and I caught them."

"Well . . . see you on Wednesday."

"Bye-bye . . ."

"Bye-bye."

Ellie put the receiver down, went into the bedroom, took off the sheepskin slippers and white socks, undressed, and walked into the bathroom, touching her tender breasts, gently stroking them. The doctor had said no showers, no baths for a day or two so as not to wet the butterfly bandages.

She went to the sink, took a towel from the rack and spread it on the carpeting; then—standing on that—turned the water on, soaped her washcloth, wrung it out a little, and began to wash—soaping her face, then rinsing the cloth in hot water and wiping the soap away. She rinsed her face a second time, then soaped and rinsed her throat and neck, her shoulders, armpits, and breasts. She was careful not to wet the bandage on her left arm. She washed her stomach, her groin—reached around to do her back and down between her buttocks—then put her right foot up on the side of the tub, washed her leg and foot, then did the same with her left, not wetting the bottoms of her feet. —When she finished, she took a towel from the rack, dried herself, then picked the other towel up off the floor and draped them both over the shower-curtain rod.

Ellie stood looking at herself in the sink mirror, took a razor from the soap dish, and lifted her right arm so she could shave that armpit. Then she lifted her left, and did that one. —Her left arm ached, from holding it up.

Still watching herself, thinking about nothing, she let her hair down, and brushed it out, moving her lips, counting the strokes. When she'd done enough of that, Ellie opened the cabinet, took out her Ponds, and stroked the cream lightly into her face, taking care to trace the faint lines around her mouth.

She turned off the bathroom light, walked naked out to the living room to turn that light off. —The picture looked very good. It wasn't wonderful—but it was a good painting. Ellie stood looking at it for a few moments, then went back down the hall for her purse, took out one of the small pink pills the Chinese doctor had given her, went to the kitchen and took it with two glasses of water. Coming back, she picked up Mayo at the kitchen door, and carried him with her into the bedroom.

She dreamed of something green, then didn't dream at all for a while. Almost awake then, Ellie felt Mayo slide from underneath her hand, her sore arm outstretched as she lay on her stomach. She supposed he was going hunting. There was a cricket in the kitchen; she heard it after Mayo left her, and its dry music sent her deeper into sleep.

Rebecca and she were walking along the boardwalk at Coney Island. Rebecca was old, but still nice-looking. Ellie supposed she must be old, too, though she didn't feel it. They'd been talking about Rebecca being in prison. "—It could have been worse," Rebecca said. "I got my marketing B.A. . . . correspondence. . . ."

Later, Ellie was alone, and looking for saltwater taffy. She asked somebody, a man with a small white dog, and he pointed to Tommy, who was sitting on a bench out on the boardwalk in the sun, looking at the ocean. Tommy was wearing his summer suit, the light blue seersucker. When Ellie walked over, he turned and looked up at her, then nodded to the sea. "—Take a look at that," he said.

In the morning, after nine, Ellie woke to the thrum of traffic across the river. She lay in bed for a few minutes, remembering that Tommy was dead . . . deciding what she'd have for breakfast. . . . Then she got up, went to the bathroom—her feet hardly sore at all—and, while she was sitting on the toilet, tested her injured arm, waving it as if she were conducting an orchestra, then making a muscle. The bandaged place was still sore, but the arm didn't ache. It didn't hurt when she clenched her fist.

She went out to the living room in her bathrobe, and found Mayo lying along a windowsill, his soft brown fur ruffled up against the screen. He was gazing down the right angle of mowed grass that opened onto the spaces of the river. The morning sun was bathing the lawn bright green—the hurricane fence below, silver white—the width of the river beyond, oiled chain mail.

Ellie made herself scrambled eggs and cinnamon toast, and had a cup of Russian Caravan tea to go with them. Then she sat at the kitchen table with her makeup kit, applied a light foundation, very light blue mascara and darker blue eyeliner, and tea-rose lipstick.

She went back to the bedroom, put on her bra and panties, dressed in dark brown wool slacks, a coffee blouse, her white running shoes and white socks. She went out to the hall, took the Smith & Wesson from her purse, brought it back to the bedroom and put it on the bed while she got into the shoulder-holster harness. The harness had two wide fitted loops for her shoulders—the left one supporting, fairly low, the small holster the Smith required—a narrow elastic strap running across her back to hold both loops firmly on, and another strap descending from the holster on the left to her belt, to hold that gun-weighted loop in place.

Ellie put her left arm carefully through its loop, wrestled her right arm through the other more casually, shrugged to settle the elastic comfortably across her back, then reached down to her left side to snap the retaining strap to her belt. She bent over the bed, picked up the pretty little pistol, and tucked it away well under the curve of her left breast.

The holster rig—with her bra—made for considerable harness, and Ellie had never liked it.

She went to the bathroom, brushed her teeth, then came out to her closet, picked an oversized, cotton-knit cardigan sweater-jacket—dark brown—pulled it on, then went to the dresser to do her hair, twisting it up in back into a French knot, pushing a tortoise-shell keeper through it. The sweater had a collar, but Ellie lifted her blouse's collar out and over it, and that looked better.

The tram car wasn't crowded, the rush hour long spent. Ellie stood by the window looking upriver . . . up strait, the painting, wrapped in newspaper, resting at her feet, Far below, several small boats were churning down toward the harbor, and farther from the Manhattan bank, a sailing boat, white and blue, carved a long curve through gray water. By standing closer to the plexiglass, Ellie could look back and see her apartment building on the island . . . her apartment's tiny windows on the ground floor. Mayo might be lying on his windowsill, watching the sailing boat go breezing by. Watching . . . thinking nothing of it.

The tram-car reeled down to Manhattan; the building roofs came rising on the left.

"Oh . . . that's pretty. That's so pretty!" Audrey Birnbaum stared at the painting as Ellie held it up for her to see. "—Aren't they pretty, Toddy . . .?" Ellie saw she had trouble focusing her eyes; dull black, no longer glossy even in morning light, their gaze drifting away to glance here or there as if Audrey were frightened of being surprised by some intrusion. She looked smaller than she had before.

"They're bright as sunshine," Audrey said, and closed her eyes. "Bright as sunshine . . ." Ellie put the picture down against her chair.

"It's beautiful work. . . ." Todd Birnbaum said. He was wearing a dark blue three-piece suit, white shirt, maroon tie, and black loafers. He looked older than he had when Ellie and Nardone had seen him at his office. Older by the day. "Thank you very much, Ms. Klein. —Where would you like it hung?"

"It's Audrey's—it's up to her."

"Over there. Where that chair is . . ." A brown stick rose from the sheet to point.

"We have those adhesive-tape things. . . ." Birnbaum said.

"Three of those ought to hold it," Ellie said. "—The frame's already got wire across the back to hang it from. It's still drying, so you'll have to handle it gently. It'll need a coat of finish varnish in a few months. . . ." Ellie was sorry she'd mentioned months.

"Toddy . . . you be sure to get that done. They're so pretty. . . ."

"I'll come and do it," Ellie said.

"I won't be here, darlin'. —You go to Toddy's, and put that . . . varnish . . . on. Toddy's goin' to hang this paintin' right over the piano in our livin' room."

Birnbaum had nothing to say.

Ellie sat and visited with them, but not for long. This morning, there didn't seem much of Audrey left—not enough for two people to talk with. —They'd heard about Rebecca and Susan Margolies; it was in the morning papers . . . on TV. Birnbaum was upset.

"It isn't just hard to believe—it's impossible to believe. I've known Susan a hell of a long time . . . too long not to get to know her very well. I don't think she *could* kill anybody—if you'll excuse me for saying so—circumstantial evidence or not."

"Shit, darlin'—lots of people goin' to kill somebody if

there's money comin', an' they can get away with it. That bitch. 'Doctor' Margolies, my sad ass . . ." The brown skull turned, its eyes slowly opened to observe them, puzzled, as if it had almost forgotten why they were there. "Poor Sally . . ." said the skull, showing fine teeth and ashy gums. "—Any person loved livin', it was her. Killed by those two motherfuckers for her money. . . ."

A few minutes later, Ellie kissed Audrey, said good-bye, and was thanked for "My sunny flowers." "—You can see that wind," Audrey said, "—blowin' them away. . . ."

Birnbaum came out into the corridor with Ellie, walked with her to the elevators, and thanked her again. "—Especially just for coming to see her," he said. "You know, she's very lonely all day, with no visitors. The nurses say they've found her crying, sometimes, and then she gets very upset and says if they touch her tears, they'll die. —They've told her that isn't so, but she doesn't believe them."

"I'll come over when I can," Ellie said.

"She's been terribly alone, all her life," Birnbaum said, "—except for people who wanted to have sex with her. She's had to live on the moon, all alone . . . and now this."

"Perhaps they'll be able to pull her out of it. . . ."

"Not now," Birnbaum said. "—After I met her, you know, we both lived on the moon. . . ."

CHAPTER 14

The administrator at the Ninety-sixth Street methadone clinic was a pretty woman, with short beautifully cut light brown hair, gray eyes, and dark down along her forearms. She'd reminded Ellie of Clara—and when she spoke, very much.

"Paula Dillon," she'd said when she shook Ellie's hand, and thereafter, in conversation, had smiled and looked at Ellie in a way that made her uncomfortable. Ellie thought Paula might be one of Clara's friends, or know someone who was, or who Clara might have talked to. —Thought the woman might be imagining things about her. In consequence, Ellie grew gruff, got directly to the point, and was worried about blushing when the woman, still smiling, at her ease in a small, cluttered office, looked at her too directly.

Paula Dillon, it turned out at last, did know someone Ellie knew. She knew Lennie Spears, and had worked for him several years before, in ATDC. She had heard of Ellie's old encounter with the Puerto Rican mother who burned out devils.

In any case, possibly because she enjoyed Ellie's company, her shyness . . . perhaps enjoying her long, white throat, Dr. Dillon was cooperative, believed the tale of Major Crimes needing some further information from the case files on Maurice and Clayton Garrison, made notes of Ellie's shield-number and ID, and went to get the files herself, possibly so that Ellie might watch her as she rose, passed near in pearl-gray silk, and walked away. Dr. Dillon had a soft, round ass, and long, strong legs.

She'd brought the file folders back, laid them out on a table against the office's left-hand wall—a TV and VCR took up the table's other half—sat at her desk, and watched Ellie, bending, take her notes.

There were medical records, dosages, initial authorizations—many of those—and copies, additions, and comments. Physicians' forms, enables, dosage recommendations, psychological profiles and psychological profiles updated. Additional comments. Referrals and recommended actions. Personal data and family data and family history. Addresses—many of those over the four years attendance—the brothers occasionally at the same address, usually not. Relatives' addresses—a number of these as well, and, occasionally, phone numbers.

Ellie pretended to jot notes as she read along, turning pages, but really only wrote down two: the addresses of the Garrison brothers' grandmother and aunt. She'd already written the grandmother's when she saw the stamped *DEC'D.* at the end of the paragraph. —The aunt, apparently, was still alive.

Ellie had thanked Paula Dillon for her cooperation, shaken her hand again, received a smile as warm as summer, and left.

At the corner, a block west, she found a working phone, and called Leahy.

"You restin'?"

"Yes, I am. I went out for a walk. . . ."

"Well, you got three, four more hours to rest—then go on down to court. Arraignment's goin' to be at four o'clock, room nineteen."

"Both together?"

"You got it . . . and the D.A.'s people are goin' to want to talk to you after that. They'll bullshit with you a couple, three hours, just goin' over what we already did. O.K.?"

"O.K."

"Now—you sure you feel all right? —How're those injuries?"

"Fine. —They're not bothering me."

"Well, they shouldn't bother you—'cause you're a very successful cop. You an' Tommy. —They got preliminary prints off that Bloomingdale's cash—Anderson put the squeeze on 'em to hurry it up."

"What was it . . . ?"

"Platt's prints—and the Gaither woman's. Not many, either one—but enough. First time prints did us any good in a long time. . . ."

"That's a relief."

"That's right. Before now, you had a case. —Now, you got an open-an'-shut. Nice work."

"Four o'clock?"

"Four o'clock. Room nineteen."

The taxi driver was from Peru. He was very small, large-headed, and a mild purple color—with the blackest hair Ellie had ever seen. It lay on his head like night.

"Harlem—I don' go."

"Police . . . *policía,*" Ellie said, and presented her shield. "—Yes, you do."

Mrs. Perry lived in the building on the corner of 115th Street and Frederick Douglas, and the cab driver drove Ellie there, and let her out between two parked cars, after muttering in some language—not Spanish—all the way uptown.

"Wait for me," Ellie said, gave him five dollars, and got out, "—and remember I've got your name and number, you little shit."

She walked to the building stoop, heard the car's transmission shift behind her, and turned to see it pulling away. "—So much for the majesty of the law," she said to a small black boy—five or six years old, who sat on the top step of the stoop, staring at her. He wore a clean T-shirt, ironed jeans, and brown running shoes with white rabbits on them. A number of other older black boys and girls (all of whom should have been in school) were playing some stickball game farther down the sunny street—a few jumping, running, scattering between the two borders of parked cars—but most occupied in game commentary, sitting on car hoods. A few of the bigger boys had turned to watch her.

Ellie walked up the last two steps, through the glass-paneled door (several panels broken, one kicked out entirely) and on into the building's entrance hall—dark, high-ceilinged . . . mustard-yellow plaster walls cracked, marked, the wood flooring splintered, settled, and worn to slight, winding narrow ridges by more than a hundred years of passage.

Ellie walked up the stairs, into a strong smell of frying pork. Pork and something else. Some spice . . . cardamom, or curry. It smelled good.

The stairs were narrow—too narrow for two people abreast—the risers worn in shallow curves, the fat railing chipped and rutted by whittling. The cooking was being done on the second floor; Ellie heard a number of people talking behind the door of 2-D. People laughing. —She thought the cooking was being done in there.

As she started up the staircase to the third, Ellie heard down the well the building's door slam shut below, hasty steps crowding down the hall, then drumming up the stairs. She climbed faster—hurting her feet—reached the landing, and stood against the wall as three large teenage boys rounded the banister post and ran up the stairs to her and past her—one, a tall, grinning mahogany boy with a rattling, beaded hairdo, saying "*Boo . . . !*" to her as they hustled by.

It didn't seem that any cooking was being done behind the door of Three C. Ellie pushed the doorbell, but it had been painted over long ago. Mud-brown . . . oxblood. It was hard to tell. —She knocked.

"What do you want?" The woman was in her late thirties, dark honey-brown, sharp-faced, big-bodied in jeans and white blouse, her hair shaped and smoothed to leave a long, neat center part. She'd left the chain on the door—stared out through the gap.

"I'm a police officer," Ellie said, took out her ID.

"Shit . . ." The woman closed the door, took the chain off, then opened it wide. "You want to come in, right?" She stood aside, and Ellie walked past her into the apartment. The living room was small, painted white, the two windows white-curtained. —Mrs. Perry had tried to make a small space bigger. There was a furniture suite—two armchairs and a couch, cream-colored and covered with heavy plastic.

"You takin' inventory?" the woman said, "—or you got somethin' to say?" She closed the door and locked it.

"I need to sit down, for a start. —O.K.?"

"Go right ahead."

Ellie sat in the nearest armchair, and Mrs. Perry sat down heavily on her couch, making the plastic squeak.

"I already had a visit from you people, last evenin'," she said. "They wanted to know where my nephews are. —That's what you want to know, isn't it?"

"That's what I want to know. —My name is Klein . . . Eleanor Klein."

"Well, my name is Lula Perry, and I don't have the slightest idea where those boys are. —I'm tellin' you that; I told the other cops that, and I would like not to have to keep sayin' it."

"There is something I'd like to ask you, though."

"Umm-hmm . . ."

"Did they tell you why they wanted to know about Clayton and Maurice?"

"Oh, sure . . . sure they did! Said they wanted them for witnesses to some junkie gettin' killed. Said there wasn't no charges against those boys at all. . . . An' I got to tell you, I believed that shit right away—a bunch of nasty old cops comin' up here to find those boys, just so they can witness to some no-name junkie gettin' killed? —Now, I work hard all week, Miss Whatever, filin' a ton of paper that cuts my fingers . . . an' I would really appreciate you tellin' me *your* lie, an' then gettin' on your horse an' gettin' out of here, so *I* can get out of here an' be with my friends."

"Almost two weeks ago," Ellie said, "a detective named Classman, and his mother, were killed in their apartment. Classman shot one of the people, wounded him . . . killed him . . . we don't know. It looked like a junkie killing . . . came in to rob the place."

"I read about that," Mrs. Perry said, "—and I'm sorry and so what? Unless you're sayin' it was my nephews did that crime? An' if you're sayin' that—you got your head right up your ass. Those boys don't hurt anybody!"

"A day later," Ellie said, "a black man, a big man who wore glasses, drove up to the methadone clinic while Maurice and Clayton were standing outside. Some men with him dropped him off around the corner. But Clayton happened to see the other men—they were white, and they looked like cops, so when the big black guy approached them to deal . . . they said no. —And it was lucky they did, too, because the man went on to talk to a Puerto Rican named Jesús Chávez—took him around the corner to that car, drove him up to the Bronx, took him into a burned-out building up there, and shot him to make it look like that dead cop had done it—so that would look like a junkie killing and nothing else. Then, he and his friends threw Jesús off the roof."

Mrs. Perry looked at her watch.

"My partner went over to the clinic, after that. He couldn't catch Clayton—"

A smile from Mrs. Perry.

"—but Maurice told him what they'd seen. And, night before last, my partner was murdered in the subway by three men. Two white . . . one black."

"I saw that on the TV . . . an' you're sayin' that's what that was all about?" Mrs. Perry said. "Well . . . you sure do lie better than those other ones."

"Don't call me a liar."

Mrs. Perry got up off her couch. "I got to go. —You sayin' those people are after my nephews? That what you're tellin' me?"

Ellie got up, too. "Two of them are dead. My partner killed them. The third one isn't. I don't know if your nephews are in bad trouble, or not. —But they've seen that third man's face."

"I got to go—I got people waitin' for me." Mrs. Perry walked out of the living room, then came back carrying a white soft-leather purse. "I don't know about Clayton," she said. "—That fool could be in Alabama. . . ." She opened the front door, and motioned Ellie through. "But Maurice is workin' drivin' a truck over in Vineland, New Jersey. He's workin' for a farmer over there, man I used to know. —Name's DiNunzio. Michael DiNunzio."

Out in the hall, Mrs. Perry double-locked her door. "An' if you lied to me, to get those boys"—she gave Ellie a cold look—"I hope you die of a cancer."

Downstairs, Mrs. Perry nodded an unfriendly good-bye, and walked away on 115th Street toward Adam Clayton Powell. Ellie went the other way, to Morningside, to walk down to Cathedral Parkway for the bus. Taxis were getting expensive.

Morningside Park still climbed green up its long hill, only beginning to be touched by autumn. The leaves at the tops of the trees showed lighter and lighter, the highest leaves going brown to gold among the others in long loose falls across the green. Ellie exercised her hurt arm as she walked along, swinging it, holding it up and out, feeling a small ache, a slight tug where the bandage was. A black couple was walking ahead of her, with two little girls—four or five years old—tagging along in identical red parkas (too warm for the day), and venturing in their parents' wakes small excursions into the shrubbery, onto the narrow, worn, littered lawns.

There wasn't time to drive over to Vineland today. —The arraignment, and D.A.'s people. She could drive out tomorrow. Might call first . . .

"Well, Tommy," she said aloud, walking along, watching the little girls ahead of her, ". . . you're gone." She could see the top of the cathedral above the small park's trees. They were building on that again, supposedly . . . stone cutters.

"Hey . . . !"

Ellie looked right, up into the park, but didn't see anybody.

"Hey! What the fuck's the matter with you?"

She turned to look behind her, and saw a car drifting slowly along the curb four or five yards back—a dull blue Plymouth sedan. A big man in his forties, unpleasant-looking, mustached, had his head out the front passenger-side window, staring at her. He was wearing a light blue sports coat.

"Are you deaf—or what?"

A cop.

Ellie stopped walking as the car pulled alongside and stopped.

The mustached cop was staring up at her as if she'd insulted him. He turned to the driver, and Ellie heard him say, "—You believe this?"

The car's rear door opened, and a tall, bald man in his late fifties got out. He was wearing a baggy gray suit, and had the drawn, humorless, considering face of certain Irish priests. Ellie recognized him from the Chávez scene, up in the Bronx.

"Come here," the bald man said to Ellie.

She took a step toward him—then, as if she'd felt it, remembered Tommy's hand on her arm when Ambrosio had ordered her to him. "—Where you goin'?" Tommy had said. She stood still.

The bald man was very intelligent, very quick; he didn't call to her again, order her to him a second time. He walked on over as if he'd never noticed any disobedience, had never had an order disobeyed.

"I'm Captain Connors," he said. "—I'm commanding an M.C. and Homicide team for assigned cases . . . the Nardone thing." Connors had a deep, soft, expressive voice, and a rough old-fashioned New York accent. Friends of Ellie's father had talked that way.

"I think I saw you up in the Bronx, Captain."

"Yes, you did . . . yes, you did." He put a long-fingered hand on Ellie's shoulder, and turned her to walk beside him, strolling slowly down the sidewalk. The Plymouth drifted along behind them. "I should tell you," Captain Connors said, "—that I've had for many years a soft spot for that Italian wild man we've lost."

"Yes . . ."

"To lose a partner is bad enough. . . . To lose an absolutely honest police officer is infinitely worse." He turned his head, looked down a long, long nose at Ellie as they walked. —She noticed he'd cut himself shaving—a slight nick in the soft, thin wattles at his throat. "—My people were surveilling this Perry woman. I felt her nephews might come to visit, believing themselves to be in trouble. . . . Young blacks are often raised by grandmothers . . . aunts. —And you got her address from the clinic files? I suppose you lied to them." They had walked almost to Cathedral Parkway when Connors, precise as a soldier, executed a to-the-rear march—Ellie turning the wrong way, stepping to catch up—and they strolled back the way they'd come. They passed the Plymouth, and the car stopped, shifted, then slowly began to back along the curb, keeping place, as it had, just behind them.

"These officers saw you go into the building—and one of them recognized you, and called me," Connors said. "Ordinarily, of course, in a major case—where a police officer had stepped so far out of line as to interfere in an ongoing investigation . . . to trouble a potential informant, whether from injured pride, or personal feelings of some sort—ordinarily I would have that officer up on Departmental charges. I'd see any person like that broken, and, if possible, dismissed." His hand rested light as linen on Ellie's shoulder.

She said nothing. Heard the car's engine whine softly behind them.

"In your case, I'm inclined to make allowances—for two reasons. First, you're a woman, and you've been shocked by the loss of a friend and partner. Second, you've been recently injured making an arrest. Where did she say those boys are . . . ?"

Ellie started to answer, and almost did, but her mouth seemed to seal itself—as if, open, its tongue would be endangered.

"Are they still in town . . . ?"

Several more steps.

"Why aren't you answering me, Eleanor?"

Ellie felt close to tears . . . so stupid. It was all she needed—to start crying in front of this man. "—Because I think it could have been cops. And they're not going to get away with it." Her mouth had opened for that.

Connors stopped walking. He looked down at her for a few moments, and said nothing. Then he started walking again, and said, "—Now, what in the world makes you think that?"

"Because Classman and Tommy were killed by disciplined men."

"But all police officers are fingerprinted—and no records found of those prints by us—or the FBI."

"Bullshit," Ellie said, surprising herself, "—men like that always have their prints taken, sometime—in the service, or by the cops, or *on* the cops. If you don't know that—then what the fuck do you know?" She turned away from under Connors' hand, and started walking toward Cathedral Parkway. She didn't look back.

"You're in very serious trouble," Connors called after her, raising his voice only slightly. "And that's a shame. . . ."

Ellie walked down to Cathedral Parkway, across it, then down the hill to the bus stop. Her heart was thumping, and she felt a little short of breath, but otherwise O.K. —I can always paint, she thought. I can go to a little town up in New Hampshire, and get a job as a waitress, or maybe a town constable . . . and I can paint. She imagined herself—as she waited for the bus—a different person, divorced from the New York City Police Department, no longer wife to that swarthy, dangerous, coarse society that comfortably contained both thieving brutes like Charley Ambrosio, and the righteous Captain Connors, a blue priest.

She waited at the stop on the lower edge of Harlem, as any white person might stand at the border of another, darker country, and didn't envy white and Hispanic policemen their patrols up there. Perpetual strangers, all of them, no matter that a few, she'd heard, loved black women, and married them, and lived buried in those blocks; it wouldn't be their country. —In that country, she supposed, a policeman had better be either brute or priest. Reason would have little place.

The bus came, and Ellie climbed aboard, showed her shield, then went to the first empty double seat on the left, and sat by the window to watch the park go by. The seat just behind her—she'd seen them before she sat down—was occupied by a beautifully dressed woman in a beige suede suit, sitting with her three- or four-year-old son. Mother and son had gleaming hair, so light a gold as to be nearly silver. Something dreadful had happened to the woman's face—a traffic accident (Ellie thought of her trotting deaths, pacing the thruways) or perhaps a fire. —Or a disease that had destroyed her bones. This tall, slender lady, a wife, and almost certainly rich, had the round monstrous face of an owl, the nose beak the only protrusion out of a deep, scooped, boneless dish of skin—the eyes, very separate, dark, round, liquid. Ellie had seen this face that wasn't—had looked away much too fast, she felt sure, for the woman to have caught her staring, then had taken her seat before them, under the owl's gaze, if the owl that had been a woman chose to do it. —Braver than I am, Ellie thought. —Braver even than Tommy, to have combed out, spun out her splendid hair, to have dressed in her beautiful suit, called her handsome little son downstairs, and gone for a ride on the Fifth Avenue bus, to do some shopping. —Which bus, bearing Ellie, this brave woman and her boy, sighed, waddled, and farted its way along the top of the park, then made the sweeping turn downtown at Frawley Circle, and heaved through traffic a mile down Fifth.

At Eighty-third, Ellie got up, went to the rear door without looking at the woman and her son, and got off. She walked down to the Metropolitan Museum, climbed the steps to its front doors, went in, and found phones on the right. New Jersey Information showed several DiNunzios in Vineland, but only one DiNunzio Produce. Ellie called that number, and a young woman answered, "Garden Delights . . ."

"Sorry to trouble you, but I'm a friend of Maurice Garrison's. I heard he was working there. . . ."

"Oh, that's all right," the young woman said. "Maurice isn't here, though. He's up in Tuxedo, delivering."

"Well, it's nothing important. Is he going to be back this afternoon . . . ?"

"More like tonight, late," the young woman said. "He may just come in Saturday morning."

"Do me a favor . . . don't tell him I called. —O.K.? We're old friends. I thought I'd drive over and surprise him."

"All right. Sure . . . I won't tell him."

"I appreciate it. Thanks a lot."

"O.K."

"Bye-bye . . ."

There was a chance, of course, that Mrs. Perry had already had second thoughts, and made a call of her own. —A chance, then, he'd decide never to come back from Tuxedo. But if he did, and came in on Saturday, Ellie saw no problem driving out there early enough—to be there waiting for him. The problem was—what then? She'd have no standing in New Jersey. No paper to bring any material witness in. . . .

She walked through a scattered crowd across the great, airy, marble space, past the central information desk to the ticket booths, lined up, and when it came her turn, gave the girl a dollar for a small tin button, colored pumpkin. Then she walked back into the hall, turned right, past a huge vase of leopard-spot lilies, then a gift shop, on through a large rectangular room where the heads of Roman emperors—variously noble, dopey, snarling like vicious dogs—were set on their small columns

. . . and through that down a long, wide corridor, lined on either side with early Greek statuary, all the figures bearing elaborately braided hairdos and slight smiles. Ellie thought they'd had that smile carved into them so people would think these lifelike things friendly, not awful and full of curses. In the old days, she'd read, the statues had been painted . . . skin sun-browned—lacquered, maybe, for the gloss of sweat and oil. Hair, beards painted black or reddish brown, depending on the tribe. And the eyes . . . pitch-bitumen, cochineal, beetle-wing blue. The smile faintly lipsticked. Breechclouts, yellow. Sandals, leather-brown.

Hercules, in the other room, would wear his lion hide tinted tawny. Light olive-brown, clear as tea, for his club.

Ellie waited in line at the cafeteria, regretting the lost fountain pool, its water dancers—selected a tuna salad, milk (for calcium to keep her from getting a hump), and a piece of cheese cake for the hell of it. She took her tray—an expensive lunch, for not being much—and sat along the west side, at a table for two beside the railing for the absent pool.

Ellie sat and rested . . . had a long lunch. Sat and watched the people walking by. She thought of talking to Leahy before Connors called Anderson, as she assumed he would. —Perhaps they'd let her go to New Jersey . . . arrange extradition for Maurice, if he didn't want to come back with her. . . .

And maybe pigs could fly, too—if they lost weight, and grew wings. . . . *You're in serious trouble.* Ellie supposed she was. Tommy had thought a lot of Connors—thought he was very clever. . . .

When she finished her cheese cake, Ellie got up and went to get a cup of coffee. Her feet didn't hurt at all. Her arm was still a little bit stiff, right there where she was cut. —But not on the surface. Underneath. It felt as though right under there, down in the muscle, was where it was stiff. She hoped that Chinese doctor hadn't made a mistake, and left her with that for the rest of her life. . . .

It was a luxury to have the whole afternoon off when it wasn't scheduled . . . and knowing the rest of the Squad was working, keying in reports, or out driving some jerk in from the airport, or talking to consulate people, or

U.N. people, or out talking to dealers or sharks or bookmakers, trying to make a case of negligence against some Internal guy. —It would be so much more pleasant to work for the museum . . . restoring, or something. Just a regular job amid all this strenuous and complete art. No gallery bullshit. —Most of this had been through all that centuries and centuries ago . . . all the begging, and scheming and stealing. The years had washed most of that away, as the sea scrubbed a beach, and left above tide a perfect blue-green dish, a sword blade fine as ice, a wrought-iron wall lacy as falling water.

Quietly working, doing her job (and staying out of the office politics), liked by the people here, loved by a shy, handsome man—a scholar, curator of Middle Eastern art. Settled into a safe life—surrounded every day by the best that men and women had ever been able to do . . . no one knowing that she painted. Until—for the modern American collection in the American Wing—they bought a new painter, Klein, no one considering *that* Klein might be Ellie.

Her lover would discover it . . . would go with a number of people on the museum staff to watch the painting hung—her traffic triptych? Maybe something else, maybe a garden . . . paintings of a garden. A garden of flowers never seen before, and seen now by different light. A garden on another planet, but immediate, imperfect, existent. Only the odd shadow of the gardener, seen against nearly roses. . . . Her lover would see this garden, hung in its separate panels against a wide creamsilk wall. Would see it, and standing in the crowd of people—all important, knowledgeable, almost all gentle—would know, would say "Ellie . . ." out loud. And the only one who noticed would be the curator of modern art—fat, nasty, brilliant, who in that instant would also know, and love her till the day he died.

Their Ellie would become *Klein.*

Her life would be changed . . . her quiet life would be over. From hero detective, she would have changed as if from some ferocious larval stage into a cocooned creature, quiet, restful, valuable—and from that to a thing that flew, iridescent . . . famous. She and the curator of Middle Eastern art would live in Connecticut. —They would give her an office in the museum, though. People would recognize her, sometimes, when she walked through the halls . . . cashmere sweater, tweed skirt, black Javanese pearls . . . her face as severe, lovely, perfect, her blue eyes as brilliant as her work. . . .

Ellie finished her coffee, and walked back up the long corridor of smiles, then through the room where the emperor's heads sat as they had sat for their sculptors, vain, calm or impatient in uncomfortable chairs set in clear shade off sunny porticoes, their guards standing still in summer-warm armor, red kilts, badges and medallions for Headquarters Service, flies buzzing over a silver bowl of fruit . . . the artist smelling, beneath perfume, the personal odors of the Lord of the World-That-Mattered—sweat, oil, garlic, fried mushrooms . . . snowy cotton, bleached with sun and urine. . . .

Then into the great hall again, past the glorious lilies, and left onto the grand staircase, and up.

At the top of the stairs—she'd felt the tiny pressures of the butterfly bandages against the soles of her feet as she'd climbed—Ellie walked left down the passage to the Andre Meyer Galleries, went to visit Degas' little ballerina, and then commenced her accustomed round of miracles observed—surprised and pleased, as usual, that she was able to understand the strokes they'd used, comprehend very well the colors . . . puzzled and annoyed that the unity of each scheme had not suggested itself to her.

She spent two hours in that gallery—rushed, as usual, when it came to the French landscapists at the rear—then walked back to the picture she almost always saved for last. Her apple trees, by Monet. An apple orchard in late spring . . . two small, propped trees closest, in the middle ground, exploding silently into pink-white, blue-white, green-white blossoms on a sunny day, but not a brilliant day. A breezy day, but with no strong wind. The small trees marched away to the right up a gentle slope, each blossom caught, every shade of green in the shivers of the light. Ellie imagined herself in the painter's day. Herself in a white dress, in the picture. —An American friend of a friend, and asked casually if she'd care for a day in the country—if she wouldn't be bored. Had said in her poor French, "*Bien sûr,*" and been included . . .

helped pack the lunch—long, thin loaves, a tomato salad with basil, fresh dill, a fat cold spiced sausage, two small round sweating cheeses from the village, a cold dressed hen roasted the night before, and little white frosted cakes, also from the village (baked by a Madame Davouste, nervous, thin, ancient and mustached). Had gone out in the spring morning with the others, sitting at the side of the slow-wheeling wagon, swaying on cracked leather horsehair cushions, listening to the musical mysteries of French, their swift trilling talk. Then, hours later, after a lunch of hours, while something else was painted, had walked a steep, sunny path to the little orchard. There, sweating slightly in her long white-lawn dress (ruffled at the throat), sleepy from wines barely in the bottle, she had lain down in the shady orchard grass, head on her arm, her long hair escaped as she dreamed of home . . . and wakened to laughter—the others watching as he painted her among her apple trees.

"I wish to apologize to you, personally, Sergeant." The Colonel lay in disarray—white shirt, beige slacks, and black socks only—on the spare bed. He'd checked out and moved down from the Algonquin, and was drunk. "'*An eye for an eye, a tooth for a tooth* . . .' was the quotation I was given by our lords and masters, when I told them I'd been informed by our source that our friends in blue were apparently not yet discouraged, were still digging for those two witnesses. I reminded them this game was getting quite expensive . . . asked them if they were going to give us any help at all. . . ."

Tucker had had reason to suspect before—that teary funeral in the *campo* behind El Paraíso—that the Colonel, silly in so many ways, felt personally responsible for his men. Tucker suspected as well that his Colonel, though physically quite brave, had no strength for bearing losses. A tender officer, a cracked vessel. —This consideration gave the sergeant such a surge of pleasure, so deep a joy, he couldn't conceive a reasonable source for it.

His object now sighed, said, "And the letters, Tuck . . ." rolled over to turn his face to the wall—revealing a slack and aging bottom in pleated pants—and added, "For God's sake . . . please be careful. . . ."

* * *

The arraignment started only an hour late—surprising almost everyone, and causing a small bustle in the hall outside number nineteen. This was a modern room, drop-ceilinged, indirectly lit, the benches padded, colorful (light blue), and even less comfortable than the dark, solid wooden brutes they replaced. Ellie—who'd been talking in the corridor with a cop named Sarakian, an almost elderly officer in permanent service to the courts—hurried in with a small chatty crowd of reporters, mildly interested in what reporter Avril Reedy classified as a four-pussy case (victim, killers, and cop) and rare as a four-leaf clover. Reedy had talked to Ellie—catching her as she walked into the courthouse—and asked for some details (with as much gravy as possible) on the two lesbo thrill killers.

"It wasn't like that at all," Ellie said.

"I didn't ask you what it was *like,* honey. —I want you to tell me what it *could* have been like, with lots of gravy."

"I'm not commenting on the case, Avril."

"Not very good. Not very cooperative, Detective Klein. —Don't you want a friendly press?"

"More than you know."

"Meaning? —What does that mean?"

"Nothing."

"Is your no-longer-chicken but still shapely ass in some sort of sling?"

"Not that I know of."

" 'Not that you know of . . .'?"

As she walked away, Reedy called after her, "Sorry about Tommy, honey.—He was one of the good ones."

The arraigning magistrate was a black woman, Margaret Baxley, and she didn't appear to intend to waste much time with it. She called the Assistant D.A., a big, blond young man named Richter, who had a hiprolling limp and used an aluminum cane; he called Ellie and swore her, and Ellie answered his questions—one, two, three. He'd done his homework. All through this, Rebecca, in a dark blue dress (no jewelry permitted), sat beside her attorney—a thin, balding young man Ellie didn't know—and smiled at Ellie encouragingly (exposing two broken teeth), made confirmatory faces, once rolled her eyes in disbelief, and gave the thumbs-up sign (her hands bandaged) as Ellie left the chair.

Susan Margolies, seated separately at the table's other end, sat in a dark gray suit, her head down, and didn't answer when Birnbaum, sitting beside, spoke to her. A man and woman sat just behind them in spectators' seats, uneasy—the man resembling Susan a good deal. —Her son, Ellie thought . . . and couldn't remember the name.

Having ordered the defendants held on a charge of murder in the first—no motion for bail being considered, though both attorneys made that plea—Judge Baxley remanded the defendants to the custody of the state in a rapid Brooklyn patter at odds with her ponderous body, her deliberate manner of moving onto the bench—and now, after a snappy rap of her gavel—off it. Friday, late, was not a favored time for judicial duty.

Rebecca first, then Susan, were led away through a side door by stocky women in blue skirts and white blouses—Rebecca looking over at Ellie, mouthing, *Come . . . see . . . me* . . . as she went through the door.

"I'm sorry," Todd Birnbaum said. "I hope you don't think I'm being ungrateful in representing Susan. . . ." He'd persisted through the casual crowd, and caught Ellie at the door.

"No, I don't—"

"She's such an old friend. —It would have been too cruel not to."

"Counselor—it doesn't bother me at all. Susan's entitled to be represented—and who by, is none of my business."

"O.K. —I just didn't want you to think I was being an asshole. . . ."

"I don't—"

"You're not the asshole here, buddy," Leahy said, the fat man having appeared and taken Ellie by the arm. "The asshole around here's somebody else entirely. —Excuse us. . . ." He tugged Ellie out of the crowd, started her down the corridor toward the stairs, walking beside her without talking, then took her arm again to steer her to a space past several phones. There was no one near them.

"I'm sorry, Lieutenant. . . ."

"Don't even say that," Leahy said. He was wearing his trench coat, its blue complementing his eyes' light, furious color. "—Shit like that is just a waste of time. What do you have? You have some idea doin' this Gaither thing makes you special around here? Makes it so you can go an' fuck up a major investigation, 'cause the guy was your partner? You think that, you been watchin' too much TV. You understand me? —You are headin' right for a Departmental trial, and I'll tell you somethin'—you earned it. You got me in bad trouble; you made the whole Squad look lousy."

"But I got something up there. . . ."

"You got shit."

"I know where their witness is—is that shit?"

"Who do you think you're talkin' to? I'm your fuckin' commander. —You lie to me?"

"I'm not lying." Two lawyers walked past them, arguing, briefcases swinging at their sides.

"—No? Anderson just happened to tell me Connors *asked* you if you got anythin'—guy was willin' to let you walk!"

"I didn't tell him."

"Oh, I know you didn't tell him."

"If I tell you—what then?"

"Oooh . . . you gotta be out of your mind! What's the matter with you? What am I dealin' with here? —The change of life, or what?"

Ellie laughed. It was a relief to be able to laugh.

"Ha, ha—you think that's funny? Well, I got news for you, you better come up with *somethin'* medical, or you could lose your shield over this. I already tried you were still in shock from that scramble you had yesterday—an' let me tell you, Anderson didn't buy that one for a minute. Oh—an' there's somethin' else. Anderson wants those letters that whore wrote her kid. He wants 'em right up in his office—but quick."

"But there's no need—"

"Don't give me that. —Just obey a fuckin' order for once!"

"But I promised I wouldn't—unless we needed it. There's no evidence in there for a court, Lieutenant—

there's just some personal stuff that would be embarrassing for her daughter. Stuff that doesn't need to be on the public record!"

"That's great—that's what you want me to tell Anderson, so he can tell the Chief?"

"I don't care."

"*'I don't care. . . .'* Who the hell do you think you are—fuckin' Joan of Arc? You think because we worry about you, you get cut up—what do you think? You think you're different from everybody else 'cause you got tits an' you lost a partner? You better wise up, lady. You are a policewoman—and you obey your orders, or you get your ass off this police force. Period!"

"I don't think I'm better—"

"You shut up. You said enough."

"The witness is in Vineland—"

"Shut up! I don't want to hear it!"

"Vineland, New Jersey. It's Maurice Garrison; he works at DiNunzio . . . Produce . . . something."

"Christ . . . Thanks a lot," Leahy said, his fat face flushed. "I really appreciate your shittin' on my shoes like this. You had to tell me—right?"

"—And I'll say you ordered me not to interfere in Tommy's thing in any way. . . . You take it to Connors, Lieutenant."

"Great. I see. It's all right if I make an asshole out of myself, tellin' Michael Connors his business. —You didn't want to do that, I notice. You got a habit, you know, lettin' other people take the shit for you. . . . This Gaither thing is the one an' only you did on your own—and now you fucked up with Connors, stickin' your nose in where you didn't have any business."

Ellie said nothing.

"So? What's this—no wise-ass answer? No excuses . . . ? Well, I got news for you—tomorrow mornin' eight-thirty on the dot, you're goin' to be up in Anderson's office talkin' to Connors again. That guy in Vineland an' all the other shit you got to say. You—not me, an' not anybody else, either."

"I don't trust him. . . . I think it was cops—"

"Oh, please, *please* don't give me that 'cops' shit!" Leahy paused as a group of people came by . . . jurors, they looked like. "—I think Tommy got that all wrong, an' I think you got it all wrong. An' when you're talkin' about not trustin' Connors, I know you're full of it. I know about Connors. Everybody knows about that guy. —Connors would book his mother, he caught her playin' wrong bingo. The guy's so fuckin' honest he's a royal pain in the ass! —You can't trust him, let me tell you, you can't trust nobody."

Leahy turned to go, then turned again. "You get up to Anderson tomorrow—eight-thirty. An' I don't mean eight-thirty-one! An' even if you kiss enough ass up there you don't get bumped, I don't want to see you in the Squad for anyway a week. You had enough fuckin' congratulations in there. You had maybe too much; maybe we been treatin' you like a fuckin' baby in there—'you will do this, you won't do that'—so Tommy had to work for the both of you, sometimes. You think I don't notice who's in that office gettin' the shit work done? —You been ridin' free a long time, lady"—and lumbered swiftly away to the head of the stairs, and on down them, the tail of his blue trench coat flapping behind him.

"Detective Klein?"

Ellie, her face hot, knowing she must be blushing, turned and saw the young Assistant D.A. some distance down the hall. He must have stayed back when he'd heard the tone of Leahy's voice.

"Yes . . . ?"

He walked over in his rolling, dipping gait, leaning heavily on the cane. "I didn't want to interrupt . . ."

"I was getting my butt kicked, Mr. Richter."

"Happens to the best of us. . . ." Richter said. "I thought the boss was going to murder me last week. I forgot to prepare an indictment. —I just plain forgot it." He was trying to make her feel better.

"What can I do for you?"

"Two things. I need to go over the case with you, step by step—not the paperwork, that was very complete. I mean the little things . . . what you felt about each defendant, what made you particularly suspicious of them . . . . anything specific they said, even if it doesn't seem germane. In other words, anything you have that you didn't put on paper. Point is, you knew them before they were defendants—before they had lawyers. I need to know what they were like, then. —It's fill-in, shouldn't take long. . . ."

"O.K."

"That was the first thing. The second thing is, I'd like to cover this stuff over a drink. —This is not a pass; I'm married. I've just had a long day . . . and I'm buying."

"Counselor," Ellie said, "—you've made a friend for life."

Tucker, in white shirt and gray tie, a dark blue suit and gray raincoat, rode over the river just after dark. It was his first trip on the tram, and he loved it. It was like flying, without flying's unease. The machinery, he'd heard, was Swiss—and that was a country another NCO had told him was loaded with trams and funiculars, which made sense with so many mountains. White man's machinery at its most reliable, he hoped—took off his dark glasses and put them in his raincoat pocket. He'd used ice packs, and his face was looking better, felt a little better, too.

Below him, the East River, glossy black, held all the lights of its banks—but elongated, shimmering out from the shores in long, wavering fingers of blue and red, yellow and green. This would be a great trip for the kids. . . . He turned and excused his way through the passengers to the downstream side. Through the windows there, the Queensboro Bridge loomed from another age—all brutal iron in angles and pillars, riveted, welded and hammered together, bearing, as Tucker watched, an entire hurtling train, up out of the subway tunnels and high into the air—and at other levels, a steady threading of cars, trucks and buses, all lit, as the train windows were lit in endless small shuttling rectangles, by lights of their own. Headlights, running lights, tail-lights, brake lights in every shape and shade of blue-white, yellow, orange and ruby-red. It would be something for the children to see, Tucker thought, worth keeping them up a little late. It was his experience that gorgeous things rich with light, seen young, stayed with men and women all their lives—as the sun, the out-islands and sea of South Carolina had stayed with him.

At the island end, when the tram car sank down to

dock, Tucker walked off and along the ramp, passed the parked bus, and crossed the street to stand back against a fence, out of the light. When the bus pulled out, he watched the way it went, then strolled after it through the cooling night. On the main street, after a few minutes walking—the street well-lit, fairly busy with shoppers, people going home—he paused beside a travel agency (Hawaii posters in the windows . . . Diamond Head, Maui, the Pipeline . . .) to glance at a small piece of paper, put it back into his raincoat pocket, the same pocket with the glasses. The posters reminded him of Schofield . . . all those times.

He found the building, right on this main street—looked to be the only street they had—and walked past it, turned around a little farther on, came back and walked past it again. There was a night security-man on the desk.

Tucker crossed the street, and walked all the way down it, this time, to the mall beside the big parking garage—empty except for two couples walking home on the other side—then turned left, went down to a low fence along a strip of grass above the island's edge. He strolled there until he found a narrow shadow thrown by a streetlamp's pillar, then walked along this shadow to the fence, put his hands up on the wire, the horizontal pipe supporting it, vaulted over and down into the grass on the other side, and walked away into deeper dark.

Behind the buildings, though, the areas were lit. Tucker paid no attention. People rarely looked out their windows at night—reflection was all against it; the coziness of warm, lamp-lit rooms turned people inward in their views.

The apartment, numbered for the ground floor, had to be one of two.

Children—a small boy, a smaller girl—were watching television in the back bedroom of the first.

In the second, there was a cat on the windowsill, a woman singing in the kitchen—a melody to no song he could recall.

Tucker reached into his other raincoat pocket, took out his Swiss Army knife, opened it, and lightly sliced the window screen in a large L, across the bottom, and up one side—then folded the blade, and put the knife away. When he pushed this flap aside, the cat, quite small, leaped past him and out into the night. Tucker took the cat's windowsill place for a moment, then was in.

The singing stopped, and Tucker stood still in the living room—then heard a pot clatter, eased his raincoat off and let it fall, and walked across the room, smelling cooking potatoes. . . .

He paused beside the kitchen door, looked along the short hall, lit by a ceiling fixture . . . noticed a dark doorway to the left—into the bedroom, he supposed—and felt the rest of the apartment empty. The woman was humming, now. A pleasant sound.

Tucker walked through the door as she turned from the stove—and saw a big saucepan behind her, and a Teflon frying pan with two hamburger patties starting to brown.

"Who the fuck are you?" Barefoot, startled in a white terry-cloth bathrobe—frightened, but still in balance. His tie, his blue suit helped.

"I'm a police officer," Tucker said to this small, dark woman—not the one he'd come for—and still saying it, stepped into the kitchen, reached out and got her by the hair.

He'd intended something neater, a blow of some sort, but the woman fought him handily, savage as a small animal, saying, "Oh, no . . . oh, no . . ." while she bit and kicked. Finally, for room, he dragged her out and into the hall, and, after a tussle, managed to hug her hard with his right arm to hold her still, catch her frantic head in a simple lock with his left—squeezing to choke off her commencing scream—and twisting one way with one arm, the other with the other, broke her neck or something deeper down, feeling and hearing faintly her spine's muffled crack and split.

She grunted and shuddered as though he'd fucked her, then a little muddy shit ran down her legs—and though Tucker bundled her up into her robe, and carried her into the dark bedroom right away, there was some of it left in the hall.

In the bedroom, he turned on the bedside lamp to take

a look at her, be certain she was gone—reached down and rolled her to him. Nothing on, under the robe . . . a nice-looking girl. Both her eyes were open, though one, the right, showed only white. In her left eye, the pupil was a gulf of black. The bedspread, dark blue, showed smears of manure from her legs. Brown. Shit brown . . . shit black . . . Is that, Tucker wondered, feeling a little odd as usual in the circumstances—is that why they despise us so?

He thought of searching for the letters—getting that much done while he waited—then remembered the feces in the hall. The right woman would be armed and was due. . . . It seemed stupid to alert her with turds in her hallway. Tucker turned out the bedside lamp, went back to the kitchen—where the smell of cooking french fries, hamburgers, now fought the other, less pleasant one—collected a bundle of yellow paper towels, and went out in the hall to clean up.

He'd gotten it off the floor (hardwood floor, thank God, and not a carpet), had thrown those towels in the kitchen trash, turned off the hamburgers to keep them from burning—and was looking under the sink for ammonia for the smell, when he heard a key in the front-door lock.

Ellie opened the door, still in the midst of deciding whether to apologize in the morning, somehow without begging—or just to tell them to kiss her ass. Leahy had frightened her—not such a funny fat man, now. Had made her feel guilty, too, saying Tommy had done her work . . . which, sometimes, he had. The thought of losing her shield made her almost sick. She couldn't believe they'd do it. . . . But if they tried, those fuckers would think it was World War Three. She'd get hold of Avril Reedy and she'd beat those motherfuckers to death with him. . . .

She closed the door behind her, wondering where Mayo was . . . and smelled an odor of shit, right in the hall—and cooking, of all things. "—Mayo, you little bastard," she said. ". . .You *better* hide!"

As she put her purse on the hall table, she saw a brown cardboard sign propped there. *—Direct from La Guardia* *for farewell dinner—Your Ex. P.S. Used your shower for old time's sake; no seduction intended.*

"Clara . . . ?"

Ellie walked down the hall to the kitchen.

"Clara?"

A big black man in a blue suit was leaning against the refrigerator. Something was cooking in a saucepan on the stove. There were hamburgers in a frying pan, too. The big man smiled at her. "—Clara's in the bathroom," he said. "My name's Bryant. I'm a cop. —Anderson sent me to pick up those letters. . . ."

"Where's the cat?" Ellie said.

"She took him in to clean him up. —Little accident."

"You look as though you had an accident, yourself," Ellie said, and turned her head to call, *"Clara . . . !"*

"She's in the bathroom," the black man said, "—the cat was sick."

"I don't think so. . . . Who hit you in the face?"

"Guess," the black man said—and came at her like a storm.

If she hadn't ducked under his arm as he reached for her, Ellie would never have had time to draw her gun, but the big man didn't seem to care. He reached out again as she fell back against the broom closet, swatted the revolver out of her hand—sent it clattering, skidding under the table—received her desperate kick on his right thigh, then closed with her, got her right wrist tight—and slapped her terribly hard across the side of her head, slapped her again when she was trying to scream, and knocked the scream into a yelp and out of her. Ellie hit at him with her free hand, tried to get her fingernails in his eyes, and he said something she couldn't hear and hit her again—with his fist this time, she was sure, because it made her float for a moment, as if she were becoming something lighter. Then, from behind, he put his open hand over her mouth and nose, and she couldn't breathe at all.

She kicked back as hard as she could, wishing she was a horse and could kick him to death, and he lifted her up off the floor by her right wrist and the hand over her face, and slung her to one side, then the other, so when she kicked back, there was nothing there. She was feeling sick from not being able to breathe, and from the way the kitchen was spinning slowly around. He was handling her very roughly. She tried to breathe as hard as she could, and scratched at his hand with her nails, but he didn't seem to care. She tried to bite the hand, but it pressed hard and flat against her nose, her mouth, and there was nothing to bite. She was glad it didn't cover her eyes. —That would have been worse than anything. Her eyes were hurting, and her chest was hurting, too. If he wasn't careful, he would kill her. She said that to him, against his hand, but he didn't seem to notice.

He threw her to one side and she hit against the refrigerator. She hoped that would knock his hand away, but it didn't. *"Tommy!"* —She thought she was able to call Tommy right through the hand, and Tommy would be in from the living room and that would be that. . . . The big man had set her down on the floor; she was almost sure her feet were on the floor. When she looked right in front of her, everything was becoming black in the middle; she could only see on the sides. She thought Mayo would grow huge and come and help her, and she would see his sudden head in the kitchen doorway, great as a tiger's. She stopped trying to breathe, because all that did was hurt. —Mayo won't come help me, she thought. —This man's too strong. She thought he was wonderfully strong—though not as strong as the fire had been, and she'd done all right then. —I did damn well, then, she thought. Now, whirled back to the stove, trying to look to the side of that blackness, just along the edge of it, Ellie thought she saw something like the saucepan, something cooking in there. She reached down with her free hand, picked the saucepan up, and threw what was in it over her left shoulder—screaming into the hand right away as something went broiling down her back.

Then—as if she had done something perfect—the hand was gone, and Ellie lay on the kitchen floor, already feeling better, breathing deep, whooping breaths. Everything would have been wonderful, except that her neck and back were burning. That was what made her scream the way the big man was screaming, standing fiddling with his eyes. But he stopped that, and so did she, and Ellie saw him reach to a shoulder holster, bring out a semiautomatic pistol with something odd added to its muzzle. A silencer, she supposed. Whining, stepping slowly in place—his left hand plucking at his eyes, tending the skin on his face that still popped softly, sizzled—the big man bent and turned a slow half-circle, listening . . . searching blind . . . blistering head cocked to hear. Then thought he heard—and began to fire his strange pistol.

Ellie saw the shooting, but heard only soft, sneezing sounds. In almost silence, she crawled on her belly through scorching oil and small chunks of potato, past his feet. He wore big black smooth-toe oxfords that stepped and shifted as he turned while she slid past. She heard only that sneezing for gunfire, but its effects were all around her, showering down in fragments as glass smashed, wood split and splintered, metal achieved sudden dark dots.

Under the kitchen table, beyond the cat-food saucer, the Smith & Wesson lay almost against the wall. She crawled in, reached for it with her right hand, but her hand lay wrong, and wouldn't go there, so she reached again, and got it with her left—then scooted around so she could see out from under. As the big man, who apparently had heard, fired down through the tabletop above her (she felt the floor jump by her hand where the round went in) Ellie shot him once, up into his chest. The sound, a ringing crack, deafened her so that her second round—going much too high, blowing a hole through her dish cupboard—hardly sounded like a shot at all. She paused for an instant, steadied down, and put the third into his belly. This last round apparently went through and broke his back, for his legs kicked out from under him and he sat down hard, shaking the floor—and stayed sitting there, lax in a ruined blue suit, his silenced pistol fallen free.

Still alive, though. She saw his left hand crawling by his side, trying—she supposed—to get back to his face, his eyes. He was turning his head very slowly from side to side, taking deep, snoring breaths.

She rolled out from under the table—hit her right arm on the floor, and felt a bone shift inside it. Down under her elbow. The bone was grinding on something there. She got up on one knee, and felt nauseated, but that passed after she rested a little while. She holstered her revolver, left-handed, then reached out to collect the man's pistol—put her left hand, the gun in it, on the tabletop, and pulled herself up all the way, until she was standing in drifts of gunsmoke, swaying, leaning on the table. —There was shouting in the hall.

The big man sat sagging against her stove in a small spreading puddle of rich red, still heaving in his difficult breaths. He was trying to hold his head up, trying to see through ruined eyes.

"You're under arrest," said Officer Klein—and gave him his rights from memory.

ABOUT THE AUTHOR

Mitchell Smith, a veteran of the U.S. Army's Counter Intelligence Corps, has written a dozen paperback novels under various pen names. He has two movie scripts currently under option. A former New Yorker, Mr. Smith and his wife now live in northeast Georgia.

(0451)

ON THE EDGE OF YOUR SEAT!

- ☐ **PRESSURE DROP by Peter Abrahams.** Nina Kitchener has no idea what lay behind the disappearance of her baby from a New York hospital. And nothing will stop her terror-filled quest for the donor who fathered her child . . . nothing—not even murder. (402359—$4.95)
- ☐ **ICEMAN—A Jack Eichord Thriller by Rex Miller.** The Iceman's in town and as a toll of atrociously assaulted victims mounts, serial murder detective Jack Eichord vows to put this killer too savage for man-made justice out of action. "Dynamite."—Stephen King (402235—$4.50)
- ☐ **NO LESSER PLEA by Robert K. Tanenbaum.** A vicious double-murderer has already slipped through the cracks in the system once, and now handsome DA Roger Karp won't rest until he gets a guilty plea. But Mandeville Louis laughs at the law, and even in the security of a mental hospital his killing spree is not over yet . . . "Tough, cynical, funny" —*Booklist* (154967—$4.95)

Prices slightly higher in Canada.

Buy them at your local bookstore or use coupon on next page for ordering.